PRAISE FOR THE WRITING OF GEMMA FILES

"Gemma Files has one of the great dark imaginations in fiction—visionary, transgressive, and totally original." —Jeff VanderMeer

"She is, simply put, one of the most powerful and unique voices in weird fiction today." —Paul Tremblay

Experimental Film

"*Experimental Film* is sensational. When we speak of the best in contemporary horror and weird fiction, we must speak of Gemma Files." —Laird Barron

A Book of Tongues

"Boundary-busting horror-fantasy . . . This promising debut fully delivers both sizzling passions and dark chills." —*Publishers Weekly*

"Truly one-of-a-kind: violent, carnal and creepy." —Chris Alexander, *Fangoria*

We Will All Go Down Together

"What makes *We Will All Go Down Together* so riveting isn't its ideas or imagery, as richly atmospheric and detailed as they are. It's the author's voice. Colorful, powerful, and charismatic, her characters are rendered in bold strokes and poignant nuances." —NPR.com

EXPERIMENTAL

FILM

EXPERIMENTAL FILM

GEMMA FILES

OPEN ROAD

INTEGRATED MEDIA

NEW YORK

Copyright © 2015 by Gemma Files

Cover design by Ian Koviak

ISBN: 978-1-5040-6388-3

This edition published in 2020 by Open Road Integrated Media, Inc.
180 Maiden Lane
New York, NY 10038
www.openroadmedia.com

I dedicate this book to everyone involved with the films I've seen thus far in my life, whether behind the camera or in front of it. Though I may not be able to name you all directly, I can honestly say that your labour, invention and inspiration went into the making of this story, along with almost every other story I've written, or ever will write.

CONTENTS

EXPERIMENTAL

FILM

Last evening I was in the Kingdom of the Shadows.

If one could only convey the strangeness of this world. A world without colour and sound. Everything here—the earth, water and air, the trees, the people—everything is made of a monotone grey. Grey rays of sunlight in a grey sky, grey eyes in a grey face, leaves as grey as cinder. Not life, but the shadow of life. Not life's movement, but a sort of mute spectre.

—Maxim Gorky, 4 July, 1896

I need a world filled with wonder, with awe, with awful things. I couldn't exist in a world devoid of marvels, even if the marvels are terrible marvels. Even if they frighten me to consider them.
—Caitlín R. Kiernan

The body is our first haunted house. We live in it. We haunt it. We are literally our own ghosts.
—Michael Rowe

TITLE CARDS

You could argue—as I have more than enough times, as part of my Film History lecture—that, no matter its actual narrative content, every movie is a ghost story. A film's production forms a time capsule, becoming a static window into a particular moment of a particular era. Even period pieces often tell you more about the times they were made in than the times they depict; think of Julie Christie's quintessentially 1960s white lipstick and modified beehive hairdo in *Doctor Zhivago*, versus the semi-accurate vaginal wigs worn by the female slaves on Starz's *Spartacus* series, to conceal the actresses' actual routine porn star-level pubic waxing.

As time passes, the cast and crew go the way of all flesh, though their celluloid echoes remain—walking, talking, fighting, fucking. After enough time, every person you see onscreen will have died, transformed through the magic of cinema into a collection of visible memories: light on a screen, pixels on a videotape, information on a DVD. We bring them back every time we start up a movie, and they live again, reflected in our eyes.

It's a cruel sort of immortality, I guess, though it probably beats the alternative.

Framing is where you make your most important narrative decisions, in film—that's something else I used to impress on my students, or try to. *What's inside the frame versus what's outside; what's actually shown versus what's only told.*

Of course, what that means is that I'm already at a bit of a disadvantage here: this is a book, not a movie, so I can't really *show* you anything. I have to rely on my words, and your imagination. I have to assume that you have one.

And yes, if you're wondering—that *is* the sort of thing I used to say in class, far more than I should have. It may even be why I never got asked back after the Toronto Film Faculty, my old place of employment, finally reconstituted itself. I don't know; I expect I never will. Life is full of these little lacunae, these empty places. Not every problem it sets is actually solvable, at least by you.

Begin with action, always, I'd tell them, which is pretty much Filmmaking 101, though you'd be amazed how few aspiring directors ever seem to have considered it. *Set the scene. Every frame asks a question, even if what you first see onscreen appears to be completely static—intention already informs it, a series of choices. What do we see first; where am I, and what's that? Why am I being shown it? What comes next?*

What sort of movie is this going to be?

No film is ever entered into cold; packaging alone will always tell you something. Trailers, in particular, are notorious for preemptively shaping a movie inside your head, providing context for content—blatantly manipulating audiences by adding music (often not in the finished product), layering snatches of dialogue against each other to make you think three lines are one, even giving away whole plot twists while the announcer's voice vies with the intertitles, each telling you what to feel, how, and when. Blu-ray and DVD boxes, on the other hand, are like Rorschach blots, relying on you to supply the mood. Every still provides a window onto another world.

Go small, therefore, and then smaller—smaller even than that. Think of these few paragraphs as a single frame, an aperture, a tumbler's tiny hole. Stick in the key and watch it turn. Then watch whatever opens . . . open.

So: *Where am I?*

* * *

Some one hundred thirty miles, give or take, and almost three hours' drive north from Toronto, an unnumbered rural route leads off of Highway 400 into a deeper part of the province's back country: the Lake of the North District, between Midland and Huntsville—a region old, remote, and obscure enough it's never needed a more elaborate name. Ten miles past Overdeere and three miles north of Chaste, just outside the town of Quarry Argent, lies an overgrown estate that reverted to local council ownership over eighty years ago. The empty manor house that sits silently at the centre of that estate is nearly a century old, built for Mrs. Iris Dunlopp Whitcomb by her doting husband, mining magnate Arthur Macalla Whitcomb. But no one calls it "Whitcomb Manor" or anything like that. Even on the application forms submitted to Heritage Canada to have it declared a historical site, it's called, simply, the Vinegar House. And this is where we'll start.

Why?

Because this is where something important happened to me, and since I am the protagonist—not the hero, never that—of this story, it matters that I tell you about it. Because it will set the tone, creating shock and suspense, before I double back to fill in character details and backstory. Because it will give you a taste of things to come, a valid reason to sit patiently through all of the exposition that unfortunately has to follow.

What comes next?

Well . . .

As to that, you'll just have to wait, I guess. And see.

But Ms. Cairns, you ask, *come on now, really. What sort of movie* is *this going to be?* To which I can only answer, very simply—

Mine.

ACT ONE
―――――――――――

FILM HISTORY

ONE

This all started a very long time ago for me . . . longer than even I could remember at the time, though since my mind is a black hole of influences, little that gets sucked inside its orbit ever fully escapes again. Because stories lie hidden inside other stories, and we always know more about any given thing than we think we do, even if the only thing we think we know is nothing.

For example, if I'd Googled Mrs. Whitcomb's name at the beginning—not that I would have had any reason to—here's what I would have gotten, probably on the very first hit, from Hugo J. Balcarras's *Strange Happenings in Ontario* (Hounslow, 1977):

> No account of Ontario's classic unsolved mysteries can be complete without making mention of the presumably lamentable fate of Mrs. Iris Dunlopp Whitcomb, wife of Arthur Macalla Whitcomb, discoverer and owner of the now-defunct Quarry Argent Lightning-Strike Silver Mine. An avid amateur painter, photographer, collector of fairy tales, and life-long follower of the Spiritualist creed, Mrs. Whitcomb had led a hermit's life since the tragically unsolved disappearance of her only child, Hyatt, who suffered from developmental disabilities.
>
> Though his bed was first found empty one morning in early 1908, Hyatt Whitcomb was only declared dead seven

years later, in 1915. Unable to persuade his wife to accompany him, Arthur Whitcomb relocated to Europe, where he funnelled the money from his mining concerns into the development and manufacture of munitions, perhaps anticipating the outbreak of World War I.

Meanwhile, electing to stay in their former home until she had proof of what had happened to Hyatt, Mrs. Whitcomb pursued comfort through the Overdeere-based Spiritualist congregation of medium Catherine-Mary des Esseintes, for whom she bankrolled an increasingly expensive series of public fundraising events and private séances. She also "took the veil," affecting a variety of opaque and heavy full-body mourning, which covered her from her habitual broad-brimmed beekeeper's hat to the hem of her skirts, dressing first in all black, then all grey, and eventually all white. Although acknowledged to be kind and pleasant in person, she became a figure of superstitious legend amongst the children of Quarry Argent, who viewed her approach with dread.

On the morning of Saturday, June 22nd, 1918, Mrs. Whitcomb surprised her attendants by calling for a motorcar. Wrapping herself against prying eyes, she demanded to be driven to the nearest train station, where she bought a return ticket to Toronto, waited an hour and a half for the train to arrive, then boarded. All she took with her was a sizeable, rigid leather case with heavy straps, the contents of which remain unknown.

After having her ticket clipped, Mrs. Whitcomb telegraphed ahead, informing the final station on her route—Toronto—that she would be arriving shortly, and expected to find food and lodging waiting. She gave no hint of the reason for her journey, and retired to her private compartment. This was the last anyone ever saw or heard of her. Thus she disappeared from both the train and from official record, completely and irrevocably.

(Reprinted by permission of the author.)

I interviewed Balcarras during my research phase, back when I was preparing to write . . . well, not *this* book, but the book I thought I was working on, at the time. He was in his late eighties, physically frail yet clear-eyed and alert, his enthusiasm for the topic wholly un-withered. He was only too happy to tell me why. "Because, you see," he said, "there's a lot more to Mrs. Whitcomb's story, and I've always wanted to tell it—but I could never verify much, not *directly*, and Hounslow's lawyers were sadly obsessed with backing things up via documentation. Still, there *was* a witness to Mrs. Whitcomb's presence on that train . . . in a manner of speaking.

"In 1953, when the Whitcomb Estate's funds were running out and the house was in the process of repossession, an Overdeere woman named Gloria Ashtuck came forward. When she was eight, she said, she'd travelled from her hometown to Mixstead, Ontario to visit her paternal grandmother, and had only just then realized that the train she'd been riding on had to have been the exact same train from which Mrs. Whitcomb vanished.

"According to Miss Ashtuck, she was on her way to the train's washrooms when she passed a first-class compartment whose interior blinds had all been carefully drawn. She paused, attracted to the compartment by an unfamiliar noise issuing from inside—one strange enough that she felt physically compelled to stand there for a few minutes, trying to work out what it might be. It sounded 'mechanical,' 'repetitious,' somewhat like the rattling of chain. The sound was accompanied by an obscured yet hypnotic flickering of light leaking out through the tiny crack in the blinds. Then, as she lingered, she saw the handle of the door begin to move, something rustling around behind the blinds, as though whoever occupied the compartment were about to emerge . . . at which point she turned and ran all the way to the dining car, where her parents were waiting, as though every devil in Hell were chasing her. Held it the rest of the way to Toronto, or so she claimed."

He spread his hands ruefully, an embarrassed showman. "Needless to say, nobody she told gave it much weight—the memory of a frightened eight-year-old, decades past. As far as they were concerned, the Whitcombs were all exactly as dead as the law needed them to be."

"What do you think she was so afraid of?" I asked him.

Balcarras simply shrugged. "No idea. But I can tell you this much, young lady: she *stayed* good and frightened, right up till the day she died. Said it gave her the screaming meemies just thinking about it." He raised his wispy white eyebrows. "Still, you understand the import? This was on the final approach, somewhere between Clarkson and Union. Most people uninterested in the supernatural tend to assume Mrs. Whitcomb simply disembarked, unseen, at another station. But if Gloria Ashtuck was correct, *somebody* was still in her compartment that day, well after their last chance to leave had already passed."

I hesitated a second or two before asking the next question; I was still trying to keep my ideas confidential, back then. But I had to be sure.

"Did you ever hear about Mrs. Whitcomb making movies?"

He studied me, shrewdly. "Funny you should ask. When they opened up the compartment in Toronto, they found exactly two things inside. One was a scorched, discoloured sheet, hung up by pins across the window, which was odd, because—as I said—she'd already pulled all the blinds. The other, meanwhile, was the melted remains of a machine no one could easily identify, probably because it wasn't something exactly in widespread use back then: a portable film projector, one of the earliest models. I saw a drawing someone on the case had made of it, and was able to connect the dots. Mr. Whitcomb sent his former wife a hefty allowance every few months or so, right up until the end; makes sense she'd have been able to buy herself the very latest toys, she only took a mind to."

"So her trunk might have contained this projector, along with a film reel—something she was going to watch while in transit."

"It seems likely. And given the period, that also might explain where the fire came from." In the pages of his book, spread open on the coffee table between us, Balcarras tapped a black-and-white photograph, so grainy with copy reproduction and age it looked like a piece of cross-stitch embroidery. "Clear signs of heat damage, but little accompanying smoke. The investigators agreed afterwards that this indicated a brief but intense conflagration, possibly chemical in nature. Oh, there were the usual rumours, of course." He waved a dismissive hand. "A kidnapping gone wrong, perhaps conducted by Industry-hating anarchists and Fenian protestors toting explosives, all that. But I think you and I, Mrs. Cairns, are of like mind as to a far more probable cause.

"How much do you know about silver nitrate film?"

I pushed back the urge to say *It's Ms., not Mrs.*; evidently, he'd seen my wedding ring and made up his own mind. "It explodes?"

"Somewhat volatile, yes, which explains why it's no longer in use. Because, amongst other things, the nitrocellulose stock would occasionally *ignite* when run through the gate of a projector. The silver in the emulsion would act as an accelerant, continuing to burn until the film was entirely consumed, and leaving very little trace behind. Doesn't require oxygen to stay alight, either; it'll keep burning completely underwater, at over three hundred degrees, and it produces toxic gases. It was a nitrate film fire that caused the Dromcollogher Burning in Ireland in '26— forty-eight people killed outright, many more injured. Burned the entire building to the ground."

"That still doesn't explain what happened to Mrs. Whitcomb," I said.

"No, it obviously doesn't. But at the time, people genuinely thought that silver nitrate fires were so hot they could consume a human being entirely—somewhat like spontaneous human combustion, to cite another, equally foolish superstition." He settled back in his armchair. "Interesting you asked about her little hobby, however; far more people making 'flickers' at home than you might think, especially if they could afford the equipment. But that was something else they made me take out—wasn't *relevant*, they said." He snorted.

I came close to spilling it all then, betrayed by that excited delight you feel when you realize, yes, *somebody else knows* about something you thought only you had stumbled across, that you've finally met somebody who'll *understand*. But at the last second, I chose not to—clinging, still, to the dark ambition at the core of that excitement.

It was my name on the line, here. Balcarras had had his day.

"They've recently recovered a few fragments of stuff they think she might have produced," I said at last, which was not technically untrue. "From 1914 to 1917, by preliminary dating."

Balcarras nodded, unsurprised. "Hadn't heard about *films*, per se, but I do know she shot footage at Kate-Mary des Esseintes's performances, her 'Thanatoscopeonic Resonance Gatherings'— documentary records, to prove these things she and her group got up to were real."

(As mentioned in Balcarras's piece above, des Esseintes was a North Ontario spirit medium, fairly famous at the time, some-body who'd followed the Fox Sisters' lead and combined Spiritu-alist beliefs with public demonstrations, though she mainly did cabinet work and ectoplasmic materialization rather than simple table-rapping. She formed the community centrepoint for many contemporary Spiritualist "seekers," with Mrs. Whitcomb one of her most fervent supporters, financially and otherwise.)

"Of course, by that time, Mrs. Whitcomb was also enmeshed with Kate-Mary's little protégé, the one she adopted, later on . . . Vasek Sidlo. Fifteen years old at the time and sightless since birth, supposedly. Kate-Mary called him an imagist—spirit photogra-phy, all that. He was going to be her link with the new generation of Spiritualists, their very own Edgar Cayce, or what have you. And Mrs. Whitcomb was quite besotted with him too, though in a different way, of course."

"Are you saying they were—involved?"

"Oh, no no no!" He waved his hands. "Not on her side, at least; she had a very *maternal* interest in young Vasek, probably because he'd been brought up in the orphanage her mother had founded. And just like with Kate-Mary, she thought he might be able to get her closer to solving the mystery of what had hap-pened to poor Hyatt. . . ."

"But on Sidlo's side?"

"Well, she was beautiful, everyone agrees on that. It's too bad no one ever took pictures, before the veil."

"He was blind, though."

"*Supposedly*. And even so—blind, not dead."

At the time, I thought Balcarras had gone off on a tangent, obsessing on gossip so old it was almost mummified. However, as with so much about this story, I'd eventually find out otherwise . . . but not until much later.

"What do *you* think happened?" I asked, flipping open the last page of my notebook.

"With Mrs. Whitcomb? Might've been a multitude of things, some more likely than others. But I'm inclined to think she took the easy way out—just stepped out of the wreck of her life, doffed her famous veil, and left by the doors, along with everybody else. Without the veil, no one would ever have recognized her. She'd have been free."

"Free to do—what?"

"Oh, I'd like to believe she settled down, changed her name, had more children. Anything but the obvious."

"Which is?"

"That train was going full speed, Mrs. Cairns. To get off mid-jaunt would have been suicide, literally. But then again, maybe that's what she wanted, eh? To be with her boy again."

"Best-case scenario, sure. If he was even dead."

"Exactly. We don't know—and odds are, we never will." Balcarras shook his head, sighing. "Poor girl. Poor, foolish girl."

We sat there together a moment while I tried to think of anything else to ask. Then he leaned across the table, giving what he might have thought was a charming leer. "You're very easy to talk to, my dear," he told me. "Who was it you said you wrote for, again?"

Lip Weekly I could have said, at one point; *Deep Down Undertown*, had I wanted to tell the truth. Instead, I found myself blurting out, before I could think better of it: "Oh, well . . . these days, myself, mainly. I guess."

"No publisher's contract yet, eh? All this work done on spec, so to speak?"

"Not really, no. And—yeah."

"Hmmm." He patted my hand, as if in consolation. "Something to look forward to then."

I walked back from Balcarras's Cabbagetown house with my mind racing, eyes full of stars from suddenly re-emerging into daylight from the dim, paper-parched atmosphere of the old man's book-lined office. I was organizing words in my head, cutting and pasting, trying to figure out where to put what I'd learned. Chapter One, maybe? How long could I make people wait, trusting them to read along while I blathered toward some point, without even a hint of the mysteries to come?

These narrative structures have to be thought out beforehand, you see—strategized, methodically, according to content. Because a story, in the main, dictates its own telling.

In hindsight, it wasn't my fault that I just didn't know what kind of story I'd been dropped into, head first and kicking.

That book I thought I was writing would've made my meandering parody of a career: as a former film critic and pseudo-film historian who'd somehow managed to stumble into teaching the subject for ten-plus years without the benefit of a film studies degree, or any other sort of qualification beyond an autodidact's instincts allied with having already watched upwards of three thousand movies while taking notes upside-down. It would've been a triumphant tale of luck, anecdata disguised as objective fact, like almost every other Canadian cinematic text. The strange but true tale of how, while reviewing a program of experimental films shown in downtown Toronto, I had accidentally discovered that Mrs. Arthur Macalla Whitcomb had apparently made a series of early motion pictures employing special effects techniques similar to those of science fiction and fantasy film pioneer George Méliès—thus making her Canada's first female filmmaker, and the Vinegar House (not only her home but her production studio) a site of great historical significance.

Documentaries, awards, speaking engagements . . . everything, all the time. The impossible dream. That book would've been my legacy.

Not this one, though. Not in the same way. Which is just how things work out sometimes—completely the opposite of how you thought they would. The chance comes, and then it's gone; the moment turns and you don't know why. Nothing's ever the same.

Still, it's not like I'm not sort of used to that happening by now.

TWO

The night I saw one of Mrs. Whitcomb's films for the first time, I'd already made my son cry twice. It was Friday, yet another goddamn P.D. Day—first of a three-day weekend—and as usual it hit me like an unpleasant surprise, because I hadn't been paying attention. It'd been in his communication book, right there, written down in black and white: *Friday off, no school. Make arrangements accordingly.* But my mind had been elsewhere, on other things—I'd filtered it away, pretty much the same way he did all the time, with everything.

"You should've asked," my mom reminded me, as though I couldn't possibly have connected those dots myself. "You'd've probably seen it if you checked the Toronto Catholic School Board website, too. They put notifications like that on page one."

"Yes, Mom. I know."

"Then why didn't you?"

"Because I'm a fucking idiot?"

"The problem is, Lois, that that just isn't true."

Selfish then, rather than stupid. That we could certainly both agree on.

That morning, Clark's brain was full of static. He jumped and ran and laugh-screamed up and down our tiny apartment, caught in a perfect storm of reference and imitation, sliding from Kesha to *Star Trek* to *Frozen* to *Law & Order: Special*

Victims Unit to various random TV commercials "OH DEAR!" he yelled, as I tried to simultaneously shoehorn him into a pair of pants and force him to eat his bacon. "OH NO! *DO YOU WANT TO BUILD A SNOWMAN? SPACE, THE FINAL FRONTIER!* BRUSH MY TEETH WITH A BOTTLE OF JACK! SEXUALLY BASED CRIMES ARE CONSIDERED PARTICULARLY HEINOUS! *CEE ESS EYYYYE NEW YORRRRK!*"

I'm aware that it looks pretty funny, written down like that. Sort of like how he always looks cute while doing it, thank Christ.

Songs and stories, rhymes and repetition—that's what my son has, instead of a vocabulary. He speaks mainly in echolalia; haphazardly grafting great chunks of memorized dialogue from movies, cartoons, commercials, and songs together to get a point across. Sometimes he succumbs to what I've come to call "jazz speech," imitating the rhythm, pitch, and intonation of a phrase so expertly that meaning completely disappears, treating it like a phrase of music, or lyrics in another language.

Clark is a lovely child, his teachers write on every alternative report card he's ever received. *Always singing, polite and happy, kind. Clark is a joy to have around.*

To which I can only think, well—in small doses, I'm sure he is. But that "politeness" is mainly imitation, that "kindness" is him choosing to not interact with you, and isn't it nice that you get to give him back at the end of the day, when his exhaustion and anxiety reach their fever-pitch and he loses every shred of language, however hard-won? When all he wants to do is stamp in a circle and babble, jump up and down in front of the TV, then fall on the floor and scream till we put him in bed?

And I have help, for which I'm duly grateful. And he's so much better than he used to be. Better all the time. But every step forward brings new traumas, new difficulties; as his understanding of the world widens, his ability to deal with it fluctuates wildly. He cares what we think, and that's wonderful, but he also worries, and we have no way to soothe him. He loves us and he shows it, and that's precious—unbelievably so, considering the women I've sat next to in various waiting rooms, unable to tell if their sons even know they're present, if they can tell the difference between their mother and a nurse, or their mother and a lamp—but he also gets angry when we ask him to do anything more than whatever it is he wants to do at that exact moment, yelling, kicking, weeping. Heartbroken by his own inability to be other than he is, especially when levelled against the world's inability to do the same.

And I know how he feels, but it really doesn't help. Nothing does.

Nothing ever will.

"Hey," I said, tapping his cheek. "Hey! Look at me."

"DON'T LOOK AT ME!"

"I'm going to have to go, bunny. I need—"

"YOU'RE NOT GONNA HAVE TO GO! DON'T NEED!"

"Well, wouldn't it be nice, but I am, and I need you to be— *hey! Look* at me, Clark. I need you to be good for Daddy, while I'm gone. I need—"

"DON'T BE GOOD FOR DADDY!"

"*Look* at me, and *do* be good, *do you understand? DO YOU UNDERSTAND ME?*"

Which is, and always has been, the question.

I still remember the day Clark was diagnosed, when the nurse practitioner watched him climb single-mindedly up onto a chair next to the bookcase on top of which she'd stuck the only one of his toys he'd shown any interest in—a talking Thomas the Tank Engine, predictably because little boys with autism love Thomas; it's the huge faces, the dichotomous freeze-frame mobility of the features, the way you can always tell what they're thinking. He stood there teetering dangerously, making grabby hands. He knew three adults in the room, all of whom loved him equally, and it never even occurred to him to ask any of us for help, or even "mand" us . . . grunt, point to what he wanted, pull us toward it. He might as well have been alone.

That this is, in fact, the very definition of the term in question—autism, to be forever alone, either shunning interaction or unable to sustain it—is an irony that is by no means lost on me, or any other parent of a child on the spectrum. But it is what it is—that's all you can ever say about it, and simply wishing it wasn't will never make it so. If my aunt had nuts, she'd be my uncle; if things weren't the same, they'd be different. You just have to deal with it, which I do—mostly. Inadequately, probably, a lot of the time.

Around the same time we discovered exactly how Clark was, what schools now call "exceptional," Asperger's Syndrome— hitherto classified separately—was folded back into the black rainbow of autism spectrum disorders. Since then, people have increasingly lobbied to further extend that spectrum, embracing things like OCD, ADD, and the like, which I can understand, in theory; all of them share a certain amount of apparently infinitely recombinant symptomology, albeit with mysterious and baffling variations, giving rise to the truism "If you know one child with ASD, you know *one* child with ASD."

"We're lucky," Simon says, and I agree. Clark sleeps through the night, and always has. He thinks of eye contact as a hilarious game. He has emotional affect; he makes jokes, rudimentary and repetitive though they might be. He is, in the main, sweet-tempered: he doesn't strike out at others; he isn't self-injurious. He rarely has full-bore public meltdowns anymore, probably because we know what the danger signs are—crowds, echoing spaces, or having too many choices, or too much noise—and plan around them. Still, we can't avoid everything. No one can.

"Wouldn't it be nice if he could just snap out of it?" a supposed Educational Assistant once said to me, at the school just before the one he goes to now. She was an older Hungarian lady, used to babysitting "special" children of a very different variety, raised to the status of professional intervener because they had literally no one else to fill the position. And I remember how passionately angry that comment made me, even though on some level I recognize it's something I've thought myself.

Wouldn't it be nice? But he won't, and I know it. And sometimes it hits me, like a wrecking ball—the fact that my clever, charming boy can't be fully evaluated in terms of intelligence, because he's (currently) incapable of taking standardized tests. That at the same age he clings to picture books like *Frog and Toad* and *Home for a Bunny* is when I was reading at a Grade Thirteen level (back when there still was such a thing). Those are the times I look at him and wonder if he'll ever hold a job, ever live even semi-independently, ever love or be loved by someone other than me and Simon.

Superimposed overtop, I see a future vision of a tall, handsome man with bad teeth (because he won't brush them unless you make him) and a full beard, wandering down the street singing Disney songs, while everyone around him laughs and points. In the distance I see cops kept from tasing him only by the fact that he's white. And next to him is myself, a grim little old lady, still leading him through life by the elbow.

I expect to still be worrying about all this when I die. Which—after all these years of rote, existential dread—has actually begun to terrify me more than simply knowing I'm going to.

Are my intentions good? I'd like to think they are. But I know myself well enough to know that intent doesn't always matter, not the way it should. What *matters* is getting things done, walking the line between caring and micromanagement, the way you would for any other kid. Making them aware that the world is full of other people, all of whom have expectations and most of whom don't love them, or even know they exist. So I struggle to shape myself for him, to keep all this in mind and work from cue to cue. Because I love him, because he's part of me. But this is all so far away from what I find natural that, a lot of the time, I find it physically baffling to deal with—I want to reject it, to yell at him, to refuse to play along. And—

—sometimes, I do. More than I should, no doubt. But sometimes, I just can't help myself.

It's how I'm made.

Because I was born fucked up, too, and I always knew it, though I guess in retrospect it never mattered quite as much as I thought it did. But my version of fucked up was never going to be enough like his to help us meet in the middle; I come from the other end of the spectrum. And I remember sitting next to my mom, going down the list of Asperger's Syndrome diagnosis points one by one, showing her how much they reminded me of how I'd been as a child, an adolescent, before socialization kicked the worst of it out of me. "Little Professor Syndrome," check. Rabid enthusiasms, check. Inability to converse without monologizing, check. Vocabulary far exceeding normal age standards, check. Frustration, check. Inability to form friendships, check. Violent tantrums, check. Self-harm, check. Check, check, check.

"Don't you see?" I asked her. "This is why this happened. Because I'm just like him, except it's all on the inside."

She looked at me then with what might have been sympathy, but what I read (at the time) as contempt, the way I'm prone to do. Because—another check—I've never really been able to tell what other people are thinking just by looking at their faces, unless those faces are up on a movie screen.

"Come on, Lois," she said. "It's bad enough as it is. Don't try to make this all about *you*."

Back in the here, I could see tears in Clark's eyes; my own stung my nose, making me even angrier. Making me repeat, in turn: "*Do you understand?*"

"YOU DON'T, YOU DON'T, IT'S SILLY—"

"Enough! *Do you understand?* It's a yes or no question! *DO*—"

From behind, Simon's hand touched my shoulder. "Listen, hon," he said, soothingly, "I've got this." Which was Simon-speak for *stop, you're making it worse, you need to go.* Or maybe not. Maybe that *was* all just about me, like everything else.

The problem with thinking you're the centre of the world is always wondering why, if that's so, do you palpably not control a single goddamn thing?

So I shook my head, shut my mouth, and I went.

I was desperate back then, I know that now. The weird thing is, however, that you can apparently live a very long time being desperate and not even recognize it. It's as though the hypersensitivity of your emotions, the constant fight-or-flight reflex, grinds away your nerve endings until all you can register is a sort of dazed, vaguely focused absence. I certainly wasn't happy, but I wouldn't have called myself actively *un*happy—sort of like how you can be "not sick" without truly being "well." I simply didn't have time to be anything else.

What I was supposed to be doing that night—October 3, 2014—was covering a screening at the Ursulines Studio of new experimental film and video works by local Toronto artists, for the aforementioned *Deep Down Undertown*—a new sub-site on Alec Christian's *Virtual Cinema* domain, specifically aimed at pushing Toronto indie culture on a new generation of Internet-savvy blogtivists. Though the gig didn't pay, as such (Christian's boilerplate contract let him return a certain amount of click-through advertising revenue to content providers, once he'd deducted the cost of archive maintenance), it at least provided me with an excuse to leave Clark with Simon and get out on my own for a while. Better yet, it guaranteed that whenever I Googled my own name, stuff still actually came up.

I'd been out of steady work since mid-2009, the same year the Toronto Film Faculty shut its doors, which also just happened to be the year Clark was diagnosed—a useful turn of events, in its own way, since the sudden influx of free time allowed me to become Clark's full-time intermediary, negotiating the often con-fusing network of autism services offered in the general Toronto area. But it was ten years down the drain, too: a decade of teaching screenwriting and Canadian Film History, the two courses nobody wanted to take, albeit for different reasons. Ten years of dealing with people who'd been lied to by their intake handlers, convinced to spend eighteen months of their lives incurring thirty thousand dollars' worth of government debt and training for "entertainment sector" jobs that would never materialize, not once they erupted into the industry proper and discovered that their graduation cer-tificate wasn't worth the paper it was printed on.

"I've learned not to tell people I went to the Fac at all, Miss Cairns," Safie Hewsen had told me the last time we collided with each other in line at Starbucks. "You tell 'em you went to the Fac and they think you don't know *anything*." "Good call," I'd agreed—because it was, sadly enough. And also because I don't think anyone at the Fac taught Safie much she hadn't already known, me included.

I turned forty and the Fac went under; it was almost exactly that fast. At Christmas we were all standing around at the office party, listening to Jack Worram—our Dean—tell the representative from the mother corporation how good things were going: *Oh, we did this, we got that, we rented a whole new floor of this building, we've got all this donated equipment, enrolment is presold all through next year* . . . and the whole time this guy just stood there nodding, waiting for a conversational break so he could say: *Uh huh, that's great—yeah, actually, we're shutting you down.*

The final mass email cited "recessionary measures," but I know for a fact that was only partially true, mainly because Jack sat alone in his office for almost a week afterwards, getting drunk enough that when I walked in and asked, he just went ahead and told me so. Basically, he said, there were two things FACilitation International wanted from their Toronto initiative that we just couldn't give them: to start offering online classes, which we didn't have the infrastructure to support; and to be able to call what we gave out at the end of each year-and-a-half a *degree*, not a certificate. But the Ontario Board of Education assumed, quite rightly, that the Fac was basically a diploma mill, and they weren't about to sign off on anything that would allow us to pretend we weren't.

It was bad enough that all our equipment was ten years out of date, if not more; and that the screenplay template program we "gave" students was an unregistered sample that wouldn't work anywhere except on the school's network, so not only could they never print or save more than ten pages at a time, everything they *did* print had a massive logo watermarked across it. But film is expensive, too, even if you're also offering the option of shooting on video—post-production alone runs into thousands, much of which students were paying out of their own pockets. Word got around, which ate into our enrolment. That's the sad truth. Everyone wants to do film because of the Hollywood angle, not that we were preparing them for anything close to *that*. But what they just don't seem to get going in is that film is basically the most expensive art form there is.

By June of 2009, I was all "taught out" and watching my students—Safie included—move on to their last, production-heavy semesters before graduating, knowing my involvement with the educational system was history. Only a year and a half back from maternity leave, I'd already spent the previous months feeling almost constantly ill and exhausted, as well as increasingly worried there might be something not entirely neurotypical about Clark. Then came the diagnosis, a punch in the gut for Simon and me, though at least now we *knew*.

But even before that, I found myself looking back at my life and thinking: twenty years of writing about other people's stuff, and what did I have to show for it? All those films I saw, working for *Lip*. All those screenplays I checked over, in and out of school. I could look at something and tell you what was wrong with it, even tell you how to fix it, but had I ever really built anything, from the ground up? Would there ever be anything I could call *mine*?

It didn't help that one of the last courses I taught that semester was (as ever) Canadian Film History—a curriculum I'd designed myself from the bottom up, incorporating knowledge gained over a lifetime of comparing and contrasting Canada's insular, barely functional moviemaking system with the glamorous over-bearing spectre of American mass media. I used to call it the semester-long downer. Because so much of the Fac experience was about enabling people's dreams, however self-delusional, and I had to be the one standing there going: *Well, see, things don't really* work *like that, up here. That's why James Cameron got his dad to move to L.A.*

Back when I was working full-time for *Lip*, covering Canadian film often felt like I was documenting and promoting a film culture made up of people mainly working for "the enemy," day-jobbing on commercial "runaway" films driven by American production companies—who came up here and stacked their crews with Canadian Content in order to qualify for a certain amount of points on the CAVCO (Canadian Audio-Visual Certification Office) scale, thus allowing them a double-shot of federal and provincial tax credits—and then waiting in vain for

February, when things went slack enough to allow them to perhaps work on something for themselves. The first time someone explained this to me, I remember thinking *wow, that's gotta suck.* And believe me, having been a part of it ever since, it really, really does.

To make your own film, meanwhile, you need government funding, because most businesses haven't seen Canadian film as a good investment since the Tax Shelter Era of the 1970s and early 1980s, when the Bank of Montreal took a bath over their investment in the making of total stinker *Bear Island* (up to then, at twelve million dollars, the single most expensive Canadian film of all time). But Telefilm doesn't give you money if you want to make anything that looks even vaguely like your average Hollywood product—instead, they expect us to define what makes a given thing "Canadian" enough for financing negatively. Which means no genre, no budget, everything small and indie and incredibly specific—as close to non-commercial as you can possibly come, and preferably with ridiculously obvious Canadian Content signifiers attached. Like *Men With Brooms*, that epic curling comedy, in which our heroes have to stop the car at one point because a random herd of beavers is crossing the road.

It's different in Quebec, where a raunchy hockey movie called *Les Boys* once beat out *Titanic* at the box office. But that's mainly due to the idea that anything shot in French *has* to be inherently Canadian by default—language defines culture, which is why they can keep theirs separate, and ours gets stepped all over by America, to the point that we ourselves can hardly tell the difference between any given American film and any given Canadian film, except that the American is usually the one that looks better. Not to mention how Québécois films come with a ready-made captive audience attached; in Quebec, it's genuinely considered cool to want to see films that reflect your reality, because nothing else coming in from the world around you does. And in English-speaking Canada . . . it's the exact opposite.

I just wanted something I could put my name on, something permanent. Something people could pick up in a bookstore and say: *Man, Lois Cairns found out something nobody else knew.* And

I guess the idea of gaining that sort of validation from anything to do with Canadian film is pretty goddamn funny, in retro-spect—Canadian film, whose "history" is a bunch of conflict-ing testimony most people don't even bother to cross-reference. Canadian film, where we save and then dump documentation seemingly at random, because nobody really cares. Canadian film, which most people don't see and don't care about either, no matter which side of the camera they're on.

I'd written articles like the one I was preparing what felt like a hundred times before, and at that very moment—sitting in a streetcar on my way to the Ursulines Studio, looking forward to a program of skippy, blurry, badly lit brain droppings curated by a local filmmaker I could barely stand to talk to, let alone interview—it frankly felt as though every word I'd ever written might've all been for nothing.

When I was in my teens I never thought I'd see my twenties, and I spent my twenties utterly convinced that if I hit thirty with-out being married I'd never marry at all, let alone have kids—a set of mixed assumptions that'd been neatly punctured when I found myself first married at thirty-five, then pregnant by thirty-six. Now I was forty-four years old, and slowly realizing that everything I'd learned thus far—at school and afterwards—was obsolete. A defective person raising a defective child, with noth-ing to show for twenty years of professional life. A teacher no longer teaching. A film critic no longer reviewing films. A film historian with nothing to show for my efforts but theories and anecdata all centred around a genre no one cared about, not even the people who sustained it.

Thinking back, I couldn't remember exactly what it was I'd thought I was going to turn out to be, if I ever lived to the age I was now. But even so, I was still pretty sure this probably wasn't it.

THREE

I'm assuming, perhaps inaccurately, that whoever's reading this probably doesn't know much about what makes a film "experimental." I didn't know all too much about it myself until I had to put together that particular lecture, which always began with me asking whatever class I was teaching if they'd heard of *Un Chien Andalou*. "Luis Buñuel and Salvador Dalí, 1929? Or how about Maya Deren, *Meshes of the Afternoon*? Anything by Kenneth Anger?"

"No, miss."

"Okay, then. University of YouTube it is."

After that, I'd hook my laptop to the overhead projector and cue the relevant visual accompaniment up. *Un Chien* opens with a shot of a straight razor being stropped; the guy doing it is Buñuel himself, not that it matters. A title card says: "Once upon a time," in French. The guy tests the razor on his thumb then opens his balcony door and steps out, fingering the razor idly while looking up at the full moon. From this, we cut directly to a close up of a young woman's face. She's held to her chair with the man's hand resting on her shoulder, waiting calmly. As a thin cloud bisects the moon, the man appears to slit the woman's eyeball open with his razor, its vitreous humour spilling out like popped egg yolk.

The rest of the film, which according to title card takes place "Eight years later," is a stream-of-consciousness parade linked only by poetic metaphor. A lot of it will seem familiar on first viewing, because—much like Dalí's paintings, or the repetitious, dream-inside-a-dream-on-a-train structure of Buñuel's *The Discreet Charm of the Bourgeoisie* (1972)—its imagery has since become shorthand for "surrealism" as a genre. There's a wound with ants coming out of it and a man pulling the literal baggage of a Catholic upbringing behind him: two grand pianos filled with rotting donkey-corpses, the Ten Commandments, and a couple of bewildered priests. There's a fight between doppelgangers, extraneous sudden nudity, a man's mouth turning into armpit-hair, a death's-head moth—sexuality, religious guilt, Jungian-Freudian imagery run wild. Like Anger using gay porno tropes such as sailors in public toilets or having an actor unbutton his fly to reveal a lit sparkler, or Deren returning again and again to a key, a knife, and a hooded Grim Reaper-esque figure with a mirror for a face, the point of the exercise is *not* to tell a linear story while simultaneously getting as much of a rise out of the viewers as possible.

Supposedly, when *Un Chien Andalou* first screened, Dalí and Buñuel showed up with rocks in their pockets, which they planned to use for self-defence if and when the audience attacked them. This wasn't as crazy as it sounds; it'd only been fifteen years since the riot that accompanied the premiere of Stravinsky's *The Rite of Spring*, and Surrealist leader André Breton had supposedly been overheard telling people they should "sabotage" the film's debut. But that night's movie-goers actually liked it a lot, causing Buñuel to complain, "What can I do about the people who adore all that is new, even when it goes against their deepest convictions, or about the insincere, corrupt press, and the inane herd that saw beauty or poetry in something which was basically no more than a desperate impassioned call for murder?"

Well, it's always annoying when people like things you don't want them to. But the point I was trying to make (and that I'm now trying, however ineptly, to paraphrase) is that it doesn't really matter what any given experimental film is "about," because the genre as whole rejects narrative, conventional or otherwise, in favour of hypnagogy; it *wants* to bore you, to annoy you, to put you in a trance and force you to meet it halfway. We're storytelling creatures. Give us a bunch of seemingly random images and we *will* try to organize them into a linear progression: tree, apple, head, bruise, gravity . . . a man sat under a tree, an apple fell on his head because of gravity, a bruise appeared, the end. We just won't be able to help ourselves.

For me, the epiphany I experienced regarding experimentalism came while watching Derek Jarman's film *Blue*, which I had to attempt to review for a *Lip* retrospective. Made when he was already blind and dying from AIDS-related complications, it consists of almost two hours of a bright blue screen unrelieved by images of any sort, accompanied with a layered and fascinating soundtrack. Watching people's faces as they reacted to the film— or struggled *not* to react to it—was a revelation in itself.

Now, there's little more useless and baffling, conceptually, than a blind filmmaker—I don't think anyone would argue with me on that point, Jarman himself included. Nevertheless, I'm pretty sure Jarman knew that while people were watching his film, he could still conduct things inside their brains—that during the entire experience, they'd be desperately trying to conjure a "movie" where none existed, just to keep themselves sane. I remember the first time I showed one of my classes Soraya Mousch's installation *As Heaven Is Wide*. And then I asked if anybody had any questions, to which this guy in the middle row put up his hand and said: *Uh, yes, miss—like, what the eff was* that?

Well, folks, I replied, *that was the* third *stream of Canadian film, neither Telefilm nor Québécois; it's the one you can make almost completely by yourself, no help required, government or otherwise—though the government'll probably give you grant money for it, if you ask. Because experimental film is as far away from exploitative Hollywood genre narrative film as humanly possible.* The point of showing experimental films, for me, was to demonstrate that if they were only willing to step outside the established system, it was perfectly possible for any filmmaker to get away with not actually *having* a "point." That they could, in fact, defy the Hollywood rules that stated they even had to have one in the first place. Because in experimentalism, the film *itself* was the point, the question and the answer, all in one.

In its purest form, done right, watching an experimental film is the closest you can come to dreaming another person's dreams. Which is why to watch one is, essentially, to invite another person into your head, hoping you emerge haunted.

I'd already covered enough screenings at the Ursulines Studios to know the quickest way to get there, without springing for a taxi: catch the northbound bus up Sherbourne, then hop a streetcar west along Carlton until it turns into College and keep going. Best place to get off is at Augusta, just before Bathurst. From there it's just a brisk walk north to Nassau, in the heart of Kensington Market, where the Ursulines occupies the whole top floor of a former industrial garage.

Founded in 2004 by a coalition of multimedia and performance artists who were tired of never being able to find proper venues for their art, the Ursulines has since become a fixture of Toronto's alternative cinema and a meeting place for both those who make and those who consume films from the fringes of the system. Though its overall budget receives generous bi-annual support from both provincial and federal grant-giving bodies, the costs of a typical week are paid through a combination of user fees, box office, and money made from the operation of an equally community-oriented bike shop sharing their location. Throughout the day, they fix bikes down at street level, or give maintenance lessons—teach people how to make their own, too. At night, they pull a gate across, lock it, then open the second storey for business: single-artist installations, festivals, "world premieres" seen by eighty poor bastards on fold-up chairs a pop. They even turn it into a mini-studio every summer and do a month of workshops on Super 8 film, mentored by guest artists from all around the world; for two hundred bucks you get a rig and a reel, they show you how to cut in-camera and develop, and then you get to force whoever's dumb enough to show up to sit still for your masterpieces. I got a pretty good article out of the experience once, in my *Lip* days.

Under current management, the Ursulines also produces a small quarterly magazine about the experimental scene (*Some Do Harm*) and runs the Stream Store, a web-based distribution company that releases films featured at and developed through the studio. You'd think they'd be a little artsy-fartsy for an area like the Market, not to mention apolitical; this is a place that's been radical since the 1960s, seemingly composed of nothing but anarchist bookstores, vegan restaurants and thrift shops far as the eye can see. It's also a neighbourhood that consistently attracts a high student and immigrant population, and is stridently anti-corporate despite some of its most vocal residents being surprisingly upper crust—self-exiled fugitives from Toronto's media and financial elite.

It was one of this latter group playing as headliner/programmer for that night's dubious roster of entertainment—a man whose work would set me on my path to the Vinegar House and beyond.

Wrob Barney was born Robert James Barney in 1962—he added an extra letter to his name in high school, hoping to distinguish himself from his three older siblings, Richard, Robin, and Reid. A former resident of the Lake of the North area, much like Mrs. Whitcomb, he was born in Chaste then raised in Overdeere. He first appeared on my radar after his 2006 debut at Inside/Out, the Toronto LGBT Film Festival, and joined the Ursulines Studio collective in 2010, replacing withdrawn member Max Holborn.

(I'd heard of Holborn but had never really seen anything he'd done, and didn't know him enough by sight to nod at him across the room. Alec Christian was a big fan, but I mainly categorized him through his association with Soraya Mousch, whom I'd interviewed back when the two of them ran the Wall of Love—another experimental film collective—and who later became a mentor for my former student Safie Hewsen. Actually, I don't think anybody'd seen Holborn directly for about a year by the time of the Ursulines screening, including Mousch. First his wife had died, and then he and Mousch had some weird falling out over their last project, and then he just sort of dropped off the map. Mousch had at least switched disciplines, as she liked to say, and though she no longer did anything involving film, it wasn't like she didn't work. But for all people knew about Holborn, he might've gone into his house, locked the door, and never come back out.)

Looking back, I can admit now that I was pretty—okay, *highly*—uncharitable to Wrob Barney, from my first review on. His affectations annoyed me, to say the least. And God knows, I have a not-unwarranted reputation for disliking people almost at random, sometimes for not much more than *screw you, that's why* . . . But in my own defence, this was a pretty much universal opinion; Wrob rubbed a *lot* of people the wrong way, sometimes without even trying.

The thing is, in Toronto, those who do experimental film basically fall into two categories: there are the zealots, people who've decided for philosophical reasons not to practise or cooperate with the commercial storytelling oligarchy—the Griersonites, I call them, after John Grierson, the dude who started the National Film Board of Canada. Same guy who once said "Fiction is a temptation for trivial people." Them I have some respect for, because that's a freakishly, perversely hard row they've chosen to hoe. I mean, make an even vaguely commercial movie in Canada—something that tells a story from beginning to end, fits a ninety-minute slot, conforms to broadcast regulations—and you can have yourself a nice little career in TV. But the stuff the Griersonites do? Doesn't get you shit.

On the other hand, some people do experimental film because it's the smallest possible pond and they enjoy being a big fish, no matter where. And Wrob Barney fell squarely in that second camp.

Wrob applied for grants even though he came from money— that was an open secret. After a boating accident killed his grandmother and step-grandfather, Barney's father Russett somehow wound up the unexpected beneficiary of a large "charitable donation" from the eccentric Sidderstane family, which he soon invested in what would eventually become the Ramble Barn mini-empire, a successful chain of quality outdoor gear shops with outlets in Toronto, Ottawa, and Burlington. So young then-Robert did indeed grow up in plenty, and it was his elder siblings' early commitment to maintaining the family business that freed him to pursue his artistic dreams. They were the heirs, ranked in descending order of importance; he was the spare, consistently supported but otherwise ignored, and acted accordingly.

To his credit, he had good taste; however, he couldn't *generate* anything. He did "collage art," sampling, like the Beastie Boys' album *Paul's Boutique*, where every song is basically nothing but samples on top of samples. Still, there's a reason they got sued for making that album, and there's a reason that suit gave rise to regulations which now stipulate samples can't be more than a certain length. Because when you build a house out of bits and pieces of other people's houses, you can't claim to be surprised when the whole fucking thing falls down.

I remember he used to compare himself to Max Ernst when he was first starting out. Back in his Dada days, Ernst made entire books out of cutting images from magazines and recombining them. Difference was, Ernst could actually *paint*, and after a certain point in his career he gave up on the whole *Semaine de Bonté* routine entirely, whereas I never saw anything in Wrob's films that I'd call original. The best parts were always stolen from somebody else.

His offering that night was called *Untitled 13*, thirteenth in a series of similarly title-less films. It was roughly ten minutes long, and at first contained nothing but the various "artistic" flourishes I'd learned to associate with product released under his name: intercutting CBC documentary footage videotaped off TV screens with loops of hardcore gay porn; using stop-motion photography to puppet around a series of naked dudes wearing *papier-mâché* masks made from vintage *Blue Boy* magazines in blown-out 16mm—tricks that aimed to shock, only to stumble over into cute or trite. Or both.

Right in the middle, however, things changed.

It started with the framing, which suddenly shifted, moving inwards. Took me a minute or so to figure out that what he'd done was poach an idea first developed in 1971 for Józef Robakowski's "camera-free" film, *Test I*: punch physical holes along a length of opaque 35mm film, then project it using an exceptionally bright lamp, allowing the strong light behind the film to "attack" the viewer and generate afterimages mimicking the flicker of film frames—like cigarette burns in reverse, all-white versions of those hovering black dots that often appear on the film-strips of older movies, just before a splice.

So Wrob was using essentially the same technique, but also intermittently widening the holes until they "ate" almost the whole frame, then using blurring and light-flare to mask the transition to a different film altogether. These secondary edits were initially brief—a couple of seconds each, just enough to suggest an image without allowing for interpretation—but became steadily longer, *wider*, until I was finally able to figure out the mechanics: he'd burned a physical hole through a piece of black cardboard, mimicking the *Test I* sprockets, then fitted it over his camera's lens and filmed a *second* set of images, presenting them as though they were appearing in the "window" of the hole itself.

Even as I connected the dots on Wrob's methodology, I was also watching this new footage emerge, politely at first but a bit restively, squinting to get some sort of purchase on what I was seeing, then with growing interest. By the last flicker, less a fade than a smash cut to black, I was riveted.

Now the thing is, I could fill this whole chapter with film-critic jargon if I wanted to, all cues and references and shorthand. But I learned the hard way how most people—even ones who actually work in the industry—just don't care about that sort of accuracy. I remember one class, early in my teaching career, where a student to whom I'd just returned a script covered in scribbled comments raised his hand and asked: "Miz Cairns, you said here that the character development was 'cursory.' What's that mean, exactly?"

"It means you didn't have enough of it. Did a half-assed job, basically."

"Then why didn't you just write 'half-assed'?"

"Because there's a *word* for it. And that word is 'cursory.'"

Rather than drowning you in cinematographic esoterica, therefore, I'll give you my most immediate impressions from that first viewing—the actual notes I scribbled down while still squinting up at the screen, done on a Staples notepad I rummaged out of my pocket.

> *very bright black + white, looks more like grey/silver*
> *bits come away? like its moulting*
> *scratches pops dropped frames*
> *this is old/1920s? silent film*
> *older?*

I remember what looked like sheaves of grain waving back and forth, or the shadows of very tall grass, sharp under a pitiless sun that must surely have been an effect, since battery-powered electrical lamps were not available during the period in which Mrs. Whitcomb made her films but a painted backdrop could be made to look flatly three-dimensional, as if going away into the distance the theatrical suggestion of a field, with people onstage in front of it, wearing archaic, fairy tale peasant-type clothes—smocks and leggings, jerkins, hoods that hid their faces, mediaeval, like a Dance of Death.

And then there was a woman, stepping out from behind them, either around the backdrop's edge or through a cunningly hidden slit cut *into* it. She was brighter than everything else yet far harder to see in any true detail, covered as she was in a whitish veil that draped from her head to her feet and dazzled, sewn perhaps with glassine sequins, or tiny shards of mirror. She leaned down to whisper in one figure's ear, dwarfing him—was he played by a child? A child with a false beard, recoiling from her with his hands up?

Cued, her own hand came out from behind her back, and I could see she held a sword, angling it to reflect till it had almost turned white: curved and sharp like a sabre, like the blade of a scythe. So bright it hurt the eyes.

At which point, the screen went black.

* * *

"Typically uninterested in any film except his own, Wrob Barney gives pride of place to *Untitled 13*," my *Deep Down Undertown* article begins, "a waking dream of troubling things, done flammably, in light and poison." Then again, though, I really wasn't one to talk: there were ten other movies on that program, and I barely remembered any of them—Alec Christian got on my case about that, later on. I just couldn't stop thinking about the way Barney's piece made me feel, itchy in a good way, like the grit before the pearl. I needed to know where that *came* from.

I got home around one in the morning. Clark had probably been asleep since eight-thirty or nine, and Simon had dozed off in bed with the lights still on, a roleplaying game module balanced haphazardly on his chest. I could hear the two of them sawing counterpoint from either end of the apartment, a wracking, swollen-tonsils duet that wasn't doing much for my burgeoning migraine. The older I get, the more I find that any sort of barometric pressure shift goes straight to my sinus cavities, ruthlessly crossbreeding what sometimes feels like a near-constant case of PMS with the general side-effects of crap vision versus watching movies all day (and night) to create organic lens-flares. I knew I'd need a potentially dangerous amount of Melatonin, muscle-relaxants, and recreational web surfing before I could safely count on being able to dodge a full-blown bout of insomnia.

So I started the usual late-night round of chores—load of laundry, load of dishes—and set my laptop up on the "dining room" table, an unwieldy glass-topped ironwork monstrosity Simon's parents had bought us in anticipation of parties we'd never throw and meals we'd never make, not once it became clear that sitting still for social situations was something Clark seemed unlikely to ever do for more than ten minutes at a time. I transcribed my notes, moved stuff around, dashed off two thousand words' worth of description and analysis, then signed onto our WiFi, readying the article to post.

Throughout the process, I kept on thinking about the film, replaying it in snatches till it overlaid the mundane details of my life. It was seriously driving me nuts, because the masks, the costumes, the hint of a story . . . it all reminded me of *something*, and I just couldn't remember what. *Not* a movie, I knew that much; I thought maybe a photo, or a picture, so I hit PUBLISH, then pulled out my reference books and started going through them: stuff on fairy tales, stuff on mythology, on the occult, woodcuts, engravings, chiaroscuro, collage—Ernst, Magritte, Khnopff, Bosch, Leonora Carrington, Remedios Varo. Movie stills. Comic books. Surrealists and Decadents of all descriptions.

Slowly but surely, as my perception narrowed, the presentiment of pain I'd been wrestling with became pain itself, dim but distinct: my eye sockets lit up, muscles on the back of my skull humping and crawling. I got sick, sleepy. Eventually, I had to force myself to sit down and stay quiet for a while, lids lowered, taking deep, slow breaths. Press my thumbs against my nasal bridge and watch the patterns form, hypnagogically recursive—red spiralling away into black, thicker and thicker, making it impossible to tell which was which.

Olfactory hallucinations came next, tinnitus garnished. To my left, I smelled hay and smoke and mould, a whole burning barn of fragrances; to my right was wet earth, cold green shoots, frozen decay. A forest, deep and dark, after the late autumn rains.

Quiet, then. A long, grey pause, empty of almost everything.

When I opened my eyes once more it was almost four in the morning, but the pain was gone. Better yet, I finally knew what I was looking for.

I still have the text in question today, bookmarked between pages 112 and 113, where the section titled "Dreams & Nightmares" begins—a battered trade paperback with fraying laminate corners, the cover a murky reproduction of Emily Carr's 1931 painting *Among the Firs*, called *Finding Your Voice: Creative Writing Prompts and Projects, Grades Three to Eight* (edited by Luanne Kellerman, copyright 1979 from Seedling Press, Toronto). It's a compilation of fifth-grade English class prompts that struck enough of my fancy to make me "forget" to bring it back at the end of the year, all based on poems and essays, myths and fairy tales; mostly Canadian Content, too, because that must've been the most affordable option. It usually is.

Nothing to show what I wanted it for, at least not on the outside. But we all know the spine of a book tends to crack where you've read it most, even if it was so long ago it now seems unfamiliar, from the inside-out.

So when I opened it, *this* is what I found.

LADY MIDDAY
A Fairy tale of the Wends
Collected and Translated by Mrs. A. Macalla Whitcomb
First printed in The Snake-Queen's Daughter: Wendish
Legends & Folklore

Once, a young boy was ploughing a field to ready it for planting, during the noon hour. How hot it was, and how he wished he could be elsewhere! His whole hatband was soaked with sweat. But his father was dead and his mother took in sewing to pay their way, and there was no one else to help him with his labours.

Soon enough, when the sun was at its still point above him, there came by Lady Midday, so tall and fine with her long white hair and her blazing eyes, and a terrible great pair of scissors in one hand, with blades so sharp and polished they threw back the sun's rays like lightning.

"It is a hard day for ploughing," she said to the boy, "and you without even a cup of water. Do you not wish for rest and comfort?"

But the boy's mother had warned him of Lady Midday. So he kept his eyes to his task, bowing low in deference at the same time, and replied: "No, milady, for this field must be ploughed and planted, so that my mother and I may have crops to sustain us this winter. I need nothing, though I thank you for your kindness."

At this, Lady Midday's eyes flashed like a sword heated red-hot, thrust deep into the very heart of the fire, and she bent herself double to put her face right up next to the boy's so that her hair fell around them like a veil. Whereupon the heat of her was so great the boy thought either he would smother, or that his cheek would crisp like bacon.

"Oh," she said, so sweetly, "but you are a good boy, to do your mother's bidding thusly! Do you not wish to stop and drink a bit, if only to refresh yourself once more for the work you have yet before you? See, I have brought water in a cup, cool and deep. You may have it all, if you will only turn to look my way."

Yet the boy did not, shaking his head and bowing still further. "No thank you, milady, for I cannot turn myself from my work, and am not fit to look upon such sights—for how is it that I, a poor boy, could count myself the equal of such a personage?"

"You think me fair?"

"I know it, milady."

"But only by report. Turn now, and see."

How he yearned to do so! Yet the heat of her was so dreadful, parching his mouth and setting his skin to sizzle, and the light she gave as bright as though the sun itself sat on her shoulder, an ornament for her long white hair—hair which was neither plaited nor tied, but dropped straight down to her feet, so bare and dainty, whose nails were great claws made from brass.

"I cannot, milady," he answered. And he closed his eyes in fear, though he ploughed on, that he might not have to see the terrible scissors descend.

All at once, however, Lady Midday withdrew her attentions, and her voice became gentle, though no more like a human being's.

"Because you have been diligent and polite," she told the boy, "and answered me with the courtesy due my station, I will give you for a gift that so long as the sun's eye falls upon it, your field will flourish. And I will not bother you again."

And indeed, after that, she never did.

Further on, a grown man ploughed his field, cursing his

lot and the sun's pitiless stare. He beat his mule hard enough to draw blood, complaining all the while, instead of giving his task the attention it merited. And since the noon hour was not yet done, the sun at its still point above him, there came by Lady Midday in all her awful finery, to ask—

"It is a hard day for ploughing, and you without even a cup of water. Do you not wish for rest and comfort?"

The man raised his eyes from his task and looked at her straight on, haughtily. "What a stupid question!" he replied. "It is hotter than the hobs of Hell out here. Is that water in your hand?"

"It is. May I take it you find me pleasant to look on?"

"Indeed, you are a fine, tall baggage. But how foolish you must be! Can you not see I am dying of thirst? Give me that cup, and quickly!"

"I think not," Lady Midday told him. "Yet because you have not answered me with the courtesy due my station, I will give you for gift something very different."

With that, she attained her full height, blazing so bright that the man went blind. Which is why he did not see to duck when she brought her scissors down with a great snip, cutting his head clean off.

"Now go home, if you can," she said, "and have your wife sew this back on for you. Then wait until your sight returns and do your work with more diligence from now on, living the rest of your life in fear, for there are those in this world far less merciful than I."

The man made his way home in terror, by long degrees— stumbling wild with his head hugged tight in his arms, unable to see where his feet were taking him—and never more dared to step outside until the sun had fallen. But for the rest of his life he felt Lady Midday's eye upon him, always fearing to look too far up or too far down to avoid it, lest the stitches rip and his head fall clean off once more.

FOUR

I'm supposed to be objective here, right? One assumes. That's
certainly what they try to drill into you at journalism school.
But the thing is, it's never made all too much sense to me, this
idea of trying to divorce yourself from any hint of personal
reaction—keeping stringently to the facts, ma'am, just the facts.
Which may be why I drifted into being a film critic in the first
place; why shackle yourself to fact checking, on exactly how
close to the truth you can parse things, when you can just get
paid for voicing your opinion instead?

One way or the other, I knew I'd read "Lady Midday" before.
Had to have. Why else would I have kept the book? How else
could I have connected the dots? But—

When I think about the stories that have stayed with me throughout my mythocentric life, which shaped me as both consumer and
creator, this just wasn't one that floated automatically to the top. It
seemed familiar, yes, but only in a pattern-recognition sort of way—
i.e. I recognized *sections* of it, echoes of other folk-tales and fables,
other hard-judging, unreliable supernatural mentor-archetypes:
Mother Holle and Mrs. Gertrude, from Germany; Baba Yaga and
King Frost, from Russia. The latter, very much.

Are you warm, maiden? Are you warm, or are you cold?

*Yes, thank you, King Frost; I am warm, thanks to your munifi-
cence. I am not cold, not at all.*

Ah, but you shiver. Your lips and hands turn blue. Are you sure *you are not cold in truth, pretty maiden?*

No, thank you, great king.

The maiden suffers politely, beautifully, deferentially, so King Frost—impressed by her polite lies—gives her a reward. Her shrewish stepsister complains, like any normal human being, and is frozen alive. The young boy gives Lady Midday her proper respect, survives, and prospers. The older farmer mouths off and gets his just desserts.

A familiar idea, except for the trappings. And there was something about it which reminded me of *The Golden Bough*, James George Frazer's compendium of pagan lore and tradition. The idea that most fairy godparents were really former *gods*, small-d deities of place locked to various community-sustaining natural phenomena—the earth, the harvest, the wind that shakes the barley—run through a Christian repurposing machine, reduced to creatures whose malice can be averted through basic cleverness, cold iron, and rote Church cant. For *I said my prayers all out in a rush*, Henry Treece concludes, at the end of his poem "The Magic Wood," *and found myself safe on my father's land.*

All I can tell you, in the end, is this: the more I studied "Lady Midday" line by line, seeing almost every phrase of it reflected it my memories of Wrob Barney's *Untitled 13*, the extent to which it already disturbed me began, at length, to disturb me even more.

Still does.

So: riddle solved, sort of. But what to do with this information?

I brushed my teeth, went to bed, and slept till eleven, disturbed only briefly by Simon on his way out, wedging Clark into his clothes for that Saturday Social Situations course he was doing at the Trebas Institute, while the end credits of *Thomas* gave way to the title sequence of *Star Trek: The Next Generation*, with Clark doing his best Jean-Luc Picard imitation: "Stardate 24608.5. I am sending an away team down to the surface of planet Rigel Four, the Enterprise is filmed in Panavision." What eventually woke me was my mom, her timing impeccable as ever, phoning about whether or not I knew if Clark was signed up for summer school yet (no, the Catholic School Board wouldn't send confirmation until probably the week before, just like last year, and the year before), or if I wanted to bring him over to her place once the Institute dropped him off that afternoon. "Sure," I told her, still sleep-stupid. "That's, yeah—no problem. I can do that."

"Are you all right, Lois?"

"I'm fine, Mom."

"You don't sound 'fine.'"

"Had a migraine last night, that's all. Took me a while to get to sleep."

"Hmmm." A beat, while I literally bit my tongue to keep from responding. Then: "That's happening more often, isn't it?"

"More often than what?"

"Lois, I *know* you know what I mean—you had one just last night, remember? Around this same time, actually."

"Yeah, I know."

"Well, even so; it's not normal. Maybe you should see somebody."

"Maybe," I agreed. And hung up.

A shower and some coffee later, I was sitting in front of the computer tapping a pen, trying to rough out a plan of attack. If there really was any sort of link between Mrs. Whitcomb's story and the footage Wrob had spliced into his film, then the easiest way to confirm that might be to go directly to the "source"—i.e. get in touch with the man himself, start a conversation, then drop hints hoping he'd simply admit it. So I accessed the Ursulines' website and clicked on the phone number provided, straightening as it began to ring; raked my hair into place for the web-camera, grateful I'd at least had the sense to put on pants beforehand.

User is offline, F2F told me, eventually. *Would you like to send a message?*

"Yep," I replied, out loud, and switched to voice-text: "Caught *Untitled 13* last night, comma, my review should be up this afternoon, full stop. Would like to follow up with an interview, comma, are you interested, question mark? Please mail or call, comma, Lois Cairns."

I waited for a few minutes after hitting SEND, just in case, then poured myself a cup of coffee and started Googling: Mrs. Whitcomb (wife of Arthur Macalla, artistic career, Spiritualism, disappearance, Balcarras's *Strange Tales*, etc.), *The Snake Queen's Daughter* (privately printed, one copy listed at the Toronto Public Reference Library, in the restricted-access stacks), the Wends or Wendish people (inhabitants of the now only German-speaking parts of what used to be the larger region of Old Lusatia, in Eastern Germany), Lady Midday . . .

Also known as Pscipolnitsa, Poludnica, Polednice, this Slavic noontime demon warns harvesters to pay attention to their duty or suffer the consequences. Generally pictured as a beautiful woman dressed all in white, she carries a pair of shears and roams the boundaries of the fields like a whirling dust cloud, attempting to engage labourers in conversation during the very hottest hour of the day. Any incorrect answer or unprompted subject change will result in a beheading, perhaps a symbolic representation of heatstroke. She may also appear as an old hag or twelve-year-old girl. Even today, the threat of encountering her is often used to scare children away from valuable crops.

In Wendish mythology, she is known as Mittagsfrau, "Lady Midday"; in Brandenburg, a related mythological spirit called the Roggenmuhme or "lady of the rye" makes ill-behaved children disappear on hot summer days, while in the Altmark the Regenmöhme—"with her heat"—who abducts kids foolish enough to distract their parents from their field-work. Around Lunenberg in Lower Saxony, the name of this bugbear is Kornwief or Kornwyf, meaning "woman of the corn."

Sounded like the same person. There was an accompanying illustration that made me sit up a bit straighter, too: all-white bristling hair, sun-rayed in every direction; light-bleached face reduced to a pair of fixed, staring-owl eyes; a fiercely set mouth. Were those wings at her shoulders or a cloak blown out in two great flaps, scudding the cloudless sky? Everything had an odd Impressionist shimmer to it, like a haze; I could almost hear cicadas buzzing in unseen trees, smell the baked metal tang of sweat as the plough passed by, gleaners following behind. I shook my head then, sharply, a shiver of last night's migraine wincing through my temples. And heard the chime of an F2F reply, appearing in my screen's bottom left corner: *yokay sounds good how bout tonite 6pm sneaky dees @ college/bathurst*

"Can you make it seven question mark?"

will do txt when ur onsite byeeee

"Byeeeee to you too full stop," I muttered, clicking voice-text off. Adding: "Asshole."

"That's . . . pretty similar," Simon observed, looking at the four clips from *Untitled 13* Wrob Barney had put up on his site and comparing them to my own transcription of "Lady Midday." We'd agreed to meet for coffee earlier in the day, him heading over to get Clark from Mom's, me with a good fifteen minutes before I really needed to hustle in order to get to Sneaky Dee's on time; I planned to take a cab anyhow, rationalizing that twenty bucks we didn't really have as a pretty good investment if you factored in the whole "might change my life" element.

"I know, right?" I took a sip of coffee. "It's kind of uncanny."

"In the truest sense, yeah. You have any evidence he actually read this story, though?"

"Nope. No evidence this supposed silent film footage isn't really his work, either . . . but I do know Wrob Barney's done it before and more than once—copied stuff from various sources just to stick it inside his own shit, like flavouring: *Untitled 5, Untitled 7.* He tends to go for stuff that's out of copyright or porn, or both—stuff nobody's exactly going to contest."

"Seriously?"

I shrugged. "Sure. That's how he lost his job at the National Film Archive—somebody walked in on him screening old films and videotaping them off the monitor to get a degenerated image, cutting in camera. Chris Coulby told me."

Chris was a guy I'd gone to Figtree Alternative High School with, once upon a time; he'd graduated York University with a degree in Film Studies and Production, the way I'd originally planned before hedging my bets and going to Ryerson instead for Magazine Journalism. He and his fellow classmates had exploded out into the world during a recession and ended up going in very different directions—one formed a band, in which Chris briefly sang backup, before working reception and ticket sales at the NFA. He'd been my inside man ever since, never directly quotable yet the source of much information.

Simon sat back. "Okay, sounds legit. So what next?"

I thought about that for a minute. "Well, going by what we have here," I began, finally, feeling my way through the thesis out loud, "it looks like someone made a movie out of 'Lady Midday,' probably shortly after the story was published. And since there's no way it was widely known, given it was published privately, then that person . . . might have been Mrs. Whitcomb herself. Which would be kind of a deal."

"And you're gonna ask Barney about that?"

"Where he got the clips, at least, and maybe not directly. I don't think I need to talk about Mrs. Whitcomb per se."

"Wait and see if he brings it up?" I nodded. "Okay, but what if he doesn't? You still need to prove the link, obviously, to get people on board. . . ."

"Obviously, yeah."

"So how?"

"Noooo fuckin' idea."

He nodded slightly, and we sat there again for a moment or two in companionable silence. Simon and I had known each other for a good seven years before we ever hooked up. Part of the appeal was that friendship; though people always claim it's good to be "best friends" with your significant other, it does tend to reduce your circle of acquaintanceship pretty severely, especially once you have kids. *Especially* if said kids are like Clark, and looking back, how could they have not been?

People still ask me sometimes what I think "happened," like they're asking me to place blame, to point to something I did or something that was done *to* me—to identify what exactly was the glitch that fashioned Clark, made him who/what he is, so they can avoid it. Was it vaccination, pollution, too much electricity in the air? The only thing that has ever made sense to me is a theory put forward by Sacha Baron Cohen's brother (also Simon, hilariously), who attributes it to simple genetics: the fact that for at least fifty years now, people have been choosing their mates by affinity rather than economic considerations, allowing geeks who test a few points off the spectrum like me and Simon to fumble our way toward each other. A double payload of geekery, therefore, and you get Clark, the über-geek, so subsumed inside his own enthusiasms that on a bad day he can barely acknowledge the outside world—though even on a good day, seemingly, there's little to nothing beyond the circle of his own skull appealing enough to distract him for long.

Simon is good at math, loves role-playing games and puzzles, and calculates point scores for fun. His father is a deacon and his uncle a priest—the same priest who married us—so it shouldn't be surprising that his thought patterns register as Jesuitical, or maybe Thomistic; he used to like to argue for fun, once upon a time, though these days he finds it wearing. He can put on a better social face than I can, but he bruises easily; his emotions are closer to the surface than mine, or possibly just less ground down, less disconnected. On the other hand, he's really good for bouncing things off of, because he thinks logically, not metaphorically. We're both pattern makers, albeit of very different types.

"You better go," he said, finally. "Mind if I think about this for a while, on my own? I might be able to come up with something."

"Please. I'll take all the help I can get."

He smiled. "Excellent! See ya later, then. Love."

"Love," I replied, kissing him goodbye.

Ten years plus since Toronto went smoke-free in bars, as well as workplaces and restaurants, Sneaky Dee's is the kind of place that still smells like the inside of an ashtray—dark-painted walls inside and graffiti mural on stucco out, all cartoon cow skulls, cacti, and cowboy hats outlined in blacklight-sensitive DayGlo paint. Weekends, they hold Eighties Music Night meet-and-greets; weeknights, it's a rotating roster of local nu-punk, black metal, and ghost house bands, cut with the occasional white suburban rap crew. I texted Wrob as the cab pulled up, then fought my way upstairs where I found him crammed into a booth near the back, all long limbs, tousled greaser-black hair, and deep-set glazed, glinting eyes, as far from the stage as possible. He was studying tonight's flyer and working on his second beer. "Tonight: Prolapse," he said, shoving it toward me. "Ever heard of 'em? I think they used to be Prolapsed *Something*, and if so, they really suck. But I'm just not sure."

I looked at the logo, shook my head. "That's the same font Fudgetongue used to use, but other than that, couldn't tell you."

"*Fudgetongue?* Jesus. They're the guys with the moog that sounds like a kazoo, right?"

"I think that's Fudge Tunnel."

"Well, one way or the other, we probably should get this over with quick." He raised his hands, semaphore-ing the waiter. "Yo, Lloyd! Two more beers!"

"Not for me, thanks, I'm wheat-sensitive."

"Make that one beer, and whatever your best girly drink is!"

Wasn't often anybody called me girly, parts aside, so I decided to take that as a compliment. "Mind if I record this?" I asked, sliding in beside him. "Alexander does a podcast sometimes, but don't worry, if I can't clean the sound-file up enough for hosting standards I'll go transcript instead—I always back my interviews up with notes."

Wrob leered. "Oh, not a problem! Makes me feel *infamous*."

I threw in for the next round, then the next, and let him talk. Wasn't hard. He was his own favourite subject, after all.

Leonard Warsame, Wrob's then-partner and assistant, once told me that Wrob "had this thing he used to do, whenever he was interviewed—he'd take it as a license to tell these outrageous . . . not sure if I'd call them lies, since I think they usually contained at least some element of the truth, but fibs, let's say, about his childhood and adolescence, growing up queer and arty in rural Ontario. Called them 'True Tales of Dourvale.' I figure he must've gotten the idea from Guy Maddin. Back when I first met him, I thought they were true, because I didn't know that much about Canada to begin with—I moved here from Somalia when I was fifteen, never really left Toronto until I was twenty. But I did some asking around and found out that not only did he *not* grow up in Dourvale . . . he actually grew up in this other town ten miles away called Overdeere, I think. Dourvale doesn't even exist."

"Excuse me?" I asked, taken aback.

"Well, it exists, I guess—physically—but nobody actually lives there. It's a ghost town. Which is just *classic* Wrob."

Afterwards, I went through the Dragon Dictation app recording of the interview, cross-checking it with my notes for anything that seemed like it needed to be corrected. The conversation ended up looking a lot like this:

WROB: So, read your review. You really liked *Untitled 13*, huh?

ME: Best thing you've done so far. Better than *Untitled 1* through *12*, by a long shot.

WROB: Yeah, yeah . . . don't oversell it, okay? I know you think I'm a parasite, a tapeworm dug deep in the bowels of Can-Con, or whatever—

ME: What? No, I don't think that.

WROB: Suuuurrre you don't. But fine, let's lay that by—I still know what you're really here to ask about. You want to know about the inserts, right?

ME: They were . . . very powerful. Almost looked like you did them on silver nitrate.

WROB: Uh huh.

ME: But that's not really possible, right? I mean—

WROB: What makes you think I couldn't get my hands on some unexposed silver nitrate film, Lois? I'm rich, after all. Could even pay somebody to *make* some, if I really wanted to. Of course, it probably wouldn't have that same kinda flaky quality, like it's starting to come off a bit. Like it's step-printed on a fire hazard. (Pause) No, you're right, of course. The clips come from something I sampled, before the NFA bounced my sorry ass.

ME: What was it?

WROB: Long story. Longish. Definitely calls for another drink.

By the end of his NFA tenure, Wrob told me, he'd been working "very closely" with Jan Mattheuis, head of the Ontario Film Recovery Project. Mattheuis had started as an academic, teaching Film Studies out of Brock University, where he'd written a couple of surveys of early Canadian film that brought him to the attention of Piers Handling, Director and CEO of the Toronto International Film Festival. Handling brought Mattheuis in to curate a couple of programmes and the rest is history—he became attached to the NFA, where he developed the OFRP from the ground up, with the help of a network of volunteers and fundraisers. Their mandate was reclamation, categorization, and digitization of found footage dating anywhere from the late 1800s to the early 1920s. Wrob claimed to have bought his way in at the bottom through a hefty donation, then set his cap for Mattheuis, even though he was "not really my type, per se—waaay too old," dazzling him with his double knowledge of digitization technology and potential recovery sites, especially in Lake of the North region.

WROB: Jan was particularly interested in locating any lost or hidden caches of silver nitrate footage, because given its chemical composition alone, there just doesn't tend to be much of it left. So he really perked up when I told him about the studio in Sulfa. You might remember this one too, or maybe you don't— the Japery? Opened up in 1918?

ME: Sure. One of the bandwagon-jumpers, after Canadian National Features of Toronto started supplying shorts and second-reel features for the Allen Brothers theatre chain.

WROB: That's right. An intense but sadly fleeting period of success in the industry. Jay and Jule Allen went straight from owning a store-front nickelodeon into an exclusive Canadian distribution license for all those glamorous, proto-Hollywood Goldwyn and Famous Players-Lasky films, and their success then gave birth to a whole bunch of envious imitators leaping up like mushrooms across Ontario, Quebec, the West . . . till they ran afoul of Adolph Zukor, that is, the Famous Players magnate.

ME: I know the history, Wrob.

WROB: 'Course you do—the part that's public record, anyhow. Zukor refused to renegotiate the distribution deal unless the Allens took him on as a partner, but they refused, naturally enough, and that tolled the bell on their entire business model. The Trenton studio was gone by 1920, and it took them four years to recoup even a fraction of their losses by selling out to the Ontario government. All its progeny soon followed likewise . . . *except* the Japery, which met a very different fate.

ME: Uh huh. Which was?

WROB: It burned to the ground. And the fire that gutted it? Began in its own little warehouse of completed movies, which just so happened to be located—un-strategically, in hindsight— in the facility where its silver nitrate reels were processed.

ME: Jesus, place must've gone off like a bomb. Anybody die?

WROB: Oh, it happened at night, well after hours. By that time, they'd mainly switched over from making their own films to copying other people's, cobbling work-prints and sending them down along the store-front and church basement circuit, all up and down Lake of the North. Actually, there was a rumour maybe the Allens might've *paid* to have them torched, in order to limit competition—or Zukor, even, you want to get all conspiracy theory. But frankly? I think both sides of that struggle had bigger fish to fry.

ME: And Mattheuis thought he could find, what? Some leftovers?

WROB: No, we both knew how unlikely that was, given the way that shit burns. What he thought—well, what I *suggested* to him—was that if Japery was still delivering prints right up until the end, then maybe there'd be some point to checking the stops along what used to be their old supply route.

ME: Which turned out to be a profitable idea, I take it.

WROB: We ran across four different caches following that protocol, all silver nitrate—maybe four and a half if you count some stuff Jan bought from the Quarry Argent Folk Museum, donated from various private collections: one under a hockey rink in Chaste, when they knocked down what used to be Gersholme's nickelodeon; one in somebody's attic, out by Your Ear; one in God's Lips, inside a meeting-house wall; and one . . . well, Jan should probably tell you about that one himself. It's a funny story.

ME: So, the clips for *Untitled 13*—you stole them from Mattheuis's stash?

WROB: Please, Lois: sampled. You know my methods. During cataloguing, before restoration. I basically filmed it off a monitor with my Super 16, put a mosquito-netting drape over it and moved it back and forth while I did it, deformed the subtextual. Sick effect, right?

ME: And what'd Mattheuis think of that?

WROB: Not much, which is why I'm not working there anymore. Truth to tell, we were probably gonna break up soon anyways; he's not a lot of fun after hours, or during hours, either. But it was worth it. I mean—you saw. (Pause) Look, from my point of view, I feel as though Canadian film belongs to *everybody*. And it *repulses* me that most Canadians don't feel the same way, which is one of the reasons I got involved with the Archive in the first place, with Jan. And the reason I feel this way is that when I was a kid, back in Overdeere, I saw this bunch of dickheads stack maybe seventeen separate silver nitrate prints in a pit and set the whole thing on fire, let it burn till it was gone. They found 'em in an old church on the outskirts of town, where I guess they used to show films sometimes—the canisters were rusted shut, so they had to beat 'em with tire irons and shit just to pry them open, and when they did they found that half of 'em had turned to goo . . . God, that smelled awful, like pickled dead bodies or something. But the other half, they were *fine*. You could see it even from the sidelines, the safety perimeters they were keeping all us looky-loos back behind. One guy held up a reel so the light shone through it, and if you squinted you could *almost* see little tiny silver pictures on each frame, moving just a bit, like they were vibrating—that's how it seemed to me, anyway. And I wanted to know why they'd just *destroy* something like that, something so old, so . . . beautiful, so important. Why they'd have to throw it away like garbage, burn it like a wasp's nest. But the local fire chief told my dad it was too dangerous to even try and store, that it was a wonder it hadn't gone up already: "This stuff *spontaneously combusts!* It gives off *poisonous gases* when it burns!" And my dad . . . he said he was right, stop your bitchin', it's nothing special anyhow. Think about it, Lois, 'cause I know you get what I'm saying: this was history, *our* history, and nobody cared enough to try to preserve any of it.

Was it a put-on, an act? I couldn't tell, even close up; Wrob was like that, I guess. He had genuine tears in his eyes, though God knows, that might've been the beer. Or the music.

At any rate, dude wasn't making a whole lot of sense, to the point where I actually stopped recording. But he just kept on talking about how he liked that particular film—that particular bunch of films—because they were all in such bad shape you kind of had to look at them at an angle, side-on, just to figure out what was happening. How if you looked at it straight on, it just hurt your eyes. Like there wasn't anything there? I asked him, and he laughed. Said, oh, there was something *there*, all right, something the person who made it didn't want you seeing. So you kind of had to sneak up on it, romance it a bit. Wait till it poked its head out when it thought you weren't watching and *trap* it.

Eventually, Leonard Warsame turned up, took one look at Wrob and rolled his eyes; he grabbed Wrob by the arm, told me he needed an early night, and that was that. So I called another cab and went home.

"So what's his angle?" Simon asked me later that night, as we got ready for bed. Clark had gone down comparatively easily, as he often did, with Daddy playing good cop; I was flossing over the kitchen sink as Simon brushed his teeth, since our bathroom wasn't really large enough to accommodate two adults at the same time. I rinsed, spat, then replied—

"Seems to me like he wants to present himself as some sort of activist, maybe seed the interview, get his side of the story on

record as a counterpoint to something Mattheuis is building up
to: a press release? That big a batch of silver nitrate, all digitized
and catalogued, so it doesn't ever have to be screened physically
again . . . that'd be something. You could do an exhibition at the
Lightbox, or even an installation at the AGO—big fundraising
bucks, potentially. *Great* cultural cred. I can see why he'd want to
get in on that, 'specially if he feels like Mattheuis shut him out."

"Sort of the same way you want to get in on proving Mrs.
Whitcomb made that film," Simon pointed out, gently.

"Well, yeah," I agreed. "Except how *I'm* not doing it mainly to
piss off my ex-boyfriend—"

"For which I'm very grateful."

"—and playing the victim, putting on a show for the media,
if you can even call me 'the media,' these days. And I'm just not
interested in helping him out with that sort of petty personal
backstabbing, seriously."

"So you're not going to talk to Mister, what's his name,
Matthias?"

"Mattheuis—and oh no, I'm definitely gonna talk to Jan, if
he'll see me. 'Cause I need the other half of this, given it might
help me build *my* case."

"That's what I thought."

I snorted. "You know me so well."

"It's almost like we're married."

So he went to bed while I synched my iPhone to my laptop,
got the sound-file all squared away, then stayed up transcribing
my notes and listening to the soundtrack from Darren Aronof-
sky's *The Fountain* on infinite loop. My eyes were burning, probably from all that residual smoke. Around 3:00 A.M. I saved,
shut down, and lay back on the couch for "a minute," then almost
immediately found myself deep in a dream: winter light, a light
dusting of snow on the ground, yellow tape marking off a safe
distance from the same pit Wrob had described to me—a jagged-
sided, split-lipped mouth full of black soil and coiled, shimmery
loops of film, gummed together by an iridescent, stinking muck
of wept-off emulsion. Firemen in full drag stood by with sand-
buckets, their faces obscured by respirator masks and helmets,

as Ontario Provincial Police uniforms held the crowd back. Somewhere in there, I knew, was the boy Wrob Barney had once been, protesting this injustice to his father, but I couldn't pick him out. Instead, my eyes went to a figure standing on the farthest outskirts, under the trees and black, overhanging branches, almost hidden by jostling spectators. A dim blur dressed all in white from top to toe, every part of it—her? But how could I know that?—equally shrouded as though enveloped in a massive bag, a beekeeper's costume without the broad-brimmed hat, a bleached-out Afghan *chadri* complete with grille . . . a veil.

Of course I know now who she must have been. Let me remind you, though—this was *before* I'd spoken to Hugo Balcarras, before I'd seen the only extant portrait of Iris Dunlopp Whitcomb, in her peculiar version of full mourning. Before any of that.

Yet there she was, burnt on the inside of my eyelids, wavering at the very edge of my sight. Raising one fine, slim, white-gloved hand, to shape a gesture I found singularly hard to interpret, especially at a distance: was that her palm turned outward like a warning—*halt, go back, this it not for you?* Or was it the back, beckoning me closer—*yes, come here, don't be afraid, show yourself—and be shown. I know your face, Lois; I know you. There is . . .*

. . . something . . .

. . . I want for you to see.

One finger extending then curved and sharp as a twig, as a claw. Pointing downwards, toward my feet.

And when I looked, helpless, unable to stop myself from following that finger's angle, I saw that the fire inside the pit was already lit, the film cache already burning, bright as a hundred thousand candles. There was something else blooming in its centre, brighter still, so much you could hardly stand to look at it: a curled absence, a hole in the world's hide, throwing off sparks. Something that shone solid, less an eye than a doorway through which a void could be glimpsed.

Curled until it wasn't. Until it spread and resolved, growing limbs. Until it reached out, four-legged, to grasp the pit's sides, its unstable rim. Until what might have been its shoulders bunched, arms flexed and pulling. Until the part that must have been its head tipped back, assessing, reckoning how much force it would have to exert to free itself. Until, slowly, so *horribly* slowly—

—it began to crawl, carefully, up. And out.

I woke in an instant, choking on my own spit, goosebumped all over; my temperature had fallen during sleep, the way it always does, chilling my sweat till it slicked me like ice. Turned on my side, foetal, and coughed so hard I felt like I was retching. When I finally recovered enough to make my way to the bathroom, my eyes were glued together with sleep so thick I had to scrub at them with a moistened facecloth—at which point I looked in the mirror and almost screamed, because my sclera were suffused with what looked like classic petechial haemorrhaging: no whites anymore, just creamy pink, inflamed every micro-millimetre or so with broken threads of pure red.

As I sat in the doctor's office the next morning, waiting to hear his diagnosis ("Looks like you've been crying too hard," he remarked, with what I felt was a startling lack of sympathy. "They'll go away eventually."), I checked my phone only to discover a message that'd probably arrived just after I turned it off for the night and hooked it up to charge—one of those creepy ones that starts out as a text, then ends up a robot voice reading the text back to you on voicemail, like if Stephen Hawking did telemarketing. The thing itself is lost to time, since I deleted it automatically after hearing it, only later realizing that might not have been the best idea. However, I believe it said:

> *jan can tlk bt I think I always hd more right to tht film than him*
>
> *not least cause he still dsnt even know what hes got*
>
> *like he even pt the wrong name on it.*

FIVE

"Did you ask Dr. Goa about the migraines and the insomnia?" my mother wanted to know. "I did not," I replied, still deeply engaged in Googling Hugo Balcarras's contact information—a thankless fucking task from the get-go. The only thing listed was his publisher, Houslow, who hadn't been active since the early 1990s. So I was eventually reduced to calling up a former colleague of mine who now wrote jokey celebrity commentary for the *Toronto Star*'s Saturday edition, and begged her to reverse-directory it; that got me his latest phone number, which got me the interview excerpted in Chapter One. But I wasn't about to get into all *that* right then and there, not with Mom already on the metaphorical warpath.

"Oh, Lois, you were already *in* the clinic, for God's sake. Why wouldn't you?"

I sighed. "'Cause I was mainly concerned about the thing with my eyes, 'cause every professional thing I do is kind of contingent on me being able to see? Besides which, you know he doesn't like it when you ask about two things at once—"

I could almost see Mom's gesture, shrugging this off as though flicking away flies. "Pssh! I don't care what that man *likes*; this is his job, and he'd better damn well do it, if he knows what's good for him. You've got Clark to look after—can't be running on five hours or less all the time. You need to get this solved."

"I know I do."

"Do you?"

"*Yes,* Mom, Christ. You think I *want* things this way, tired all the fucking time? Think if there was a switch I could turn to reset my own clock I wouldn't?"

"You know, you're impossible to talk to when you get like this."

"So you've told me," I said, and hung up. Adding in my head: *Too many times to count, in actual fact, and most especially when I'm—*

Could you really call it "working," though, if nobody was actually paying you to do it? This was the wall Mom and I kept slamming up against, weirdly and contradictorily from my angle, considering she'd been freelance longer than I'd been alive. But acting was—is—an art form, and artists keep odd hours, routinely giving to get back, treating their careers as a type of infinitely extended gamble; journalism just isn't. *Film criticism* isn't. Except for how, these days, it really is.

What I was doing right now I saw as being like applying for a grant—studying the body in question's internal jargon, its lingo, before finding the most socially acceptable way of saying what I needed the money for. The primary person I'd have to apply to would be Jan Mattheius, of course, and I didn't want to go in there empty-handed. I wanted to go in armed to the teeth, my thesis unshakable, all guns blazing; till I could, I'd just have to keep on researching. And that struck me as far more important than whether or not my sleep cycle remained screwed up, considering how long I'd already had to live with that particular reality.

But you have a child, Mom would have said, had I ever been stupid enough to voice any of the above to her. *A child with special needs, who needs* you, *his mother. How can you be so selfish, so careless with your own health, your own time, your own life? How can you justify it?*

Well: when you put it that way, I suppose I couldn't, so I didn't. Because I'd already learned a long time ago how the way other people thought about whatever I was doing at any given time was always the most important thing, and that when it came to my own desires—my own *needs*—there was no contest, none at all; they came last, always, not first. She'd done it for me, after all, so now she got to police me as I did it for somebody else—i.e. Clark. And that was just called being a parent.

What you need to understand about my mom and I is that for a long time, we were everything to each other—all either of us had, often quite literally. She met my dad—Gareth Cairns—at theatre school, at the age of seventeen; he was seven years older, here from Australia to escape the draft, rightly reckoning that Canada was about as far away as you could get from Vietnam. She married him by the time she was twenty-two, had me at twenty-four. It took them seven more years to divorce, and she was the one who initiated it. "Only good thing ever came out of us being together was you," she used to say sometimes, back in her drinking days, when she'd finish off a six-pack alone and demand I sit up with her, having long conversations she couldn't remember afterwards. How could I disagree, exactly? If she'd never been with him, I wouldn't exist, no more than Clark would if I'd never met Simon. No matter the relative heartbreak both births may have caused, therefore, I can't say I'm ever inclined to favour either of those scenarios.

Sometimes she wanted me to sing to her, stuff like Juice Newton's "I'm Dancing As Fast As I Can," or Linda Ronstadt's cover of James Taylor's "You Can Close Your Eyes," and we'd both cry, hugging each other. But it didn't really mean anything; nothing got any better or worse because of what I did or didn't do, not until she finally wanted it to. Much like my own later flirtations with addictive behaviour, that part of her life probably lasted exactly as long as was needed, and while the mere fact of my existence might have had some theoretical bearing on her eventual decision to clean up, none of my direct actions seemed to make a single bit of difference. In retrospect, the most useful piece of advice I ever picked up concerning other people's problems was from one of the books Mom read while she was in recovery, a self-help text called (I shit you not) *If You Meet the Buddha on the*

Road, Kill Him!, which pointed out how you can't really change anything *for* anyone else, no matter how much you love them. All you can ever do is make yourself available in terms of emotional support, while they do the majority of the heavy lifting themselves.

Then again, maybe I'm talking out my ass, as usual. One way or the other, I've never found anyone's emotions as easy to process as my own—and considering how goddamn hard I find doing *that,* even at the best of times, that's really sort of sad.

That was the day I went to see Balcarras, after which I set up an interview with Jan Mattheuis because I definitely wanted to hear his version of that "funny story" Wrob Barney had alluded to. Much like old Hugo, Jan got back to me far quicker than I'd expected, which was excellent—and better yet, he set the time for ten the next morning, with Clark already safely off to school, thus giving me exactly as much time to quiz Mattheuis as he was willing to cooperate with.

Located in an outwardly undistinguished office building two doors from the corner of Yonge Street and right where College turns into Carlton, the NFA is an astounding research resource that most Torontonians (predictably enough) remain unaware even exists. The Archive was founded in 1995, partially as a response to then-Ontario Premier Mike Harris's virtual scuttling of the Ontario Film Development Corporation's budget back in 1993—according to his so-called "Common Sense Revolution," the making of Canadian films was a culturally protectionist luxury, unworthy of draining provincial funds during an economic downturn (though to be fair, he also slashed the amount of money made available for the Ontario Film Investment Project, our tax-rebate program, thus eating into runaway production profits as well). Since then, the NFA has managed to weather various governmental changeovers by keeping itself well-insulated within a cocoon of private monies, selling itself to private investors as a good donation recipient for both reputation-boosting and tax shelter purposes.

I'm always amused by the fact that at no point along the curve, however, has any of this money gone into installing some sort of lobby-level sign indicating where exactly to go for people walking in off the street. Instead, they're supposed to somehow pick up, via osmosis, that if they wander up a flight of stairs at the back of the elevator-bank waiting area, they'll eventually reach a pair of glass doors flanked by cabinets full of classic CanCon props: on your right, the titular faux-Aztec face covering from Julian Roffman's *The Mask* (1961, Canada's first 3D movie); on your left, the cursed Catholic oil dispenser from Harvey Hart's *The Pyx* (1973, with Christopher Plummer and Karen Black). It's like a J.K. Rowling riddle: if you have to ask, you'll never know; if you know, you don't have to ask. And I already know.

Upstairs, Chris Coulby was at the front desk, like usual. "Jan's in his office," he told me. "Coffee?"

"Got some already," I replied, raising my cup. "But thanks."

"Yeah, go ahead and make me feel useless, why don't ya."

I rubbed thumb, index, and pointer together at him, as though playing the world's tiniest violin. "The tears of men are tasty, boyo," I remarked as I passed, to which he simply snorted, shooting me the double finger.

Mattheuis was a smaller guy than you'd expect, given his reputation—smiley but broad, with heavy glasses and a greying, slightly furled goatee, sort of the Gimli of Canadian film studies. "You mind?" he asked, and then gave me a brief yet apparently sincere hug. "Lois Cairns! Been an age, hasn't it? I used to turn to your pieces first, back when; *Lip*'s definitely suffered for your absence."

I smiled. "Must be why they're *The Centrist*, now."

"No, I'd put that down to a classic case of Web versus Dead Tree, myself. But if we're going to talk shop, let's make it about a slightly more interesting subject. I hear you want to know about our silver nitrate initiative."

"Wrob Barney dropped a few hints about it during our inter-view, re: *Untitled 13*. Sounded intriguing."

"Oh yes, that'd be the way he'd phrase it, I'm sure. Given the amount of sheer *intrigue* he channelled into concentrating our attention on Lake of the North over the last few years."

"Turned out fairly well for you, though, didn't it? In terms of—"

"Sheer yield? Absolutely. Wrob's almost as good at giving people what they *think* they want as he is at getting what *he* really wants. It's practically his superpower."

I sat down, pulled out the tools of my trade, and got to it. "So," I said, as he did much the same, "what you're saying is, Wrob's goal all along was copying the footage?"

"Frankly? It's hard to tell. I mean, I knew he had to have a hidden agenda of some sort, right from the moment he first offered me the possibility of finding Japery's back-stock; the goodness of Wrob's heart is an entirely negotiable concept, as I'm well aware. Which makes what happened my fault entirely, in that even when the warning bells were going off loud and clear, I simply ignored them." A beat. "What he took . . . you've seen it, of course. The clips."

"Striking stuff."

"No one can claim Wrob doesn't have an eye. Interestingly, I'd never worked hands-on with silver nitrate before—afraid to, really, given its reputation. But Wrob has a positive knack for it. His digitization is pristine."

According to Mattheuis, Wrob had already catalogued nine different complete, partial, and fragmentary one-reel films he believed to have been produced by the same filmmaker by the time he was caught "sampling" red-handed and fired. "But there was a scene when he left, typically, and after that we were reduced to working from his notes—he wouldn't take my calls. The notes were handwritten, and that man has the worst chicken-scratch I've ever come across, outside of someone with an honest-to-God medical degree."

"Did he work with all four caches?"

"Mainly the last one, actually. I suppose he's told you about that."

"Not directly."

"Well." Mattheuis hesitated then glanced away, as though gathering himself—like he expected his next words, whatever they might be, to cost him. "It's an . . . interesting anecdote, I suppose. Especially so for me."

So I've been told, I thought, but didn't say. Just waited for him to elucidate, which—eventually, in slightly halting fashion—he did.

According to Mattheuis, he'd already bought up the Quarry Argent Folk Museum's little back-stock of silver nitrate films and was planning to drive back to Overdeere, where he was staying—at Wrob Barney's old family house, as it happened—when he somehow managed to get off-course and found himself hopelessly lost in the woods on what locals refer to as the "Dourvale shore" of the Lake of the North. "Now, I don't know how much you've already heard about that area . . ."

"Let's assume nothing."

"Yes, me either. But apparently, it's a bit of a legendary dead spot; cellphone service tends to go out, as does GPS, and—on occasion—cars just tend to, uh, stop. Like mine did."

Mattheuis thinks it was about 10:00 P.M. at this point, but has trouble narrowing things down further, since he doesn't carry a watch, and after a few minutes fussing with his phone it simply went black. The sun had fallen, leaving only a few deep purple streaks near the horizon as the full dark of the country took hold: cicadas, crickets, a dense cacophony of buzzing, rustling, and vague animal noises. He didn't even have a flashlight in the glovebox.

"When I finally did get to Overdeere, most people informed me that if I'd been born in the area, I'd've known to just lock my doors, stay in the car, and wait for morning. But since I was a city boy, I wasn't having any of *that.* I needed to take charge of the situation."

So Mattheuis got out and walked up and down the road a bit, "maybe thirty paces in either direction," without much joy. He was about to give up when suddenly he thought he saw lights moving through the woods to his left—faint but distinct, a kind of "globular, dim, intermittent" brightness which waxed and waned as it travelled in and out of the trees. "I won't say it looked like *people,* exactly, but what else could it have been? Like . . . hunters, maybe, or somebody from a cabin, a campsite, searching for the perfect place to use as a bathroom. So I made the decision—rather silly, in hindsight—to go after them."

Much like Little Red Riding Hood, therefore, Mattheuis stepped off the established path (or road, in this case) and into the brush, calling out that he was lost, in trouble, could anybody help him? The lights didn't seem all too far away, so he forced himself onwards, making brisk progress, but to little effect. Soon, he found himself far enough from his point of entry that he could no longer tell which direction he'd originally come from— he was surrounded on all sides by thorn-bushes, gnarled trees, and uncertain footing. One way was choked with mud, the other with what he thought he recognized as poison oak, and the misty night was getting progressively colder.

"Eventually," he continued, "I ended up at the edge of what seemed like a swamp or a sump—there's a lot of that around Lake of the North, very alkaline, very unreliable. I didn't want to risk my shoes any more than I already had, so I leaned back against this tree and just stayed there, stock-still, almost frozen. The lights were gone. I don't know how long that lasted; might've fallen asleep a couple of times, I guess. Finally, around five or six in the morning, the sun came back up, and everything got grey. Which is when I turned around and realized that all this time, I'd been *right next to* one of the famous Hell Holes, those limestone shafts that open up suddenly underfoot and seem to go down forever. Like, close enough to step right into it if I'd gone just a few more inches."

The tree Mattheuis had been leaning against grew up out of the Hell Hole, its roots clinging to its interior, and it was "not healthy, by a long shot—I mean, I'm no tree surgeon, but this thing looked *diseased.* Had a big, open, rotten gap in the trunk, far down enough I hadn't been able to feel it. But as I recoiled, I went far enough I wasn't blocking the sun anymore, and I saw something glint: dull, but obvious. Metal. Rusty, old . . . really old."

He looked at me then, as though daring me to interrupt; for emphasis, the way some people do. Like calls to like, they say—he and Wrob Barney were definitely the same sort of drama queen. But then again, so was I. So I just waited.

"I don't know why, even now," he continued, finally, "but I put my hand in, felt around. It was all soft in there, like fungus.

Mushy. Wet. And then I closed my fingers on something that felt like an edge and grasped hard. I pulled it out."

It was a canister, obviously—film. Silver nitrate stock.

With the sun up, the path back to the road became obvious. Acting on instinct, Mattheuis kicked open the hole in the tree further, exposing what would turn out to be five separate reels, and wrapped them in his coat, using it as a makeshift sling. He then humped this bundle through weeds and stickers, deadfalls of browned-out milkweed and Queen Anne's lace, a poisonous harvest of deadly nightshade berries bursting underfoot. Dropping it in the back seat, he turned the key in the ignition and heard the car turn over, catching perfectly; though his phone had also turned back on, he didn't even need to call CAA—he simply drove back to Overdeere, calling Wrob to tell him he had potentially exciting news.

"What did they say happened?" I asked. "I'm assuming you had it checked out, afterwards."

He nodded then shrugged. "No idea. Like I said, apparently it just goes like that, sometimes. *Shore don't want us,* that was the mechanic's diagnosis. *Car's iron-made, and they don't like that.* Whatever the hell *that* means."

"'Iron-made'?"

"You got me. That car was a Prius, steel from one end to the other. *Metaphorical* iron, at best."

The canisters did indeed turn out to contain the fabled fourth cache of silver nitrate film. "Five reels, like I said, and according to Wrob—if he can be believed—they matched up with four of the Quarry Argent Museum films, in terms of content, methodology, and what he calls 'signature.' Basically, they shared the same sort of intertitle cards, which appear to have been hand-lettered. The museum films all had Japery's mark, as though they were copies struck through Japery and sent out along the circuit, which made a sort of sense; the community apparently used to show them for free to area kids on Victoria and Dominion Day, right up until the 1960s when somebody finally went 'gee, maybe that's not the very *best* idea, given they might explode if they get too hot.' The films I found in the woods, however, have no mark at all—they're originals, not copies. And I can see why Japery probably didn't want them, because they are . . . *odd,* to put it mildly. Not exactly blockbuster material."

"How so?"

Again, Mattheuis hesitated. "I'd probably have to show you," he said, finally.

And now you're probably thinking: *That's an amazing amount of coincidence.* Which is true, I guess, but history thrives on coincidence, as does archaeology. Sometimes all it takes is being in the right place for the wrong reasons, then moving just a little only to find you're standing on top of something you weren't even looking for, something you never would have found otherwise. The theory of parallel development is a useful one to keep in mind, too. That's how Edison and Tesla could be working on electrical current at the same time. How Eadweard Muybridge could be using his "camera-gun" to capture and reconstruct movement through sequential photographs in British Columbia at exactly the moment that Étienne-Jules Marey was doing so in France, with only slightly different results. Or how it was only the fact of Louis-Aimé Augustin Le Prince's own still-unsolved disappearance—off a moving train, freakishly enough—which prevented him from "inventing" the motion picture camera five years before the Lumière brothers did.

So many individuals in different places, all with the same good idea. All, in their own ways, attempting to use light on a wall to open a window into another world. And how odd is it that the two guys who made the first viable motion picture happened to have a surname that means "light"? Still just coincidence?

More like synchronicity.

Enough of that, however, and people almost inevitably start talking about magic.

It doesn't take long to watch a bunch of amateur silent films, even five of them, given that George Méliès's ground-breaking *A Trip to the Moon* (the world's first science fiction film) only lasts fourteen minutes. The ones Mattheuis found in his tree were all less than twenty, definitely meant either as second features for whatever they might have been programmed to accompany, or simply to fulfill their mysterious director-producer's own purposes. Better yet, they were all just slightly different versions of the same damn story, though each became progressively more ambitious, less narratively integrated, and (say it with me now) more *experimental* in execution: field, apparition, weapon. A visitation at noon, a warning ignored, followed by violence—always off-screen, implied not shown, played out in mime and shadows—and horrified reaction. "Lady Midday," in the proverbial nutshell.

Wrob appeared to have pulled his clips from the first film in the batch, the one with the mirror-veil, the painted backdrop and real sheaves, the mediaeval-dressed children. In the second film, the veiled figure wore an additional *papier-mâché* mask overtop its head, stylized and severe, features so reduced as to be hieroglyphics; in the third film, that same mask had also been set with mirror pieces, catching the light from every angle, a blazing blur. In the fourth film, the veiled figure was the only human player, with all other character represented by puppets—a weird sort of mishmash of traditions, their limbs manipulated from below on sticks like Balinese shadow dancers, heads worked from above like marionettes. The final film, meanwhile, was all stop-motion, a combination of ink-on-glass drawings that assembled themselves between each shutter click and paper silhouette animation, like Lotte Reiniger's legendary *The Adventures of Prince Achmed*, though necessarily cruder. It must have taken ages to put together, so the idea that whoever made it—Mrs. Whitcomb?—was so unsatisfied with the result that they apparently tried to throw it down a hole afterwards made me vaguely ill.

The light-wrapped central figure's weapons changed as well, one for each iteration: sword, sickle, scythe, and something even more hooked, like a pike, or Billy Bob Thornton's famous sling blade. By the animated version, it had become a generalized ray, bright and razor-sharp, which emerged from the figure's hidden sleeve as though replacing her hand, five fingers fusing to form a cutting implement that probably cauterized on contact. It was like watching somebody anticipate thirty years of Japanese magical girl anime in one brief shot.

"Why would anybody try to *destroy* these?" I couldn't quite keep myself from blurting out.

Mattheuis laughed. "Good question! I can only assume that no matter how impressive *we* find them, they simply weren't delivering exactly what their creator was going for."

"No one who made something like *this* would ever stop exploring artistically, though. You'd agree with me on that point."

"Oh, absolutely, but people do switch disciplines; sometimes they move out of their comfort zones, play around for a while, then stop and move back again, take whatever they started with back up. They might have been a painter—those flats and curtains look hand-made, for example, and the animation's definitely in the same style. That said, I can't think they were well-known, or we'd have run across them elsewhere. Maybe a gifted amateur."

"And you have *no idea* who that might have been."

"Like I said, Wrob claimed the Hell Hole films have certain elements in common with some of the Quarry Argent Museum cache, and I'd agree, to a point. But if they ever kept detailed records of exactly who made those original donations, they're gone—a fire and two floods put paid to half their back-files, according to the woman who runs it."

"That's too bad," I replied, reaching into my bag. "Actually, can I show you something?"

His laugh tapered off into a smile then, somewhat ironically. Inquiring, of the air: "And how did I somehow know you didn't come here just to see *me*?"

I took out my copy of *Finding Your Voice*, passed it over—the "Lady Midday" section clearly marked—and sat there waiting as he read through it. "Intriguing," he allowed, setting it down again. "You and Wrob obviously think along much the same lines."

"Come again?"

And here he drew out the notebook in question, a half-filled pocket Moleskine whose leatherette cover had been collaged over in newspaper and magazine clippings, random words and phrases layered haphazardly in between Cronenbergian chimerae cobbled together from National Geographic photo spreads and glue-stick glitter. Inside, Wrob's handwriting was indeed just as bad as advertised, as Mattheuis demonstrated by flipping to the second-last page, where he seemed to have been making a list of potential candidates for the tree cache's mysterious filmmaker. Halfway down, underlined several times and legible only if you squinted hard, was the name *M[smear] A. M. W[it] tc[u]mb.*

"Wrob once told me he had a syndrome called uncontrollable hypographic pornocentrism," Mattheuis remarked, dryly, while I bogged at the spelling. "Which I suppose I can understand in terms of stuff he just jots down, but I think he's reprogrammed the spell-check on his email, too, which can get kind of . . . unsafe for work."

"God, that's so wrong."

"In all senses of the phrase." Mattheuis was still flipping through *Finding Your Voice*, eyebrows faintly drawn. "Though as a half-educated guess, tapping Mrs. Whitcomb's not bad: highly unlikely that smear stands for Mister, since Arthur was mainly a patron of the arts rather than a practitioner, and that only on his wife's behalf. The museum has a whole room of her paintings, though I must admit I didn't pay much attention to it while I was there. Did find an interesting little sidebar, though, when I went looking for references to her—a canvas by Gustave Knauff, one of Odilon Redon's favourite fellow Decadents, who set himself on fire in Bruges in 1909, the year after she and Arthur passed through on their honeymoon and arranged to pay their respects to him at the Café Brumaire, his usual haunt. I'll send you a link to it tonight, if you want."

"She did have a camera, though. And she did make movies."

He shrugged. "Shot documentary footage at séances, if you can call it that. There's no proof she ever did anything this elaborate."

"Okay, but what about the similarities between these films and 'Lady Midday'?"

A sigh; Mattheuis closed the book, marking his place with a finger. "Look, I'd love for it to be that easy, Lois. We're talking about the very start of moviemaking in North America, so in theory *anyone* could just start turning these things out at home— and did, if they could afford the equipment and stock. And yes, I'm far more likely to think the Hell Hole films were made by someone like Iris Whitcomb than by the sort of person who could get a distribution contract with a studio like Japery, no matter for how brief a time. Though I suppose that's not impossible either, not entirely. . . ."

"Hugo Balcarras also has a theory about Mrs. Whitcomb's disappearance, which relates directly to her supposed filmmaking forays."

"That she was watching a homemade silver nitrate reel in transit on her portable projector and what, combusted spontaneously? Please."

I smiled as though I agreed, then continued on anyhow, ignoring his growing look of annoyance. "Gotta say, though, I can count the number of times I've seen a thematic resemblance like that mean *absolutely nothing* on one hand, especially in cinema. You?"

He sighed. "Well, I didn't want to point this out, but . . . would you say that for these films to be both the work of Mrs. Iris Whitcomb and based on this Wendish fairy tale of hers, the fairy tale would probably have to pre-date the films themselves? Her version of it, anyhow?"

"Probably, yes."

"Then look at the copyrights index. The 'previously published' information."

He handed the book back to me, two fingers already slipped between the relevant pages. And there it was, right under his index: *The Snake-Queen's Daughter: Wendish Legends & Folklore*, privately published . . . 1925. The same year Mrs. Whitcomb was finally declared dead.

The shock—the disappointment, both in this revelation and in myself, for provoking it—was so intense that it really did take me a moment to recover. "I'd still like to see those other films for myself, if I could, later on," I told him, at last. "The Japery ones, from the museum."

"And we'd love to show them to you. Just call and set it up." I nodded, gathering my stuff, while he sighed again, striking a sympathetic pose. "Sorry to end on such a down note. I really wish things could have lined up the way you wanted them to, but sometimes it simply doesn't work out that way; you've done your share of research, after all. *You* know."

"Uh huh."

"You did get a fair deal of background on the *Untitled 13* clips, though, yes? So that's useful."

"Mmm. And something's always better than nothing, right?"

"A *very* good way to think about it, I've always found."

I just nodded again—smiling back, shaking his hand, striking a pose of my own. Thinking, as I did: *sure you have. You sanctimonious prick.*

That night, Clark sang and sang as he twiddled a clothespin with a piece of wicker stuck in its jaws in front of his eyes, danced up and down while flipping his head back and forth to simulate the world around him being fast-forwarded. He clicked and hooted and made noises like a computer resetting itself over and over and over. He sang "Accidents Will Happen," from *Thomas the Tank Engine*. He sang the "Rescue Pack" song from *Go, Diego, Go!* He sang the title theme from *Play With Me Sesame*, until I frankly wanted to dig Jim Henson's corpse up and punch it in the face. It didn't help that something horrifying was going on with my stomach and bowels at the same time, cramping me as though my guts were trying to shed their lining. Finally, after a half hour on the toilet, I retreated into our bedroom, dry-swallowed a palmful of Robaxacet to numb myself, and cranked my earphones up as high as they'd go, blasting Jocelyn Pook directly into my brain. I spent the bulk of the evening transcribing and collating notes while Clark jigged at the periphery of my vision, desperately trying to get my attention—because much like a cat, my son never wants to be near you when you want him to, but the minute you don't want him interacting with you it's all "Come back for Mommy! *Mooooommmmy!* Mommy, can you dance? *Mommy,* you have to *kiss* him!"

Simon dealt with it, mainly, the way he always does when things get really bad. He got Clark out of his clothes and into a bath, fed him Nut-Thins and bacon, and sat on the toilet replaying the same damn scene from Disney's *The Princess and the Frog* while Clark laughed like a maniac: Dr. Facilier's downfall, his patented Friends from the Other Side coming to collect after Tiana breaks their precious blood talisman, triumphantly pointing out that what she's covered in isn't *slime*, it's *mucus.* While I sat in front of a screen, refreshing my Tumblr over and over with my eyes starting to cross and my nerve-damaged shoulder humming—I separated it early, in elementary school, then developed a degenerating disc in my neck by the end of college, for which I take anti-inflammatories that cyclically accelerate my digestive ailments—and brooded yet again over just how unqualified I was to be anybody's mother, let alone *this* little boy's. Just how little I obviously had to offer anybody, myself very much included.

Jesus Christ, I thought. *You'd think these fucking films were* mine, *any of them, the way I'm obsessing over this shit.*

But they weren't, of course—no more than they'd been Wrob's—and equally "of course," that was the entire goddamn point. Because unlike Wrob, I didn't even have the chutzpah to "sample" a few bits and pieces, stick some shit of my own around them and claim I'd made something new, let alone the balls . . . or wasn't that what I'd been trying to do, really, in my own sad way? What Mattheuis had seen, and laughed at, if only to himself?

This basic white girl's urge to stick a random pin in a map, make up a name, and claim I'd "found" something that'd always existed—to sail someplace and tell the people who'd always lived there that I owned it now, so get the fuck out. *Nothing more sad than some bitch who can't even find something real worth writing about, in a whole world full of forgotten wonders,* I thought, grimly, as I finally drifted off next to

Simon, knowing my jaw would ache the next morning from grinding my teeth all night.

No dreams that night, thankfully, and when I woke, my eyes looked clearer. I took it as a sign, which, in hindsight, it might well have been . . .

. . . though probably not the kind I thought it was at the time.

SIX

Writing up the interview with Wrob took an hour and a half, maybe two. I did it while sitting in my favourite coffee place, Balzac's, down the side of the St. Lawrence Market; had to cut around the Mrs. Whitcomb angle entirely, obviously, given the way my conversation with Mattheuis had ended, though I did make sure to mention just how much Wrob owed the "unknown Canadian filmmaker" whose work lent *Untitled 13* so much of its mysterious allure. "He won't like *that*," I remember muttering, under my breath—then thinking, almost immediately adding: *Which probably makes it a good thing I don't give all too much of a shit.*

Pressing PUBLISH, I closed out and accessed my email, compulsively checking to see if anybody had left new comments on my previous review. A tone told me I had mail, which proved to be from the NFA: that link Mattheuis had promised me, the one to Knauff's painting. I clicked on it, revealing a gaudily odd-coloured interior (mainly blue and grey, rich navy for the shadows with details rendered in teal-touched argent) full of angular figures that was half Toulouse-Lautrec, half Jan Toorop—the famous Café Brumaire, I could only assume. Layered in shafts of light and darkness, its background characters reduced to mere smears and haphazard pixilation, the scene shared some of the same feeling as Belgian symbolist Jean Delville's "occult" portraits, with their narrow, glowing features and ecstatically upturned eyes: a veiled woman in green sat just off-centre from the close-packet dance floor, playing solitaire at a rickety little table with one hand hidden inside a fur muff dyed the same shade, the other dealing out, its naked fingers tipped with delicately hooked black nails.

In the bottom right, meanwhile, sat a couple I could only assume to be Mr. and Mrs. Whitcomb: he was tall, broad-shouldered, and slightly stooped, visibly older, arm thrown protectively across hers in the light from a single, slightly smoking oil-lamp; she was also tall, and stately, enough so that her shoulders and his sat almost level. She was dressed all in white, with an unfashionably modest lace snood or cap pinned over the coiled wealth of her heavy, honey-cream hair, a filmy shawl wrapped up high to mask the bottom of her face, and her narrowed eyes, too pale to hold any one particular shade, though her pupils stood out like pinpricks. She appeared to angle her head—seen in three-quarter profile—as though listening to some off-canvas conversationalist.

What's he telling you? I wondered. *Something you want to hear? Or the exact opposite?*

Acknowledged as his most well-known work besides the infamous "Black Annunciation," the few lines of text beneath the .jpg began, *Knauff's "Réunion de Nuit" recalls both the nighttime Impressionism of Manet and the thematic obscurity of Jean Delville. The May-December romance featured in the foreground may depict two Canadian admirers Knauff corresponded with briefly throughout 1908, while critics have attempted to draw a parallel between the striking "green lady" of the middle field and contemporary advertisements anthropomorphizing absinthe (Knauff's drug of choice) as a seductive yet toxic lover. As Henrique L'Hiverneux points out in her 1997 paper on Decadence in Bruges, however, an almost identical figure can be found in Degouve de Nuncques's "Au Café Brumaire," sitting next to a smearily rendered man sometimes identified as Knauff himself.*

Later, I picked Clark up and took him over to my mom's, a process that took far longer than it should have, mainly because he kept stopping to twirl in the middle of the sidewalk every five steps. It's not as though he was unhappy, or being deliberately obstreperous; he'd virtually bounced off the school bus, yelling "Bye, thank you for helping, see you next time!" to the bemused driver, and dived straight into the (in)convenience store at our building's base, as is his wont, where I paused to get money out of the ATM only to hear him call: "Mommy! Do you want to kiss him?"

"Yes I do," I said, keying my PIN number. "Just a minute, bubba."

"Moooooommmmmy!"

"Just a *minute,* bun."

But Clark likes what he likes, and he has a very specific schedule for post-school decompression: run upstairs, strip to his underwear, plop down in front of Daddy's computer, put on his frog-face headphones, and surf YouTube till he's so jacked up he can't stop himself from laughing inanely and singing along, which sort of negates the whole headphones concept. At which point I'll say: "Time to stop, log off, go do something else," and he usually will, albeit under protest.

"You don't have to log off!"

"Yeah, you kinda do, actually."

"Don't do!"

"*Do* do, and *now.*"

"*Aaaaaagh!*" he'll shriek then tell himself, mimicking me, even to the tone: "Don't scream, there's no reason to scream." And he'll run away to the bathroom, or his room, slamming the door either way. Cue the sound of either frenzied peeing or frenzied dancing, and we're off to the races.

That's a good day, by the way. Typical. The kind of day when, if he notices how much he's driving me nuts, he'll sometimes suddenly appear by my side and kiss me—knock his mouth against my elbow or my stomach, face-first, like a pecking bird. Then grin and sing out some nonsense phrase ("I didn't mean to burp!" "*Koo*-do!" "BAD ROBOT!") before scurrying away again, like he's the Road Runner and I'm the Coyote.

Taking him to Mom's breaks that up, though, leaving him off-balance. It's not that he doesn't like it there once he's there, or that he doesn't like *her*; he *loves* her, unreservedly. But there can be weeks on end during which he refuses to express that in ways she's willing to accept, and that's when things tend to get testy. "He doesn't want his old Nay-Nay anymore, I guess," she'll remark to me, and I'll feel the urge rise in me to snap: *Yeah, that's right— I'll just work on training him to say the right things when you press his buttons, shall I, like a parrot? Because that's the most important thing, not teaching him to self-regulate, or making him use his words; we need to get across to a kid whose entire vocabulary is made up of Disney dialogue how essential it is that he not only* feel *grateful, but also* act *grateful. To at least get him to say "I love you, Nay-Nay," even if we can't make him act like he means it. . . .*

Oh, and I *know* how I sound when I blurt these things out, I absolutely do—which is why I struggle not to. Especially when the very next thing that always occurs to me is: *But why should you get what I don't even get, most days? What makes* you *so special? You're* my *mother, not his.*

Yeah, that's never a conversation much worth having.

Spinning and spinning, trudging and trudging. I took his hand, trying to urge him along, and he fought me; I held on like grim death, not quite dragging him. By the time we reached Mom's building, my shoulder was in an uproar. She let us in, he rushing past her with barely a glance to try and monopolize her computer, only kissing and hugging her when she extorted it out of him; I lowered myself onto her couch with a grunt, rolling my neck, unable to bite back further noises as things cracked and strained. "You look like you're in pretty bad straits," Mom said, to which I just half-nodded, unable to shrug. "Seriously, are you *okay?*"

"Much as I ever am, sure."

"Well, that's a pity."

"Probably, yeah."

"I just mean that it seems like you should be getting *better*, doesn't it, considering how long it's been going on? All . . . this."

"Mmm, uh huh. And yet."

(Thinking: *Sorry if it offends you how I'm always in pain, Mom; life's like that, at least for me. Can't do much about it except*

*what I'm already doing, in between all the other shit on my plate,
but from now on I'll do my level best to try and make it a bit less
obvious.*)

"You're in a bad mood, too. How'd that last thing you were
doing go?"

"It went."

She gave me a shrewd look, but didn't press, for which I was
grateful. "I just wish you were getting paid for all your hard work,
Lois," she said, eventually. "That's all. Given the effort you put
in . . . and what it seems to take out of you."

"Well, me too, Mom, but it's an investment. Like when I
started out—remember that? You prove yourself, do something
for nothing, then trade up. . . ."

"That was a long time ago."

I sighed. "What goes around comes back around. Blame the
economy."

"Interesting times, in other words."

"Exactly."

A few minutes later, she offered to take Clark overnight, thus
freeing Simon and I up to go out on one of our increasingly infre-
quent "dates." I accepted, then texted Simon, telling him to meet
me at her place after work. We spent some time after that trying to explain what was going to happen to Clark, which was an
exercise in frustration, as ever—he refused to even acknowledge
it right up until the moment Simon appeared, at which point he
suddenly announced: "Daddy, Mommy, Clark—we're a happy
family! And now it's time to go home."

"No, bunny. You're staying at Nay-Nay's, remember?"

"Don't remember!"

"Yeah, we already talked about this. You have to stay."

"You don't have to stay! You have to go!"

"Nope."

"Don't, don't, it's heinous! CEE ESS EYYYYE!"

"Look, man, it's gonna happen no matter what you say, so just
roll with it, okay? Have a good time with Nay-Nay and we'll see
you tomorrow, do you understand? *Do* you? *Clark!* Look here,
here. *Do you understand me?*"

Simon took him aside, murmuring, as I struggled back into my coat, trying not to wince. "He really seems to be annoying you, these days," Mom observed, to which I could only reply: "Okay."

"Please don't do that, Lois. I'm just saying you need to be careful what you say around him, how you say it. Children pick things up."

"Yeah, they do—and you know what? I actually *want* him to pick up how there's more people in the world than just him, and sometimes things don't go the way you want them to, 'cause that's just life. Besides, you know how he is—all 'no Nay-Nay, no Nay-Nay!' until we leave, and then suddenly you're the best thing ever. It'll be the same tonight."

"That doesn't excuse your behaviour, Lois. You're his *mother*."

"Uh huh, and *nothing* excuses me, like nothing excuses *him*, either. Must be genetics."

I regretted saying it the instant it was out of my mouth, not least because of the glance my mom shot me then, so much more hurt than angry—but right that very moment Simon reappeared, timing suspiciously on point, sporting that too-cheerful smile he puts on whenever he's trying to defuse tension (a lot like Clark's fake "Disney smile," come to think). "I've set him up with *Make Mine Music* on your DVD player, Lee, and he's got bacon," he said. "We should probably go, right?"

She nodded, eyes still on mine; I wanted to look away, but didn't. "Tell him goodbye, though, before you do. Don't just disappear."

"Of course."

(*Of course.*)

"That didn't sound good," Simon observed, carefully, on our way down in the elevator. "Talk? Or just forget about it?"

"Forget," I replied, still staring resolutely forwards, studying the dull, scratched inside of the elevator doors like I thought if I only did that long enough, a reflection would appear: not mine, perhaps, but *somebody* worth looking at. Already knowing, however, that I probably wouldn't be able to.

* * *

Do you ever wonder when you started to hate yourself? I felt like asking Simon as we sat there in our favourite sushi restaurant, waiting to order. Except for the fact he'd most probably answer: *No, but I do sometimes wonder when* you *started to hate* your*self, let alone why*—a question I knew damn well I'd never be able to answer, at least not in any way he'd find enlightening.

I was thirty-six when I fell pregnant with Clark, old enough that the gynaecologist judged my womb "geriatric," and on the night I went into labour he was already two weeks overdue, so they'd been talking about inducing me the next day anyhow. I weighed more than two hundred pounds at that point, a lot of it fluid, and my hands were covered in pruritic urticarial papules and plaques, a rash often found in first-time mothers—benign but incredibly uncomfortable, like tiny, crunchy, air-filled subcutaneous blisters that hurt anytime I moved a finger. There'd been a series of scares in that last month, everything from a sugar test hinting at prenatal diabetes to a false water breaking, but now we were finally at the precipice. Things were going—well, granted, I had nothing to compare it with, but it seemed all right, probably because I'd taken the epidural the minute they offered it to me.

On one of my second or third pushes, stuff gushed out of me in a flood without any hint of warning, like I'd pissed myself, so suddenly I didn't even feel embarrassed; Simon held my hand as I bore down then stopped to recoup, whoop-gasping, before bearing down once again. And that's how it went from then on: repeat, repeat, repeat.

Thirteen hours later, Clark had crowned but little else and the doctor could feel his neck starting to twist, as if he couldn't decide which way to face while exiting. She recommended a caesarean, which I'd wanted to avoid, and eventually I signed off on it. I remember being wheeled into the operating theatre, sobbing like a drunken maniac and apologizing to everybody I saw. I remember the frame around my hips, a sheet placed so I wouldn't be able to watch them cut me open, them lifting Clark free and putting him in my arms. He was covered in my blood, slightly yellow and swollen, eyes bulging like a bemused frog's; his full head of black hair was plastered down, and he held his hands up to the light, fingers spreading delicately, whimpering. Nine pounds eleven ounces: "the little stud," they called him. A friend had knitted him a cap with a skull and crossbones on it, which he wore for all his first photos. He couldn't latch on, probably because my breasts were so massive and deformed—five years later I'd have to have a breast reduction, because they never quite deflated—which meant the nurse literally had to hold his head in place while I nursed him for the first time, half-asleep. The hangover lasted for days.

It was traumatic, for both of us—but then again, birth always is. In another era, neither of us might have survived. What I'm trying to say, though, is that I never resented him for any of it, never suffered from post-partum depression the way some of my friends did, never blamed him for the pain or the irreparable damage to my body, the staple-studded scar that ran twice as long as normal under a stomach pendulous enough it was impossible to clean without help, so it became infected almost immediately.

He was my child, a part of me, and I recognized that immediately; we lay in bed together for what seemed like months after, rarely separated by more than a few feet. He smiled early, laughed early, crawled early. When I wanted him to sleep, I'd put something I'd worn into his bassinet, knowing the smell would comfort him; when he heard my voice, his eyes lit up. I never doubted that he loved me, or that I loved him.

In my darkest moments, though, I have to wonder: how much of our affection, as parents, is for the child we think we're *going* to have, the child we think we're entitled to, instead of the one we actually end up getting? I mean, I'm pretty sure Mom and Dad didn't see *me* coming, either: the kid with the black moods, the kid whose mind was always elsewhere, flinching from real life as from a bruise. Who wanted to lay a fiction-filter on top of everything and pretend it was something else just to keep the sheer disappointment of it all bearable: this limited, empirical experience of ours, trapped inside a decaying shell of meat, mainly able to perceive that nothing lasts, even in our most pleasurable moments.

That future I saw for Clark, though, when he was a baby . . . that was gone. It wasn't coming back. That left only the present, which felt unbearable on occasion, though it wasn't, because nothing was. Sad but true.

"Penny for your thoughts," Simon offered, and I shook my head. "Wouldn't want to waste your money," I replied.

"Hey, it's mine to waste."

"Oh well, *okay*. No wonder we don't do our own taxes."

We'd already established there wasn't anything showing in Toronto worth enduring two hours in a movie theatre seat, so edamame and assorted sushi rolls plus a bit of mild flirtation, followed by whatever we'd PVR'd earlier in the week, seemed like the next best thing—good for an hour or so, anyhow. Still, as we walked home, I found my mind sliding back to Mom: the impossibility of a last word, ever, when both of us were just so *certain* we knew better—about Clark, about life. About each other.

"I just wish she'd admit I might *occasionally* know what I'm talking about, that's all," I told Simon, closing our condo door behind us. To which he basically shrugged, moving to flick the kettle on, and pointed out, in return: "But she wants what's best for Clark, right? And it's not her fault she doesn't know what that is, any more than either of us do—it's uncharted territory, here. We're all feeling our way, Clark very much included."

". . . Yes."

"So." A beat, then, while the steam gradually mounted. "If what you resent is her wishing you wouldn't push him quite so hard, I have to be honest and say on that particular issue, I kind of agree: he's a *kid*, first and foremost. Self-control's always gonna be an issue."

"Most kids grow out of it, though. He . . . might not."

"He will. Slower than some other kids do, probably."

"'Probably?'"

"We don't know! Anything, really. People make leaps; he's autistic, not stupid. What I do know is that no matter how long it *seems* to take, one day, he's gonna be an adult—which means he'll end up living in the real world soon enough no matter what we do, or don't do."

"Yeah, I know. I know that. But . . ." I paused. "We're not gonna be around forever. One day, we'll be gone—her too, sooner than that. And he'll be alone."

"What're you afraid of, Lois? That no one's going to love him but us? Look at him, man: he's lovable. Very much so."

"He's innocent."

"You say that like it's a bad thing."

"'Cause it *can* be." He blew out a breath, annoyed. "Tell me I'm wrong, Simon."

"I can't, obviously—but you're not *right,* either. Not totally."

We stared at each other for a long minute then, neither willing to give an inch on the subject, till the kettle's spout finally began to sing. Till I sighed, letting my eyes drop, and thinking, as I did:

We'll see.

So we had tea, mainly in silence, and then we picked up a bit—shuffled all those various bits and pieces Clark tended to leave behind everywhere back to where they were supposed to go, the DVD cases and the random toys, the plastic cups that'd once held water and the coverless Tupperware containers containing nothing but cereal crumbs or pretzel salt. Eventually, as I loaded the dishwasher, I felt Simon draw near, clearing his throat; I looked up to see him hiding something behind his back, and smiled in spite of myself. He smiled back.

"Well," he began, "I *was* going to give this to you at the end of the evening, but since I think you could use the pick-me-up now. . . ."

"Thank you," I said, feeling absurdly touched, and a little surprised—Simon rarely gave me gifts out of the blue, mostly because by the time I'd talked enough about something I wanted for him to clue in about it, it usually turned out I'd bought it myself already. I recognized the Amazon packaging right away as he handed it over. "No guessing," he said.

"Aw."

"*Seriously.* I think you'll find it's worth the wait."

I shook my head, smiled, and obliged, popping open the cardboard flap at the end and sliding out a flat, bubble-wrapped package; tore open the bubble-wrap, slipping it off to reveal a startlingly old-looking hardback volume no more than six inches high, bound in dark green fabric, spine worn and pages yellowing, like something from the older and dustier shelves of a university library. No title on the cover. Genuinely puzzled now, I opened it and found the title page.

In the centre, drawn in black ink, a massive snake curled about a little girl in a frilly Victorian-style pinafore; both the snake and the girl wore crowns, and behind them, a dark forest rose on either side. Above this picture were the words *The Snake-Queen's Daughter*; below, *Wendish Folkore & Legends*; and below that, in smaller letters, *Translated and Compiled by Mrs. A. M. Whitcomb*, and smaller yet below that, *Edited by Charles Pelletier, M.A., O.B.E.* And opposite, on the printer's page, my eyes drawn magnet-sharp to it even though I knew exactly what I was going to see: © *1925, printed in Toronto, Faber & Faber.*

"I'm sorry about the condition," said Simon. "I had to buy it used because the seller only ships to Canada by priority mail, but I figured, well, like you said—it's an investment, right? In a project that could really be something important . . ." He trailed off, maybe noticing at last that I wasn't squeeing with delight as he'd obviously expected. "Hon? Is—this not it?"

"No—no, this is definitely the one, and that's great; I'd have gotten around to it, I guess, but the fact you already did . . . that's amazing, thank you so much. That's excellent."

"Um, all right."

"No, it's just . . ." With a sigh, I flipped the cover open again. "When I was talking to Jan Mattheuis, I showed him my book, the one I found the original Lady Midday story in—and he pointed this out." I tapped the copyright notice on the printer's page.

"The date?" I nodded; he rubbed his face, clearly thinking hard. "Look, this doesn't *disprove* anything. It's still perfectly plausible she could have made the films, then wrote her source material down—I mean, she wasn't involved with this book either way, right? She was already gone. This is this other guy's baby, this Pelletier. . . ."

"Maybe, sure, but it doesn't matter." I leaned against the counter, hard, welcoming the distracting pain as its granite edge creased my skin. "What I want out of the NFA is a *contract*, money for research up front rather than afterwards, and Mattheuis isn't gonna shell out that kind of dough for 'plausible.' Which means I have to find another way to make the connection, if such a thing exists."

"It does. It will."

"We don't know that," I replied, throwing his own words back at him, 99.9 percent unconsciously—then realized what I'd done, and went a little white. But he simply shook his head, took me into his arms, hugged me hard. Laid one hand on the back of my neck, warm and soothing, and let me dig my face into his collarbone.

"It will," he repeated. "*You* will. I have faith."

I woke up at four-thirty in the morning.

Simon was snoring, duvet wound around him, sheets underneath sweat-hot; like Clark, he runs at a fever pitch, particularly when unconscious. By contrast, I was naked to the waist, clammy, frigid—I'd somehow managed to bend my arm up behind my head and lodge it there, cutting off the circulation so my hand felt gloved in needles, all their pricks turned inwards. The room was dark, my eyes unfocused, perceptual lag-trails hovering everywhere like worms sketched in light, a thousand blinking spirals. A drawn breath rattled in my throat, pulse hammer-fast.

Abruptly, I found myself upright, hand on the bedroom closet's light-switch. One flick and a wash of light showed our apartment exactly the way I'd left it: no crouched figures, white-eyed and grinning; nothing extruding from the walls; no ceiling spiders. I pulled on a robe then scrabbled around in bed for my glasses, where they must've fallen off in my sleep. A huge smear bisected one lens. I rubbed it clear if not clean on my collar, thinning the grease so I could look through without squinting. This lent a weird, pale light to everything, including

The Snake-Queen's Daughter, which still lay on the glass-topped dining table.

Shivering, I sat down and picked it up, resisting the urge to re-read "Lady Midday." I studied the table of contents, which was laid out in a small, crabbed font with occasional smearing. Thirty titles, each slightly weirder than the next: "Why People Today Die Their Own Death," "In Spring We Drown The Winter," "The Green Boy," "She Washes Your Feet With Her Hair," "Prince Worm Sheds Twenty Skins," "The Pots With Candles In Them," "Nightingale the Robber," "There Were Eyes In The Knots of Trees," "The Iron Trencher," "The Drowned Dog," "The Princess Who Was One Hundred Animals," "Lamentation of God." "Never Trust An Old Man With A Frog's Mouth," was the last. "No shit," I heard myself mutter as I turned the page, revealing Charles Pelletier's Afterword.

The process of editing the volume you now hold in your hands has been a quizzical one, it began, *not least because the transcriber of these tales was as curious a figure in life as she was in her, if not death, then certainly ending. Mrs. Iris Dunlopp Whitcomb was, in her time, a painter, scholar, helpmeet, and mother; a charitable institution, a seeker after occult knowledge whose tireless chronicling of the Unseen all similarly inclined personages must sure feel grateful for—*

My knuckles went white.

—and such further records as were left behind in the wake of her "departure" serve to reflect both the truly mercurial and impermanent nature of all such talents. The tales held within these pages are not the result of any formal study in the folkloric field, but rather the efforts of a gifted amateur; they comprise the contents of a series of notebooks found at the famed Whitcomb Vinegar House and thought to be Mrs. Whitcomb's private aides-mémoires, ranging from early 1899 to mid-1918. From these journals' perusal, it becomes clear that Mrs. Whitcomb's interest in the Austro-Slavic mythology of her Wendish ancestors was a lifelong body of work, though she did not begin transcribing fully-translated versions of

the stories until the year 1905, possibly as an entertainment for her lamented only son Hyatt, before his own vanishing.

Started the stories in 1905, my brain repeated, idiotically. Before Hyatt; before the train. Before she took the veil. *Long* before those films were made . . . before *she* made those films, goddamnit: there it was, in black and white. My proof.

A massive yawn took me by surprise; my eyelids felt like iron, vision blurry and balance wobbly as I pushed myself to my feet, letting the book fall. Maybe I should go back to bed, look at it in the morning, take some time; not like there was any great rush, now. I turned back toward bed, toward Simon, not meaning to wake him so much as snuggle up and murmur in his ear, apologize for my depressive agnostic's lack of belief.

Thinking, my whole body humming: *This is going to happen. I'm going to* make *this happen.*

(*Please don't.*)

I looked up at the sound—the *thought,* more like—and caught sight of my own reflection in the double window that ran ceiling-to-floor along our living room's front wall, blinds un-pulled to show a mostly black cityscape with occasional light pollution; the balcony of the guy across the road, where he sunbathed every summer. Superimposed, however, came a single, horrid, micro-moment's blink of something else—behind me yet in front of me, suddenly *inside* my silhouette, some bad idea made manifest. Another figure impossibly occupying the chair I'd only now vacated, legs sprawled and skirt awry as a dropped doll, looking up through a thickness of veil: sequin-eyes flashing cold, white brightness, palely lit, like glass in noonday sun.

At the sight, I released a completely involuntary sound, gasp-choking—spun around, staggered back. My foot slipped on something, a toy of Clark's we'd managed to miss in our scramble—a puffball-shaped green creature with big plastic eyes, one patched like a pirate's: *Arrrr, matey, walk the plank!* it exclaimed in a tiny, tinny electronic voice as the wrench threw everything about my body out of balance: hips, neck, back. My shoulder gave an actual spark, shocking as any touched wire.

Heart-punched, I slumped against the wall, cursing. Made myself look, and saw—nothing, obviously. An empty chair, slightly dented from my own ass.

Back inside our bedroom, Simon turned over. And—

Two days on, I turned up back at the NFA armed with a spreadsheet tracking imagery from every *Snake-Queen's Daughter* story, and Mattheuis and I went through the rest of the Japery films, connecting the dots. One of the biggest surprises? *All* of the Quarry Argent Museum cache turned out to be probably Mrs. Whitcomb's, given their content—the funny ones as well as the morbid: one must've been her riffing off the "Old Man With A Frog's Mouth" model, a creature I'd since ascertained was called a *vodyanoi,* smoking his pipe by one of those Lake of the North alkaline swamps and leading travellers astray, sending them into the clutches of sexy *rusalki* who used their long hair like a fishing net to trap unwary young men. By the end, Mattheuis was literally rubbing his hands together, and I couldn't stop myself from grinning.

"So Wrob was right," I said, at last. Mattheuis snorted, replying, "Oh, fuck Wrob, Lois—and I say that as someone who has. *You* were right."

Yeah, I thought. *For once, I was.*

I got my contract, my money, my project. Simon kissed me when I came home. Mom congratulated me when I called to tell her. Clark danced and sang. Granted, I don't think I had much to do with that last part, since I rarely did—but for once, it was a lot of fun.

The next day, I found another text message from Wrob Barney on my voicemail, that same flat robot monotone: *congrats on yr coup cairns.* He'd found out, just like I'd suspected he would; *Wrob has his sources,* Leonard Warsame would warn me, eventually. But even without knowing that yet, I still ignored it.

Five minutes later, as I was checking Facebook, my phone rang.

"So," Wrob said, as I picked up. "You really *are* as big a bitch as people say."

I flinched, but kept things light, shooting back: "Yeah, probably. Care to get specific?"

"Uh, all right. *Specifically,* I handed you Mrs. Whitcomb on a platter, and *specifically,* you took me up on it, to the tune of Jan fronting you, what—was it ten thousand? Twenty?" *Twelve,* I automatically filled in, not answering. "Solid like that rates a thank you, I'd think, at the *very* fucking least."

"Well, okay, Wrob: thanks, a lot. Very much. Are we done?"

"Like fun, we are. Already wrote a review *and* an interview linking *Untitled 13* to this big discovery of yours, Lois, which means I'm in this already, balls-deep. Think I'm gonna let you ret-con it so I'm not?"

"Of course not! You did all the digitization, the preliminary cataloguing, and I'm going to give credit where credit's due. I want to be fair."

"Which is why you're gonna talk to Jan for me, right? Get me re-hired."

"What? Um . . . no."

"Why not?"

"Because that's between you and Jan, Wrob. It's got nothing to do with me."

"But . . ." he trailed away, genuinely nonplussed. ". . . he's never going to let me back on unless you push, and if I don't get back on, we can't *work* together."

"I've got my own people in mind, Wrob."

"Like who?" Again, I just waited. Sharper: "So you don't *want* to work with me—is that it?"

"Not on this, no. Sorry."

"Yeah, right. 'Cause saying that makes it all better."

Now it was my turn to get shirty, standing straight up, pulse already starting to jitter. "Look, you want me to say it right out? Then okay: frankly, I don't trust you, and you want to know why? Because the one thing I know for sure is that *by your own admission,* pretty much your first impulse after seeing Mrs. Whitcomb's work was to jack random bits of it—"

"Sample!"

"—then smuggle them out under your shirt and, well . . . I

won't quite say 'pass it off as your own,' 'cause there's no way you could, but definitely try and use it to make *your* pretentious crap look a little better."

I heard him huff, then take a beat before replying, teeth audibly gritted—

"You know, legally, those films don't belong to anybody. Not her, not me, not you, not *Jan.*"

"No argument there. Who they belong to is all of us—everybody. To Canada."

"'To Canada,' really? *The Maple Leaf Forever!* Oh, grow the fuck up."

"I'm sorry—am I crazy, or did you actually say *exactly that* to me at Sneaky Dee's, drunk or not? Wait, I know: yeah, you did. I've got you on tape."

"You stole this from me."

"I *stole* from you, right—stole the thing *you* stole from your boyfriend, which is why you're not attached to this anymore in the first damn place. The thing you spun into a film that you went ahead and showed in *public*, where anybody with half a brain could see it and pick up the connections. . . ."

"'Connections'? Fuck you, I *gave* you all that! Don't pretend like you're the Sherlock fuckin' Holmes of CanCon, Lois—"

"Look, just shut the fuck up right there, okay? Because at no point in our conversation did you say the words Mrs. or A. Macalla *or* Whitcomb. You said Lake of the North, yes, Quarry Argent, yes, but *I* was the one who remembered 'Lady Midday.' And I really doubt to hell and back that *any* other random critic could have done that, especially somebody down on their luck enough to get sent to watch some no-budget programme of experimental fuckin' films at the goddamn Ursulines Studio."

"Lady *who*, now?"

I laughed. "*Exactly.* Holy *shit*, you need to get over yourself."

"Pot to the kettle, baby."

"Whatever, *Wrobert*. Thanks again, better luck next time. Hanging up, now, and by the time you try to call back, I'll have your ass blocked."

I thumbed the icon, sat down again, and took a long breath. Palms were clammy. Felt the charge prickle as it faded, warming me from the inside out, and felt . . . better than I had in ages, actually, like I was finally awake, alive. Like I was *whole*. The person I barely remembered once having been, back when.

I didn't tell Simon about any of this, naturally; he's big on reconciliation, not burning bridges, my sweet Catholic boy. Besides, it didn't seem to matter, aside from the brief natural high. I had work to do.

So I opened Contacts, ran my thumb down to "S," and called Safie Hewsen.

FILM

SEVEN

When I was a kid, I used to dream about angels. Some people might find that comforting, but I didn't—mainly because the way I was brought up virtually guarantees that "angels" mean something substantially different to me than whatever they probably mean to you.

"Here is the world, Safie-girl," my Dédé Aslan used to say, "and our place in it. Here are seven angels, one with peacock feathers for wings and a crown, but no devil. And here also is God, behind it all, who created both Himself and them, whereby everything else was created. Yet there are other things as well, you must remember—things which have always been, which fools without true religion sometimes choose to worship, or trick themselves into worshipping. Small gods for small minds, trapped in small places. And while these creatures' scope is narrow, as with all half-made things, their reach can be long, long . . . just so long as their names are still known in this world, so they may hear them whispered somewhere, recognize themselves, and come calling. . . ."

My Dédé knew all about weird religions from personal experience, and he passed that knowledge on to all of us, or at least tried to. That's what made me want to make films in the first place.

That's from Safie Hewsen's pitch doc for *Seven Angels But No Devil*, the film she made as her Practical Production course thesis project. I still remember reading these words and feeling an immediate stab of sympathy, a sense of kinship, because I'd had very similar dreams all my life—though me being me, they were really more like nightmares.

I'd find myself back in the McLaughlin Planetarium, closed since 1995 due to provincial budget cuts at its sister institution, the Royal Ontario Museum; I'd sit there staring upwards with my neck slightly crimped, as if in a dentist's chair, while the central Zeiss-Jena projector (since sold to the University of Toronto for the grand sum of a dollar, then broken down for parts) ticked back and forth, casting star-maps up onto the domed darkness. The movement was vertiginous yet weirdly lulling, white holes of light in a fake black "sky" blending and flowing without pause, brightening intermittently to form constellations—Orion's Belt, Ursa Major and Minor, Draco—while a soothing voice I could never quite recognize droned faintly on about how long light from those same stars took to reach Earth.

On bad nights, the maps would gradually shift, showing how universal expansion would eventually deform each pattern far beyond recognition, as the sun swelled to engulf our world before shrinking to a cinder, a gravity-torn hole sucking everything into itself till it simply went out. Or they'd turn negative, revealing various deep-sky objects hidden within these cheerfully familiar mythological constructs: galaxies, dwarf or otherwise; quasars and pulsars; dark cloud constellations. The Great Rift, a series of dark patches in the Milky Way, more visible and striking in the southern hemisphere, where Australian Aboriginal star charts described an "emu in the sky" between the Southern Cross and Scorpius, its half-lifted head formed by the Coalsack Nebula. . . .

And on *very* bad nights, the angels would come.

Looking back, I eventually realized the seed of this particular vision was probably planted during my actual visits to the Planetarium, either during summer—since Mom made it known she wouldn't object to anything that took me out of the house, no matter how far downtown I had to travel—or around Christmas, when we'd often attend their annual show about the Star of Bethlehem, which never entirely succeeded in reconciling biblical canon with scientific theory. This might explain why "my" angels always seemed Byzantine in design, long-faced and claw-fingered, with tiny, stern mouths and distant eyes; cruel parodies of the far rounder, kinder figures routinely stencilled on Christmas ornaments rather than along the edges of illuminated manuscripts, managing to evoke two thousand years of Christmases Past in one simple silhouette.

One way or the other, they would take shape as the darkness peeled away around them, lightening to a scaled or studded curtain of gold, uniform yet infinite: so massive they blocked out everything, even the projector. Their presence remade the Planetarium's dome into a globe, a self-contained pocket universe, with no easy way of knowing which way was up or down, left or right. And from the moment they took shape, it seemed to go on forever, halo-glare-lit and shrouded in a double-cloak of feathers, half-spread wings hanging poised but shadowless between two useless horizons.

Be not afraid, they told me, uselessly, even as I shivered in terror, wanting to vomit myself hollow. *For unto you I bring great good news, forever and ever, Amen. Forever, and ever, and ever.*

I'd never quite been able to convey all this—not to Mom, only imperfectly and occasionally to friends, and certainly not to Simon, who'd only nod in sympathy but no real empathy. But reading Safie's thesis was the kind of wonderful gobsmack that happens all too rarely: the instant realization that somebody else just *gets it*; that you're not alone in your dislocation. That you've finally, *finally* found somebody else you can talk to without having to *explain* to.

For all the practical and mundane reasons I had to turn to Safie Hewsen for help, that shared and secret terror was the thing that really made the choice for me.

As you may have gathered, in the normal course of events I wouldn't willingly hang around with most of my former students, let alone invite any of them onto something as important as filling in Mrs. Whitcomb's background. This was, in large part, a reflection on the whole Fac process: the place essentially ran on selling OSAP grants to people who, for one reason or another, either couldn't get into or weren't willing to invest their time and money in "real" colleges, which meant we got a pretty amazing spread of candidates. Sometimes it was technically adept but academically weak people who wanted to get into the industry and saw the Fac as a jump-start; sometimes it was people coming straight out of high school, often with various learning disabilities, whose educational experience thus far had consisted of being warehoused and talked down to, people to whom "teacher" was a synonym for "person who thinks it's their job to make me feel stupid." In the latter case, reframing the Fac as a service industry gave them the impression that because they were supposedly paying my salary, I'd let them treat me like a waiter. Not so much, really, but we could usually come to some sort of working agreement—a position of mutual respect—at least long enough for me to make sure they graduated.

"You're always acting like you know something I don't!" one kid complained, to which I replied: "That's because I *do*. I'm the teacher."

The older ones were always more difficult. I taught people—guys, mostly—who were twice my age, who'd already had a long-term job or even owned a business only to see it fail from underneath them, forcing them into a midlife career change they weren't ready for; they tended to have odd ideas about exactly what making movies entailed, especially on a practical level. I remember once giving my normal lecture on the difference between Hollywood and Canada, pointing out that in Hollywood a movie budgeted at less than six million dollars was considered "below the line of visibility," unable even to budget for self-promotion, and how this explained why so many English-speaking Canadian movies came and went without a trace—*their* average budget was five million and under (more like two point five to three, at the time). One fifty-plus dude at the back immediately raised his hand and said: "Wait, *three million dollars* isn't enough to make a movie?"

"Not usually, no. Not in Hollywood terms."

"Well, what do they usually cost?"

"Twenty million and up."

"Twenty million! That can't be right. What do they *spend* it all on?!"

The best students I ever had were either immigrants who came from cultures where teachers were automatically accorded respect (though even then, because the Fac never vetted applicants properly, I often found myself dealing with more than a few per term who desperately needed an ESL course or two, or the occasional autodidact with a true artistic drive—people who would have been writing, shooting, and editing visual narratives no matter where they ended up. The real deal, in other words. The kind of obsessives even the Fac couldn't discourage.

It was this last category that Safie Hewsen fell into, embodying it so beautifully that even after she was long gone, I continued to refer to it in my head as "the Safie slot."

Seven Angels But No Devil was partly documentary, built around interview footage Safie had shot with her great grandfather before he died, which she augmented with some truly gorgeous and (yes) experimental animation achieved through a process of still photography, rotoscoped digital footage, and video step printing—sort of Chris Marker meets Richard Linklater meets Wong Kar-wai. It was incredibly ambitious, especially considering that much of it, even the clips she came in with, had been recorded on a Fisher-Price PXL-2000 she picked up when she was fourteen, a toy camera released the year after she was born that records video and audio onto a standard audio cassette tape. A flop on the market, this odd piece of stillborn technology was pulled from the shelves because of the low resolution, inherently slow-motion black-and-white images it creates—the same grainy, dreamlike visual shorthand which later led to its revival as a popular format for hipster video artists like Sadie Benning and Michael Almereyda. Now considered highly endangered cult items, PixelVision cameras routinely fetch up to $600 on eBay, which tells you a little about Safie's family background, above and beyond the whole diasporic Armenian Yezidi thing . . . she's a very nice girl, but much like Wrob, she didn't exactly grow up hurting for cash.

Safie's great-grandfather, Aslan Husseniglian, was born and raised in the Kurdish village of Sipan in the Aragats District of Armenia's Aragatsotn Province. Back in the 1900s—the man lived to be over a hundred—he fell in love with a girl named Gayane Hovsepian and chose to marry her, even though she was Christian and he knew it'd make him an outcast; it was a big deal, because he was Yezidi, and the Yezidi used to think everybody else in Armenia—the world, really—was mistaken at best, and wilfully evil at worst. Then again, a lot of Armenian Christians still think the Yezidi straight-up worship the Devil, so I guess it sort of went both ways.

Without community support they were forced to immigrate, avoiding the genocide of 1915 to 1918. Eventually settling in the Don Valley Village, Aslan and Gayane let their name be "Canadian-ized" to Hewsen and had seven children, one of whom would be Safie's grandfather Petrak, who called himself Peter. Aslan started off working construction, then built up a home improvement business that mostly catered to Armenians, and was a great success. By the 1960s, the same time Safie's father was born, Peter cashed out his share of the company and started up a suburban real estate develop-ment venture, moving out to Mississauga, where it cost surprisingly little to buy into, build, and occupy a two-block "neighbourhood" inside a gated community that's still known as Hewsen Estates. That they also happened to be right next to a newly developed GO Tran-sit line made the area popular with upwardly mobile immigrant families from all ethnic backgrounds throughout the 1980s.

Peter's son, however, had come far enough from his assimi-lationist origins not to feel as though he was shooting himself in the foot socially by calling himself Barsegh instead of Blake, nor did he have any qualms about marrying a non-Yezidi girl—Safie's mother, Domenica, an Italian-Canadian. In 1986, Safie was born. "Perfect suburban childhood, ridiculously well off, all that," she told me, during an early chat between classes. "We spoke English at school, Kurdish and Armenian at home, and I guess we were pretty insular, but it wasn't like I could tell."

"Did you always want to make films?"

She nodded. "Ever since I got my first video camera. I used to play like I was a reporter for CITY TV, trying to interview everybody I came across. Dédé Aslan was pretty much the only one who'd put up with it."

"And were you raised Yezidi?"

"Not really, no. Mom's Catholic, Dad's . . . nothing, I guess. Now that Dédé's dead, I think Granddad and Grandma probably drop in at the Anglican church down the road every once in a while, but I don't exactly ask."

"He was your one link to the faith, then."

"Yeah, that's right." She paused. "Everybody in the family's one link to it, and there just aren't a lot of other Armenian Yezidi in Toronto, period. So he wasn't totally one of a kind, but he was definitely something special."

Most non-Yezidi tend to interpret the figure of Malak Tâwus—the "Peacock Angel" who was, according to myth, the leader of the angelic task force assigned by God to create the world and look after humankind—as analogous to the Judeo-Christian Devil, or the Islamic Shaytān. *Seven Angels But No Devil* was written as a direct refutation of this idea, and begins with a close-up of Aslan quoting the truism that "today all Yezidis are Kurds, but there was a time when most Kurds were Yezidis, and Yezidis are still considered the living memory and conscience of the Kurds." As the film continues, various sequences "interpret" the imagery of Aslan's religion literally, yet with a haunting sort of sketchiness— Malak Tâwus, and the other six angels to which he gave birth, are translated as different species of birds: the dropped Cosmic Egg of Xwedê ("The One who created Himself", or Yezidic Universal Spirit) as an artificial pearl cooked until it starts to crack; and the five cardinal elements of Fire, Sun, Earth, Water, and Air are all represented by their most immediate domestic and natural examples: a lit match, a window-kindled reflection, flowerpot dirt, melting snow, trash devils blown across an intersection. When finally completed, *Seven Angels* turned out to be a pains-taking, intensely personal work that took Safie on a film festival circuit tour, winning her awards from coast to coast. The film was solitary and a bit oblique, but I enjoyed it a lot.

"I get tired of people calling my relatives witches," Safie tells the camera, near the end of the film. "Yezidi were massacred and denounced under the Ottoman caliphates for hundreds of years, and continue to be treated as pariahs even today. But the truth is, they practise equal rights, ecology, and consider honesty, pacifism, and tolerance of other religions the highest moral principles. Yezidi don't even believe in a personification of Evil, because to them, both Good and Evil coexist under God's control. So we should always be held responsible for our own actions—not God, and definitely not the Devil—because we were all created with the ability to think and decide for ourselves, whatever the consequences."

Since then, I'd kept in touch-but-not-really, tracking Safie's sad lack of professional progress mainly through Facebook posts, plus the occasional IM exchange. Those latter would have been the quickest way to reach her again, but an old-fashioned face-to-face sell session was what I really wanted—ideally, one where I didn't have to try to explain things in IM or Facebook message boxes.

A lucky coincidence brought me my chance. I Googled Safie's name to see what else she might be attached to locally, and was pleased to find her listed as one of the contributing artists in the upcoming Nuit Blanche art festival: a free event that takes place every October in Toronto, featuring dozens of interactive art installations all over the city on display from sundown to sunup. Safie was providing technical support for a "sound collage installation" by Soraya Mousch, Max Holborn's old partner—another former filmmaker who'd supposedly sworn off the medium entirely in the wake of . . . whatever the hell had happened to Holborn, and (one assumes) to her.

Safie's alliance with her made sense in hindsight—she'd done a biographical essay on Mousch for my Canadian Film History class, I now recalled, actually looking her up in the phone book and calling her directly rather than relying on Wikipedia like most of the other quote-unquote "kids" in her class. It's yet another way people fail to realize Canada isn't like Hollywood: Canadian industry types tend to be far more accessible, providing you're polite. Then again, given the size of the community over-all, it probably did help that they were both Armenian. Mousch invited Safie over to her place, showed her the old-school flatbed rig in her living room she used to do reel-to-reel editing on, and became a bit of a mentor to her—if I recall correctly, she actu-ally gave said rig to Safie as a present after whatever happened with Max Holborn, not that I think Safie ever used it. They kept in touch, Safie consulting with her on a variety of professional issues. When Mousch phoned her up with the outline for her Nuit Blanche piece, Safie jumped on board. As she later told me: "It's not like I had anything better to do."

"That's a rousing endorsement."

"Yeah, well: she *was* paying, at least."

Previous to that, Safie had just wrapped final edit on a film called *Drink Me*, an artsy softcore that wanted to crossbreed Ham-mer Horror with *Alice in Wonderland*. "Thirty hours of boobs, blood, and blurred-out privates compressed down to seventy-six minutes, and I'm not even getting official credit for work done," she complained; their Internet Movie Database page still had her listed as "3rd Camera Assistant," even though she'd apparently been the *de facto* editor ever since the real editor "went literally crazy" in post-production—stopped coming in, changed all his contact info, dropped off the map. But they'd kicked her a few thousand extra under the table, if nothing else, and she'd plugged the money straight back into making Mousch's aural "vision" as fully realized as possible.

Since I already knew I'd be up, and it was close enough I could walk there from our condo, I got to the area indicated on Nuit Blanche's official map—an office building lobby just off Yonge Street, about ten steps down from Yonge and Adelaide—at roughly 2:45 A.M., when attendance was just starting to taper off; we were entering the "dead hours" between three and five, the event's last spasms before sunrise. I'd emailed ahead to tell Safie I was coming. Opening the door, I found myself immediately con-fronted with a twisty grey structure made from sound-retardant

materials, a tunnel whorling inwards like something caught halfway between either the world's most massive ammonite fossil or
a human ear blown up large enough to crawl through. ENTER
HERE, a sign instructed. After a moment's hesitation, I bent my
head and did so.

Inside, the passage beyond curled back and forth across itself,
a mini-maze. I was forced to bend in increasingly creative ways
to gain access. I soon began to wish I hadn't brought my backpack, especially when the ceiling shrank even further. Eventually
I slipped it off and pushed it in front of me through the narrow
canal, soldiering grimly on. Behind me, the entrance first muffled,
then effectively cut off all trace of ambient noise—distant traffic,
weather, the hum and clank of machinery, the chatter of passing
crowds—and scrubbed my mind's palate clean, opening me up for
the equally subtle intrusion of Mousch's sound-mix, which seeped
up through speakers set in the floors, meeting more layers of noise
sifting down from the roof, now on my right hand and on my left,
now making me shy from whatever lay ahead, now driving me
forward with an awful sense of mounting pursuit.

It wasn't music, exactly. Just tones and drones and spatters of
muffled dialogue; conversations filtered through the walls, noise
and effects overlaid to create some sort of ever-moving internal
landscape of almost-glimpsed sequences. And when the passage finally widened, giving way to a room beyond, things didn't
much improve: the blackness was total, womb-like, with no hint
of which direction to turn. I stumbled with hands out, feeling
my way, constantly afraid I was going to encounter something
else that would grip me and pull me into . . . what, I don't even
know. Another dimension, some dreadful night-time abyss. The
silent, dust-piled bottom of some long-dried ocean full of skeleton fish and glowing, floating jellies, blind seekers with mouths
open wide, waiting to bite down and swallow.

Like the Orphic Mysteries, conducted in Grecian caverns, my
brain told me, while I shuffled blindly about. *Like that cave in the
jungle, the one they've identified as the working model for Xibalba,
the Mayan Underworld. Quite fascinating, really; you'll be okay,
I'm almost sure. . . .*

And then—at the edge of my total lack of vision, a waft of scent, borne on some invisible breath. It broke over me all at once, weirdly familiar: green shoots, turned earth, burnt hay. A hint of perfume—something musty and antique—impressed upon old clothing like sweat. Was that tuberose, perhaps? Lily of the Valley?

Don't move, a voice seemed to say, right against my ear, warming the lobe. *Keep your eyes shut, stay still. Don't look. The risk is great; avoid it. Do not—look—*

Spurred, I reeled back, arms flailing; touched the wall on one side and spun toward it, gripped hard, almost fell. Reached out in the darkness, only to feel another hand meet hers.

"Ms. Cairns?" a familiar voice asked.

"What's with your eyes, Ms. Cairns?"

My hand went reflexively up to touch my glasses. "Oh, shit—is it that obvious?"

"Well, in here, yeah." Safie and I had adjourned to a nearby Starbucks, which like many local shops was staying open all night to take advantage of the Nuit Blanche crowds; compared to the darkness of Safie's display, it had seemed dazzlingly, tear-making bright.

"Crap. I thought they were looking better."

"Um, well. Depends on how they looked before, I guess." A beat. "So how'd they look?"

". . . Worse."

She shot me a look, like: *You don't change, man, do you?* Which was valid, I guess; I've always been prickly, and teaching brought that out in me extra hard, especially when people got *really* stupid. I remember this one guy in my general film history class who literally didn't seem to understand the distinction between star and director, who thought *Cast Away* was a film *by* Tom Hanks rather than a film *with* Tom Hanks, thus making Robert Zemeckis and his crew just, what—friends of Hanks's who got on-screen credit for standing around admiringly while he simply dreamed the whole movie into existence, or spun it out of his ass like a spider? And yeah, if you're wondering, I did

say that last part out loud, in front of all the other students—
Safie included. I can still see her trying not to laugh, and failing
miserably.

"I can see fine," I reassured her. "Not that that was much
help, back there . . . you had anybody freak out, yet? Nobody's
been an asshole and dared their claustrophobic significant
other to try it?"

"Not so far. We *did* put a warning sign up at the front, you
know, 'People with Phobic Responses to Darkness or Enclosed
Spaces *Strongly Cautioned* Against Entry'—I guess you didn't
notice that. But just to be safe, we've got night-vision cameras in
a couple of places, and there are sections designed to lift straight
out if we see anybody about to lose their shit." Safie sipped her
cappuccino. "Once you get past the opening flat, most of the
structure's just wooden frames with sound-baffling foam layered
three or four sheets deep on chicken-wire backing. The foam's
the most expensive part, weirdly, just 'cause we needed so freaking *much* of it. We rented the speakers and the board, and Soraya
and I did the sound mix ourselves on her home system." She
brushed her hair back from her brow then asked, with slightly
too casual a tone of voice: "So how'd you like it?"

"Honestly? It scared the crap out of me."

"I seem to recall that's a compliment."

I grinned. "Yup. I mean, I'm not even phobic about this stuff,
mostly, and I was still seriously creeped out. How'd you do the
scents thing, by the way? Atomizers, set up to pump stuff in at
key places?"

"No, we didn't include an olfactory component. What did you
smell?"

"Um . . ." It was surprisingly hard to put words to it now.
"Organics, mostly. Warm. Like flowers in the countryside,
maybe. But if you really didn't do it, it obviously doesn't matter.
Some neurological thing, probably; memories firing, et cetera."

"Maybe you should go see a doctor," she suggested, unknow-
ingly mimicking my mom.

"Not unless one of the things I smelled was burnt toast." I
finished my chai. "Anyhow, what's next for you after this? You

planning to go on with that project you've been blogging about—
the *Seven Angels* sequel?"

Safie looked down; I saw the thin skin 'round her earlobes red-
dening, olive flushing darker. "That's . . . not really finished yet."

"The clips you put up on your site look pretty good."

"Yeah, those are—that's just for promotion, I guess. Proof of
concept. I don't really have much else, besides those; applied for a
Canada Council grant, so I could get back into it full-time."

I snapped my fingers. "Right, I remember you made a post,
talking about all the ridiculous questions on the application
form—" But as ever, I put two and two together just a fraction
too late to keep my foot out of my mouth "—and you didn't get
it," I finished. "I'm sorry, man."

"Thanks," Safie said, in a low voice. "Yeah, the letter came two
days ago, but with all our prep I didn't get the chance to read
it till this morning. So, um, I don't know what's next. Might be
nothing."

"Well, if you're looking for options, I *did* just get some funding;
from the NFA, as it happens. Which sucks it was me and not you,"
I added, hastily, as her eyebrows went up, "and if I'd been making
that decision, I might've gone the other way. But it's something I
could really use your help on, something I really think—I *hope*—
you'll find at least as cool as I do." When she didn't answer immediately, I went on. "Look, you know me—my field of study is pretty
esoteric, to say the least. I care a lot about stuff most people don't
even know exists, and even when they do, it's not like they're going
to *pay* for it. This is probably the only money I'm ever going to
make from doing this research. But if I give some of it to you, then
at the end of the day, I'll—*we'll* have rediscovered one lost Canadian filmmaker, and helped another make the leap from invisible
to visible—hopefully, anyhow. No guarantees. Nobody's ever going
to see your film unless you shoot it, right?"

Safie bit her lip, looking thoughtful. "Why me?" she asked,
at last.

"You always handed in your work ahead of time, and you
always did more than I asked you for; also, I like your stuff. As I
believe I've already told you, on numerous occasions."

Safie looked down again, this time turning slightly away, sheepish. "I guess I thought you were just being nice about that," she said.

"I'm a lot of things, Safie. None of them are 'nice.'"

That got a sidelong look and a slightly opened then closed mouth, meaning clear: *You said it, Miss, not me.*

We repaired back to the tech room at Mousch's auratorium, or whatever, because it had WiFi and Safie could stream the *Untitled 13* clips from my laptop, putting them up on a big screen. It was 3:30 A.M., and the only person there was Soraya Mousch herself, manning the board while Safie and I had our chat. Alec Christian used to rave about her all the time—called her "international model-glamorous"—and I could certainly see why: tall, willowy, with long black hair and beechwood-coloured eyes. But she looked thinner than I was entirely comfortable with, so much so that when she impulsively hugged me, I could feel her bones.

"Safie's told me a lot about you," she said. "And I remember your reviews, of course."

I laughed. "You and a grand total of maybe five other people, I think, but thanks. I remember *your* stuff too, from back during the Wall of Love era."

"Yes, me and Max. Those . . . were good times."

"Too bad you guys don't work together anymore."

She nodded, shrugged, took a beat. "Well," she said at last. "You just don't know, do you? What's going to happen, or why. If you did . . ."

. . . *You'd never get out of bed,* a creepily familiar voice supplied, or seemed to, from the back of my skull. I felt myself twitch, almost shying from the sound of it. She noticed, smiled to cover it up, but didn't get a similar gesture in return. *Yeah, and screw you too, lady,* I found myself thinking, uncharitably—then shook my head to dispel the bad energy and turned back toward what Safie and I had already been doing.

"Got any FireWire?" Safie asked her, rummaging through one of the boxes underneath the main workstation; Soraya nodded, and passed her some. A little more technical fussing and she emerged victorious, synching my laptop to the screen's flat blue glow. I pointed out the relevant icon and she clicked on it; from the corner of my eye, I saw Soraya's hand literally whip up to cup her cheekbone, like she was honest-to-God shielding her eyes from the dreaded sight of something potentially film related. *The hell you think I'm going to show her here?* I wondered. *A turn-of-the-century snuff film? Vintage porn?*

"Just fast-forward, say, five minutes," I told Safie, who nodded. "That'll get most of Wrob's bullshit out of the way, and things'll be really obvious from there on out."

"'Kay, cool." Raising her voice, keeping things studiously light: "Hey, Soraya—you do a walk-around anytime recently?"

Soraya shook her head, eyes still blocked, downcast. Replying, flatly,

"No, you're right, thanks. I should go do that."

"This won't take long," I assured her. "Maybe eight minutes from now, we'll be done."

"Okay, great. I'll see you then."

She retreated out the installation's back door, kicking it closed behind her. I heard a tourist cry out as they must've stumbled against her in the dark, then the hushed sounds of her calming them. Onscreen, meanwhile, the silver-bright figure of Mrs. Whitcomb as Lady Midday took shape amongst the sheaves, a shadow turned inside out, up-rearing to scare the child peasants in her glittering, fold-hung mirror cloak, her filmy white mourning veil.

"You know, I'd pay money to find out how this phobia of Soraya's kicked off in the first place," Safie murmured. "It's pretty intense, though, I know that much—I can't even get her to watch cat videos on YouTube."

I frowned. "Wait, wasn't there . . . you know, I think Alec Christian told me once it had something to do with that urban legend, the guy who shows up in everything. Background Man."

"Dude with the red necklace, right? Or the cut throat, depending."

"That's him."

"Mmm. Well, that *is* kinda spooky. What am I looking at here?"

"Digitized copy of a film shot sometime before 1918, on silver nitrate stock. Might even date back as far as 1908, which'd put it among the earliest examples of Canadian moviemaking, plus part of the oeuvre of someone I think could be Canada's very first *female* filmmaker. A whole chunk of completely unreported Canadian film history, in other words, so my job—yours too, if you opt to help out—would be to track it down, package it up for public consumption."

"That's . . . kinda cool as shit, actually."

"I *know*, right?" I felt my lips curve in the darkness, shaping a smile of private (yet not totally undeserved) triumph. "Wrob tripped over it as part of the Ontario Film Recovery Project, hooked it out from under Jan Mattheius, and *this* is all he thinks to do with it. Lost his damn job to make this film, such as it is. But Mrs. Whitcomb here's the real deal, the real story—you couldn't make this shit up, man. Tragic life, eccentric habits, mysterious disappearance . . ."

"Seriously?"

I nodded. "It's all in my notes. I'll email 'em to you, minute I get home."

Safie was still staring at the screen, though the clips had ended at least a minute ago; she tapped fingertip to bottom teeth, thoughtfully. "And you wanna move quick, I take it?"

"Well, yeah. I've been asking around for a month already, give or take—talked to a lot of people, one way or the other. Wrob already knows, and Jan, and Hugo Balcarras. In my experience, once you start connecting the dots, a thing like this doesn't stay secret for very long."

"*Buried Treasure: The Films of Mrs. A. Macalla Whitcomb,* by Lois Cairns and Safie Hewsen?"

"By Lois Cairns *with* Safie Hewsen, I was thinking, but sure— we can negotiate, as long as you're in." A beat. "So, are you?"

The answer's probably pretty obvious, by now. But nevertheless:

". . . Yeah, okay," Safie replied.

EIGHT

What I didn't know when I left Soraya Mousch's installation was that Wrob Barney already had people following me. I know, this sounds paranoid; it isn't.

Much later, after everything still to happen . . . happened, Wrob's then-boyfriend/assistant Leonard Warsame and I sat down together and exchanged frankly on exactly how, to paraphrase the Talking Heads, we got here. I filled him in on the various details of my search for Mrs. Whitcomb, while he told me what Wrob had been doing during the same time period—reading texted reports on me and fuming, mostly; trying to figure out how most effectively to undermine me, to steal my work and take credit for it. And all this while Leonard attempted at first to talk him out of it, then gradually stopped doing so, then started to scheme ways to withdraw himself from the situation without Wrob realizing he was doing so until it was an actual *fait accompli*. That he never quite managed to get there wasn't really his fault, and I certainly didn't resent him for it, but I have to admit, I kind of wish I'd known it was going on. Because he might have been a fairly useful person to call upon, in context, once things began getting *really* bad.

"It's not a good idea to turn your back on Wrob if you have something he wants," Leonard told me, sadly. "Believe me, I know. . . ."

And here he went into a long anecdote about another guy
Wrob had been involved with, before either Leonard or Jan Mattheuis—this dude who'd approached Leonard out of the blue,
trying to warn him off Wrob by telling him how, when he'd tried
to launch projects of his own instead of simply supporting Wrob
in his dubious ambitions, things suddenly began to go subtly yet
horribly wrong in every other area of his life. Oh, Wrob was sympathetic throughout, but that didn't really help; the guy ended up
losing both his day job and his health, plus a lot of his friends—
a downward spiral that culminated when he came home one
night to find that not only had the cult video store he lived above
burned down, effectively destroying all physical copies of his artwork, but that it had done so as part of an apparently deliberate,
barely controlled burn designed to clear a whole half-block of
Queen Street West. The area was then bought up for gentrifica-
tion, costing a bunch of people their livelihoods, and the guy in
question was forced to move back home to Nova Scotia, where
he worked in his parents' hardware store for the next three years
in order to pay rent on his former bedroom.

"He had no clear proof Wrob was involved, and he understood that completely," Leonard said. "As I recall, he prefaced
everything by saying: 'You're not going to believe a word I tell
you right now, and that's okay . . . but please, keep it in the back
of your mind for afterward, when things that sound familiar start
happening, because *they will.*' And I blew him off, of course,
exactly like he already knew I would; Wrob was everything to
me, my best friend, not just my boyfriend. But—"

"He was right," I filled in. He nodded.

"*So* right," he agreed.

Across town, meanwhile, and back in the here and now, Safie was
helping Soraya Mousch strike as the sun came up: not the whole
ear-whorl maze of flats and padding itself, since that was frankly
beyond both their physical capacities and would have to wait for
a brawny bunch of movers scheduled for sometime that same
morning, but the network of electronics, speakers, and night-
vision cameras that supported it. As she packed the last box of

bells and whistles into Soraya's truck and turned for the subway, yawning, she felt Soraya's hand on her sleeve.

"Let me ask you something, Safie," she began. "Do you trust Lois Cairns?"

Safie frowned. "Trust her like how?"

"Well, let me put it another way. Is she reliable?"

"Uh . . . she's weird, that's for sure; always has been. But weird in a good way. Like she cares too much."

"She looks tired, to me. Maybe a little sick."

"Said she's been having a hard time sleeping. I don't know if you noticed her eyes or not, but that happened pretty recently, I think."

"After she saw Wrob Barney's film?"

"Yeah, I guess." Safie stopped and thought for a moment. "And that thing about smelling stuff that wasn't there, too, in the installation . . . that was whack."

"I overheard, yes. Now I'll ask you something else. How do you feel, having also seen it?"

"I don't—"

"Watching Mrs. Whitcomb's film, for the first time. How did it make you *feel*?"

A simple enough question, on the face of it. Safie stopped, made a concerted effort to think her less intellectual reactions through, only to quickly find the flickering images had given her less a jolt of recognition or curiosity than a gradually dawning sick feeling, as though she were starting to perceive something incipiently dangerous drawing ever closer. That by the time the playback had stopped and she'd looked away, it had been with a lurch, a gasp—as though she'd been holding it, ever since the few tiny sections I'd shown her of what Jan Mattheuis and I had come to call *Lady Midday (Version One)* began.

"Why do you ask?" she replied after a moment, only to watch Soraya give the same weird smile, this time with even less humour behind it.

"Oh," was all she finally said. "No reason."

That night, Safie eventually told me, Soraya contacted her on Facebook, warning her: *I would be careful on this project, if I was*

you—keep your eyes open. Other people's obsessions can be fasci-
nating, but there's also an element of pull. A current. Don't want
to go any deeper with it than you need to. Might be you're inviting
something in without even knowing it.

Like what? Safie sent back. She waited for a reply but none
came. *Look,* she continued, *it's not up to me, anyways. You said*
that stuff to Ms. Cairns, she'd just quote David Cronenberg at you.
Be all, "where I need *to go with this is all the way through, right to*
the end. I need to see."

Some things you don't *need to see, though. Like some things*
shouldn't be *seen.*

Don't know what you're talking about, S.

I get that.

Maybe it was because she didn't know me that Soraya went to
Safie first. Christ knows I have that effect on people, sometimes.
Or maybe, just maybe, it was because she knew better, from
hard—and entirely personal—experience. Because I reminded
her enough of herself, or someone else she'd once known, to
understand it wouldn't have made a damn ounce of difference
either way, even if she had.

"So that's the deal," I told Mom the next afternoon, while
Simon watched as Clark bounced up and down on his tram-
poline in the background, hooting frantically along to his
favourite album, They Might Be Giants' *No!* "Safie drives me up
to Quarry Argent and plays videographer when we get there.
We gather as much background material as we can from the
museum, then visit the Vinegar House for more—footage of all
Mrs. Whitcomb's paintings, any photos we can scavenge of her,
her son Hyatt, or Mr. Whitcomb, stuff about the séances. We'll
try to find where she might've shot the films and check that out
as well: Méliès had a specially constructed studio made of glass
in a steel frame, to let in as much light as possible; the Vinegar
House's plans say Mr. Whitcomb built a greenhouse but never
used it, so I'm betting that was probably Ground Zero. Then
we come back, go through *all* the NFA's Lake of the North silver nitrate films again and match them up with the fairy tales,

digitize anything Wrob Barney didn't get around to . . . it's gonna be amazing."

"Mmm. How much are you paying her for this, exactly?"

I huffed, took a beat. "You know it's not *my* money being spent here, right? That's sort of the point of a grant."

"I know what a grant is, Lois, thank you. I also know you've never done anything this big before—or have you? Am I wrong?" I shrugged. "That's what I thought."

"Safie's trustworthy, Mom. I wouldn't have involved her if she wasn't."

"Which you know how?"

At that, I really did have to laugh, though I saw Simon shoot me a warning glance as I did. "Because I just *do*, and I guess you're just gonna have to believe I know what I'm talking about! I mean, you either do or you don't, right? It's not rocket science."

In fact, though Safie probably didn't rely entirely on her family anymore, it seemed likely she wasn't hurting quite as badly as some of my former students, which kept her motives strictly un-mercenary. I knew this because she'd accepted my first offer without a qualm, let alone any attempt at further negotiation: a 500-dollar retainer, plus forty dollars per hour logged for her initial assistance, to be raised if the research period exceeded two weeks. Jan Mattheuis had told me it was pretty standard boiler-plate, and she'd have to return a signed copy of the agreement to him before we could leave for Quarry Argent. We were plan-ning to go up over the weekend, travelling Friday, exploring and shooting Saturday-Sunday-Monday, then back on Tuesday by the latest.

"The Archive is going to want to do a tie-in documentary for their website, which could lead to an expanded documentary for the CBC," I explained. "That's why I need someone with Safie's skills."

"But you don't *know*."

"I know if I do this fast enough my name's going to be on it, and if she helps, hers will, too. That was my sell, and it worked." Mom looked at me again, sceptically. "Listen, I'm not asking you for anything here; I'm telling you what's going to happen.

I signed a contract, worked out a schedule, so you're not going to see me around for the next few days because I am going to Quarry Argent, with Safie Hewsen. Me informing you is a courtesy; this is me, being courteous."

"Oh, mmm-hmmm. Very."

"As I can be, yeah."

Dryly: "I could debate *that*." Her gaze shifted up over my shoulder, pinning Simon, one eyebrow lifting. "And you, you're all right with this?" He nodded. "Health issues and everything else, you're *fine* with her going out of town with someone you don't know from Adam, where anything could happen."

Simon gave her his patented earnestly placatory look. "Honestly, Lee, I really don't think it's as sinister as you're making it sound. It's Northern Ontario, not Beirut, and they both have cell phones; no worse than going up to a friend's cottage for the weekend. Lois and Safie'll be fine."

"I could care less about this Safie person." To me, again: "You're not *well* these days, Lois, in general. Would you agree with me on that at least?"

I snorted. "C'mon, Mom. I mean, I've had some trouble sleeping. . . ."

"Constant insomnia, migraines. That's not nothing."

"It's inconvenient, sure; annoying, absolutely. In practice, though, it's just—so I don't get a lot of sleep here or there, what's the difference?"

"Did you go back to Goa yet?"

"No, I did not. I haven't had a migraine for weeks, seriously. Haven't had time."

"Right, because you've been too busy driving yourself to distraction."

"I've been *working*, and this is what I've been working on. An actual job, just like the old days. Freaking *finally*."

Mom opened her mouth to refute me, but right at that same moment—behind us—Clark bounced extra-high, gave a whoop, then stumbled against the front window, ankle turning; he started to buckle, skull angled toward the glass. Luckily, however, Simon was there to catch him as he came down, fast enough he didn't get exactly how close he might've come to disaster. "Whoa, doggy!" Simon exclaimed, and Clark laughed maniacally, hugging on tight.

"Clifford is SO big!" he sang-yelled in return. "The Big Red Dog, *wooof!*"

I looked back at Mom, who sighed before gathering up her purse and coat.

"You have a job already, Lois," is all she said as she turned to go.

"Am I being an asshole?" I asked Simon that night, snuggled up in bed together—a rarer occurrence than I liked these days, as my insomnia usually kept me up well past his latest. "To her? To Clark?" This close, I could almost see his face clearly, even without my glasses. "To you?"

Simon shrugged. "I think you're in a lot of pain, and that makes it hard to be patient. But I don't think a four-day trip counts as material for a heartbreaker country song." He abruptly grinned. "'My wife, she done left me with an autistic son/He sings on the YouTube while she's on the run!'"

I snorted. "I'm trying to be serious."

"This is *se-wious*," Simon said promptly, in a toddlerish falsetto lisp. Then he yelped as I ran my hands up under his armpits, proving once again how Clark's helpless ticklishness didn't come from *me*; I stopped after a moment, to let him get his breath, and he rolled onto his side to face me. "You want serious, hon? You've looked happier these last few days than I've seen you in months, which I think is worth a few headaches."

"Mom doesn't think so."

"She's just worried about you. 'Cause that's *her* job."

I closed my eyes. "Yeah, that would come off more plausible if she didn't phrase it to sound as if me taking a research trip means deserting Clark, somehow falling down on my responsibilities to him. Because nothing *I* want matters anymore, right?"

"Well, nothing *either* of us wants matters if it conflicts with what Clark needs . . . but I honestly don't think this does." He tilted his head. "Besides, and no offence—you don't really have a record of knowing when to downshift gears for your own sake. Maybe she's just taking any tactic she thought you might actually listen to."

I nodded. "Manipulating me, you mean, since I'm genuinely too thick to know when I'm not physically up to something."

He breathed out in the dark, sharply—that last part must've gotten to him, more than usual. "No, that's not it either. What I *mean* is, she cares enough about you that she's never going to give up trying to get you to take better care of yourself. Is that so unforgiveable?"

I sighed. "I just wish she'd get it through her head how important this is, and not just to me. It's not the money, not even really the fame—I mean, Jesus, it's the Canadian film industry. I just want to feel like I've accomplished something. Like there was some point to being here, in my *life*."

Simon's pause was longer this time, and again I belatedly realized how that might have sounded to him. I wanted to wince, but knew he might feel it as a withdrawal; his eventual response was dryer yet, but nothing worse. "A man with lower self-esteem might take that amiss. Fortunately, I'm protected by an impenetrable bubble of arrogance."

I felt my face heat. "You know what I mean."

"As it happens, yes, I do." He tightened his arms, wrapping us closer, furnace-warm. "Look, there's absolutely nothing wrong with needing more in your life than just one vocation. Lee's erring in favour of Clark because she loves him—loves *both* of you—so much she can't see that just yet, but she will. And while you might have to put up with some nagging in the meantime, that's just par for the course between you two."

Unarguably true, so I let myself relax, much as I could with my shoulder already beginning to whine at me. "I love you," I told him, without planning to.

"I love *you*. So does Clark."

"I hope so."

Sleepily, but firmly: "I *know* so."

I was tired—and smart—enough to know not to say: *I'm glad* you *do*. Because much as Simon's own family, and Simon himself, were evidence for the assertion, I'd never quite bought into the idea that being someone's parent or child automatically guaranteed their love or yours. Mom hadn't been able to stand her own mother by the end, as I'd pointed out to her more than once.

Gamma couldn't stand me, *you mean,* she'd said. *I loved* her, *always. I couldn't help it.*

That sounds healthy.

That's family, Lois. Healthy doesn't come into it.

And Clark . . . God help me, helpless bedrock affection notwithstanding, we just made each other so *uncomfortable*, him and me, all the time. For someone on the autism spectrum he was amazingly persistent at seeking out contact, demanding your interaction, but only on *his* terms: he'd play up to me while I struggled to keep myself even, pretend I didn't feel resentment at the interruption or frustration at so often not being able to follow his skittering attention shifts until it became impossible to ignore him. If he loved me at all, I sometimes thought, it was only because he could still be so easily distracted into forgetting our last quarrel.

Similarly, if he really did notice that I was gone during this trip, it'd probably only strike him as a bonus. More time to spend with his "friend Daddy," without that annoying, ever-pushy, ever-insistent-on-making-people-use-their-words *Mommy* around. . . .

Simon's breathing had dropped into his usual snore, body gone limp. Pain throbbed steadily under my collarbone and looped through my capsular ligament, rotator cuff puffing; I shifted, felt the blade flare uncomfortably, and cursed, but only mentally. I stayed still another few minutes to make sure Simon would remain asleep before extracting myself, slipping onto my desk chair and turning on my computer, knowing the light wouldn't wake him.

I sat there in the dark and watched *Lady Midday (Version One)* again, with the sound turned down, till I felt tired enough to go lie on the living room couch. To stare up at the ceiling, glasses still in place, before finally closing my eyes against my throbbing temple, the grind-anticipating ache in my back teeth, and the only slightly dimmer knot where my arm met my torso, trying my level best to simply slip away.

No dreams that night, however unsettling—mere dreams would've been too simple, too homey. Instead, I had a full-blown night terror episode for the first time in . . . well, not years, but enough consecutive months to make it seem so. If you're lucky, you don't know what I'm talking about, so here's some background on the concept.

Night terrors, or *pavor nocturnus*, are a classic sleep disorder whose universal feature is inconsolability on awakening plus apparent paralysis and pressure on the sleeper's chest, chased with intense feelings of terror or dread. Sometimes, especially if the sleeper somehow manages to force their eyes open while trying to wake themselves up, this is accompanied by horrifying hypnagogic visual hallucinations: floating, crawling, and looming phantom figures with rictus-frozen faces, eyes in the dark, orbs and auras, threatening shadows, and nonexistent insect swarms. Typically, night terrors tend to happen during the first hours of Stage Three non-rapid eye movement sleep and coincide with periods of delta or slow-wave sleep arousal, but they can also occur during daytime naps.

During bouts, patients often bolt upright with their eyes wide open, a look of absolute panic on their face. They scream out loud, sweat, exhibit rapid respiration and heart rate, thrash and flail. When woken, they're confused or unresponsive, unable to recognize familiar faces. Sometimes they lash out further, kicking and punching; I've never done that, but then again, I've also never experienced the one positive side effect of this syndrome— while most people with night terrors become at least partially amnesiac about their incidents the following day, I remember each iteration with almost grotesque clarity.

They used to call it being hag-ridden. In ancient Britain, it was the province of the literal night-*maere*, which rode men, women, children, and even animals through their sleep, sometimes to their deaths. Even trees were thought on occasion to be subject to this sort of bewitchment, resulting in their branches being entangled, their roots knotted, strangling each other.

My first night terrors happened in Australia, when I was still going to visit my dad every year. He and his significant other met me in Sydney and took me to the house they'd arranged to stay in—a cool, modern, single-level beach house that sat at the edge of a cliff overlooking the sea. From the outside everything looked great, if not exactly designed with the acro- or agoraphobic in mind, but once we got inside I realized that this woman apparently collected Polynesian art, which meant that every part of her home was crowded with leering, life-sized statues made from dark wood with inset shell eyes and teeth, the largest of which depicted a giant shark-god swallowing a man whole. In order to make it more habitable, Dad moved all the masks and what-not out of the main bedroom and into the living room, which was where I was going to sleep, in a window-seat bed surrounded by massive looming Polynesian death-gods on one side, and on the other the open edge of the cliff seen through windows full of unfamiliar Australian stars. I was so frightened I woke up later that same night in the throes of a classic *maere*, certain I was having a heart attack while being sexually assaulted by a ghost.

Time softens all things, however, which may explain why this particular event was gentle by comparison, if no less disturbing. At roughly 4:30 A.M., my eyes opened with what sounded to me like an audible click, and I found myself looking upwards; the room was silent, the whole apartment likewise, which was its own brand of unlikely—no snoring, no dryer, no ambient noise or traffic outside. The air in my lungs felt heavier than water, turgid, like jelly. No light—Simon must've gotten up to use the bathroom, then turned everything off on his way back—and my glasses had slipped off in my sleep, probably ending up on the floor, smeared all to hell. But I could see nonetheless. I could see everything.

And how I wished to Christ I couldn't.

Above me, something leaned in, shrouded in layers of white-turned-grey. Where its face should have been was a lace grille, fine-holed as a bee's eye; it hung limp, whatever lay behind stiller than stone and had been for years. For almost a century. And still I heard a voice, small and fleshless—a murmur, a buzz, faint and fainter. Words ant-crawling up through dirt.

Don't go, Lois. I beg of you now, face to face—not warn, not threaten. I beg, sister; please, oh please. Please, please, no.

(no)

(oh, no no *no*)

I wanted to shut my eyes again but couldn't. Wanted to flail out, to punch and scream—no such luck. Instead, I simply lay there, chest on fire, drowning in my own fear; felt each breath catch on the inside of my throat, scoring it with a thousand fish hooks. My tongue was a choke-stone, gone rough, dry and cold in a dry, cold mouth, spit gummed and bloody.

The fear mounted, mounted, mounted, till I thought my heart would burst. But . . . it didn't.

It never does.

When I woke it was morning, full sun and the normal bustle. Clark was reciting along with *Match Game* as Simon shoehorned him into his clothes. For a split second, I had no idea where I was, or who, or why—till he noticed me staring, that is, and smiled at me. "Hey, hon," he said, almost unbearably cheerful. "Sleep okay?"

I swallowed, painfully. Then managed to repeat—

". . . Okay."

"That's good." Checking his watch: "Well, bus time. Clark, say 'bye."

Clark made a noise somewhere between a buzzer and a burp, as he's wont to do when asked to participate in something uninteresting. "*Aaaarp!* 'No match. King-size, or king crab?'"

"Neither," I rasped back, swinging myself up and beckoning. "Kiss, please."

"No kiss."

"Oh, I think yes kiss."

"No kiss, you're silly! The Mommy should listen."

"Listen to who, bunny?"

This last was from Simon, but Clark just turned his head side-long, eyes meeting mine instead—a rare enough occurrence to raise the hairs on the back of my neck.

"The lady in the bag," he replied, without prompting. "Listen, don't go—she said so. Please, please, *please* . . ."

No.

NINE

In retrospect, it's probably not too surprising how little I remember about the trip to Quarry Argent, given what eventually happened when I got there. When I try to think about it now things begin all right, then get smeary and unreliable—after a certain point, I have to take other people's word almost entirely for what I did and said, with one very notable exception. Their memories, their records, trump mine. So yeah, not surprising as such, but not exactly a *comfortable* thing to admit, either; this goddamn world's empirical enough as it is without having to worry about your own experiences seeping out of your head like a sieve, no matter what trauma might have perforated it.

And yet, as I've said so many times before, with just the same impatient tone I hear it spoken in now, looking at it on the page—to my mom, to Clark, to whomever. To myself.

I remember dragging my travel suitcase downstairs, out the building's side entrance, then crossing the street to where Safie waited in a van she'd borrowed from a friend. Remember her looking up as I approached, turning down the radio and remarking, "Knew it was you when I saw you coming, Ms. Cairns. You walk like you know where you're going, I ever tell you that?"

"Thanks, I guess."

As we pulled onto the highway, Safie switched iPod playlists, trading Kanye West's greatest hits for some Tracy Chapman;

something from the more recent part of her career—"Telling Stories," maybe. I wondered who'd introduced it to her—a friend? A boyfriend? I never thought to ask, or wanted to. I didn't even know if Safie was straight or gay, or what. Irrelevant, for my purposes.

I remember sitting beside her, van humming beneath me, eyes kept level so my vague nausea wouldn't take over. Because yes, on top of everything else, I'm also prone to car-sickness, possibly as a side effect of the many medications I'm taking, prescription and otherwise.

"So, that fairy tale," she said. "'Lady Midday.' That's some pretty wild stuff."

"I've read her whole book, and they're all . . . eccentric, by modern standards," I agreed. "But I guess that must've been the one she liked best, considering she filmed five separate versions of it."

"Five? Shit." I nodded as she continued: "That veil . . . I mean, it was a costume, right? Those pieces of mirror, making herself look as much like the story as she could—but not really. It almost looked like she was hiding, from somebody she thought might be watching. Like she wanted to keep what she was doing a secret."

"Yeah, I get how you could think that, but she was just in mourning; wore it all the time, apparently, ever since her son Hyatt disappeared. And while she's definitely playing Lady Midday in the *Untitled 13* clips, she's in a lot of the other films as well, in the background sometimes, and she always wears the veil. It's *possible* it's somebody else, but I really don't think so."

"Wouldn't she have to be working the camera, though?"

"Not necessarily. Méliès starred in almost every film he made. She was already the director, the designer—the sets, the masks, they're all probably her handiwork, just like that backdrop. We'll probably find some of 'em still out at the Vinegar House, if we're lucky. And anybody could've run that kind of camera: just point and crank, make sure the light doesn't get in the wrong places."

She nodded. "Plus, she was rich, so it makes sense she would've had crew."

"I'd be surprised if we can't locate some of them, or their descendants. Small towns are like that, right? Everybody knows everybody."

"No offence, Miss, but you never struck me like a small-town gal."

"You either."

"Well, should be fun. Who knows, I might be the least white person they've ever seen. Like, not on TV."

"I'm not sure I'd go into the situation thinking that."

"You might if you were me, but don't worry. I'll be good."

A couple of minutes elapsed, the ground spinning by beneath us like the fields outside, the sun already halfway up the sky—it'd be noon soon, it occurred to me. Lady Midday's time. But the steely grey October overcast seemed worlds away from the burning white air of the clips, and the radio had switched to the twenty-first-century electronica of Daft Punk. Last night felt like it'd happened to somebody else.

(*The Mommy should listen.*)

"I wonder if any of the original notebooks are up there," said Safie. "The ones the book's afterword talked about. Be interesting to see if she drew on any other stuff, besides the Wendish material."

"Like what?"

"Well, maybe this is just me connecting everything back to *my* pet obsessions—" She gave me a wry eyebrow lift; I snorted, nodded a silent *touché*. "—but Lady Midday and some of the things in the other tales, they reminded me a lot of figures that pop up in Yezidi myths as well; it would just be neat if maybe there was actually a direct connection, somehow. I talked about some of this in *Seven Angels*, I don't know if you remember. . . ."

I shook my head. "You might have to recap. It's images, names, and characters that stick for me; backstory detail tends to kind of slide."

"Okay. Well . . . you remember the part where my Dédé says how in Yezidi thought, God basically entrusted the management of the world to this heptad of Holy Beings, who're sometimes called angels, sometimes *heft sirr*—the Seven Mysteries?"

"Given that part's in the title, yeah."

"Mmm. So they're supposed to be God's emanations, these angels, and God delegates most earthly action to them—sort of like how the mediaeval Cathars and other Gnostic-influenced sects claimed the Devil was 'king of this world,' with God's complicity. It's a system that leaves room for a whole lot of animistic deities, spirits of place or concept—the kind you get in ancient Greek, Roman, Aryan-Indian, and Slavic beliefs, or even Chinese Shenism and Japanese Shinto. And these things could be good, could be bad, could be beneficial or malign, but since they all had *God* behind them, you couldn't really get rid of 'em, not completely. The best you could do is, um . . . stop paying attention. Ignore them, walk away. Don't *ever* give them what they want."

"Which is?"

"Attention, I guess. Worship." She paused for a moment. "Which means there's a whole lot more than seven angels, when it comes down to it—and maybe more things like devils than my Dédé wanted to admit."

I frowned. "What's that mean, 'God's complicity?' Like, what . . . God *lets* these things exist?"

"More than that. It's like He *wants* them to."

"For what possible point?"

She shrugged. "Do I look like God to you? All I know is that when I went looking for source Yezidic texts in the U of T rare-books libraries, I ran across an idea that's making more and more sense to me these days, which is that there *is* a connection between the Lucifer myth and Malak Tâwus, the Peacock Angel—but it was the *Yezidi* angel that came first, not the other way around. It turns up in all Big Three monotheisms, it's got offshoots in half a dozen versions of Gnosticism, the core cosmology looks like a key inspiration for Persian Zoroastrianism, and you can find echoes in a bunch of pagan mystery cults too."

"So the Peacock Angel *is* the Devil?" I had forgotten my nausea, forgotten my shoulder, and turned to face Safie as directly as I could; I had no idea how much of this might prove useful, but I'd never been able to resist a new myth, creation or otherwise.

Safie tilted one hand back and forth, making a sort-of-but-not-really grimace. "Well, the 'origin story' for Malak Tâwus is almost exactly the same as the Muslim myth about Iblis, the *djinn* they later call Shaytan—but Yezidi *revere* Malak Tâwus for refusing to submit to Adam, while Muslims believe that Iblis's refusal to submit was what made him fall out of grace with Allah. From our point of view, God *praised* Malak Tâwus for refusing to serve something made out of dust, because he was made from God's own light; instead of punishing him, God made the Peacock Angel His own representative on earth, telling him to dole out responsibilities, blessings, and bad luck as he saw fit. And we can't question him, because he's beyond good and evil—good and evil are *human* qualities.

"My Dédé Aslan used to say that if God commands anything to happen then it just happens, automatically—*bibe, dibe*. So God could have *made* Malak Tâwus bow down to Adam, but He chose not to, and that was the right choice: human beings are flawed because we were *made* flawed, intentionally; we need to be guided by sublime beings, which is the Peacock Angel's job. It was a test for Malak Tâwus and he passed, qualifying himself to act as God's stand-in, so God doesn't ever have to worry about humanity again."

"Wow." I sat back in my seat. "What's this all got to do with Lady Midday?"

"Well, what Lady Midday reminds me of is, basically, one of those old other angels, or spirits, or gods—the figures from the cult offshoots, the beings one step down from the Seven. Things that sometimes got prayed to, sometimes just placated; things that were local to one place or time and got left behind when people died out, or moved on, or converted to something else. If you think about it, isn't that how Midday and some of the other figures in the stories come off? It's like they're desperate for attention, but they don't know how to do anything except repeat their old patterns, so they wind up harming the very people whose attention they're trying to get in order to . . . I don't know, keep going. Stay alive. Intact."

"*Can tah in can tak?*" I suggested then explained, off her baffled stare: "*Desperation*, Stephen King—he calls it the

Language of the Unformed. It means 'small gods out of a greater god.'"

"That's . . . almost exactly what I'm talking about, yeah. Weird."

I shrugged. "Tropes are tropes. They resonate. Which is why, awesome as all of that sounds, I don't know if we're going to be able to get much mileage out of it—for this project, anyway. I'd be really surprised if Mrs. Whitcomb had even heard of the Yezidi."

"Maybe. But how much do we really know about Mrs. Whitcomb's background, anyway? We know her maiden name, Iris Dunlopp, and . . . what else?"

"Not much," I acknowledged. "She was adopted—her 'mom,' Miss Dunlopp, was the woman who ran the orphanage she grew up in, and Mr. Whitcomb was a big contributor. That's how they met. Iris taught the younger children basic reading, writing, and arithmetic, plus gave art classes for local kids and tutored adults, that sort of thing."

"So, dead parents. Any information as to how, or who they were?"

"Not that I've uncovered. Balcarras might know." I thought a minute. "Actually, Jan Mattheuis said the Quarry Argent Folklore Museum had all Mr. Whitcomb's old papers, as well as Mrs. Whitcomb's paintings. He must've donated them at the same time."

"Good thing we're going there then."

"Yup."

I'm still not entirely sure what prompted me to ask the next question. It's always struck me as something too personal to ask someone who hasn't already brought up the topic, and most people who do so tend to make the answer pretty obvious. But—

"Safie," I began, carefully, "how much of this stuff do you believe? I don't mean just know about, or use to build films around, but that it's objectively true—is that what you think?"

Safie opened her mouth then closed it. "I . . . don't know," she finally replied. "All of this is more like history than religion, really. It's what makes my family what it is, which makes *me* what I am; it's always going to be there inside me, this sort of core I rotate around—the source of everything." I nodded. "It's why I ended up going to the Fac in the first place, you know? I wanted to extend what I'd already been doing into a longer-form narrative, to package it in a way people from outside my family could swallow; show them all the stuff I'd grown up with as just part of my day-to-day. And that's probably why I'm here, too." She glanced briefly at me, our eyes meeting. "Because if that's what Mrs. Whitcomb wanted, I kind of feel like I owe it to her to finish her work."

It struck me then, like a slap—how weird it was I'd never asked myself these sorts of questions. What was it she'd been doing it *for*, exactly, in the first place? What drove her to constantly return to these stories, re-interpret them over and over, especially "Lady Midday," yet still end up so unhappy with the result she literally tried to bury it? For all my feverish research thus far, I'd never once thought of her as a *person*, with goals or desires of her own that might yet be accomplished even now, through us. Someone to whom something might be owed.

I stared out the windshield, struck silent. Thankfully, Safie didn't seem to notice. "I wish I could talk to my Dédé," was all she said, wistfully. We were on some rural route now, one of only a few cars moving; Lake of the North district isn't one of the big cottage country destinations, and we were well in advance of whatever they considered rush hour. She added, after a moment, "God, I miss him."

I nodded, and just for a blink, my mind returned to Simon and Clark. Much to my surprise, given how little time had elapsed since we'd left, I found myself in complete sympathy.

As it turns out, we were both wrong about at least one thing regarding Mrs. Whitcomb—she *had* met at least one Yezidi while she was still alive, though she might well not have known it at the time: doomed Gustave Knauff, whose surviving family still traces the origin of their fortune back to the Crusades, when a certain Swiss knight brought home a beautiful woman of Middle Eastern origin and married her, claiming her parents—conveniently dead—were converts to Christianity, their documentation lost in transit from Acre. There's a tiny yet passionate sub-genre of art history devoted to tracing Yezidi themes in Knauff's paintings, especially the famous *Black Annunciation* and his subsequent *Hymnes de Paon* triptych. Not that this has much to do with anything, I suppose, within immediate context.

But maybe it does, and maybe I'm just fooling myself, because I'm afraid to do anything else. Maybe everything's linked, like atoms; all the component parts of some unknown universe, laid parallel beside our own. Maybe it was fate, always: inexplicable, inescapable.

Be nice if it was, I suppose, on one level, because then there would never have been anything I could've done—or *not* done—to make what happened . . . happen. Then it would've been out of my hands from the very beginning. From long before.

And none of it would be my fault.

That conversation with Safie is actually the last thing I remember clearly from our entire trip. It's after this point that things begin to skew, smearing together, a tangle of moments I still find difficult to set in linear order—I know certain events happened, but not when or how, let alone why. Luckily, I have Safie's footage to refer to, with its built-in time-stamp and freeze-frameable visuals, as well as her physical notes, scrawled but scrupulous, in a series of sixty-sheet Staples mini-notebooks she bought in bulk; she'd used them to track continuity on editing jobs, mostly, developing a quite amazing eye for detail. And all of that becomes even more important now, when I no longer have Safie herself to consult with.

But that's for later, right? A place for everything, with everything in its place.

Safie's notes say we reached Quarry Argent around 4:30 P.M., by which time I was pale and slightly faint from vertigo, but I refused to stop long enough to recuperate—just chugged some water, donned a pair of wrap-around sunglasses I'd bought at Shopper's Drug Mart, and set off for the museum. The person who answered the door was Bob Tierney, interim director, standing in that weekend for actual director Sylvia Jericote, who goes up to Gravenhurst every October to spend time with her family.

Tierney hadn't been there during Jan Mattheius's sojourn in Quarry Argent, but he knew the basic details, and when we showed him the clips from *Untitled 13*, he perked up considerably. The footage shows him as a square-set guy with hyperthyroid eyes and an unfortunate neckbeard, gesticulating excitedly as he tells us: "Wow, that looks *so much* like her paintings! It's uncanny, huh? Isn't it just. You know, we have the largest collection of Iris Dunlopp Whitcomb in Canada, not that she was ever so well-recognized, you understand, outside of Ontario."

"We'd heard that, yeah," I can hear myself say, from slightly outside the frame. "Love to film those, if the museum's okay with it. And Mr. Whitcomb's private papers, you have those too?"

"Right, right; we've a whole three file boxes on Mr. Whitcomb at least, down in the basement. Though two of them are mainly about the mine, and I guess you probably don't want to see *those*."

"Not as such, no."

Later, in the hospital—recuperating—I scrolled past Safie's beautifully centred shots of Mrs. Whitcomb's art, arranged earliest to latest, and was frankly amazed by their complete lack of familiarity. Oh, they all shared a certain visual kinship, obviously; all fell inside a particular spectrum of artistic influence, displaying Impressionist or even Fauvist leanings and an Orientalist design sense, much like Mary Cassatt's domestic portraits or Odilon Redon's famous "*chimères*." The colours she used were pale and slightly off, even in the studies she'd done as a teenager, as though she routinely diluted everything in her paint box with white lead or Chinese yellow. Her favourite subject matter seemed to be country landscapes that, on closer examination, proved to have figures lurking suggestively in almost every part of them—white-draped, long-limbed, oddly contorted, their faces hidden by hands, hair, the folds of their flowing robes.

One of the most evocative, done when she was only thirteen, was of a cornfield that could have literally formed the backdrop for *Untitled 13*. Indeed, when I examined them more closely and cross-referenced them with Mrs. Whitcomb's films, almost all of the paintings soon began to look like location scouting stills done in oil: the swamp from *The Old Man With a Frog's Mouth*, the dock on the Lake of the North itself from *In Spring We Drown the Winter,* the quarry where *The Pots With Candles In Them* are dug up. I remember staring at that one for at least a minute, the shot in which the chief excavator lifts a random pot lid free replaying in my memory: inside, a quarter-face with a single eye, blinking, bloodless. And the carefully lettered title insert card immediately afterwards—*Those Old Heretics Have Been At It Again, Mocking God's Will With Their Evil Ways And Feeding Their Elders To The Earth*—could that have been Mrs. Whitcomb's own handwriting, that slightly spiky copperplate?

The story that movie was based on, from *The Snake-Queen's Daughter,* ran a page long at most: *For it is told how near Riga, before Christ took hold, those old heretics used to sacrifice their old and young alike at harvest's end, to seed the fields and bring on next year's crop. How they cut them into pieces then put those pieces into pots with candles in them, each signifying the soul cast away to be eaten by She Who Gives All, who walks behind every row. And when they were taken up by godly men and asked to defend their actions, they said only: "But what better gift to give my true Mother, the Mother of everything, than that of she who bore me or he who bred me? To fold them deep in the soil's open mouth and let dirt fall down upon them like a blanket, softly extinguishing them, returning them to seeds in the darkness . . . unless it be my own child, of course, my best-loved, my favourite. . . ."*

(And that dreadful sin was practised as well, here and there, in different places. But the priests put an end to it, as is only proper, with fire, sword, and salt, and nothing ever grew again on the spot where these terrible criminals were finally done away with.)

"What can you tell me about Mrs. Whitcomb?" I can be heard asking Tierney as Safie tracks past the quarry painting to frame a miniature of a flower garden in full bloom, so small yet vivid it almost seems like a tiny window opened from one season onto another. "Does anybody know where she came from? Or why she was committed to Miss Dunlopp's in the first place?"

"Well, it's all pretty vague if you're just looking at the official documents—she doesn't have a birth certificate, for example, so she had to visit Europe under her husband's passport on their honeymoon—but we *were* eventually able to find a copy of Miss Dunlopp's register. The year that Mrs. Whitcomb was admitted, there were only three other orphans who stayed at the Home, and two were boys who got fostered out quick, apprenticed to local farmers; the third was a girl who never shows up again. It's like she just vanishes, but if she'd died Miss Dunlopp would've recorded it, because that tended to happen a lot—there was a definite protocol in place for dealing with it. So what we think is this girl might've *been* Mrs. Whitcomb, except Miss Dunlopp changed her first name to Iris and gave her her own last name, never making a clear connection between the two."

"Why do you think she would've done it that way?"

"Oh, that's because the other girl was kind of famous around here. There was a scandal associated with her—nothing she *did*, more something got done *to* her—so Miss Dunlopp probably wanted all that forgotten, to give Mrs. Whitcomb a fresh start."

"What was this other girl's name?"

"Giscelia Wròbl. She came from up around God's Lips, or maybe Your Ear; was a lot of farmland in between, with quite the little community of Wendish Anabaptist immigrants—her father, Handrij Wròbl, defected from one of their sects after his wife Liska died in childbirth. But the other Wends mainly moved away after it happened."

"After *what* happened?"

Tierney pauses. "I'll go get the file," he says, at last.

Safie's notes say we asked for copies of the stuff he showed us next, and Tierney obliged us, same way he did with almost everything else we requested; poor guy spent a good couple of hours xeroxing stuff from Mr. Whitcomb's non-mine-related box alone, later that evening, while Safie and I checked into our little room in the Gooden Tymes Bed & Breakfast down the street. But the file on Giscelia Wròbl was considerably lighter, which you can see Tierney apologize for. "We had a fire back in 1957," Safie's notes have him saying. "And then a flood, then another fire . . . you're sort of lucky we have anything from that time period at all, really. 1886 just wasn't a good year, by most accounts."

There were three newspaper clippings: one from Chaste, one from Overdeere, one from Upper New York. Story must've travelled, and I could see why. I remember doing research about the turn of the century, how there were a series of Millennialist scares as the 1800s drew to a close, though obviously nothing like what would happen in 1999, let alone what had happened in 999. Sometimes these were jump-started by actual cults—the Children of a Living Voice set their followers three or five separate deadlines for the apocalypse, for example, depending on your sources, before finally giving up on the idea. But then again, telling people the world's about to end has always been big business of a sort, though it's not as though Handrij Wròbl made any money off seeing his particular version of it through to conclusion.

According to all three articles, Handrij was such a recluse that locals first figured out he might be going a little wacky after he let all his animals go, then harvested his crops too early for them to be worth anything, stacked them together in his barn, and burnt the whole thing down. When the constabulary arrived to arrest him for endangering his neighbours, Handrij's family convinced them he'd already run off; actually, he was lurking in their root cellar, where he passed the time praying and pounding nails into his own head "like Jael with Sisera," as the paper from Chaste put it. When night fell, he collected his children and mother-in-law, leading them at gunpoint into the smoking ruin of his fields, where they spent the next two weeks waiting in vain for Jesus Christ to arrive on a chariot drawn by angels and whisk them off to heaven, hopefully without the minor inconvenience of having to die first.

On Tuesday morning of week three, Giscelia was discovered hiding underneath a pile of ashy dirt and discarded stalks, the sole survivor of the incident—her siblings and grandmother having either died of privation during their wait or had their brains beaten in. Handrij, meanwhile, was once more notably absent. A subsequent manhunt failed to turn up any leads, though a week later a man's body was recovered from a nearby swamp with its head neatly severed at the neck, the wound cauterized, as if with a red-hot implement. And two years after *that*, the next person to plough Handrij's "cursed" field broke his blade on a human skull buried a foot or so beneath the surface, with four iron nails driven halfway through its right-hand occipital ridge.

"She was blind, hysterically, when they found her," Tierney tells the camera. "Spent the next few months at Miss Dunlopp's, eventually regaining her sight, and started to paint sometime soon after. People thought it was a marvel—this uneducated farmer's daughter, no culture but the Bible, making the kind of art she did. Used to have blackouts, go into these trances and paint all day and night without stopping, like she was sleepwalking. Got bad enough they had to tie her to her bed and feed her knockout drops just to make her rest. But Miss Dunlopp said her hardship was a gift from God, so they had to let it run its course, and as Giscelia—Iris, by then—got older, she stopped doing it quite as much. Miss Dunlopp also told anybody who asked it was a mercy she didn't remember more about what'd happened." He pauses. "That last part was a lie, but again, I can't help but think she meant well."

"How would you know she was lying?" Safie asks, from off-screen. To which he shrugs and answers, "Because we have her statement—Giscelia's, Iris Dunlopp's, Mrs. Whitcomb's. From right after she was rescued." One last nod, toward the file in my hand. "It's in there, at the bottom."

Statement of Giscelia Ezter Wròbl, aged nine years & eight months, collected 1886, at Miss Guinevere Dunlopp's Formatory for Orphaned Girls and Boys (Schoolmaster Euan M'Latchey, acting as clerk):

My father said there was no point in sowing or reaping anymore, because the Lord was coming & these were End Times. So he took us all out to the field instead & there we stayed from the beginning of one week to the end of the next, fourteen whole days. We were waiting for Jesus & His angels to come get us, to take us away to Paradise on doves' wings. We were waiting for the trump & the breaking of seals.

& some of us were sick when we first went out there, & some of us got better, which my father considered a blessing & a miracle, but some of us got worse. I was holding my littlest brother when he died & my grandmother died while she was holding me. & after a time I was glad that my eyes were glued together with sickness, because then I did not have to see how both of them changed. Besides which my father would not allow us to bury them because Jesus was coming & if we tried to move he would brandish his sword at us, which he had beaten out of a ploughshare. So we all just lay quiet & still as we could & pretended we were praying.

& then things were dark, but a light came, bright as though it was noonday. Yet perhaps it was noonday, since the doctor told me later I was eaten up with fever when they found me, so time may have passed me by. Even now, even here, I do not truly know.

& then, in the midst of it, with the flies & the heat & the burnt flowers nodding, the useless flowers & the ruts all overgrown with weeds. Then a smell came, such a bad smell, so hot & dreadful. Like when you make sausage & blood drips into the fire. & I heard a voice ask my father why he was not at work.

Who are you, woman? he asked, & she said: It does not matter who I am. Who do you think you are, that you neither till nor harvest & your field is gone to ash, not crop; where is your horse, your plough? Why is this land I gave you watered only with kin-blood?

I do not have to talk to you, he told her, & she laughed. Ah, but I think you will, she said.

You will.

If she comes to you at midday do not look up, my grandmother always told us, but my father said those were old wives' tales, witches' prattle. But my father told tales of Jesus & His angels in his turn, & those were not true, either. None of it is true, before or since.

She is the only true thing.

& I did not look up, I could not, my eyes were shut, I could not see. The doctor said I should have gone blind, that I should have been scarred for life, but I was not & this is a true miracle, not one of my father's tales. A miracle that occurred when she touched me, cupped my chin in the palm of her white-hot hand & burned me to

the bone, deeper, down where no one can ever see just for looking. She came & I saw, I saw. I am still seeing.

No, nothing ever came in the field but her, whether at noonday or midnight & so I know she is real, if nothing else. Everything else is lies or tales, the sort we tell ourselves when we are eaten up with fever, when our eyes stick together, when we are too hungry to move & too tired to pray.

When light reflects off the ploughshare-sword like a mirror & there is no water anywhere, no voice but his & then. & then.

& then, hers.

TEN

Safie's notes say we made arrangements to join Val Moraine's usual Saturday tour of Whitcomb Manor, aka the Vinegar House. Outside the museum, however, she mistakenly left the camera on, even while it was pointed downwards, allowing this snatch of conversation to be recorded—

HEWSEN: The fuck was *that,* man? That story—

CAIRNS: Yeah, I know.

HEWSEN: No, but seriously. Was all that *real?*

CAIRNS: Mrs. Whitcomb thought it was, I guess. Granted, she was young . . . just been through an ass-load of trauma, too.

HEWSEN: She thought she saw Lady Midday, is what that was. Thought Lady Midday killed her dad.

CAIRNS: Wait, no. Didn't she say her eyes were shut the whole time? I mean—Tierney said she was *blind,* right? So—

HEWSEN: Blind *after*. "I saw," that's what she said.

CAIRNS: Well, we can't possibly take her at her word, 'cause that's just . . . that'd be crazy, yes? Totally. No, she was just—she remembered the story, the one her grandma told her. The fairy tale. So she saw it, but in her mind. That's what must've gone on.

HEWSEN: Right. [A beat.] So . . . what happened to Mrs. Whitcomb's dad if it wasn't . . . that? I mean, with his head?

CAIRNS: I don't know. No way *to* know. It's a great story, though. Isn't it?

HEWSEN: Great, yeah. Uh huh.

CAIRNS: Oh, it's just perfect. The perfect narrative strategy. Everybody in the world is gonna want to—what?

HEWSEN: Nothing.

CAIRNS: Safie, c'mon. These people've been dead a hundred years, long before either of us was born. Before *my* mom and dad were born. It's sad, but it's true . . . what bleeds, leads. So this leads.

HEWSEN: You're *happy* about this. That we found this out. That this is why she was doing what she did.

CAIRNS: Well, I'm pretty sure it wasn't the only reason, but yes. This is the sort of stuff we came here to learn, and I'd rather it be interesting than boring. Wouldn't you?

HEWSEN: Yeah. I guess, yeah.

CAIRNS: Don't guess, be sure, or we might as well just go home—no money, no film, no book, nothing. You want that?

HEWSEN: No.

CAIRNS: 'Course not. So. Are you sure?

HEWSEN: . . . Yes. Miss.

CAIRNS: Good.

It's definitely my voice—I hear myself say the words, and they sure as hell sound like the sort of bullshit I pull out when there's something I want that I don't want to be made to feel bad about wanting. I know it's Safie, too. But . . . no, otherwise there's just a hole, a blank. No sense of time or place. Just . . . empty.

Similarly, Simon tells me I phoned home that night—spoke to him at some length. Tried to speak to Clark, or get him to speak to me, but all he'd do was jig up and down on the bed yelling some rhyme Simon didn't think he'd ever heard before. He couldn't tell where Clark might've picked it up from, but thinks it went like this:

> Inside out and outside in
> This is how the world begins,
> Outside in and inside out
> Is how you blow a candle out.

"Dude, so *loud*," I observed, and Simon laughed, or so he says. "He's been like that since you left," he told me. "Maybe he does miss you after all."

I snorted. "Chance'd be a fine thing."

"Aw, now, hon. Stay positive."

"Well, I would, except for the fact that doesn't sound a thing like me, really. Does it?"

"Nope, you're right. Unfortunately."

> Inside out and inside out
> Knock at the door then turn about.
> Outside in and outside in
> There she stands so let her in.

I hung up the phone, and then Safie and I had supper before going to bed. Her notes say I told her I thought the air pressure was shifting, that I could feel it in my temples. Something about how there were faces moving around in the paintings back at the museum, but I didn't expect she'd noticed, ha ha. Sometime in the early morning she says she woke up to the sound of me yelling something she couldn't make out, and when she snapped on the light it seemed to hurt my eyes; I jack-knifed into a foetal position, palms slapped to shield them, covered in sweat. Asked me: "Are you okay, miss?" and I just said yes, yes, it was nothing, I was fine.

"Should I call somebody?"

"No! No problem, go back to sleep!"

She didn't, though, for which I can hardly blame her. Sat up instead, cataloguing what she'd done so far, till the sun came up and I woke for real, apparently unaware that anything at all had disturbed either of our rests.

The Vinegar House tour began that day—October 23, almost the last visit of the season—the way it always did, with an 11:00 A.M. sharp meet-up at Quarry Argent's Town Square Pub, owned and operated by Val Moraine's husband Stewie. Moraine does volunteer work for the Folklore Museum, and has been running the Vinegar House tour since she got her tour guide license from Ontario Parks and Rec in early 2000, shortly after the museum finally managed to have Whitcomb Manor declared an official Heritage Trust site, deciding to use the small annual easement this gave them to fund educational excursions around its grounds. As the house was already in an advanced state of decay, the museum's board of trustees decided against attempting anything more than minimal upkeep on the site as a whole, especially since they probably weren't going to get any more government funding to help defray the expense. Instead, they'd use it as an additional revenue source, hoping to attract just enough sightseers to keep the Manor from falling into irretrievable ruin.

We told Moraine what we'd been working on and, according to Safie's notes, "her eyes lit up." Like Balcarras had originally told me, it was no surprise to her that Mrs. Whitcomb had made films—indeed, one of her great aunts turned out to have been a staple player in the Japery movies and might even have appeared in *Lady Midday (Version One)*, though the likelihood of being able to prove it was slim, since she'd died a mere month and half earlier. If we were right, this would make Mrs. Whitcomb not only Canada's first recorded female filmmaker, but a technical and artistic savant as well. As her home and, almost certainly, her production studio, the Vinegar House would therefore be a candidate for classification as a site of "great historical significance" (my exact words) whose promotion might potentially bring Quarry Argent and surrounding townships a fair deal of welcome interest—and better yet, money. Carried away with enthusiasm (or so Safie describes me), I offered to show Val my *Lady Midday* clips on my laptop, since we were still waiting for the rest of the tour-goers for that day to show up.

You may or may not believe this, but Val Moraine was the first person to watch those clips who actually stopped the first one before it finished, and not more than twenty seconds in. "Thank you, that's more than enough," she said. According to Safie's notes she looked either sick or scared. "I see what you mean; those *do* look a lot like the paintings in the museum. And the ones on the walls, too."

"Walls?" I asked.

"Of the Vinegar House. They're all over a bunch of the interior walls, painted right onto the wallpaper, sometimes into the wood."

"Then that's where we have to go," I said, or Safie—the notes, annoyingly enough, don't specify. But from the next sentence, I'm inclined to think it was me: "That's what we have to *see*."

If Moraine answered, it didn't get written down. Presently, in ones and twos, the rest of the group trickled in—five people, all told—and we boarded Moraine's minivan-cum-bus for the drive out to the Vinegar House.

"We call it that because of the smell," Moraine told us during the drive up; in Safie's recording, Moraine's voice has the firm smoothness of a long-memorized but still-enjoyed spiel. "It doesn't smell all that bad now, not that it smells like roses or anything. But all of us who grew up around here remember hearing the legends, those stories about what happened to Mrs. Whitcomb . . . what might've happened, anyways. My old gran told me there was this stink used to hang around the place—really bad, like rotting eggs; or something poisonous, like there'd been a fire, or a big spill down at the Chaste pickling plant.

"When Mr. Whitcomb got married and had the house all dolled up, he took that old field out back and turned it into a hedge maze with a garden in the centre of it, herbs growing wild around big beds of expensive flowers with special names he and Mrs. Whitcomb brought back from their European tour. Everything was beautiful, and when things got real hot you could smell the garden all the way down the hill into Quarry Argent. But things changed after their little boy ran away. . . ."

The museum records for this period note an intermittent series of complaints to the town council about "unpleasant and pervasive" odours coming from the general direction of Whitcomb Manor, whenever the wind changed direction sharply. These complaints start in late 1908, the year that a judicial injunction allowed an empty coffin bearing Hyatt Whitcomb's name to be buried in the Whitcomb crypt; the last complaint on record was filed in 1925, the year Mrs. Whitcomb was also officially declared dead. But even at the complaints' peak, between 1916 and 1918, there's no evidence in the records that any of them were ever acted on in any substantial way. By 1926, Mr. Whitcomb had already returned briefly from Europe to sign various documents and close Whitcomb Manor down permanently, and then promptly left Canada once more, never to return.

"People understood," Moraine said. "They knew she had more than enough on her plate to deal with already. She was eccentric, sad—special, just like her boy. Never knowing what happened! And Mr. Whitcomb being always away, too, though of course he paid for anything she asked for, like a true gentleman; he begged her to come with him, but she refused. Said she was gonna wait right here until Hyatt came home, or he didn't. It's a sad story."

Our group arrived at the Vinegar House shortly after 1:00 P.M.—an hour later than Moraine customarily began her showings, because I'd made it vehemently clear that Safie and I wanted to see the (usually-unexplored) inside of the house as well. This necessitated a detour to pick up steel-toed boots and hard-hats from Quarry Argent's M'Cauley Family Hardware Store; Bob Tierney had already authorized the loan, using the museum's emergency credit card. Once we disembarked, however, Moraine lost no time in leading her charges—now including German tourists Axel Beckenbauer and Holle Abend, and a local family on a day trip from Overdeere, Max LaFrey, his wife Kirstie and daughter Aileen, as well as Safie and me—up the driveway and through the remains of a mixed-fruit orchard that had once blocked the Manor's view of Stow-apple road, providing shade and privacy, toward their destination.

I can describe the photos Safie took from memory.

Picture a strip of field, narrow and rough, suitable for wheat or rapeseed but gone untilled since the turn of the twentieth century. At one end there's a small stand of woods, too knotted for easy penetration. At the other, a house—first raised in 1885, then rebuilt to its owner's specifications in 1902—that has stood here so long it's begun to sag and split along the centre-line, becoming two rough half-mansions smashed haphazardly together, sutured only by the further process of decay. Between field and house stretch the remains of a garden verdant with weed and herb, a simple maze whose box hedges have grown so thick that access to the back door is difficult in any season but winter.

Back and to the right, however, is the ruin of another building entirely: iron struts, black and rusty, outlining what seems to be an invisible barn, a boxy greenhouse cleared of its contents shortly after Hyatt Whitcomb's "burial" and converted first into an artist's studio, and then—as we now know—a movie set by adding a stage, a series of hand-painted backdrops, and a windowless wooden shed probably used as a dark room for developing the resultant film strips. Fifty years of foul weather had broken nearly every last pane. Even the shards left behind were dull and blunt, matte grey in any but the brightest light.

"All the time I was growing up here, the Vinegar House was our main creepy landmark," Safie's footage shows Moraine telling us, as we stand outside the front door, its gleaming brass padlock the only bright new thing on the entire edifice. "Kids used to sneak over and break in all the time—almost like making a pilgrimage—but we never stayed too long, just looked around a bit and left. Nobody ever had parties here. Nobody came here to park and neck, or what have you. For myself, I haven't been inside for three years at least, and the one thing I remember is that there doesn't seem like there's *ever* been *any* graffiti in there, *anywhere*, crazy as that sounds. What bunch of teenagers doesn't scribble all over everything?"

Safie turns her camera on me at this point, and I give the lens my most obvious and disdainful eye roll. But it got harder to be snarky once we were inside, especially when we hit an unexpected roadblock; right on the front steps, the little girl, Aileen LeFray, suddenly had a complete meltdown and absolutely refused to proceed further, to the point that she started kicking and punching when her exasperated father picked her up and made as if to carry her. Her parents gave up, and the mother took Aileen around the back—"See if there're any crabapples ripe enough to eat," Moraine suggested. Then, lighter by two, our group made its way past the doorframe . . .

. . . and there really *wasn't* any graffiti. Not, as Moraine gleefully pointed out, "a scrap."

But that's not to say there wasn't any decoration.

We came in down the House's main hall, checking constantly for sags and gaps in the floorboards. "This floor can be treacherous," Moraine said. "Five years back, a kid from Overdeere was here doing his thesis and fell right through, up to his hip. Got stuck there overnight. It was so cold that year, he was almost blue when they found him!"

For all her morbid glee, however, she seemed as relieved—and unsettled—as the rest of us, once we finally got to where we were going.

The "paintings" we found ourselves confronted with were actually a series of freehand-drafted murals covering much of three walls in what was once the Whitcombs' grand dining room, located at the rear of the house. Its main table—now missing all its legs due to rot, almost invisible upon the rubbish-strewn floor— would have once been angled toward a set of four large windows looking out onto the maze garden and glass house alike, flanking a set of double doors which give way to the terrace. The murals start at the baseboards and rise to a height of roughly eight feet, which suggests they were finished by someone already fairly tall (as a young woman, Mrs. Whitcomb stood five feet, eight inches) using a ladder to boost her reach.

The original paints appear to have been white lead-based, which perhaps accounts for their surprising durability under harsh circumstances. On the video, you can see that although there's a lot of mould and peeling, the general shape of these images remains clear, along with enough fine detail to give a dis- tinct impression of what Mrs. Whitcomb must have had in mind. (To rebut critics who speculated she must have had help while installing them, the museum dug up records showing Mrs. Whit- comb only brought in local men to help her lay the foundation before sketching over it in charcoal and dividing each wall into sections, which she then personally filled in over a period of two years, 1907 to 1908.)

I don't know yet if it'll be viable to get any of the photos or still frames from the footage into this book, or whether it's even worth trying. Nothing we took that day does the place justice; nothing really captures that room's queasy power. What few European artists and critics took note of the pieces produced during Mrs. Whitcomb's honeymoon tour all mention her odd, wavering figures—thin-limbed and indefinite under haloes of diluted washes, outlined in receding layers of pale green, violent yellow, or stark white, as though viewed through eyes squinting against a bright light. If her earlier work was mainly Impression- ist and only tentatively Symbolist, the Mural Room friezes seem to transcend these influences—to take them and wring them out, boiling them down to bare essentials, pure, weird, and stark.

Set against a background of a thousand tiny colour points and arranged in a sort of procession moving inward from either side, faces cast down but hands upraised as though in supplication, the figures range from child-sized to adult but have few other signifiers—possibly universally feminine or simply androgynous. Some appear to carry farming tools like rakes and scythes, while others tote sheaves of fruit, grain, or flowers. All have something in common with both Jan Toorop's Indonesian shadow puppet-inspired "soul" figures and classic Byzantine ikons, up to and including their use of three-quarter semi-profile and full-body *mandorlas* or glories, outlining light clouds similar to the effect observed in Kirlian spirit photography, which supposedly reveals the human body's aura, or life-force.

But they're also attended by what seem to be "shadows" done negatively, in even brighter colours—green shading upwards to viridian, yellow to citrine, white to palladium. Slightly larger than the figures that cast them, these "shadows" are thin and predatory, almost skeletal, with long hands and nodding, wide-mouthed heads, blind and seeking. Their bottom halves terminate in tails rather than legs, coiling and twining with each other like snakes or tentacles, in some cases seemingly attempting to ensnare the feet of the individual figures to whom they find themselves attached. As in the famous illumination from the *Liber Scivias* showing Saint Hildegard von Bingen receiving a vision from God and dictating its content to her personal secretary, the processional figures are also linked by a five-tongued flame emanating upwards from their eyes, which joins into a vine or tree-branch above them.

On either side, these branches merge with the gigantic central figure—not immediately apparent on entering the room, since you have to turn around to see it—whose body is mainly composed of the yawning aperture of the dining room door, two flaps of a pale cloak or pair of wings falling to either side of the frame, and a veiled, almost featureless face with blazing white eyes fringed in gold glaring down at visitors from just above the lintel.

No flaming sword, Safie's notes read—margin-scribbled, almost a footnote. *But it's Lady Midday all the same. Who else?*

I don't remember exactly how long we held up the tour in that room, though it was probably a good thing Aileen LaFrey had ended up staying outside with her mom, given the awestruck, breathless, and totally obscene exclamations I kept making. Our fellow tourists Axel, Holle, and Max were all too ready to leave before long, but as Moraine explained, insurance regs meant she couldn't let anyone out of her sight; so long as one stayed behind, everybody had to. To get us moving, Moraine finally had to lean between Safie and me, and offer—

"Hey—want to see Hyatt Whitcomb's secret place? Upstairs?"

Because he spent the latter half of his short life increasingly subject to debilitating seizures, the Whitcombs' only child lived in what Moraine called "a glorified closet" next to his parents' bedroom. "They wanted easy access to him at all hours, just in case," she said, as we trudged carefully up the stairs, "so they took the doors off and hung up a curtain. He was seven years old but he still slept in a kind of a crib with a lid over the top they could latch every night, because sometimes he would get up in his sleep and wander off. They'd already hired a girl to go everywhere with him when he was awake—her name was Maura Sauer, from God's Ear—so they made her a bed in there that was right up against the side of his crib, hoping if he *did* get up, she'd be there to catch him."

Much like his mother, Hyatt Whitcomb was artistically gifted. Whenever he was ill, which was often, he would lie inside his crib sketching on long rolls of rag paper with soft chalk. A lot of those drawings are in the Quarry Argent Museum's back-shelves, only a chosen few on general display. What neither of the Whitcombs could know, however, was that Hyatt had already found a way to get out of the crib and avoid his nurse's detection.

"That little cubby's right back against where part of the roof comes down to meet an outer wall, close to one of the chimneys," Moraine said. "And if you take the wood panelling off, you can get into an access ladder-way the builders left to make it easier to clear blockages out of the flue. There're rungs cut right into the big load-bearing beams, going all the way to the ground and a little service door out the back. Well, poor little Hyatt must've figured out one of those panels was loose, or maybe he kicked it loose during one of his fits and nobody noticed, I don't know. One way or another, he finished prying it free, dropped it down the ladder-way, and tacked up a bunch of his sketches to curtain it off, so he could come and go as he pleased. Boys do things like that, no matter how 'special.'"

Discovered after Hyatt's disappearance, the top of the access shaft was left open throughout Mrs. Whitcomb's subsequent tenure in the bedroom (she moved in a month after Mr. Whitcomb's departure for Europe, and was never known to sleep anywhere else from then on), only to be sealed up with the rest of the house in 1925. Though it's clogged now with cobwebs and blocked off at each floor with wire mesh, with a flashlight you can look down all the way to the bare earth, three floors below. The rungs Hyatt used can still be seen, incised into the foot-thick vertical beams, wood worn smooth—possibly slippery—with age.

And if you lean into the shaft and wait for your eyes, and your camera, to adjust, you will see that almost the entirety of its interior has been covered with crude yet recognizable yellow, white, and green chalk scribblings—sketchy parodies of Mrs. Whitcomb's finished product downstairs.

Stay in the shaft long enough, Moraine told us, and a smell begins to collect in your nostrils: faint but acrid, something hot and rotten that stings the eyes. Not everyone reports this scent, apparently—Safie didn't smell a thing and says I claimed not to either, though Axel, Max, and Holle said they did—but nobody who has reported it was ever able to identify it, or find any kind of biological or chemical source for the stench. Whatever it was, or is, it drove Holle out of the room in five minutes, loudly exclaiming that she wanted to puke. Axel went back downstairs with her, as did Max, who went outside to join his wife and daughter; this time, Moraine didn't try to stop them.

Safie says that when I asked Moraine if anybody knew which *particular* sketch or set of sketches had camouflaged the shaft, she told us they were simply views of the maze garden and the field beyond it, as seen from the dining room's windows. The chalk drawings Hyatt made while *inside*, however, obviously served as prototypes or "raw" versions for the processional and shadow figures in the Mural Room, as well as its overhanging central image, suggesting that Mrs. Whitcomb almost certainly deliberately incorporated them into the Murals after her son's death.

"You can see a lot of crossover, true enough," Moraine acknowledged on the recording, after I asked her about this. "Probably went both ways—he grew up watching her paint, after all, and she'd been doing that since before he was born. Maybe by way of being a memento, as well, after his death. But there's a long way between Hyatt's drawings and those paintings."

From our own review of the shaft's artwork—or what our camera captured of it—the image Hyatt repeated most often was definitely the veiled, glaring face his mother painted above the dining room's main door: a disturbing design, especially when you consider it was drawn by a child of less than eight. I've read other people's accounts of visiting the Vinegar House, and a number of them have asked the question (rhetorically left unanswered, perhaps because it's unanswerable): of all the works her son produced, why would Iris Whitcomb choose this one above all others to memorialize?

Then again, given their origin, the murals gain further troubling context from the fact that the maze garden they frame, Hyatt Whitcomb's favourite source of daytime entertainment, is also the place where his parents and nurse eventually found the last trace of him ever discovered: his abandoned nightclothes, partially buried in the earth just beyond the maze's far edge, bordering that final strip of field between the Vinegar House grounds and the woods.

According to at least one report I turned up, Hyatt's nightclothes had somehow been pushed so hard into the ground that they became jammed in a cracked chunk of granite and had to be cut free.

When I listen to Moraine reeling off Hyatt's range of symptoms, even after re-viewing the footage as many times as I already have, I still feel a sick sense of recognition mounting in me, narrowing my throat; I can only think the same thing must've happened then, even if I can't remember it. Which might explain why the next thing I hear myself asking Moraine is—

"So—Hyatt Whitcomb was on the spectrum, right? What I mean is, from the way you describe him, he must've been autistic."

"That's what they'd call it today, probably, yes. Why?"

Here Safie suddenly decides to pan around the room, maybe trying to avoid my face, though I can see myself start to look down just as her lens switches away. Hear myself start to say, softly: "Well, I . . . that is, my son . . ."

"What about him?" The barest pause here, just a fraction of a breath, as she suddenly realizes what sort of hot button she's tripped across. "I, oh; oh, I'm very sorry. Is he—"

"Never mind," I reply after a moment, voice gone quieter yet. And Moraine breaks off as well, switches subjects like the pro she is, hastening to avoid giving any further offence; turns back toward the door, beckoning with a bland, cheerful, empty sort of smile, the kind oncology ward nurses must practise daily. "Well, anyhow," she says, "let's go back outside, shall we, since the light's still with us? I'll show you two the maze."

"That'd be great," Safie agrees, readily. While at almost the same time, I put in from the side of the frame—

"You know, I'd actually much rather see what's left of the greenhouse, thanks."

"Thought you wanted to do that together," Safie says. I shrug.

"No problem," I tell her, easily enough. "It's getting late—might as well split up, get as much as we can, come back tomorrow if we have to. That'll work, right, Miss Moraine?" She nods. "Yeah, see? That's why God made iPhones."

Safie's notes say Moraine, Safie, and I came out through the dining room doors, picking up Holle and Axel as we went. The LaFreys were already over by the maze, little Aileen kicking a half-bitten crabapple 'round the first corner like a soccer ball then chasing after it. As Moraine led the way toward the glass house, Safie, who'd been itching to get footage of the maze—the memorial plaque set up where Hyatt supposedly disappeared, in particular—parted ways with us, taking some shots of the maze entrance and its interior's first few paces with Axel and Holle posing in it, to lend perspective. True to my word, I took out my iPhone and switched it to video, recording two longish clips I saved to memory before starting my final go-round. These aren't all that interesting, in hindsight; the best part of the second one is when Moraine, who's showing me around, brushes a dirt-stiff tarp off of what proves to be a stack of flats from Mrs. Whitcomb's Lady Midday period.

"Didn't even know those were there!" Moraine's voice exclaims as I start to flip through, using only the barest edges of my right-hand thumb and ring finger; dust puffs up in clouds, making us both cough. Thus revealed, the artefacts in question are bleached-out and stained—edges nibbled, gummed together with a winning combination of insect by-products and bird crap—but the bottom-most one still shows traces of Mrs. Whitcomb's trademark hypnagogic design and psychedelic colour scheme. Interestingly, as I thumb through the pile, these tints fade away completely, as though she's figuring out that using shades of grey with the occasional white highlights will suit her method of shooting far more accurately: almost a negative image of what she wants to achieve, pre-jacked so it registers for maximum impact on silver nitrate stock.

But I don't have a lot of time to study the mechanics of it all. Because something is about to happen. *Is* happening already. Couldn't stop it if I tried, not that I'd know to want to.

So I'm talking through the colour-shift progression—retro-gression?—and Moraine's barely listening, for which I can't really blame her; she's looking over to her left, frowning slightly, saying something I can barely hear. "So much glass," that's what it sounds like on playback. Like: "Gotta make sure and get that cleaned up, someone could hurt themselves." That's nice—always thinking ahead, that Val. In this case, she's probably got her head stuck in the future, post-exposé, when everyone in Ontario will want to come see where Mrs. Whitcomb used to work her odd, silent, black-and-white magic. And I can't fault her can I? Because I'm basically doing the same, until—

I pause—stop short, mid-sentence. Say: "Ow," just like that. Then start over, and stop again. Say: "*Ow,*" once more, but harder, with a sort of wondering pain. "Oh, *oh, OW*, shit. Shit, oh *shit*. Oh *shiiiit,* my *head,* fuck *meeee . . .*"

Moraine snaps around, eyes wide but increasingly framed sidelong, as my iPhone's screen starts to droop, to wobble. "Miss Cairns—Lois? Lois, are you all *right?*"

"I dunnoh."

"*What* did you say, what? I don't—"

"Seh, I *duh.* I *doh.* I dohntnoh, dohhhhhnnnttt . . . knooohhhhwww . . ."

And then the phone falls, and *I* fall, right on the aforementioned glass, the dirty mess of broken tile over cracked stone where the greenhouse floor should be: crack, thud, *crunch.* Visuals cutting out, though sound sticks around slightly longer, picking up Val Moraine as she yells out and lunges to not quite catch me in time, shaking me even as I start to shake. Grabbing me underneath the back of the skull with both hands as I start to outright seize, to thrash and kick up dust, trying like hell to keep me far enough off the ground so I won't split my scalp open and bleed out all over this little piece of forgotten Canadian cinematic history.

And here, at last, is where I'd love to tell you my memory finally kicks back in—where I begin to filter up once more through layers of nothing much, peeling them away like dead skin to reveal the still-raw burn beneath. Except I can't tell you that, because I don't, and it doesn't, and none of the above happens. Not one bit of it.

Instead—what I do remember, sort of, is a dream. Very vivid, bright; all the details sharp enough to cut, as though they're etched in pain. The kind of dream you have when you're sick, or maybe drunk—hung over, sinuses alight and hammering hard, though you're not quite awake enough yet to realize it. When you're high on a fever, when everything shrinks and the world starts to blur, and you know just enough to understand that if you could only get your brain to work the way it should, you'd probably feel like you're going to—

—like you *want* to—

—die.

Thinking: *Hurts.* Thinking: *Just make it stop.* Thinking: *Oh God, please, I don't know what I did. I'm sorry, so sorry. I'm so, I'm so, so, so . . .*

(Sorry, sister)

(I tried, though. I *did* try. I warned you. But you, you simply wouldn't)

(*listen*)

Safie's notes say she was coming back from the maze when she saw me go down, right over Axel Beckenbauer's shoulder—keeled over and fell with a *flump*, like a sack of wet laundry, right into Val Moraine's arms. She took off running, and by the time she got there I was already having some kind of full-on attack; Moraine was yelling at Axel to get his belt off, stuff it between my teeth before I started choking, as Safie grabbed my phone from where it'd fallen, thankfully only slightly cracked across its face. Stabbing 911, she was redirected to the Quarry Argent Fire and Rescue dispatch centre:

DISPATCHER: 911, what's your emergency?

CALLER: This is Safie Hewsen, calling from the Vinegar House—that's Whitcomb Manor on Stow-apple Road, off RR #10. I'm on Val Moraine's tour, and my friend is having a seizure or something. We need help!

DISPATCHER: Okay, Safie, we're hooking you up with ambulance services now. Where are you, exactly? At the front of the house, the driveway?

CALLER: Uh, no. We came that way; the bus is still there, but we're out back now, near the glass house, that old greenhouse. At the bottom of the field.

DISPATCHER: Near the maze with the garden?

CALLER: Just past it—oh man, she's really not doing well. I think she's throwing up. Should we try to move her?

DISPATCH: No! No, don't do that. I got an ambulance on the way—they're on speakerphone. It's Mickey Vu and Loretta Coy. You can talk to them directly now, Safie.

PARAMEDIC: Safie, this is Mickey. Can you describe the symptoms?

CALLER: Val was there when it happened, not me. Val?

NEW CALLER: Yeah, okay—hey, Mickey, this is Val. She was taking a video in the greenhouse and then she just fell down, it was like—um, she dropped the phone she was using, put her hands up over her eyes like her head hurt, and she kind of yelled "ow," stumbled back, and then she fell.

PARAMEDIC: On her head, she hit her head?

NEW CALLER: No, I mostly caught her, but there's some blood still—ground out here's all covered in stones and some of them are sharp. There's glass, too, and metal, but I don't think she got cut anywhere except the back of her head. We tried to put a belt in her mouth—

PARAMEDIC: Don't do that either! Just hold off, okay? [To other paramedic] Tetanus shot, for sure. A seizure, you said?

NEW CALLER: I don't know, I don't. She's just lying there trembling, you know? Shaking all over. Her friend's with her. She's like yelling, then making sounds like she wants to puke—

PARAMEDIC: Okay, Val, we can see the house now. We're maybe two minutes away, so hold on, just make her comfortable.

NEW CALLER: Thank you, thank God. Thank you.

PARAMEDIC: What's her name, the patient? You know her name?

NEW CALLER: Yeah, sure. Lois, from Toronto. Her name's Lois Cairns.

According to Safie, the ambulance rushed me to the clinic in Chaste, because Coy and Vu judged it to be both marginally closer than Quarry Argent's own and more easily accessible by transport back to Toronto, if necessary. Safie caught a ride back to the Quarry in Moraine's bus with the rest of the tour, picked up the rental car we'd arrived in, and drove over, where she wound up playing middleman between the clinic staff and Simon, who she'd gotten hold of en route.

To Doctor Ustan Souk, who examined me first, I insisted I couldn't say exactly what was going on just before my seizure, let alone what might have set it off—a viewpoint experts at St. Michael's Hospital in Toronto later endorsed, claiming what Dr. Souk diagnosed as a "stroke-like episode" might well have left me with limited partial amnesia. But as Safie told me later, she didn't believe this could be entirely true. Apparently, she'd heard me whispering something over and over while I lay there in Moraine's grip, eyes wide and fixed and streaming tears:

"It was her. I *saw* her. Just like in the film."

I saw.

ELEVEN

I found something written in an old notebook of mine the other day—two lines, unattributed: *When the witness is ready, the ghost will appear. When things wear thin.* Possibly a quote, though from what I don't know. It also reminds me of that old line about students and masters. As for wearing thin, meanwhile—

In retrospect, I suppose my life had worn plenty thin enough to let anything in, by the time this all began to happen.

But didn't you know, *by then?* Everyone's going to ask that, no doubt, as they watch me continue to flail around, to deny what's literally right in front of my eyes. *Given everything that'd happened, for Christ's sake, wouldn't* anybody *have stopped short and said to themselves: holy shit, it's like I'm in some kind of horror movie, here?*

To which I can only reply: *I think not.* Because, as you might have already noticed, nobody ever *does* think that.

Not even when they are.

I woke up in hospital two days later, by slow degrees. Didn't have the least idea where I was, until I recognized the smell—astringent, metal-and-antiseptic—and the stiff, flex-framed feel of the mattress underneath me. Last time my back hurt this badly had been after my breast reduction. That jolt of memory was enough to kick me the rest of the way awake; I rolled my head side to side and shifted, pushing myself up a little, as bright, cold morning sunlight spilled across the floor. In a chair next to the bed, Mom sat, dozing with her chin propped up on one hand.

I tried to say something, but my typical morning-dry throat brought it out as an unintelligible rasp, which triggered a coughing fit. Mom jerked awake, sat up, and grabbed my hand. "*Lois!*" she gulped. "Oh my God, honey, thank God, thank God . . ."

I got the cough under control, worked my jaw until some spit came back to my mouth and throat, squeezed her hand back. "What *happened*?" I asked at last.

Mom opened her mouth to answer, but then her face crumpled and she began to cry instead; sounded by the tone like it might be as much relief and exhaustion as anything else. Not knowing what to say—as ever—I let her weep it out, guessing she'd probably have far too much to say to let herself go too long. Sure enough, within a minute she was wiping her eyes and swallowing, back in control.

"I'm sorry," she said. "It's just—with you here, and then last night . . ."

I stared. "What happened last night?"

"You, ah, well, you had another seizure, sweetheart. Yesterday evening, while they were taking X-rays. Not as bad as the first one, up at that *place*, but afterwards, they couldn't wake you up. Dr. Harrison said you were responsive to stimuli, though, so they said they'd try to let you sleep it off. . . ." She trailed off, perhaps finally noticing my expression. "You really don't remember?"

This time, it was me who swallowed, and it hurt. "What . . . what day is it?"

"Tuesday, that's why I'm here; Clark's at school, Simon's at work. God knows how he's keeping his head straight, but—what?"

"This is St. Michael's, right?" Though the smells *were* familiar, my breast reduction recovery room had been windowless, barely more than a two-cot closet to park people in until the anaesthetic wore off. But I'd finally matched the layout and positioning of this slightly more deluxe suite, obviously meant for somebody whose stay might be indefinite, to what

I remembered from back when Clark was born. She nodded, confirming it. "Mom, I . . . honestly don't know how I got here. Last thing I remember is, is—"

(Flash of skull-splitting agony, a grey reflection in broken glass, dirt-rimmed and dull)

"—going up to Quarry Argent, on Friday. Being in the car with Safie. We talked about . . . Yezidic texts. That's it."

"You went to Whitcomb Manor on Saturday, took the tour. That's where—it—happened."

"*What*, 'it'? You said *another* seizure . . ."

"That's right. Listen, let me call Dr. Harrison—" As she reached to press the nurse's button, I yanked on her hand without meaning to; must have done it extra-hard, because she stopped mid-gesture, letting slip a small, hurt noise. I let go.

"Shit, I'm sorry. Didn't mean to . . ."

"All right, that's okay." She patted me with her other hand, awkwardly, smile just a hair shy of a grimace. "It's fine, honey. Just let me make the call, and he'll explain everything."

So I slumped back. Moments later, a tall young black man with a Trinidadian accent was briskly checking my vitals, chart in hand. "Look up, please," he told me. "Now down. Good. How's your head?"

"Hurts, mostly."

"Sharp pain or a dull pain?"

"Dull, I guess. Like a bad hangover."

A nod to the IV stand, which held two bags, one half-deflated. "That'll be the dehydration; we've had you on fluids since Sunday, but that's just enough to keep the wheels greased. Are you hungry?"

"Um, maybe. Need the bathroom, though, pretty bad."

"I'll help you," Mom said, eagerly. But I shook my head, wincing, and waved her away as Harrison levered me up. "I've got it," I said, and limped off to the john, dragging my glucose behind me.

One incredibly long, verge-of-ecstatic pee later, Mom all but forced me to sit back down on the bed before allowing Harrison to fill me in on exactly what I'd missed.

"Before we start, should I introduce myself again?" he asked, without any sort of embarrassment or impatience. To which I flushed, feeling enough for the both of us, and replied, "Probably."

"Thought as much: Guy Harrison, intern." He offered me his hand so we could shake, and then turned my wrist over to check my pulse. "All right, that's better. You were airlifted here from a clinic in Chaste, after an episode at somewhere called the Vinegar House. . . ."

"Yeah, that much I've gathered. Any idea why?"

"Well, good news first—we gave you an MRI, and there's no sign of epilepsy or tumours, plus no ischemic effects, so there's not likely to be any immediate alterations to your overall health. That said, *bad* news is, we're still not sure *what* caused the seizures, and since we're talking more than one, that's worrisome. Blood work hasn't shown any signs of natural allergens or poisons, though I'm not too happy with the amount of medications you've been mixing on the regular."

"Medications? I mean, Mobicox and Tecta, that's basically all I'm on—"

"By prescription, yeah. Except you told me yourself you've been topping that off with all sorts of over-the-counter pills: Robaxacet, Maxidol, migraine-level ibuprofen. Robaxacet alone you're not supposed to take more than three caplets per twenty-four hours, and you've been taking upwards of six, seven, eight. Add in the others, and that's quite a tolerance you're courting."

"How would you—?"

"Because you *told* me, Ms. Cairns. 'Keep going till my lips go numb, that's the standard.' Ring any bells?"

Again, the quote did *sound* like me. I didn't want to look at Mom, to see her reaction to this little piece of information, so I looked at the floor instead. "Are you saying that had something do with . . . whatever happened to me?"

"There's no proof of that, no." Continuing, as I opened my mouth: "But before you speak, there's no proof to the contrary, either. We have no idea what set your first seizure off, let alone your second; every person's biochemistry is unique, and mixing medications is generally a bad idea. My recommendation, therefore, is that you try to cut back as much as possible—reduce your doses, scale down. Maybe even stop everything *except* the prescriptions."

"I . . . just don't think that's going to work, for me. I mean . . ." I exhaled through my nose, thought a moment, then continued. "I have a job, a kid. I need to be functional, for both of them."

"You can *be* functional. It might take time to detox, but—"

"Detox? For Christ's sake, I'm not an addict!"

"Anything you do alone, anything that becomes unmanageable, anything you regularly lie about to others, or yourself . . . that *is* an addiction, Ms. Cairns, no matter how low level it seems right now. But you don't have to beat yourself up about it; we all want control. Things like these are your body and your mind fighting each other *for* control, and developing bad habits along the way."

From the corner of my eye, I saw Mom nod, and felt a wave of unreasonable anger lap up over me: oh yes, of course, classic Twelve-Step jargon. *We understood we were powerless against our compulsions, took a searching and fearless moral inventory of ourselves, turned ourselves over to a higher power as we understood it.* Next thing I knew, it'd be meetings and sponsors and what have you, spilling my guts to strangers in church basements full of bad coffee. All of which had worked just fine for *her*, thankfully—but me? No. The only therapy I'd had thus far had always been on my own terms; if I wanted counselling, I'd damn well pay for it.

"There are lots of programs for chronic pain," I only then realized Dr. Harrison was saying at the same time—great minds, as ever. But I just shook my head and snorted.

"'Chronic pain' sounds a little . . . elevated, frankly," I told him. "Like describing a bad review as bullying. This isn't anything I can't handle, but believe me, if it ever gets to that point, I'll take it under advisement. Right now, though, I just—"

"'Don't have the time,' yes, a lot of people say that." Harrison sat down, leaned back in the chair, eyes fixed on me. "You know, people say men are the stoics, but you'd be surprised how much effort it takes to get some women to think about themselves for a change. Look at your situation objectively. Your physical condition is bad enough to cause habitual sleep disruption, you spend hundreds of dollars on pain relief you can't even claim on your husband's health insurance, and by your own admission, this has been going on for *years* now. As the parent of a special-needs child, you're under exceptional mental stress, while your emotional state sounds borderline manic-depressive."

"Again, *no*. I had a friend who was manic-depressive. That's something chemical, something *real,* diagnosable. They gave her pills for it."

"Ah. And what happened then?"

I sighed. "She'd even out, stop taking them. Eventually, she jumped off a bridge."

He smiled. "Well, at least you haven't done that." To which Mom chimed in from behind him: "Not *yet*."

Not fucking helpful, I wanted to snap. But the fight had already gone out of me, all at once: a body-wide slump, breath hissing out, energy sapped like a switched-off light. Not just because I knew everything he'd said was undeniably true, but most specifically because I couldn't remember telling him.

Sometimes you can tell the truth in advance—lie that you've done something, then make it so. I've done it most of my life, and I don't feel guilty. But *nothing* will put a pattern of misdirection back in place once you've been dumb enough to map it out for someone, however tried and true; it's like a cracked bone. Might heal right eventually, but you'll feel it the rest of your life, especially when the weather starts to turn.

Mom was studying me now, looking for places to press on while I was weak, to force her case and make it stick even after I'd recovered enough to rebuild my defences. But I wasn't going to give her the chance.

Harrison leaned forward, probably unaware of any of this. "What I'd like you to consider, Lois—may I call you Lois?—is that if you're in constant pain for a long enough period, your overall tolerance for stress and discomfort rises so high, any sense you might have had of what's 'normal' gets reduced to what's bearable. And by that point, you simply *expect* to hurt, so complaining about it feels inappropriate. Nobody should live like that, if they don't want to."

I laughed, wearily, bitterly. "Think that's what I *want,* huh?"

"Of course not. But if you're suffering yet you truly feel like you just can't manage to put yourself out enough to do something about it, then there's a bit of a problem, wouldn't you say?" He sighed. "Listen, I've watched your mother sit vigil, off and on, for the last two days . . . her, your husband, and that friend of yours, the girl who brought you in. Going by that alone, there *are* people who love you, who want to see your quality of life improve—but that's not going to happen unless you make it."

I looked down, swallowing again. "Fact is, though, you don't even really know what happened up in Quarry Argent. Do you?"

"No, we don't. The episode shared some commonalities with seizures triggered by high fever, or heat-stroke."

(*The* Regenmöhme, *with her heat*)

"And then I had another one, down here. How long did *that* last?"

"Less than two minutes—ninety seconds, at most. The first one went on for more than twenty, though you were only convulsing for the first five, and talking to your friend while doing it. After that you were in a trance, eyes open, unresponsive. The pattern with your second incident was very similar."

"No idea what caused it, though, even after all these tests. Either of them." He shook his head. "Okay, fine. Do I have to worry about it happening again?"

"If it was epileptic in nature, possibly. But there's no way of knowing until we figure out the variables, the inciting factors."

"Until I have another one, you mean."

". . . Basically, yes."

"Excellent. Well, I'm not staying here any longer than I have to, so—what's the out-care plan?"

Dr. Harrison glanced over at Mom, who raised her eyebrows fearsomely at him in return, perhaps attempting the international gesture of *tell her she has to stay, tell her you'll commit her, whatever it takes to make her do what we want her to.* But he wasn't dumb—none of us were—and seemed to know as well as I did that there was exactly zero point, nothing to be done in that regard. I was a legal adult with all the normal rights and privileges, perfectly free to check myself out, go home, and die on my own terms if I wanted to.

Not that I actually believed that was a possibility, then.

"Well, there's no real migraine *prevention* medication, but since you're depressed already, my instinct is to put you on a course of beta blockers known to act as anti-seizure medications and see what happens. However, I also think you need to taper off—do a sort of general system flush, preparatory to rebooting your regimen. So I'm suggesting you add Feverfew to your basic prescriptions, which may help, and I'd also recommend you continue using Melatonin as a sleep aid but commit yourself to having a full sleep clinic evaluation, sooner rather than later."

"After this project I'm working on is done with, sure."

"*During* that, if possible, which I don't see why it wouldn't be—just find some time, get it done, move on." I shrugged. "And limit your exposure to seizure precursors: flickering lights, flashing patterns, TV, computers."

"Oh wow, that's only everything I work with. Should I wear sunglasses at night, too?"

"More often, certainly."

"Kind of feel bound to point out, I had 'em on when this shit all happened."

"Nonetheless."

His frustratingly good poker face finally became enough to make me laugh again, this time for real. Tension thus dissipated, I took one more second before asking,

"Any side effects to the Feverfew, doc?"

"Well, it does tend to make you sleepy. But in your case that's good, yes?"

An hour later, I was all processed and back up to speed, Mom pushing me down the hall toward the exit in the traditional wheelchair. "In case you're wondering, I'm against this," she informed me.

"Duly noted," I replied. "Take it you probably tried to tell Clark what happened. How'd that go?"

"Not as well as I'd have liked." She rolled the chair to a stop, right across from the sliding door onto Queen Street, and slid one arm under mine, helping me up. "He was . . . um, unresponsive, I guess. Lots of singing, lots of bouncing; zero real comprehension, so far as I could tell." She sighed. "Probably better we didn't try bringing him to see you, considering last time."

"Yeah, good call," I agreed. Remembering lying there with bandages all over my chest, watching Clark ricochet from one side of the room to the next—this tiny holding space they'd parked me in, just big enough to hold two beds separated by a curtain—while Simon chased after him, struggling to keep him away from the hall and safely out of the path of any passing medical personnel. Even in my woozy, post-anaesthetic state, it'd been obvious he didn't get much of what was going on, but what he did get he didn't like; he was bouncy and nuts, gamboling all over, and I found myself subconsciously cringing away from him, afraid he'd grab my wounds without meaning to. Bad sounds, bad smells, too much echo—all anathema for little autistic boys.

We were out on the street itself, turning east. "You're very blithe about it," Mom said.

I snorted. "Less 'blithe' than 'resigned,'" I replied. "But seriously, Mom, c'mon . . . you know Clark, at least as well as I do. What did you *think* was going to happen?"

"I hoped—"

"Yeah, exactly, and that's great—Simon and I do it too, every once in a while. Push him a little bit out of his comfort zone; gamble that maybe this time, things might turn out a little bit different. And sometimes it even pays off, believe it or not. . . ."

At the corner of Queen and Church, we stopped for the light. Mom turned to look at me, forcing me to do the same, and then simply stood there a minute, like she was thinking of what to do next. "What?" I asked, eventually.

"I can't figure out what's sadder," she said. "That you think he's genuinely incapable of caring about what happens to you, or that you won't even try to *make* him care."

"Who says I think that? I know he feels for me, enough that my pain hurts him; that's why I keep it to myself, or try to. And as for him, he just . . ." I trailed off, stymied, before switching subjects: "Also, 'make' him? Like what, force him to perform some sort of—fucked-up parody of a socially acceptable emotional reaction to make myself feel better? He's got Disney movie scripts for that and he'll trip on them eventually, you give him enough time, but only so long as you don't put him in a situation where he's too over-stimulated to remember how they go."

"And that's good enough?"

"That's what I've *got*. Sure, I could insist on him putting what he's trying to say into a different language, but if I reject the echolalia completely, it just looks like I'm rejecting *him*."

"All right, but you can at least give him an idea of what's acceptable and what isn't, try to keep him to some sort of behavioural standard. . . ."

"Yeah, and I *do*. And sometimes he goes along with it, at least halfway, but a lot of the time he doesn't, and not because he won't. Because he *can't*."

"You use that word a lot, Lois."

"Like when it's appropriate?"

"Yes. And even when it isn't."

The light had changed twice by now, but we were still standing there, me starting to waver a bit, light-headed from two days of forced bed-rest. So while what I really wanted was to yell at her—something along the lines of *Jesus, can we not do this right in the middle of the sidewalk?*—I didn't. Instead, I took a calming breath and replied, "Listen, I get that you're worried about me and that's putting you on edge, which is why you're trying to pick a fight, here—just like I get that telling you not to worry is . . . impractical, at best. But think back, okay? They don't know *what* happened, let alone why, or if it's even likely to happen again—"

"It happened twice. Twice is a pattern."

"Once, then again," I corrected her, "at, like, a third of the original intensity. That's not a pattern, that's an anomaly in two parts."

That made her laugh, at last, not that she sounded super

amused. "Oh, so now you know math, Little Miss Innumerate? And medicine. You're an expert."

From the corner of my eye, I saw the light change once more, debated just crossing rather than waiting—midday traffic was light; that car sitting at the corner had its blinkers on, wasn't going anywhere—then decided Mom would just think I was trying to get away from her. So I stayed where I was. "Well, I do know there's no point getting myself all knotted up over predicting the unpredictable, that's for sure. Just like I know that no matter what happened, it had nothing to do with you telling me not to go up there in the first place."

"How is this about *me*, now?"

"It's not, I just . . . get the feeling maybe you *think* it is. Like you told me not to go 'cause something might happen, and I went anyway, and something did indeed happen, but the one didn't make the other. You get that, right?"

Mom sighed once more. "I don't know, Lois. I don't know."

"Me either. Neither of us do; no cure for that, though. We just have to keep going." A beat. "I love you, by the way."

A snort. "Oh, *fine*. Well . . . I love you too. Don't ever think I don't."

"That much, I do know."

As I glanced back at the parked car, sidelong, something tweaked at my memory. The vehicle itself was a dirt-streaked grey hatchback, driver barely visible—but as Mom drew me into a hug, close enough that I could feel most of the tension had left her, I relaxed just enough into to catch a clear glimpse of the hoodie-shaded face of the man behind the wheel.

"Whoa," I heard myself say, out loud. "Is that—?"

—*Chris Coulby?*

My hand jerked up, sketching a truncated wave, but the driver—obviously having caught my move from the corner of his eye—seemed first to stiffen, then stepped on the gas. With barely enough time for its blinkers to click off, the car swerved, pulling a sharp turn south down Church, away from us. I stared after it, mouth open.

"What was that about?" Mom asked. "Somebody you know?"

"Yeah, I—" But here I broke off, no longer sure. A sudden wave of queasiness swept over me, strong enough I had to close my eyes and take a breath, abruptly no longer interested in anything but getting home. "I think I need to flag a cab."

"Okay, sure—let me." She waved one over, opened the back door and helped me in, then asked: "Want me to go with you?"

I shook my head. "Good from here, thanks. Just call me later, all right?"

"Absolutely."

At home, Simon met me at the door, escorting me over to the couch, and went to put the kettle on. "Safie gave us your phone back," he called, from the kitchen. "It's charging right next to you if you want to check your mail, call anybody, find out what happened on *The Walking Dead . . .*"

"You know me so well."

"Pretty well, yeah. Clark'll be back in an hour, but don't worry about that—just check your mail and go to bed, okay? You need sleep."

Had two and a half days of that already, I thought, but didn't say. Replying, instead, "Always."

Though just staying where I sat was definitely tempting, given my complete lack of energy. I nevertheless decided to unplug and take the phone into our bedroom instead, where I could do a couple of things at once then get straight into bed afterwards. Opening my laptop, I signed on and clicked through—there was a message from Safie at the top, telling me how once I was safely on the medevac copter she'd gone back to Quarry Argent, making sure to grab everything we'd been promised at the museum before driving home, and that she'd already started to sort through the footage. After which I spent a few minutes deleting at will (spam of all types, much of it from media liaisons who thought I still needed to be kept informed about upcoming movie screenings), then moved on to Facebook, where I sat staring at the update box for a long moment, debating whether or not to tell anyone what'd happened, however obliquely. Could frame it as a migraine episode, I supposed, even make it sound mordantly funny in retrospect. But what if Jan Mattheuis saw it, and got worried? How would that affect the project, or my continued participation in it?

Social media's a goddamn curse, I'd just began to muse, when I heard the IM tone. I clicked on the icon and watched a box open at the bottom of the screen: *hope ur feeling better hospitals r never much fun.* And underneath that, like I couldn't possibly have guessed who it came from—

wrob.

"The fuckitty *fuck*," I said, out loud.

"You okay?" Simon asked, from behind me. I jumped then half-turned to find him standing there, a mug of tea in either hand—one of which was obviously for me. I took it, shaking my head, explaining, "Just . . . some random message from Wrob Barney, that creepy asshole. Strength in my hour of trial, or some shit."

He frowned. "How'd he even know where you were in the first place?"

"Exactly. You didn't . . ."

But the IM tone interrupted again, just as Simon asked, "Didn't what?" In the open box, fresh typing appeared, quick and relevant—almost as though Wrob could hear what we were saying—

> *vinegar house = sick nviroment f/sure*
> *stay away from now on i was u*
> *nobody gonna want t work w/u they think ur*
> *unreliable*

Simon and I exchanged a look, Simon's mouth opening—and at that very moment, on the bed beside me, my phone rang. Simon tilted his head to read the ID. "*NFA—Jan Mattheuis,*" he said.

"Mother*fucker,*" I exclaimed, slamming the laptop's lid shut.

Short story short, it was indeed Jan, and he knew everything.

"I don't know what you've been told, but I'm fine, *really*," I found myself saying for what felt like the tenth time that day. "The trip was everything we hoped, got a ton of research done, before and after. Granted, things turned a little crazy near the end, so it's good we live in the twenty-first century; modern medicine's an amazing thing. End of story."

"I'm so glad. You do understand why I had to call, though—right, Lois?"

"Absolutely. You needed assurances my health wasn't going to impact things negatively, and it's not—got released today, clean bill of health, no complications. You want more details, I can give you my doctor's number."

"Oh, I don't think that'll be necessary."

Thank Christ. "Great," I replied. "So—back on the horse."

"When can I see what you gathered?"

"I'm seeing Safie tomorrow. We can probably get something presentable together for Thursday."

"Make it Friday."

"Perfect." I hung up then blew out, shakily. "Jesus Christ, that was . . . did a fuckin' *memo* go out? Seriously, who did you tell?"

"Nobody," Simon maintained. "My parents, that's it. I mean, maybe Lee might've told *her* friends—"

"Wrob Barney doesn't know my mother's friends, man."

"Well, um . . . he could've gotten it from the Web, I guess. Like, the news."

"What, 'cause I'm so famous? Please. *Former Film Critic Lois Cairns Falls Down in Assfuck Nowhere, Ontario,* a.k.a. slowest news day ever." I shook my head. "Roger Ebert was the last name-brand movie reviewer, Simon. And he's dead."

"How'd Mattheuis know, then?"

I shrugged. "Wrob told him, I assume. Or Chris Coulby."

"Why would Chris—"

"Because Wrob paid him to? I already saw him out on the street today, following me around. Mom was there, she'll tell you . . . tell you she *saw* me see him, anyhow . . ." I stopped, sighing. "Okay, maybe don't ask her; probably thinks that was just me being crazy, actually. Considering she also thinks I should still be in hospital."

Simon shot me a concerned look. "Lo, you really do look wiped—just go to bed, okay? Like we said. It'll all look different tomorrow."

"Yeah," I said. Not necessarily agreeing.

Sleep was blessedly dreamless. I woke gradually, already feeling "better" just for being home, if not in much less physical discomfort. I had no idea what time it was, but it felt late; the apartment was dark, blinds drawn, and I could feel Simon all pressed up against me in that permanent dip in the mattress's centre, a sort of second bed, sheets tangled and hot as an oven. My arm was already under his neck, slightly numb from the weight; I used it as a pivot to hug him closer and kissed down his sweaty face, forehead, nose, lips. "Hey," I whispered. "You awake?"

"Am now."

"Forgot to ask whether or not they gave you shit at work, when the long weekend got longer."

"No, I said you were sick, and they were fine with it. They're good people." A beat. "Plus, it's not quarter-end yet, so there's that—something goes wrong with the system, they can afford to let it set a day. Best thing for it, sometimes."

"Switch it off, wait thirty seconds, switch it back on?"

"The time-honoured method." He nestled back into me, kissed my cheek, deliberately shifted to let me free my arm after a few seconds, which I did, gratefully; I moved onto my back, made the mistake of stretching slightly, and groaned. At the sound, I felt Simon stiffen.

"Back?" he asked, without surprise.

"Uhhh, no. Shoulder." I resisted the urge to shrug, adding: "Same as always."

"That bad, huh?" He rolled up onto one elbow, facing me. "You need Robax?"

I sighed. "I don't know. I mean, normally, yes, I would, but the doctor said that I should try to cut back. Stick to herbal stuff, Melatonin and—" I stopped. "Hear that?"

We both stopped, listening hard. At first there was nothing, and I found it difficult to even remember what had attracted my attention. But then it came again, that distant twang of mattress-springs shifting, a clump of toys falling, clattering across Clark's floor. And a thin, bitter wail, followed by the sound of weeping.

Clark used to wake himself up all the time, crying inconsolably. I never understood why, though it often occurred to me how the only thing worse than a nightmare would be one you not only couldn't distinguish from waking life, but also couldn't communicate to others. What little language he'd gained from echolalia was a fairly recent thing, and like I've said before, trauma tended to wipe it away like window fog—gone in an instant, nothing left behind but smears and tears.

Simon and I looked at each other. "I'll run the bath," I said. He nodded.

So I went to do that, and a few minutes later Simon brought Clark in, hiccupping, his pants sodden, clinging miserably fast to his Daddy's torso like a monkey. We put him in the tub and I ran the showerhead over his equally wet hair until it ran flat and clean while he moaned in protest. Meanwhile, Simon loaded almost everything on his bed into the washing machine, except the fold-up fire engine he slept inside. I didn't even have my glasses on, so Clark's face was just a blur with eyes, a pale tragedy mask; he sat there hunched up, bubbles to his chest, humid air ripe with lavender and ammonia.

"No fun, huh, bunny?" I asked.

"No fun," he repeated, eyes still spilling.

"No, I know. You have a bad dream?" No answer; I waited then leaned closer, a bit less patiently. "Clark, listen—Mommy asked you a question. Bad dream yes, or bad dream no?"

"No."

"No what?"

"No bad dream. Good dream."

"That seems . . . pretty freakin' unlikely, man." Again, no reply followed, so I sighed, sitting back. "Well, okay. You want to get out or stay in?"

"Stay in."

Holding up one hand, fingers spread: "For five more min-utes?" He nodded. I sighed once more, rising to set the stove alarm, only to meet Simon on my way back.

"He okay?" he asked.

"Not too happy, but yeah, I guess. Keeps denying it ever hap-pened, flipping negative to positive, like saying it's gonna make it so. . . ."

"He always does that, hon. Like when he ran straight into the wall and said 'I *didn't* hit my head,' remember? He'll be fine."

"Hope he's not getting sick," I muttered, or started to, since a second later the alarm went off. Simon didn't bother answer-ing, just went in and pulled the plug. "Okay, bud," he told Clark, "looks like you're all better, so we're going to get you back to bed. We love you. You love Daddy?" Clark nodded. "How about Mommy?"

"I love Mommy."

Simon glanced at me as if to say *you see?* I rolled my eyes. "You know that's just mimicry, right?"

"Maybe. Maybe not." He moved to one side. "Can you dry him off? I'm gonna put fresh blankets on his bed."

I nodded, letting Simon squeeze by so I could sit down on the toilet. Clark's eyes flicked up at me, then back down at the drain-ing water, as if he didn't think much of the shift change but was too tired to protest. My mouth tightened, and I felt as if I wanted to laugh and cry simultaneously.

"Oh, bunny," I finally whispered. "I'm sorry you got stuck with such a sucky mommy."

At that, Clark actually did look at me full on: eye contact, that legendary holy grail of interactivity. "It's time to kiss the mommy," he murmured, and I laughed, dipping to do so, then reached for the towel. As I pulled it down, I realized his lips were moving as he splashed, mashing bubbles, singing so quietly I could barely hear it; I pushed the washroom door closed, filter-ing out the washing machine's rhythmic clank, and tried to listen.

". . . *and outside in,*" Clark sang, "*this is how the world begins. Outside in and inside out, is how you blow a candle out.*" The near-inaudible tune was strange, a lilting little minor-key ditty that sounded only vaguely familiar. "*Inside out and inside out; Knock at the door, then turn about. Outside in and outside in . . .*"

(*there she stands so let her in*)

"Huh," Simon said, through the door's half-open crack. "That one again."

"Again?"

"He was singing it when you Skyped me from Quarry Argent." I shook my head. "Okay, well. I don't know what it is either, in case you're wondering."

"Sounds sort of . . . Wendish, going by Mrs. Whitcomb's stuff. Or just creepy pseudo-Victoriana, take your pick."

"Ain't the Wiggles, that's for sure. All right, bud—enough of that, time to step out. It's over."

Clark cracked a huge, shuddering yawn and stood up, wavering slightly; I folded him into my arms, the towel, pulling him onto my lap, no matter how much my pelvis complained at his weight. Rubbing his hair, I thought I heard him say a few more words, from under my armpit. "What's that?" I demanded, pulling away. "Say again, Clark. What was—"

Lifting his head from my chest, he studied me, bags beneath his eyes like bruises. "*Not* over," was all he said, however, before settling back down. And didn't speak again, at least till morning.

A few days later, in and between other weirdness, I was taking a couple of minutes to square Clark's room away before he came back from school—stack books according to size, soft toys on top of the Thomas the Tank Engine storage shelves, hard toys in their various bins, et cetera. Then something slipped beneath my foot, almost making me turn my ankle; I picked it up, cursing.

It took a second for me to recognize it as a toy my dad—Clark's O.G., for "Other Granddad"—had sent over from Australia just before Clark was born, a plush purple bunny with a microphone in its belly; perhaps, in hindsight, where our favourite nickname for Clark got started. When you pressed a button on its back and held it down, you could record a message; press the bunny's nose, and your own voice emerged from a speaker in its head, as though the toy was channelling you. One cancelled out the other, always, each new message recording overtop the last—no repeats.

That day, on sheer impulse, I pressed the playback button. Clark's voice emerged, singing that same creepy rhyme he'd been parroting in the bath: . . . *how you blow a candle . . . and outside out . . .*

Same old same old, I thought. But then, halfway through, another voice joined in—or seemed to. And maybe it was an echo, the mechanism wearing thin; maybe it was a fragment of an old message with a new message laid overtop, the first longer than the second, spliced Franken-style. Maybe it was low batteries or phone bleed, radio waves even, not that anyone really uses radio anymore—

Yeah, maybe. Or it might have been a woman's voice, dark and scratchy, breath-starved, each note a bare, reedy scrap of tone. Singing a third verse, one none of us had ever heard before, or since:

> *Inside, outside, more and more,*
> *Every mirror is a door.*
> *Outside, inside, mirrors break,*
> *To look has been your first mistake . . .*

TWELVE

After one thing and another, it was already Wednesday of the next week by the time Safie and I were finally able to get together; we'd spoken, obviously—I asked her to courier the Whitcomb file box over to me and paid dearly for the privilege—but various factors made a physical meeting impossible until then. Slight annoyance factor of Simon and Mom attempting to keep me on enforced bed rest aside, however, that was fine with me, because it gave me time to sort through and peruse the writings in question with only intermittent interruption, barring the usual—another They Might Be Giants album, *Here Comes Science,* in the background on continual repeat, for example, plus bouncing, and cries of, "Your turn, Mommy! Dance! *Sing!*"

"Can't, honey, Mommy's doing something," I'd call back, at which point Clark would inevitably switch to, "Your turn, Daddy!" instead, running poor Simon through his paces. And I'd go right on back to the pile, pulling sheaf after sheaf of copied material out of the same seemingly endless file, getting semi-high off the toner's barely set stink.

Eventually, however, the relevant stuff did start to float to the top . . . which is when it got really interesting.

From Arthur Macalla Whitcomb to an unnamed friend, dated 1925:

You ask me how I feel now my wife is pronounced deceased ex post facto, to which I can but reply: were it only so easy! She is with me always, even now—her presence does not fade, nor, all pangs aside, do I wish it to.

How well I still recall the day we met, at Miss Dunlopp's, her standing tall amongst all the children in their rough frocks and short trousers; she was a teacher's aide already, dressed head to toe in blue bombazine, her glorious hair wound up tight and tucked away beneath a cap like some Mennonite. Hardly a figure of glamour, and half again my age, yet I could not stop myself from staring. I wrote draft after draft to that place, completely disinterested in those other orphans' welfare, only in order to speak with her an instant here, share a stolen moment there. Once she was of age, I was able to make my offer, which she accepted—and though I never believed she would refuse, I can state with conviction that hour when she agreed to marry me remains the absolute pinnacle of my life.

In another age, the fascination she exerted over me might have been characterized as witchcraft, for she displayed a charisma which drew her on to heights of creative endeavour I could never have predicted—a certain Sibylline quality, visionary and pure yet touched by the malign, as I felt even before I came to know what losses spawned it. It drew me—she drew me—and I gave myself over gladly. I was never resentful. I could not be.

I never will be.

It was after Hyatt's misfortune, the violent blow of his— erasure—that Mrs. W. began to affect the veil she would wear forevermore, both in and out of doors. Just as she had previously feared to allow him outside unaccompanied, so she now feared to venture forth herself without its protection; as though, it struck me, she dreaded some sort of unnatural attention, discovery, recognition.

"I saw," she told me, often enough. "I shall never un-see, nor be un-seen, so what I know must be told some-how, by any means. I must remove it from my head;

*translate it to the heads of others. Perhaps then, the debt
will be paid."*

I did not know, nor do I, of what she spoke. But it meant
the world to her—and she the world to me. I would have
done her any service, far above and beyond the mere vows
of our union; she knew it well enough, from the very beginning. Yet she ceased to call upon me, eventually. I was cast
out, forgotten. Can any blame me for taking myself away,
leaving her to her own devices? Her toys and trinkets?

Well, it is all of little account now.

You ask me what is to be done with the boy, her charge—
Sidlo, that poor little blind mountebank—so I set down my
wishes, accordingly: I will continue to pay his upkeep, since
I am not inclined to throw any crippled thing to the winds,
let alone one who was so tenderly loved by the woman who
still holds all my heart, and no doubt loved her, too. He
wept bitterly enough, seven years past, when I told him that
she had gone missing; I have no doubt that if she is truly
beyond retrieval now, he will continue to mourn her the rest
of his days. Thus we will share that, if nothing else, though I
expect it will bring neither of us much comfort.

"Boy," I call him, though he must surely be grown a man
of more than twenty years. Yet perhaps I wish only to convince myself that if he did know her better than I, it was
for but a short time, and that the difference in age between
them (more markèd even than that between she and I)
would have left them no room to do aught of which I might
be required—by law, by morality, by God's own word—to
be jealous.

Nevertheless, I place no blame on him, or her—or myself,
for that matter. No more than any other human being.

Here I will break off, however, and though I am glad to
hear from you, I apologize in advance for my lack of subsequent communication. I plan on leaving Europe at last,
returning to Canada, retiring to the Manor, there to gather
my thoughts and count the seconds till my own departure.
It is my fervent hope that in death I will find the answers I

*seek . . . that she and I will be reunited, with no further mys-
teries left between us. Yet should this prove to be no more
than idle fancy, I have no grand designs left to play out anymore, and this world holds very little appeal for me beyond
the certainty of its eventual passing. I expect to neither long
survive her, nor be over-unhappy to not do so.*

    I am, as ever, yr. obt., etc. etc.

Further down in the stack, I found a photograph of Mr. and Mrs.
Whitcomb on their wedding day, seated together like some royal
couple amidst an attendant troop of bridesmaids, groomsmen,
servants—even a tearful-looking older lady who might be Miss
Dunlopp, given she herself stood surrounded by a clutch of uni-
formed kids. As usual, Mrs. Whitcomb was veiled, though far
more lightly than every other time I'd "seen" her: a fall of trans-
parent lace hung from her hat brim, tails thrown back over her
shoulders and points tied beneath her chin, embroidered with
delicate flowers that reduced her actual features to a teasing,
candled-egg blur.

    Mr. Whitcomb, on the other hand, was both fully visible and
palpably ecstatic—he was a carthorse of a man, long, tall and
bluff-featured, wearing an uncomfortable-looking celluloid collar and a walrus moustache, neither of which suited him. His
hands were large enough to engulf both of hers at once, and he
studied her with gentle, baffled eyes, so drunk in love he could
barely sit still; one of his legs was actually slightly blurred, probably from juddering with nervous energy during the no doubt
interminable exposure time.

    Whoa, man, I remember thinking, eyebrow arching slightly
at the sight. *Seriously, keep it in your trousers. I mean, she married
you, didn't she? That's about as good as it gets.*

    He definitely seemed to think so, anyways. And if she thought
something else, well—it wasn't like she was saying anything.

    Sifting down, I hit yet more correspondence, post-wedding—
happy happy joy joy: *I am enthused beyond all words at the delight
we share, now that this sweetest of creatures has consented to vow
herself mine before God and all congregants,* blah blahbitty blah.

Letters and drafts of letters, a voluminous ongoing net of back-and-forth with family and friends, business consultants and partners, basically anybody the surprisingly excitable Whitcomb admired enough to try and make a pen pal out of. If he'd lived during the Internet age, old Arthur M. would've probably ended up being labelled an unrepentant fanboy, prone to tweet or re-blog a million shots a day of whatever Iris happened to be working on, along with selfies of him mooning over her, and her blocking her face with anything handy.

He was besotted with her; that much was clear—but interestingly, his powerful attraction appeared to be fuelled as much by admiration for her creativity and intellectual acuity as for her youth and beauty. For *[t]hough many assert there be no female quality equivalent to genius, what I find in her—my Iris, my darling, my bride!—can, truly, be given no other name*, he wrote, maybe to the same dude as before—the first and last pages of that letter were missing. *She is possessed by a fierce flame of talent which illuminates all she touches, and I would have every one in the world know her as I do, through her works first and foremost, since they cannot share daily in her life . . . and indeed, all matters of mere boorish business laid aside, I own no higher aspiration but to make this so.*

Discussion followed over whether or not to stay in town while Whitcomb Manor was being renovated (fitted up for two, with extra space cleared out for when kids started coming along), or make a European honeymoon tour, the way Mr. Whitcomb had apparently promised her they would. Though Mrs. Whitcomb didn't seem to mind either way, Mr. Whitcomb suddenly started pushing the latter idea hard, mapping out a journey that would begin in England, then go through France and Belgium to Germany, ending up in those areas of Lusatia bordering closest to Hungary—the former Wendish territories, from where her family originated.

You have spoken of tracing your ancestry, he wrote to her while on a business trip to Toronto, *and so I have made inquiries up around God's Ear, hoping to discover any who might recall your former family—that foul maniac, your father, as well as your mother and grandmother, of whom you have such few, yet fond, memories. Oh forgive my presumption, please, dear girl! Though you may well deprecate my methods, I believe you will gain great pleasure from their result. . . .*

And here the tone began to shift, correspondence giving way to notes, lists, little sketches, and memoranda. A map of the area, one particular district highlighted, longitude and latitude reckoned to show the position of a village—so small I could only assume it hadn't been thought important enough to include on its own merits—called Dzéngast. (*In the Sorbian tongue,* dzén *is day, or perhaps bright, depending on sources,* Mr. Whitcomb's scribbled commentary revealed; he'd hastily written something else underneath, before scrubbing it away once more, leaving nothing but an odd smear in its wake. *Unlikely,* he'd appended, right after that, with no real hint as to what had just been so summarily dismissed.)

Well, we already knew they'd gone, right? Bruges, the check-in with Gustave Knauff, Knauff's maybe-portrait of the two of them. But when I turned over the next wad of papers, what I got was a sort of diary after the fact, one that skipped straight over the British, French, and Belgian portions of the trip. It began *in media res,* as Mr. Whitcomb would have put it: with a stopover in some hotel near Bautzen, *cultural capital of Upper Wendia, my guidebooks say. Dr. R— has agreed to meet us here, pretending we have encountered him by chance; he comes highly recommended by my cousin Adelhart, the surgeon, who accounts him the most unsung alienist of his acquaintanceship. To identify him as such to Iris would be impossible, of course, but seeing her megrims have become steadily worse since we disembarked, I see no other way forward. . . .*

Dzéngast is fifty miles from here, if that, and she must face it with as much strength as possible in order to gain the answers she so desperately seeks (for all she declines to tell me, explicitly, what those answers might be). And thus, since it is my duty to assist her—she being my very flesh and blood, the living vessel my heart resides within—I will, by any means necessary. Dr. R— is well known for his mesmeric skills, and has assured me his methods are

nigh-undetectable, even . . . or perhaps most especially . . . to their
subject. As my father so rightly observed, in such delicate matters,
it is sometimes easier to beg forgiveness after the fact than to ask
permission before.

If he can help her and enlighten me, he will; he has sworn so.
I like to think he understands the consequences to both of us if he
does not.

"*Megrims*"—that would be headaches, I thought, flipping forwards. So . . . Mr. Whitcomb wanted to hook his wife up with a
psychiatrist, basically, years before that term would come into
common usage. Have him, what—hypnotize her? Analyze her
dreams? All very Ann Radcliffe, and still more than a bit con-
troversial at the time, which was probably why he'd left "Dr. R's"
name out of the journal: to protect the doctor's privacy, or his
wife's, or both.

The next page started abruptly: *13 June. Iris accepts Dr. R— at*
face value, or seems to; she says she finds him good company and
they chatter away together, swapping fairy tales. Both keep mostly
to English, no doubt out of politeness, but lapsing on occasion into
the odd, guttural tongue of her birth. She continues to work, how-
ever, against my better judgement—claims it a salve against her
sleeplessness, which persists, though Dr. R—'s drugs allow her to
nap during the day or early evening. She sketches constantly, occa-
sionally transferring the result onto a small canvas, which she fills
at top speed then barely glances at afterwards. When they are dry
she tends to burn them, unless I object strenuously. She left behind
three in the last village alone.

The images are similar, far too much so: a storm overhanging a
field, clouds bright-lit from within; the noonday sun engulfed, all
wings and eyes. They hurt the mind to contemplate. I recall that
fellow Knauff, his hand lingering on her knee—and me nearby, the
scoundrel!—as he leafed through her folio before raising his head
to observe, sadly: "Ah, meine schöne Madame . . . I see you, too,
labour under the direction of an angel."

At dawn we travel on. One more stop, perhaps two, before our
destination.

Dr. R— says he will begin tomorrow night.

To be continued, I thought, flipping forward again.

The next document in the stack was a sideways shift, in a number of ways. A letter this time, dated from November of the same year. I recognized the name at the top: *Adelhart Whitcomb M.D.*—the surgeon-cousin. Mr. Whitcomb's writing was different, too—smaller and more cramped, obviously scrawled in haste yet somehow easier to read, perhaps because it was addressed to somebody other than Arthur M. himself.

My dearest Adelhart, it began. *Please do not let my lack of answer up till now imply reproof for your recommendation re Dr. R—, whose efforts have been unstinting, if not so fruitful as hoped. Nonetheless, things have happened in the interim that change everything, making him the least of my worries.*

You will note, for example, that my wife and I are no longer on the continent, having been forced to curtail our tour by circumstances beyond our—beyond anyone's—control.

Not long before we reached Dzéngast, Dr. R— used both medicines and counsel to establish a relationship of trust with Iris, such that when mesmerism was finally employed upon her it might yield its best result. As you prognosticated, when he judged conditions finally propitious, he placed my dearest into what he called the "monoideitic sleep," a state of curious entrancement. It was deeply disquieting to hear my beloved, normally so sharp and animate, speak and respond in such a lethargic monotone, and to see her sit so lifeless. Yet within seconds of the experiment's commencement both Dr. R— and she had lapsed into that foreign tongue they share. I could bear only some few minutes of that incomprehensible converse before excusing myself to the receiving room of our suite, attempting to read or scribe other letters, ever aware of that dull, unceasing murmur behind the not-quite-closed bedroom door.

When Dr. R— emerged, I confess I quite leapt to my feet, and only his hasty gesture silenced me till he had closed the door, joining me near the window. "Your wife, Mr. Whitcomb," he began, "is neither deluded nor deluding. She is as sane as any woman I have known."

The relief of this near finished me; I am not ashamed to say that I very nearly wept. Dr. R— proceeded to the liquor cabinet and decanted generously of the local brandy for us both before resuming. "I have placed her in a full natural sleep, from which I expect her to awake in an hour or so, hopefully much refreshed."

"Will she remember the experience?"

"Oh indeed, all of it; it would be a waste if she did not." The doctor smiled wearily. "I trust you shall not take it as a slight if I tell you I thought your wife's narrative an invention, though not a wholly conscious one—a scrim concocted by what Herr Freud calls the 'subconscious,' to shield her from the trauma of witnessing her father's death—or, perhaps, of having contributed to it. After all, the evidence in the case speaks volumes toward such an assumption, for was it not your own fear that this might be true that caused you to solicit my assistance to begin with?"

I could not but acknowledge it. "I would be a fool if I closed my eyes to the facts, since murder is a crime without limit. Yet still, it seemed so ludicrous—a nine-year-old girl, alone against a grown man, her own father. And then to do all that was done thereafter, the burial of his head, and such . . ."

"A madman weak with hunger and exposure, while she was terrified to near-madness herself? I have consulted in stranger cases. But for all her perturbations, sir, your wife has no guilt in this—not mentally, at any rate, leading me to suspect she is innocent physically of any crime as well."

I felt a great urge to sit down, and fought it back by finishing my brandy. "You are certain?"

"Very much so. She is, as you know, a woman of capacity, forever at the mercy of her own intelligence, her sympathies, and her imagination. Indeed, it is that very imagination which may prove our greatest concern. For though I may state with near-certainty that nothing criminal was done on your wife's part, that does not mean events can possibly have proceeded as she recalls them."

"Explain, sir."

Dr. R— hesitated, long enough that the fear within me grew intolerable, before replying. "The details are of little import," he said at last. "What matters is the sincerity of your wife's conviction, her firm belief she experienced something—numinous, if I may lapse into Spiritualist terminology; something wholly outside *her experience, to all intents and purposes not of this world. But she does not now recall what it was, and that lacuna has become a void her fantasy struggles to fill, conjuring up all the contents of her dreaming mind. Until she can confront that missing memory, there will be no peace for her."*

"So taking her here, to Lusatia—to Dzéngast—was the correct decision."

"The necessary one, yes. It may be that when she visits the fields outside her parents' village, so reminiscent of where her family died, she will remember only an ugly, mundane truth. But truth, however ugly or mundane, is the only thing that will heal her." And here he sighed, concluding: "The mind is full of mysteries, sir. As full in its way as the earth itself, or more so."

You may be tempted, from the detail I have employed, to think that perhaps I have been fanciful or inventive in my recounting. I assure you I have not. The events of that afternoon are etched upon my brain as if engraved, and I greatly doubt that they shall ever fade, especially when placed in conjunction with what followed.

Three days later, our journey was complete. We reached that damnable hen-scratch of a village in early evening, just in time for Iris to alight from our carriage and collapse, right there in what passed for a street. She was put to bed, where she lay like a dead woman, a wet cloth across her eyes, too much in pain even to moan. And I confess I was beside myself, since Dr. R— could apparently do nothing for her. Just as the sun sank, however, a young girl (perhaps twelve years of age, no more) appeared at our host's door, petitioning to be allowed entrance to my wife's chamber, to whom she referred by her maiden name—her original name: Giscelia Wróbl.

"The Kantorka sends her greetings," she told me, through Dr. R—, "and begs to be remembered to the sparrow-child, daughter of Handrij, daughter of Liska. She will attend her in the morning and have speech with her. In the meantime, she has sent this potion to aid with her sickness."

Dr. R— examined the mixture, declaring it wholesome. I brought it up to my darling myself, watched as she drank it down, and was amazed by the effect.

"I feel almost well," she told me, sitting up. "Who was that, downstairs?"

"She said she came from the Kantorka, whoever that might be."

"My grandmother knew the term . . . a singer, and leader in songs. She keeps the village's memory, its stories."

"Its fairy tales?" She nodded. I conjured a smile, no doubt forced, but intended only to cheer. "Perfect for you, then, my love."

The look she gave me in return was odd, however. "One might think so," was all she said.

From then on things progressed quickly, or at least seemed so, from where I stood—out of the compass of the action, wholly dependent on Dr. R— for any sense of what might be happening, or why.

We were received the next morning by the Kantorka herself, a withered and feeble old woman with a great pile of embroidered cloth on her blind, nodding head, ensconced in a veritable witch's cottage at the edge of town. The same girl as before attended her, continually simmering something vile-smelling in an iron pot over a smoking fire, watching as her mistress and Iris conversed while Dr. R— translated for me, careful to keep his voice to a polite whisper.

"You are troubled by the Noon-Witch's touch," this wretch of a peasant mountebank told my darling, "and you will be troubled always, for those She has set her eye upon" . . . and yes, I heard the capital letter used here, blasphemous and awful . . . "will never again be free from her influence, except that they find their true vocation and keep to it. Do you do the work you are intended for, my girl?"

"I do the only work I can do, old mother."

"Well, then."

"But is there nothing else to say? We have come a long way, my husband and I."

The old woman seemed to assess me, shrewdly. "I can see he loves you dearly, daughter, and that his intentions are good, but these are matters only women should deal with, not men, or outsiders. As to the other, only She can say. Yet if you make an offering at the procession tomorrow, She may yet consider your case favourably."

"Ah, and now comes the request for cash, which—luckily enough—I have in ready supply," I muttered to Dr. R—, who
hushed me, quickly.

The procession they spoke of is an annual event, apparently,
aimed at placating this aforementioned "Noon-Witch," some spectre or pagan goddess, said to haunt the fields at harvest-time. The
crop in this case is rye, winter-planted, which reaches full growth at
the summer solstice; this ceremony must be performed before they
start to reap, or dire consequences will result. Dr. R— told me that
before Christianity took hold, the fields in question were known as
the Place of Burying, where (rumour has it) Sorbians were once
wont to entomb decrepit family members alive, "feeding" the earth,
so as to keep it fertile.

(I recall how my darling told me a similar tale during our
courtship days, having learned it at her own beloved grandmother's
knee, along with many more: of the Wodny Muz or water-man,
who tempts bathers into his lake, where he pulls them down to the
bottom to drown; of the Dusiolek or Forest Strangler; the Zmora, a
female creature who kills people in their sleep; the Strzyga, a flying
monster that swoops down on people and carries them off, dropping their half-devoured parts from a great height, and the Cmeter,
who digs up people's corpses from graveyards, and eats them.)

Such terrible things to tell a child, or anyone. Was that ven-
erable unfortunate of the same lineage as this Kantorka, or are
such horrible fables what all Wendish children receive with their
mother's milk, thus explaining from where her father's seemingly
unnatural bloodthirstiness truly stemmed?

But no, I cannot think that, and so risk tarring my Iris with the
same foul brush. Not when she is so dear, so tender, so terribly feeling, always—for others, if not for herself.

I will forbid her to participate in such folly, and she will obey,
I thought to myself, knowing in my heart both statements to be
a lie, since I have never exerted my husbandly prerogative over
her in such a fashion, nor will I ever. So to Dr. R— I said instead,
"I cannot let her go there alone, unprotected, amongst these people . . . they are hardly trustworthy, with their strange beliefs; I will
not have it. Yet gold cures all things, as the old saying goes, and

marriage makes my blood hers, as hers is mine. Surely, if I offer to pay my way—given their obvious poverty—they cannot seek to bar me access."

To this, however, he simply shook his head, replying, "My friend, in some places money truly is no object, especially where faith is involved . . . this being one, as you may well find yourself forced to realize."

I paused for a minute, feeling light-headed and pukey, only to realize that was because I must've actually stopped breathing some time back, caught up in poor old Mr. Whitcomb's narrative. I made myself take a long, measured sip of air, which immediately improved everything, before continuing on.

He had the right of it, of course. I would have followed her into that nodding thicket of stalks, but they held me back. I am unashamed to say it took several of them to do so effectively; I fought them with all the strength at my disposal, for which not a few of the bastards commended me, in their way. My ultimate overthrow, I lay at the feet of the last man to join their number, my height but far wider, a veritable upright bull who so expertly slipped his arm around my collar and choked me into unconsciousness like some slaughterhouse ram drove mad by fright, yet gently enough that I woke with barely a bruise in the aftermath.

I remember seeing the Kantorka leading my Iris by one sleeve, her latest canvas tucked beneath her other arm, with the old wretch herself piloted by that assistant of hers as the hot morning sun turned the tops of the rye to gold. The procession—made up entirely of girls and women of all ages, similarly dressed in crossed-front blouses, long, flounced skirts, and high-piled headdresses of fringed, bright-stitched scarves—was led by a looming creature who might have been either one masked mummer propped up on stilts or a puppet manipulated by several revellers concealed beneath its train, like some Chinese New Year's dragon or pantomime horse.

The face of this thing was no doubt intended to seem feminine, fashioned with horrid skill from a dried, painted lattice of braided husks and other vegetable matter; its hair was a pelt or hide, falling to graze the shoulders of its cloak, whose panels were pinned all over with brass or silver tokens, glass beads, any manner of mirror *or tinsel, throwing back the light in such a way as to look almost on fire.*

One naked human hand I saw upraised claw-like, while the other hung down, slim fingers white-gripped around the hilt of a sword much like the one my darling's accursed father supposedly beat out of ploughshares—almost a full three feet in length and so heavy it dragged behind, carving a furrow through the crop-dusted earth below.

I watched as they took her into the fields, those witches, my sight fading, even as I waited in vain for her return.

Here I paused again, the same weird feeling mounting, like bile in my mouth.

Because here it was, wasn't it? At last. The image that'd haunted Mrs. Whitcomb the rest of her life, become the centrepiece of paintings, murals, movies alike: Lady Midday, *Poludnice*, the Noontime Spectre herself, shouldering her way through the crops to inquire of some unlucky farmer whether or not he was comfortable with his given task, whether or not he wished himself elsewhere. Whether or not he could feel his attention . . . slipping.

That blazing cloak, that great, sharp sword, that hidden face. And the sun staring down overtop it all, hot and pitiless, a naked white eye in an equally naked sky.

But now Mr. Whitcomb was "talking" once more.

Dr. R— cautions me to control myself, if only for her sake—set an example, as a man must, for his helpmeet's support—but I find it

(Here came another smear, perhaps two piled on top of each other and violently abraded, the paper beneath creased or possibly torn.)

When I came to, it was late afternoon, with both of us—all three, in fact—already delivered once more to our lodgings. Dr. R— stepped in from the next room, where he had been tending to my Iris; he caught me by the arm, attempting to calm me, then told me she was still in a species of fit, having fallen down in the very midst of that bloody pagan ceremony of theirs. Felled by sunstroke, or so he maintains. In Dzéngast, I later learned, they say of one to whom this happens, "he—or she—has been crowned by the Witch, forever fixed between the minute and the hour."

Apparently, the Kantorka and her attendants had allowed her to lie there in the heat and the dirt until their prayers were done, then dragged her back on a traverse made from shawls, far enough that the village's men might bear her away. When Dr. R— first saw her, she was sunburnt and filthy, her hair and dress full of rye. In that moment I thanked God I had not been conscious at the same time, for I knew I would surely have performed murder on whoever had delivered her to me in such a fashion.

As it was, I went straight to my luggage and withdrew a small pistol I kept there, for defence during rough travel. I loaded it and went to seek out the Kantorka.

"What do you do in those fields?" I demanded. "Women's business," she had the gall to reply, so I showed my weapon, brandishing it in her face, and watched her supposedly blind eyes widen. "My wife may be dying, you old witch," I told her, coldly, as Dr. R— shivered beside me (I having yet once more forced him to accompany me, to translate our discourse), "and I will have no compunctions over sending you along with her, if you continue to refuse me. What do you do in those fields, therefore, which left my darling as she is now?"

The girl who kept her fire looked pale, but the old woman merely smiled. "We salute the Lady," she said at last. "We beg the favour of Her absence, that She may turn her gaze elsewhere. And we give Her offerings." I nodded. "My wife's painting," I said, and she smiled again, more narrowly, so I could see the sharp tips of her teeth.

"That was what she brought, yes," she said, with relish, "not knowing, as yet, what else she might have to give. But I do not think that was what the Lady accepted."

The hell? I wondered, turning the page.

I paid a heavy price to extract my darling and I from Lusatia's grasp both quickly and cleanly, the next section continued, leaving Dzéngast as far behind as possible. Dr. R— advised against such haste, for the Kantorka's implications had caused him to examine Iris once more, confirming that she was indeed with child—perhaps as much as four months along, in fact—yet I could not by any *means suffer us to stay, let alone allow our son to be born within those hellish precincts. So it was, with great effort and expenditure, that we reached the nearest port and chartered a ship home, racing nature itself to make sure we reached shore before Iris might be taken to bed. I can only thank Christ Almighty that we were within time, however, for her consequent suffering proved long, difficult, and (in the end) bloody.*

Yet I do have a son now, Adelhart—an heir. His name is Hyatt. Likely the only child we will ever see, or so the doctors say. He is large and healthy, beautiful in all his parts as only befits one plucked from my darling's lovely flesh, but there is something troubling in his very sweetness, his quietness, his lack of robust protest. Sometimes he seems more a doll or a pretty toy than a boy-child, accepting whatever we put before him with the same dignified equanimity. His eyes are dreamy, turned ever-inward, like hers when caught in the throes of creation; if nothing troubles him for long, it seems more and more likely that that is because he simply does not perceive most things in the same way we do, though he is hardly blind. Sometimes he stares at nothing and smiles, laughs, as though he hears singing, or is danced attendance upon by ghostly playmates.

Worst of all, however, is the knowledge that though my wife— my Iris—tries not to show me so, I know she is disappointed, or feels she has disappointed me. That she blames herself, somehow, for Hyatt's condition—as though I would ever lay it at her feet, when there are so many other places for such a load of guilt to accrue! To myself, for example, for thinking I could solve her mysterious obsessions through some mere quest, that I could buy her lasting happiness. For sending her "home" in the first place, allowing that disgusting old woman to mar her mind further, exposing her to whatever horror they bow to between the furrows of that awful field, a place which surely deserves to be burnt to its roots and sown again with salt . . .

Well, enough of that. All will be as God wills it from now on, and always would have been. I accept that, fully and without regret, not least because I have no other choice.

My darling I will no longer over-trouble with marital attentions, I have decided, even after her recovery, seeing we have no reason or duty to keep trying. There are French methods after all, as you know; other possibilities, did she prove amenable. But she is an innocent girl still, for all her oddities, and in my own conscience, I cannot require of her anything she does not wish to offer freely— not loving her so dearly as I do, and always shall.

I am & remain yr own loving cousin, with a full heart & troubled mind,

In Christ Our Lord, amen,

Art. M. W.

THIRTEEN

Folding Mr. Whitcomb's letter, I lay back, the general sound of jumping, yelling, and tinny harmonization from the next room having finally faded, at least enough to make studying the ceiling more restful than annoying. The box lay heavy in my lap as my eyes drifted closed. Outside, the streetlights were just starting to come on.

In the red dusk behind my lids, the weird synchronicity with which my own life was starting to line up with Mrs. Whitcomb's was becoming undeniable. Headaches and insomnia, check; life-wrecking obsessions, check. Infinitely patient and supportive husband who'd do anything for her/me, check. Child with special needs, check. Seizure—sunstroke-related, supposedly—while investigating Lady Midday, check . . .

Mr. Whitcomb swum in front of my eyes, transposed from his wedding photo—celluloid collar askew, facial hair bristling, pistol in hand. He'd blamed himself, obviously, for how Hyatt ended up, just as there was virtually no doubt but that Mrs. Whitcomb had probably come to blame herself, too, over those first few months of recuperation, let alone later. The both of them stuck in painful orbit, barely able to acknowledge their own sick guilt to themselves let alone take comfort in each other—god, what a fucking tragedy.

As for the rest, though, all this gothic shit. Was that true? Could that possibly *be* true?

(No.)

He *thought* it was true, though. Why say it if not? Why write the letter at all?

Because guilt, I told myself, firmly, *or general Victorian fucked-uptitude, whatever. Guy'd just decided to never have sex with his wife again, "for her own good," and without even consulting her. No wonder their marriage fell apart.*

Through the bedroom door, I heard my iPhone ring and Simon answer it, but I tuned out when he told the caller that I wasn't available at the moment. I stayed there a few minutes more without moving, vaguely intending to get up and turn off the bedside lamp; my limbs pressed down, leaden, a mounting warm numbness spreading all over. Wondering if there was a point to walking anybody else through what I'd just read—Simon, Safie, Jan Mattheuis. Forget factual, was it even pertinent? Well, maybe as a further motivation, an explanation for the way she chose to sequester herself after Hyatt's disappearance, channelling her pain into murals, then Spiritualism, then films—

Yeah, Kate-Mary des Esseintes and her meetings, plus that *guy,* "the boy." Vasek Sidlo. I really needed to find out more about *him*.

With a tap on the bedroom door, Simon peered in, iPhone still against his face; he was wearing a flat expression that I'd long since learned meant, if not necessarily trouble, then something serious enough to require total attention. It was enough to snap me back and make me sit up.

"Lois?—okay, good. Yes, she's awake," he said into the phone, "and I think you should tell her what you just told me." He came in, handed me the phone, and dropped into his chair, watching me intently. I put the phone to my ear, unnerved.

"Hello?"

"Hi, Lois? It's Val Moraine calling—you remember, from the Vinegar House, up in Quarry Argent?" Val's voice was oddly subdued, as if trying to keep from being overheard. "I didn't mean to disturb you, just thought I should check and see how you are."

"Oh, well, that's, that's really nice of you," I said, a little nonplussed. "Nothing to report, really; tests were all clear,

I'm starting a drug regimen soon . . . Is that all you wanted to know?"

"No, I—" A pause, then a sharp huff and she went on more firmly, as if she'd finally made up her mind about something. "I'm at the museum, and there's a gentleman here by the name of Wrob Barney talking to Bob Tierney *right now* about your project."

For a moment, my mind still half on the Whitcombs and their tragedies, I couldn't process this. "What?" I finally said. Simon nodded, mouth tight.

"He came by the museum a little while ago and started right in with Bob about Mrs. Whitcomb, the films, the documentary, that book you wanted to write. Well, Bob'll give away his own grandmother to anyone interested enough in town history, so it never occurred to him to think twice, I imagine. But something just didn't ring right to me about this fellow, and at last I thought, you know, maybe I should check with Ms. Cairns myself. Do you know him? Is this on the level?"

"Oh, yes, I know him, and no, this is absolutely fucking *not* on the level." My jaw clenched hard enough to bring on a headache. But the anger itself felt liberating, so much like my old self that even that pain was welcome. "Actually, Val, can you do me a favour? Put Wrob on the phone with me, and tell him who it is before you do."

Val paused. "Think that's a good idea?" she asked, finally.

"Probably not, but I want to see what he does. Okay?"

". . . All right."

Simon, apparently realizing what was going on, straightened up. "Are you sure?" he said in a low voice. "Might be worth not letting him know we know."

"Don't care," I replied, covering the phone's mic. "If it turns out he hasn't got the balls to talk to me directly then I'll get hold of him some other way, but I'm sick of his crap. This is the last fucking straw." I turned back to the phone and waited. The pause was just long enough I started to grind my teeth again with frustration; of *course* he wasn't going to—

"Hey, Lois. How ya feelin'?" As casual as if we'd just bumped into each other in Starbucks, making half a laugh escape me, thin with disbelief. "Oh, better than I was, Wrob, but still pretty pissed off," I said. "Seriously, what part of 'You are not involved in this project' do you not get, exactly? I mean, it's one thing you got Chris Coulby to stake me out when I was in the hospital, now you can't even do your own research?"

He didn't even bother to deny it, which just made me angrier. "Oh, there's nothing here that isn't available to the public . . . and considering you'd never even have gotten started on this without what I gave you, this is really more like *my* research. Isn't it?"

"What you *gave* me?"

"In our interview, yes."

"Oh, uh huh. What you stole, you mean, and what I caught you stealing after Jan caught you first, which is why you don't have a damn *job* anymore—"

"I wasn't aware Mrs. Whitcomb belonged to anybody, actually," he shot back, loftily, to which I just had to snort.

"Ex-fucking-actly. Jan know you're up there?"

"No, but so what? Like you say, he already fired me; only gets to do that once. Besides which, you really think either of you learned anything I didn't already know? Above and beyond what it feels like to have a stroke, I mean."

"*Seizure,* and that's debatable."

"Same difference, and the question stands."

I drew a calming breath. "Oh, I kinda think I did . . . but if you want to find out what, you can just go on and buy the book when it comes out, like everybody else. Now give Val back the phone."

"Goodbye, Lois," he said, and hung up on me.

I put the iPhone down, fighting the urge to throw it against the wall, and struck my knee with my hand instead. "Fucking pretentious, gay-ass *turd*-bucket!" I exclaimed.

Simon leaned back in his chair, folding his arms. "I'm beginning to agree with you," he said flatly, which made me raise my eyebrows; I hadn't heard him sound this angry in a long time. "Did he seriously get somebody to stake out St. Mike's?"

I blew out, hard. "I don't know. I mean—I can't prove it. But why else would Chris have been there? Jesus." I shook my head. "I don't know what I'm going to do."

Simon tilted his head. "We could try to get a restraining order, for a start—"

"No, we couldn't. He's nowhere near me, man; he doesn't need to be. And he's richer than either of us, so if we go to court, who do you think is gonna win?" I waved my hands, anger collapsing into exhaustion. "Too bad it's not against the law to be an asshole." Simon's jaw tightened. I leaned forward and put my hands on his. "Look, I love that you're pissed on my behalf, but I haven't got the time or the energy, and it wouldn't do any good, anyway. I just have to make sure he doesn't get to fuck this up for me, long distance or otherwise; get it done, finished, in the can. Just . . . bear with me till that happens, okay? That's all I need."

Simon closed his eyes and sighed heavily, but his hands tightened on mine. "All right," he said at last, then let me go and stood. "Tea?"

"Please."

While Simon busied himself in the kitchen, I took a moment to text Jan at the NSA, telling him what'd just happened; didn't mention Chris Coulby, or the fact that Wrob'd all but admitted he was a mole—that sort of shit should probably be said face to face, if at all. My pulse started to soften. But then, just as I hit send, the iPhone began to ring. I checked the number: *Mom,* it said.

"*Big* surprise," I muttered to myself, hitting accept.

I've had a lot of opportunity to think about Wrob Barney and myself since then (don't worry, you'll understand why soon enough): the why/how of it all going bad between us, and so quickly. Because on the face of it, it seems like something simply chemical, straight oil and water, but in retrospect I've come to accept the truly sad fact that he and I were actually very similar people—too much so for comfort, let alone collaboration. I didn't want to see it, but I'm sure I suspected it, which is why I cast him away so violently. If we'd been different, we probably could have worked together, and . . . well, not *none* of this would have happened, because I think a lot of it would've no matter what. But at least the circle of damage would have been smaller.

It's just amazing how two people can misunderstand each other so wilfully, without "willing" it at all. Or maybe it isn't.

Back when I was a reviewer, I often had to remind myself that film is 99 percent interpretation, subject to inherent narrative unreliability. It's really hard to say "objectively, *this* is what [x] is 'about.'" Critics ask each other all the time: "What movie did *you* watch?" the same way we constantly tell each other, "You kind of have to *see* it." But can the movie you see ever *be* the movie I saw, given how perception is skewed the very moment in which we observe something?

Your perceptions are not reliable, and you will never escape unchanged.

Silver nitrate film, in particular, is the Schrödinger's Cat of cinema—you can open the box once, maybe, take a look inside, but after that you kind of have to take it on faith it ever existed in the first place. But then, all film is illusion; it's just an illusion that looks like the truth.

The problem with all numinous things is that you can't just take somebody's word about them, especially the ones you're warned away from. You *have* to look at them, eventually, to know they're really there. You look at them even though you know it's not a good idea to. You can't not.

In the end, you will always look at the thing you're told not to just because it exists, if only to *prove* it exists.

What's always funny, with me and Mom, is how the conversation can continue even when we're not in the same room—how whenever I feel especially under pressure, I almost always start to hear my own internal version of her arguing with what I think might be her internal version of me, as though I'm rehearsing our next argument in my head, playing through things I'd never have the guts to say to her in person. Except . . . maybe it's less "guts" than simple forbearance, a wistful wish to seem more reasonable than I often think I'm capable of being, plus the insight to know exactly how *crazy* most of the shit I long to spew at her would sound, if blurted out loud: how bitter, how scary. How essentially unnatural.

When did you get so unkind? she asked me, once, after I was stupid enough to tell her how I really felt about something—and Jesus, what was it, now? Oh yeah, whether or not I got anything out of Christmas besides the dubious pleasure of watching her and my in-laws attempt to get Clark to interact with them, considering I haven't outright enjoyed the holiday itself since I became an adult; all those expectations, that forced gaiety, the waste. She pointed out that it's not really about *me* anymore, which I certainly agree with, but that doesn't make it any easier. And the plain fact is, the whole thing gets Clark so high he wouldn't notice whether or not I was even there, so long as she and his "friend Daddy" were.

Not true, she shot back, when I unwisely chose to voice that particular opinion, *and you know it's not; he* loves *you, for God's sake. You're his* mother.

'Cause the one always leads to the other, huh? Except not really, I pointed out.

This wasn't about any of that, though, for once. This was about me, supposedly.

"So," she said. "You're seeing this Safie girl tomorrow, right?"

"The Safie girl whose name is Safie? Yes."

"And this is because . . ."

"Because we present on Friday, so we need to get our stuff in order. The footage we took in Quarry Argent."

"Remember what Dr. Harrison said about flickering light, TV monitors—"

"It's just sound work tomorrow, Mom, don't worry; looping, voice-over, room tone. Safie already took care of editing the clips that go with it, like she already digitized all Mrs. Whitcomb's films. I don't even have to look at the screen."

"So . . . no visual component at all."

"That's the clear implication."

That note in her voice, like: *Are you lying to me, Lois?* And the answering one in mine: *Would I be likely to tell you if I was?*

"I still think you need to slow down," she said, as though I couldn't have figured that out for myself.

"Christ, Mom, I've *been* slow, believe me! I'm off the drugs, eating well, sleeping . . . eight whole hours last night."

"A whole eight, huh? *Lois.*"

"Look, this is bigger than me, than either of us. This is important. This is *real.*"

"You're real, too."

(*Am I? Can you prove it?*)

"Well, be that as it may, I'm not gonna get any *less* real for giving this project the due diligence it deserves," I replied. "And now I have to go to bed, all right? Got an early start tomorrow, so thanks for your concern, I appreciate it. I'll be okay."

I could tell she wasn't persuaded, but on the other hand, reassuring her wasn't my job; *this* was my job, for now. Thank Christ.

"Look after yourself," was the last thing she said to me, before I clicked off. I'm somewhat ashamed to say I'd already disengaged so much from the conversation that I barely noticed.

Needless to say, instead of going to sleep, I sat up again and set about sifting through the files once more, hoping Mr. Whitcomb might've saved some of his darling Iris's ghost-busting materials. But halfway down the rest of the stack I found something else entirely, shoved vertical: a sheaf of paper folded in half and stitched up the centre to make a rough sort of notebook. The weave was heavy, the consistency fragile, tea-stained and spotted. I could see where the faded ink intersected with its surface, half-absorbed but half not, rendering part of every word a mere whisper, the shadow left behind when all its thicker parts had rotted away.

Were I able to scribe this in Wendish, I should, to save it from poor Art's prying, the first page began, *yet I cannot; my skills are in speaking and understanding that language only, with nothing written down. This too was taken from me, when he—my father—took my family.*

"Holy shit," I said, out loud.

When we came to that place at last, in the field's heart, I turned and saw a whirling dust cloud form above the rye, those nodding stalks. I saw it sweep in to engulf the procession, though the women marched on through it, impassive, and without pause. They were used to such things, I suppose. Perhaps the same phenomenon occurs each year, whether a stranger accompanies them on their journey or not.

She can appear as an old woman or a child, the Lady, *I recalled my grandmother telling me—and how odd that she should have done so, for me to recall it, walking as I was between a Kantorka so ancient she could barely move on my left-hand side, and her nimble little apprentice on my right, twelve years of age at the very most.* She can be a flash on the horizon, or the sun up above at noon. She can be a cloud moving through the harvest crops like God upon the waters, before this world was even made, only thought of.

Can the Lady be so old? *I asked her then, or think I did, for I have a strong memory of seeing her nod, lips set, as though she were afraid to speak further. As though the* Poludnice *were powerful as God Himself—or more so, my father's vision of Him. I could believe that then.*

I fear I can believe it now, as well.

"What did you find?" Simon called from the other room.

"Iris Dunlopp Whitcomb," I replied.

Next morning, Safie was waiting for me as I walked toward Earworm Audio, a coffee in either hand. "You look . . . upright," she commented, taking hers; I just shrugged.

Inside, she introduced me to her friend Malin Riegert, whom I vaguely recognized as another Toronto Film Faculty alumnus— the Fac had once been primarily about music production before adding in film and video; they'd maintained a separate stream for that up till the end, allowing Audio students to gain extra credit by working on third-semester projects so they wouldn't have to set up a competing suite of sound studios. Malin had met Safie, logically enough, by working on *Seven Angels But No Devil*, cleaning up the final mix before Safie sent it out as a festival submission. Since graduating, she'd gone specifically into digital reconstruction and analysis. "A lot of my income stream comes from packaging up CCTV footage for news broadcasts," she explained. "I put subtitles on stuff with muddy sound, or boost it back into audible range, sometimes both."

"Cool," I said, shaking Malin's hand. I took a long swig of caffeine before sitting down, orienting myself toward the monitors. "I brought a script for the intro," I told Safie. "Just the basics, but I can probably go off-the-cuff, for linkage."

"Good, great. I have a couple of sequences cut together already—clips versus stills, some of the stuff from the museum, Mrs. Whitcomb's art, plus the Vinegar House interiors. Turn out there were photos in the box, or what?"

"One, so far." I brought out my sheaf of Mr. Whitcomb's correspondence and showed her the wedding group portrait, pointing out all the major players. "We can always go back and get shots of the original, I guess, if the resolution isn't good enough."

She studied it. "No, I think that's fine. A little pixellation's good, right? Makes it look old."

"That was what I thought." I bent to rummage in my bag, brought the notebook out with a flourish. "Check this out, though."

"Holy shit," she blurted.

I laughed.

"Yeah, that's what *I* said."

While Malin got everything cued up, Safie shot footage of our main character's spiky, spidery brown handwriting, the pages blotchy as old skin. She thought we could double-expose it, use it as backing here and there, and I agreed; it would look amazing. The idea of people straining to read Mrs. Whitcomb's own words as they unspooled was an intoxicating one. Here and there, I could already catch phrases divorced from context as they skittered by, each more tempting than the last—

The Kantorka says, when a small child wanders the rows, it is known She has taken it for her own. It is pointless to set a black tracker on its trail, therefore, for her evil eye has rendered it entirely unsalvageable. . . . Her attention is known to cause freckles, and those under her gaze sleep with mouths open, allowing their souls to escape and come join her revels in the fields. . . . There is a story which tells how a woman seen sleeping this way was carefully turned over by her husband, only to be found dead in the morning—because she suffocated, Art suggests, being entirely unwilling to keep such opinions to himself.

Laying in the narration went more quickly than I'd initially expected, though that dissonance I've talked about was there in spades—the sheer weirdness of watching yourself play through actions you frankly can't remember, even though various other background details might tweak your sense of *déjà*-to-*jamais vu*. It was like one of those old slide projection systems, except jiggered so part of one image was laid over part of another—half Kodak carousel, half vaudeville-hall magic lantern phantasmagoria. Here and there I saw orbs floating onscreen, like dark spots in vitreous humour, slight corneal flaws—an occasional shimmer just beyond my visual range, too, the migraine sparkler writ tiny.

"You okay?" Safie asked. I looked up and realized she must've been watching me closely, checking for signs of another impending episode. I bit down hard, restraining myself from snapping back.

I replied, "Fine, thanks." To Malin: "You get all that?"

She nodded. "Levels look good."

"Excellent."

While Malin made sure the tracks synched okay and started laying in room tone, I filled Safie in on how Mrs. Whitcomb's notes linked up with Mr. Whitcomb's testimony about their honeymoon, Hyatt's birth, et cetera. At first she seemed to be mostly humouring me, but soon enough she was hooked, the story's inherent pull turning her big eyes starry. "Jesus," she said, finally. "I mean, *wow*. This is . . ."

"I know, right?"

"It's fucking *gold*, is what it is, Miss Cairns."

"Uh huh," I agreed, and we grinned at each other.

Beneath my thumb, more words, spooling out unbroken. I read them out loud, as Malin and Safie worked: *Women near their time must beware being caught short in the fields, for the Lady is known to take unbaptized babies as her tithe, swapping them for changelings with goggling heads, thin limbs, and swollen bellies, forever crying. These must be taken back and buried alive where they dropped, to keep the crops fertile. . . .*

"Pretty big into burying people in fields in Dzéngast, huh?" Safie commented, clicking her mouse around. "Guess her dad wanted to import the custom."

I shook my head. "Daddy Wròbl was a *Christian* fanatic, remember? This is pagan stuff, held over from prehistory. Earlier than that by a long time."

"How much, exactly?"

"Well . . . they found this headless stone fertility statue in a Cyprian cave that was made around 3500 BCE, I seem to recall—unearthed it in 1878. The Woman from Lemb, they call her, or the Goddess of Death, 'cause bad stuff supposedly happens to everyone who touches her." I flipped the page. "Then there's the Lion Man of the Hohlenstein Stadel, carbon-dated to forty thousand years old, probably one of the first anthropomorphic images ever made. They're both what your Dédé would've called little gods, cult-objects . . . worshipped in their time, just like Lady Midday."

"'Those old heathens.' The ones with the pots."

"That's right."

"Mmm." She clicked something, dragged it somewhere, saved. Beside her, Malin was nodding along to the almost-subliminal sound of my recorded voice through her heavy headphones, recognizable from where I sat by tone if not exact words. "How is it you know all this shit, anyhow, Miss Cairns?"

I thought about that for a moment. "I've always been interested in mythology, archaeology . . . history," I said, finally. "This is all three. An obsessional convergence. That must be why it seems so familiar."

"But you—my turn to ask this, I guess—you don't *believe* any of it, right?"

"I don't have to believe it myself to assume Mrs. Whitcomb must've." I turned another page. "Hell, even *Mr.* Whitcomb did, by the end. Enough that he wound up leaving her to it."

"Only after Hyatt disappeared."

I nodded. "That's true, too."

It was She I saw, in that field, in my fever, Mrs. Whitcomb wrote, *just as before—Her voice I knew at once, when She spoke to me. The only difference this time being that I looked instead of hiding my eyes, and She looked back.*

"This is weird," Malin observed, suddenly. She waved us over; Safie simply shifted her chair, while I rose and stood next to them as Malin indicated something onscreen. "There," she said. "In the mix, at the bottom—you see that?"

I didn't see anything, but was well aware that didn't mean much. Safie narrowed her eyes. "Yeah. What . . . is that part of the original track?"

"I fed in a bunch of different stuff to create a kind of generalized room tone—that place was noisy, man. Almost like it was outside, not inside."

"Might as well have been," Safie agreed. "So . . . which file did you take this part from?"

"Um, gimme a sec." She checked the log. "That'd be ten-fifteen, point two."

"Ten-fifteen was from your iPhone," Safie told me. "You know, what you were shooting right before—that thing happened."

"You can say 'seizure.'"

"Thought you said they weren't sure."

"They're not, it's just . . ." I sighed, ". . . easier than calling it anything else, I guess. Can I see that clip?"

"Sure," said Malin, who'd been listening in with interest—maybe Safie hadn't told her about that part, though I suppose there was no real reason why she should have. She found the clip in question without any trouble, opened it in a new window, started playing. And: *Fade to grey,* I could hear myself muttering through the speakers, as Val Moraine nattered on about cleaning up, tourist-proofing the glass house, making sure it was all nice and safe. *Grey with white highlights, she's working out her palette, that's really* OW, *oh.* Ow, *oh shit, fuck* meeee . . .

"Huh," Malin said, pausing it. "Right there. You hear that?"

Safie frowned. "You mean *me,* or—?"

"Either of you."

I shook my head, still staring at the screen, my own blurred face caught mid-grab, motion-smeary. "I don't hear anything," I said. "But that doesn't mean much; I've been blasting music straight into my eardrums since I was fourteen. What's it sound like?"

"Well . . ." Malin pulled up some sort of further breakdown, fast-forwarded till something caught her eye, stopped. Under the window showing the footage, the sound mix drew multiple jagged, oscillating vector lines across a black field, each in its own colour. Malin pointed to one almost flat line at the bottom edge of the field, then another, wavering in and out of visibility, right at the top. "Here; this, these. There's—something, up *and* down, just around the outer edges of what the mic would be picking up. Between the range and the volume, it makes sense you wouldn't have heard it. But I've got pretty good ears."

"Good thing, given your line of work."

"It's useful, that's for sure. Let me see what I can pull out." Safie looked at me again; I nodded. "Okay, now . . . it probably won't make much sense, 'cause I'm going to have to really push it to make it audible, and besides, it's gappy as heck. . . ."

"Go for it."

She did as asked, lip between her teeth, keyboard and mouse rapidly clicking. All the lines but the two she'd pointed out vanished, and those two then stretched out vertically, like scars straining over skin pulled tight. With a flourish, Malin pulled her headphone jack out and clicked PLAY, the white tracking cursor sliding smoothly from left to right. What came through the speakers sounded like something taken from *deep* underwater, all hiss and click and slosh. Plus a sort of—well, what sounded like a long, low, intermittent tone, echoing up through muddy fathoms.

"Is that a *bell?*" I asked Safie, who shook her head, equally baffled.

"That's about as good as it's going to get," Malin told us. "Sorry."

"Still kind of obscure," Safie agreed. "Could you convert it into something else, though? Data—an image, maybe?"

Malin frowned. "What, like a graphic? I'd need something capable of extracting visuals from a sound-recording medium."

"Do you have a recorder? For cassette tapes, I mean."

"Yeah, sure, somewhere—the system's computerized, but I can plug in pretty much any tech I want; you have to, when you're doing reconstructive and transfer work." She got up, went to the green metal shelving on one wall and began sliding white banker's boxes out to look through them. "You want reel to reel, mini, what?"

"Compact, magnetic tape, analog signal, C-30 or -60. An old-style mix-tape, basically."

"Why?"

Safie opened her mouth, but right at that very moment I snapped my fingers, finally getting it.

"PixelVision," I said, out loud.

You are under Her eye, the Kantorka told me, and thus whatever you make will be touched by Her likewise, always open to her looking and working through it, working Her will on this world; every thing you fashion will be both a mirror and a door, especially during Her hour.

I thought I knew what she spoke of; but how could I, when I did not yet know of Hyatt's very existence? My poor boy, born between the minute and the hour, who felt Her burning hand on his head even inside my belly?

It is always midday somewhere in the world, however, both day and night. And so the Lady's limits truly have *no limit.*

If I had never agreed to go to Dzéngast then we might have lived out our lives in peace, he and I and Arthur, too, for my sins. Arthur knew no better, after all, in begging me to go there, to make my peace, solve my riddle. To stare my father's crime down and spend the rest of my days praying to Christ and his father, like a civilized woman, not staying forever some weak slave of those old, bloody gods in whose names I was first baptized. . . .

He knew no better, my husband, and I know it; he loved me, as he loves me still. He wanted only my betterment, as he wants Hyatt's, never willing to acknowledge him broken since before birth, let alone vowed to another Supreme Being entirely.

Art knew no better, poor man. But I did, even then.
I did.

When Safie brought her PXL-2000 in from the car, Malin's mouth
fell open. "Holy shit, seriously? I haven't seen one of those in . . .
actually, I don't think I've *ever* seen one of those. You got a cassette already?"

"Never leave home without it," Safie told her. "I've been
recording over this one for, like three years now, watching it
degrade: sound to vision. All we have to do is put the sound on
the tape, hook the camera to a monitor, FireWire in the computer, and we can burn the footage right off the screen."

"Handy," Malin said, approvingly. "Okay, let's set 'er up."

I went to the toilet while they assembled the machinery, leaning against the wall for a moment, forehead slick on cool tile. The
static of the day was starting to mount in my head, and I could
feel my pulse like a nervous tic in my temples; not painful yet, but
uncomfortable, like I'd drunk too much coffee and was right on
the edge of a caffeine headache. But even that was weirdly exciting.

By the time I came back out, things were ready to roll.

"Here we go," Safie said, slipping in the tape as I sat back
down.

It started like every PixelVision film I've ever seen—snow
on snow, progressively dirtier. Long bars more than individual
points, gradients of grey; it's like watching something on a really
old videotape, or a slightly scrambled channel, or a dial-and-
antenna TV whose picture tube is giving out. Except here, there
wasn't even a 1920s cartoon version of me to focus on, or the
glass house's broken panes, the background flats I'd been flipping
through—no sort of *image* at all, just an ebb and flow of grain, as
if someone had left the camera angled on one of those fly-blown,
dust-crusted mirrors Mrs. Whitcomb once set up to maximize
the light for shooting.

Back and forth, forth and back, tide-eddying. Up and down
and up again like a rusty wave, dark as old iron.

That same bell still tolling, so slow and old and far away. Plus
a click and a clatter, gradually mounting—or was that just inside

of me, the rattle of my own breath? It sounded like gears grind-ing, like the handle of a Lumière Brothers chronophotographic motion picture camera being cranked, a portable projector run inside a train compartment as the train itself thundered on, unstoppable. Like a movie being constructed one silver nitrate clip at a time, barely enough footage per clip to even make up a reel—forty seconds snatched here, forty-one seconds there, and forty-nine seconds somewhere else, at the absolute most.

"Maybe we should . . ." Malin began after almost a minute, but Safie shushed her violently, a weird lizard hiss. Because some-thing *was* taking shape at last, or seeming to—turning, unfurl-ing, fitting itself together. Something unveiling itself, dark lifting away on every side like a parted curtain, to reveal—

—a wavering, inverse form, flipped white on white from grey on grey, slender and stately, candle flame-tall. Mrs. Whitcomb in her veil, glittering with mirror-shards? But then that twisted as well, flapped sidelong, and there was nothing beneath but an open hole—no face at all, just an absence so bright and cruel it made me almost sick to contemplate. And the smell, that *smell*—

Pareidolia, I thought, admirably calm. *You know, that thing where you connect the dots, see faces everywhere, Basic Iconogra-phy 101: shoes with their tongues out, light-switch noses, grinning coffee makers. Or when your camera suddenly floods with light as you reach the Vinegar House maze's centrepiece-heart, blowing out all images, so you let it droop downwards as you play with the lens and it catches a weird image on the path below, all gravel and dust, scudding cloud-shadow; a child's face looking up at you, submerged and frozen, fossilized in dirt like amber. At least that's what you think you see, playing it back—*

Wait though, that's not me I'm talking about at all; that's Safie. And she didn't show that particular piece of film to me till long after all this was over and done with, or at least the part we both had anything to do with directly. Till it was anything but a sur-prise, for either of us.

Back in the now, meanwhile, the studio lights flickered off, then on, then off again; the camera, Safie's almost-irreplaceable artefact, gave a weird sort of fizzle-*pop* and stopped working.

The sound-file image disappeared, unrecorded, never to be seen again.

Like when the film runs out, that little voice in my mind very quietly said. *Just there and gone in a flash, literally, with nothing left behind . . .*

. . . but a bright, white light.

FOURTEEN

We sat there a moment more, Malin, Safie, and I, just staring at the monitor. None of us sure what came next.

"I don't . . . think we should put that in the presentation," Safie said, finally. To which I nodded.

"Me either," I agreed.

I'd left knowing that Simon and Mom were taking Clark to a Movie for Mommies screening at the Rainbow Market Square—I don't recall the title off-hand, but the sound was always routinely adjusted down in such instances, light adjusted up, social standards relaxed enough to allow for screaming kids and semi-public breastfeeding. Plus most selections came with subtitles, making it the perfect outing for our purposes. So I texted him on my way back then sat in our building's Tim Hortons till he and Clark walked home together, getting all my ducks in a row for tomorrow's presentation. They slid in across me maybe twenty minutes later.

"How'd it go?" Simon asked.

"Very interesting," I said, with no real word of a lie. "I think Jan'll be impressed."

"Can't see that he wouldn't be, given the work you and Safie have put in on everything." I shrugged, but smiled.

As we stepped out of the elevator and came around the corner, however—Clark singing and spinning as ever, pirouetting frantically while doing his best Oogie Boogie from *The Night-mare Before Christmas*—Simon stopped dead, one hand grab-bing Clark by his shoulder, the other braced across my chest. "What—?" I started to ask, but he shook his head.

"Keep him back," he ordered, nodding at our apartment door, which I only now realized was slightly open. Granted, Simon himself left it that way on occasion, usually absentmindedly for-getting to close it hard enough to catch—but only when we were already home, when he was coming in late and laden, and even then he'd usually still put on the latch-lock we'd attached to the door's interior once Clark first started walking.

It took maybe three minutes for Simon to emerge. I distracted Clark by alternately singing along and acting out snippets of dia-logue, playing Sally, Santa Claus, or Jack Skellington to his Oogie. "Nobody's there," he said, phone in hand. "Not too sure if we should call the police, either; place looks like it did when I left, and nothing's been taken that I can see."

"You're sure you just didn't forget to lock it somehow?"

"Almost sure. I mean—" He sighed. "Look, we both know I'm forgetful, but I'd like to think not *this* much. Was there mainte-nance scheduled?"

"No, I don't . . . wait a sec." I strode in, Clark babbling along behind, already pulling off his pants, headed for his bedroom. It only took a few minutes' searching through our bedroom to ascertain my vague presentiment had been correct: the only thing missing was that file box from Quarry Argent, minus the portions of its contents I still had in my backpack.

"You think Wrob Barney did this?" Simon asked, once I'd explained what was making me laugh so hard. I nodded, still grinning. The idea that Wrob might've actually paid somebody to break into our place only to end up with nothing more than a bunch of silver mining-related business correspondence cut with Arthur Whitcomb's fanboy ravings was utterly hilarious to me, considering how easily I could string together a com-posite example of the latter: *dear [whoever,] I allow myself a great admirer of your portraiture, and wonder if you may be sim-ilarly familiar with the art of my wife, who—though female—is brilliant indeed! If your journeying ever takes you to Northern Ontario, therefore, feel very free to come to dinner at our house, even uninvited. . . .*

"What amazes me is that this is all stuff he could've just gotten his own copies of, at the museum," I said as I put the kettle on. "I mean, he was right *there* just yesterday, and that's where the originals live—we didn't even have to pay to get ours done. It doesn't make any sense." I popped a teabag in Simon's cup, pausing. "Then again, maybe he got so mad after I talked to him he just . . . flounced out, and didn't come back. That kinda sounds like him, now I come to think."

"What would be the point of stealing *your* copies, though?"

"At this late date? Man, I don't know; could be simply to slow me down, derail tomorrow's meet with Jan."

"Seriously? Is he *that* petty?"

"From what I've seen? Yeah, I kinda think he is."

The kettle screeched. I thumbed it off and poured, setting it to steep; Simon folded his arms, frowning. "I don't like it," he said. "He was in here, or somebody he *sent* was—what's to stop them coming back? It's creepy."

"I agree, no argument there. But I can't see Wrob doing, like, a home invasion. He waited till we were out, right? That tells you something."

"Yeah, like he has us under surveillance."

"Well, we already knew *that*," I pointed out.

"No, we suspected. Now we know." Simon pulled the door open, pointing. "And look—the lock isn't broken. That means somebody let him in, somebody with a key: not security, even; the concierge, the building manager, someone on the maintenance staff. Hell, he probably bribed them to."

"Makes sense. So?"

"So?" Simon flung up his hands, voice rising. "*So,* if we've established our home is now a place any random rich asshole can walk in off the street and take stuff from, I don't like the idea of our son sleeping here anymore! Or you, for that matter. Or me."

I scoffed. "He's not gonna do it again, Simon. There's nothing left to take."

"What, are you planning to just tell him that? And he'll *believe* you, of course. . . ." He flipped open his own phone, began to type something into a search engine, then stopped and shoved it back in his pocket. "You know what? Forget that shit. I'm going down-stairs—email me a picture of Wrob, if you've got one. Any good face shot will do."

"If you're still thinking of the police . . ."

"No, we don't have enough proof for that yet, like you said. But if I report this in-house, maybe somebody'll recognize his face, and then we *will* have something to take to the police. Or we can at least get him banned."

"All right, fine. If it means that much to you."

"Would've thought it'd piss you off just as much, frankly. If not more."

"I'm—sorry, I guess?—if I can't take Wrob as seriously as all that, not compared to . . ." But here I caught myself, not ready to say what really came to mind: a ghost, a god, legends, and fables. A flickering face on a freezing screen, bright enough to burn out a whole camera. ". . . other stuff," I concluded, at last.

Taking a few shots of every interview subject was second nature for me, even now, so I found the brightest-lit one of Wrob and passed it on without difficulty, accompanied by the typical "swoosh!" of a sent email; Simon heard the chime, nodded in thanks and then left, yanking the door closed behind him, hard enough to rattle it in the frame. The sound drew Clark, who stuck his head out of his room, wide eyed.

"Oh, you don't have to *bang!*" he scolded, giving his own door a couple of swats, before ducking back inside. "No *banging*, Mommy!"

I laughed, despite myself. "No banging," I agreed, and went to make some bacon.

Simon returned looking unexpectedly frazzled some forty-five minutes later. Things had resolved more quickly than he'd expected, he said; the concierge recognized Wrob from the photo, remembered seeing him talking to one of the maintenance staff, and called our building manager Janice at home. Janice told them said staffer—who also happened to be a resident—had just that

day settled up some outstanding financial issues with the building, in cash, and rang off to check up on her. Within twenty minutes, Janice called back to fill both Simon and the concierge in: the
staffer had broken down when confronted, admitting having let
Wrob into our unit; he'd given her the same story he tried on Val
Moraine, that he was working on a project with me, and I'd supposedly given him permission to pick up material. "Janice fired her
right then and there, on the spot," Simon added, voice subdued.

"And you're feeling guilty, is that it?"

"I was angry at Wrob, not some janitor lady trying to make
ends meet who made a mistake."

I nodded, hugging him, holding on till I felt him begin to
relax. "I get it . . . but that was her choice, man, not yours; she
knew the stakes. Not to mention how Wrob's still the one to
blame."

"I guess so, yes."

"I *know* so."

He nodded again and went off to say goodnight to Clark.
While I thought, at the same time: *Yeah, Lois, that's the way. Just
say it loud enough; it might even become true, eventually.*

I started to make dinner.

That night, while Simon snored beside me, I returned to Mrs.
Whitcomb's notebook, determined to read it all the way to the
back if I could, in order to answer any extra questions Jan might
have for me tomorrow. Much like my own adolescent flirtations
with diary-keeping, she mainly seemed to return to her memo-
randum book under stress, so its pages read like a litany of loss:
Hyatt first, then "poor Art," then (debatably) her own mind.

*He is gone, my sweet fool of a boy. And everything I did, all I
tried to do, to draw Her gaze away—useless, from the very beginning, seeing Her hand was laid upon him even before the start. I
knew it when we drew those papers away above his crib, revealing
the hole he had somehow scratched for himself in our walls—that
tiny church, barely fit to crouch in, within which he crawled on
bended knee to worship at Her shrine and sketch out Her blazing
face, again, again, again. . . .*

Oh Christ, why did I ever let Arthur persuade me? I should have

Another massive smear engulfed the rest, much like in Mr. Whitcomb's honeymoon account. I studied it closely, trying to see if there was anything inside the mess of greyscale that gave some hint what she'd been trying to cover up. It was like deciphering one of those 3D optical illusion puzzles—unfocus your eyes, shift slightly in your seat, move the paper at an angle. What emerged was a sprawl of half-sized letters, so close-cramped they bled together, reading—

(but perhaps it would have been better to not be born at all, for him and me both)

I felt a cold thread curl up between my shoulder blades then shook myself slightly, dispelling it. Listened to Simon snort and growl on my one hand, while simultaneously straining to make out Clark's similarly raucous throat music as it filtered down toward us from behind his bedroom door.

Remembering how, on those few occasions when he fell so deeply asleep he went silent, I sometimes stood in his room with the flap on his fire engine bed thrown back, watching him till I saw his chest rise and fall slightly, to reassure myself he was still alive.

Though life with Clark was hard—full stop, no negotiation— I knew that life without him would be impossible. I couldn't even contemplate it.

Back to the document then. The matter at hand.

Arthur will never accept Kate-Mary, the next page began, *whom he calls the Witch of Endor, and that within her hearing. I understand his misgivings, which come mainly from frustrated grief, though I am sure some business instinct as well. Yet I must admit my own assumption to have been that if she truly were the fraud he wishes to brand her, it would be far more efficacious on her part to pass me "messages" from Hyatt without regard to their plausibility, rather than doing what she has at our last three meetings: emerge slowly from her trance's toils, sadly shake her head and apologize, telling me she will accept no payment because she has once more failed to deliver on her part of the bargain.*

Seemingly against all evidence, she maintains she cannot *contact our son, our dear lost creature, and that the reason remains unaltered, if baffling . . . for according to her, she simply cannot* find *him, neither in our waking world nor in the realm beyond.*

Not here, but not there, in other words. Somewhere else. Elsewhere.

"You must make your own methods," she tells me, offering no advice, allowing no coin to change hands between us. If this be the connivance of a charlatan, therefore, in my opinion it is ineffective, to say the least.

"Pretty sure Mr. Whitcomb disagreed with you on that one," I muttered out loud, and paused to shut my eyes for what I thought was a moment before scanning further down. My lids were getting heavy, a dull ache outlining the sockets; sparks had already begun to fizzle at the corners of my gaze, slow-mounting. I needed a break.

The subsequent transition from reading to dreaming was almost instantaneous. I found myself in a long, dim room, vaguely familiar—its atmosphere crisp and sere, paper-parched, lit mainly by a series of upright display cases full of spread books, plus an angled lamp on the desk I sat at. This last part was what tipped me off: the Toronto Public Reference Library's restricted stacks area, a place I hadn't been physically since the age of nineteen, probably, researching something for one of my Ryerson University journalism program electives. Augustans and Romantics, maybe; Pope's "The Rape of the Lock," Blake's *Songs of Innocence and of Experience*, Byron and Shelley and Keats (oh my).

But when I looked down, of course, what I was actually reading was probably Mrs. Whitcomb's next entry, framed through half-shut lashes. It wavered in and out like heat haze, age-browned ink semi-visible at best, and I had to squint to make much sense of it: something more about Kate-Mary, about Lake of the North's very own Spiritualist circle? Yes, but other stuff too, sentences popping out at me like automatic writing in constant revision, shaping and re-shaping themselves before my eyes.

How I do miss Arthur, his vast presence, one sighed, almost audible, even in the dream library's desiccated air. *He sends news of his European doings whenever the post allows, almost monthly, along with his love, and various diversions. This last packet came accompanied by a very new item indeed, one of M. et M. Lumière's cameras, designed for the capture of images in motion. I may use it at Kate-Mary's, with her permission, for those events should be chronicled, if they can be.*

Spring again, with Hyatt gone two years. We are almost at Her time. In Dzéngast—

No, I will not think of that.

I could see my own hand taking notes, skin like bluish cheese, mould touched; see it, not feel it. The air full of orbs. A sudden empty pain all through my head, nostrils freeze dried, the white-gowned librarian leaning over my shoulder, face inverted and head on fire, to murmur: *We have to keep it dim in here, you see, so the paper doesn't degrade . . . these old documents are so fragile, you understand. Like—mummified skin.*

(yes, oh yes)

It's nothing personal. Nothing to do with you, *at all.*

(oh no, I didn't think it was)

Beneath my fingers, the pen scratched on, spitting out words in clumps: this Sunday's circle, our fellowship, join hands, the spirit cabinet, coughing out ectoplasm. *I feel so sorry for these other mothers,* Mrs. Whitcomb wrote, interior voice buzzing in my spit-less throat, *clinging to their grief, loving it publicly as they would their own absent chicks, if they only could. Yet I envy them, too—hate them, almost, when my blackest fits are on me. Sometimes I watch their tears take shape in the developing solution, reduced to unstrung frames, then deliberately hold them up to open light before the fixative sets, and laugh to watch them melt away forever.*

Amongst her visiting protégés, *I see none with even a portion of Kate-Mary's gift, which gives me a bitter satisfaction. Yet this new boy is different, or so she claims; his talent, like mine, expresses itself through the lens—a true mechanical prodigy, a child of this new age, as far removed from the shaking table or* planchette *as I now am from M. Knauff's noxious daubs and horsehair brushes, the paint-encrusted palette knife with which he slit his throat. Some*

*Slavic name, reminding me strongly of God's Ear, before my father's
oddity drove us forth . . . Sidlo, yes. Vasek Sidlo.*

Were there photos? I couldn't recall seeing any. Thought
about rummaging through the box, then remembered it wasn't
here anymore—fucking Wrob. Plus, this was a dream.

(*a dream, just a dream*)

Shit, my head was really *killing* now, sparks cascading every
which-where. The librarian flickered in and out, her aura gone
coronal. Beneath my still-scribbling hand, the print turned
white, the pages black; Sidlo's name humped up, a gasoline-filled
anthill bulging and splitting under pressurized heat, fiery insect-
letters blossoming in all directions.

And now the "librarian" was Mrs. Whitcomb once more,
all dog snarl, corpse lips and nude teeth under her flowing beekeeper's veil, crowned with a nodding mask of bleached flowers.
Leaning closer still, and whispering in my frozen ear—

*I took up Kate-Mary's challenge, gave him an image to play
with for proof of his ability, my hand on his brow like Hyatt in some
fever, or the Lady's on Hyatt's, inside me*

*and sister, sister, when I ran the printed film through its chemi-
cal bath I saw him bloom again, my lovely boy running through
the maze and laughing, my own thoughts pulled like silk through a
skein from my skull to Vasek's, Vasek's to the reel he held*

*Hyatt in miniscule, shadow-rendered, engraved in poison and
flammable with love, with grief*

*my memories struck long distance, match to a ceaseless flame,
and* oh

so impressive

Impressive, yes. That was the word she used. As in, "to
impress."

Vasek Sidlo pressing his mind against the unexposed silver
nitrate film, only to leave his lovely patron's—Mrs. Whitcomb's—
mental fingerprints behind.

Too painful to look up now, so I looked down instead. Back at
my hand. Wanting to lie down in the dark, a wet cloth across my
eyes. Wanting to be anywhere but here—stumbling around blind
through some unfamiliar house, bruising myself on the furniture

to escape what trailed behind with its skirts in the dust, train rattling like snakeskin—

my poor blind child, poor Vasek

yet I was grateful he need never see what I sought to birth back into this world

invisible made visible, lost once more found

—then breaking out through the door into daylight, the black behind my eyes suddenly turned red, straight into a spiky clutch of close-pruned hedge twigs. Feeling my way handful by handful, gravel underfoot, 'round one corner then another, another, another . . .

Further in and faster. Still blind, staggering, too quick to catch myself as I went down, knee popping. The swish of cloth like tearing paper, icy air on my nape.

There is no one who wants you here, sister. Not even yourself. Yet still you come, over and over.

What will I have to do, to drive you away at last?

So bright, so hot. I knew that voice, and desperately wanted not to. Everything hurting just as badly, especially my fingers on the pen I held, wrist bent as though I'd swapped right hand for left. Two completely different sorts of writing, neither anything like my own, trading back and forth like question versus answer, a conversation. Minutes from a meeting I'd never had.

Will it work?

YES

Should I try?

NO

Why not?

NO GOOD WILL COME OF IT

And if I do so anyhow?

WHAT WILL BE WILL BE

Automatic writing, maybe, from one of Kate-Mary des Esseintes' meetings . . . Spiritualists swore by it, if I remembered correctly. I could almost see Mrs. Whitcomb sitting there in the dark, watching Kate-Mary write these lines out: advice from Beyond, dictated by ghosts, or angels. It was her final enterprise she spoke of, I knew in my bones, the one she'd needed Sidlo's help to complete—the train film, burnt up on projection, her only true work. The answer to Lady Midday's fatal enquiry at last, posed under the lit sword's glare, in the field's terrible heat; that awful smell, and that voice. That voice Mrs. Whitcomb had only ever heard once, but had never forgotten.

dare the sword and be spared, then, with Hyatt regained if I do right

(if he still can be)

Down at the very bottom then, this final set of notations, in tinier letters even than the smudge-hidden message I'd plucked from that first entry:

I must, then. It will be as God wills.

As She . . .

Later, looking for proof this phantom conversation ever existed, I'd find only a section of Mrs. Whitcomb's notebook, torn away years—decades—before, all brown and ragged along its edges. But for now, as I snapped awake, I felt nothing but a sense of relief so strong it verged on nausea as my incandescent migraine pain peeled away on contact, leaving me chilled and shaking but otherwise fine; just part of the same dream and nothing more. My skull felt light and dim, empty; I bent forward, panting, palms braced on knees, almost letting the notebook fall unheeded to the floor before I caught it and laid it carefully to one side. Simon must've felt me move, because he turned on his side, groaning— he flopped a hand my way, patting me absently on the thigh, like he thought that'd give me some sort of comfort.

"Y'okay?" he asked, muffled. "Sounded . . . not good."

"Yeah, I just—fell asleep working, I guess. Had a bad dream."

"Thass never nice."

I sighed. "Nope."

Nearby, somebody made a miserable little noise. I looked over to see Clark standing there, almost close enough to touch; his hair stood straight up, sweat-spiked. His wandering eyes were big and glazed, bruisey both underneath and around their edges, while a big blue vein I didn't think I'd ever seen before ran the length of one temple, pulsing slightly. "Oh my God, bunny," I exclaimed, staring, as Simon—spurred by the note in my voice—managed to heave himself upright. "You scared the *crap* out of me, seriously. Are . . . are you okay?"

"I'm okay," Clark claimed, wavery voice sounding anything but. Then he leaned forward, without even a second's warning, and puked all over me.

Though St. Mike's was closer, we eventually ended up at Sick-Kids Hospital, because not only did Clark's vomit smell absolutely horrifying—it had a greenish-black consistency, like dirt and rotting tubers, wholly incompatible with anything we'd actually seen him eat that night—but he was also burning up, so hot that taking his temperature made my hand tingle. Step one was a hasty clean-up and new clothes while Simon called a cab; Step two had us all in the back seat, Clark humped and moaning over our largest plastic salad bowl. By the time we got there, we had more than enough fresh samples for the ER staff to look at. They rushed Clark off, leaving us to wait. I called Mom after composing myself enough to not sound crazy.

"I'm coming," she said, brooking no disagreement. Not that I had any, for once.

The SickKids' waiting room is a massive, echoing space bordered by McDonald's and Starbucks on one side, and downtown Toronto's most central source of gluten-free and non-allergenic snack foods on the other. Here and there, big flat screens blast continual Treehouse TV, though they thankfully turn the volume down at night. Simon and I sat holding hands, neither of us looking at each other, while I looked down at the few things of Clark's I'd thrown into a shopping bag before we left: two fresh changes of clothes, his furry white blanket, various soft toys, some books he liked, his iPad.

"I don't get it," Simon said to nobody in particular. "He seemed fine earlier. Didn't he seem fine?"

"Seemed fine to me," I agreed.

"These things come on fast though, I guess, with kids. They run hot and high, burn through them quickly; I did. I mean . . . I think I remember Mom and Dad saying I did."

"Yeah, I think your mom told me something about that once. Some fever you and your sister got, knocked you both out for a week."

"Uh huh." A pause. "I should call them, probably. Just to keep them in the loop."

"Probably, yeah. You have your phone?"

". . . No."

"Okay, that's okay. Take mine."

"Thank you, hon," he said, voice breaking slightly. I pressed his hand as I passed it over, trying to transmit whatever comfort I could through sheer contact. We both knew that since Simon's parents lived in Mississauga, that'd make getting to SickKids' more difficult for them than for Mom, though hardly impossible; they'd appreciate being copied in, though, even without an immediate diagnosis. Hell for all I knew, Mom had called them already, on her way out the door.

She turned up a few minutes after, just as I was paying for coffee, and hugged me so hard I almost dropped it.

No guilt, not even any questions. Just my mother's arms around me, the way I sometimes tried to put mine around Clark, till he got too uncomfortable to accept it: gave his fake little Disney laugh, vibrating and babbling, then fought his way free again. Leaving me to laugh as well and call him a creep (*I'm not a creep, I'm a dangerous creep, Mommy*), something she never liked, and wasn't exactly afraid to say so—*you think he doesn't hear you, Lois, but he* does; *you need to understand that, and act accordingly.* But what she never got was how I *had* to do it, to minimize the hurt bouncing back my way, this pain I'd long since absorbed—the idea I had no right to feel. To play Bad Mommy to the hilt and wear that title like a joke, call myself it, before anybody else could.

Always thinking, as I did: *I hold as much of my son in my heart at any one given time as I can, Mom, and I'm sorry if that seems like it's not enough. But I have to protect myself, first and foremost: not from him, but from my own . . . disappointment in him, over things he can't even help, over my own reactions to those things. The sheer poison of it. I have to keep myself just far enough apart from him to be able to love him at all, knowing it'll never be as much as he deserves to be loved. And that's not because he's broken, no. Not at all.*

That's because I am.

It'd been three in the morning when I first woke, or thereabouts. Around six—just as the sun was starting to think about coming up—the pediatrician assigned to Clark's case finally came out to talk to us.

"I see he has ASD," she began, flipping through his chart. "Has he ever had a seizure before?" That made us all sit up.

"No!" I snapped. "Did he *have* a seizure?"

"Mrs. Burlingame, we're just not sure. Things got fairly ischemic-looking around the same time the fever broke, but with these kinds of episodes it's about establishing a pattern. Except that we don't really want to *do* that, so . . ."

. . . no way of knowing until we figure out the variables, the inciting factors, Dr. Harrison's voice chimed in, in my head. Followed by my own, replying: *Until I have another one, you mean.*

(*. . . basically, yes.*)

"My *name's* Ms. Cairns," I started to point out, but Mom waved me silent. "Please, doctor," she said, "my daughter's just upset, obviously. You see—"

"She was hospitalized over last weekend, at St. Mike's, for something very similar," Simon hastened to put in as I glared at Mom. "Though, I mean . . . I wouldn't think that was *catching,* exactly."

The doctor blinked. "*You* had a seizure?"

"That's debatable," I muttered, as Mom clarified, helpfully: "Two, actually."

"Um, well—I'm surprised you didn't put that on the intake form."

"Seriously? Why would I? The circumstances were completely—" I shook my head, huffed. "Let's put it this way: high fever aside, I had no reason to connect the dots. We don't even know what happened, let alone why."

"All the more reason to mention it, I'd think. I'm going to need to talk to your physician."

I gave her Harrison's contact info from my phone, which she copied down. She told us there would be tests, surprising exactly no one, then cast disapproving eyes on me and walked away. In her wake, Mom looked my way like she definitely wanted to lodge some criticism of her own—but thankfully, Simon's phone chimed before she could.

"That's Mom and Dad," he told us, checking it. "They're coming down, should be here by ten. They're taking Dad's car."

Mom nodded. "Good." To me: "I still don't understand why you wouldn't—"

"Yeah, I get that, Mom."

"I mean, come on, Lois. Didn't it seem . . . pertinent?"

I looked at her for a long moment. "No?" I said, finally.

"Lois . . ."

Simon raised his hands, placatory. "Not all autistic kids have seizures, Lee; very few, in fact. The ones who do, it usually starts early, before diagnosis, even. And Clark's never done anything like this before, not even when he was a baby—remember that ear infection, back when he was three months old? That's the highest fever he's ever had, until now."

Mom shook her head, clearly frustrated. "There's no consistency," she said. "'One kid with autism . . .' Oh, *shit*." She turned away and sat down abruptly, burying her face in her hands. Simon sat down too, and put his arm around her, saying nothing.

I've never been able to figure out if that was a guy thing, a Burlingame thing, or just Simon—that reflex instinct to distract yourself from your own pain by trying to console someone else—just like I've never been able to figure out whether I find it more endearing or off-putting. Right now, though, even as I fell back into myself in my own autonomic response (always to shut down, hard), I realized that more than anything else—I envied it.

Simon was right, I told myself: our presenting symptoms were wholly different—Clark never blacked out, never acted as if he had a migraine; I'd had no preliminary fever, no nausea. And up till last week nothing like this had ever happened to either of us, so what was the likelihood we shared some neurogenetic time bomb that only went off now? It was stupid; it was impossible.

The two things couldn't have anything to do with one another, really. . . .

Unless they do, a small, flat, pitiless voice from the back of my brain said while I stared as though hypnotized at the empty chair across from me. *The same way whatever happened to Hyatt Whitcomb had* something *to do with what happened to Mrs. Whitcomb, in her father's field, or that town, Dzéngast—because she thought it did, didn't she? So much so she spent the whole rest of her life trying to set that story straight,* record *it, like a warning: making the film over and over again, writing down the fairy tales, telling and re-telling it. Like she was trying to get something right . . . trying to* fix *something.*

But no. Because even if she had thought that, all it meant was that she was wrong. Or crazy, like so many brilliant, creative people. Or desperate, like anyone in her place would be. Because stuff like that just didn't *happen.* Ever. And even if it did—

(*even if it does*)

—it surely didn't happen *again.*

And now I really did feel something—not just annoyance, not just emptiness. I felt cold, ice filled. I felt . . . scared.

Slowly, over this mounting sense of horror, I gradually became aware Simon was murmuring to Lee, his voice oddly threaded with laughter. For a moment I found myself flashing back to long childhood rides stuck in the backseat of my parents' car, telling myself stories to live inside while Lee and Gareth argued, focusing so intently on the pattern of the seats it felt like I could fold myself down inside it and disappear for hours. More than once, they'd had to yell at me to get me to re-emerge. But then Mom laughed, too, a chuckle, watery but real, and I relaxed.

I leaned forward, turned my head slightly, and saw that Simon was flipping through photos on the iPad—the latest photos Clark must have taken in his endless ongoing series, fifty to a hundred mostly repeated images in a row: dust-bunnies under the bed; close-ups of the slightly decayed wicker trunk in the bathroom where we kept our towels; the too-bright smiling faces of his Thomas the Tank Engine shelf buckets; light through the window of his fire engine bed-tent. Then, some reverse shots he'd obviously taken on my laptop's webcam, posing and chatting away, flirting with himself: Disney prince faces, Disney princess faces. Sometimes he applied effects. He was particularly enamoured of the psychedelic colour shift that made everything look like a Kirlian photograph, all vibrant lime green and purple auras, but he also liked the doubling mechanism, which made one half of the screen mirror the other.

"What's *that?*" Mom said, suddenly.

I was already drifting away again, expecting Simon to answer her. But the seconds stretched out and he didn't, until—finally, he did.

"I . . . really don't know," he said, tone unnerved enough to jerk me awake. "That's weird."

"What?" I asked.

They both glanced over, startled. Mom opened her mouth, but Simon forestalled it by handing me the tablet. "Have a look," he said, and sat back.

I studied it a minute, maximizing the photo in question— Clark, dancing in his bedroom, the iPad propped on his bed, angled to record while he watched himself in his screen—and turned it in my hands, this way and that. Trying to figure out exactly what I was supposed to be looking at beyond the obvious: my son's bony chest and flappy, jigging limbs, his welcome crocodile grin . . .

And then, all at once, I saw it—recognized it. What it had to be. It, her: She.

She, with a big "S."

In the corner of Clark's room, by the door, stretched almost two-dimensional—so flat, somebody who didn't know his room might've mistaken it for a painting on the wall—was something almost exactly like what I'd seen on the monitor with Safie and Malin: the sound-file image, Safie's PixelVision spectre. Except instead of shades of grey, it was in brass and gold and fierce, bright silver-white, so pale it was almost blue tinged.

Lady Midday, standing in the corner of Clark's room with her wings hanging down around him, looking in at him, eyes fixed and inhuman, sharp as a stooping hawk's. *Every angel is terrible,* as Rilke says, with her no exception to that rule.

And Clark was *smiling* up at her, with full eye contact like he knew her, like he welcomed her. Like she was his usually invisible friend. As widely as he grinned at his "friend Daddy" . . . or, once in a while, at me.

"What's wrong?"

I almost didn't recognize Simon's voice. At the sound, however—as angry as it was worried—everything inside me locked up; I could only imagine what my face already told him. But I couldn't think where to start, how to say any of it, without proving I was exactly as crazy as I was already terrified I might be. I couldn't not look at him—owed him that, at least—but even as our eyes met, terror meeting confusion in a crackling spark, the only thing I could manage by way of a reply was: ". . . Nothing."

Broadcasting to both of them, as I did, with my hunched shoulders, avoidant gaze, knotted hands, and drawn-taut mouth: *don't ask don't ask don't ask . . .*

Simon would've probably have backed off if it had been just him. But not Lee. Not my mom, with her innate knack for picking up on exactly what people least wanted to give away, and her utter lack of any reluctance to call them on it, especially when she thought it mattered.

"Answer the question, Lois."

"Nothing," I said. "I—" My phone beeped with a calendar alert—thank Christ—prompting me to look down, almost to smile. I stood up, grabbing for my bag. "I gotta go."

"Excuse me?"

"*Go,* that's what I said. I have to—"

—get away from you, from him. Because if I can get far enough away, maybe this thing will go with me, and leave you guys alone; it's followed me this far, after all. It, she—

(*She*)

Unlikely. I saw the word inscribe itself across the inside of my head, in Arthur Macalla Whitcomb's looping scrawl: letters run together, brain knit with bone. *So, so very . . . unlikely.*

"—go, I have to *go.* I have an appointment."

"No you don't!"

"Yes, I do." I shoved my phone at Simon so he could read the message alert, and then stood and gathered my coat in one arm while shrugging my knapsack half on with the other. "At the NFA, Mom; nine thirty meeting, Safie and me. We're presenting to Jan Mattheuis, to get him up to speed on the Mrs. Whitcomb project. It's been set up for a week."

"You've got to be kidding."

"No, I'm really not—Simon, you remember, right?" I appealed to him, and while he didn't exactly nod, he didn't *not* nod, either. "C'mon, Mom, what do you think I've been doing this all for? I *have* to. This isn't the kind of appointment you can miss."

"Your son is in *hospital,* Lois. I somehow think they'll understand, if you—"

"No, they won't."

"You don't know that."

"Oh no, you're right, of course; what was I thinking? 'Cause there's nothing in this whole wide world that *I* know, and you just don't."

Mom recoiled a bit in her seat, as if from a slap; the venom of my words even splashed onto Simon, who stood as well, putting a hand on my sleeve. "Lois," he said. But I was still looking at Mom, her face gone rigid in a way that made me want to snort, or maybe give a nasty little grin. Neither would be the smartest move in the world, but after the night I'd just had, I have to admit I wasn't feeling all too smart.

So—

"What is it you think is gonna happen if I don't stay?" I asked her. "Like if I'm not within a certain physical range of him the whole time, he'll never wake up again? All we know is they don't know *anything* yet, so he'll either get better or he won't, full stop—and nothing I do, here or anywhere else, is going to make a damn bit of difference. Any more than you being there, or Simon *not* being there, in St. Mike's, made a difference to what happened with me."

My voice had gotten louder than I'd intended; both Simon and Mom had backed up a step. Simon was taking the slow deep breaths he used to stay calm, and I could half-read his thoughts already: *Easy, easy, she's just blowing off steam, don't take it personally.* But Mom just blinked, mouth working like—she couldn't figure out what to say, for once. At all.

"Why would you say that to me, Lois?" she said at last. "This isn't you. It's *cruel.* You were never cruel."

Fear, I guess, I thought. *And pain. And disappointment.*

The thing I heard myself say, however—voice gone suddenly hollow; tired, as though pithed—was: "I don't mean to be. But I'm going, Mom; least I can do, so I'm doing it. I'm always good for that."

'Bye.

And I shrugged my backpack the rest of the way on, turned, and left.

I think I might've been half-hoping one of them would say something; I was mostly relieved, yet simultaneously depressed, when they didn't. Still, as so often happens, reality conspired against my dramatic exit when, outside by the elevators, I heard rapid footsteps and turned to see Simon trotting up to me. "Oh, God," I sighed. "Simon, I'm so sorry about all this—all *that*, too. I didn't mean—"

"Lois, look, it's okay—" He caught himself, with a snort. "Well no, actually, it's *not* okay, but we'll talk about it later. Here." He held out my iPhone and I swore; I'd completely forgotten giving it to him. "It's Safie, for you. She called about ten seconds after you left."

I swore again then thanked him and took it.

"Hey," I said. "Sorry if I'm late, I was just on my—"

"Forget that," she replied. "You seen the news yet?"

"No, why?"

"Just watch it, Miss."

"Um, all right. What station?"

A pause passed between us, stretching far longer than I expected it to.

"Any should do," she said.

That was how I found out.

SCREENING

FIFTEEN

It's amazing, really, when you think about it: film has a language all its own, a vocabulary of visual storytelling, and it was people like Mrs. Whitcomb and her contemporaries who invented it over an amazingly small period of time. Everything since has been nothing but elaboration, technical change. George Méliès laid the basis for every special effect we have today.

I'd love it if real life came equipped with those sorts of narrative short cuts, you know? Especially when things get complex, start to accelerate, just like they will—like they *did*. Irises, fades, dissolves, wipes . . . smash cuts to black.

If life worked that way, then that's where this chapter could start, right now: a black screen then a title card—TWENTY-FOUR HOURS LATER. Because that'll be when I wake up, back in hospital again. And the light's on, I can tell it is; feel it on my skin somehow, like a warm touch, a red intimation inside my skull. But I can't see it, because I can't see anything.

I'm blind.

And somebody's sitting beside my bed, holding my hand very gently. And I want to believe it's Mom—I really do. But even then, even right then, I know it's not.

And then there's a breath, near my ear. Somebody leaning in. That voice I know so well, inside the hollow of my own ear. Saying, sadly—

Sister, I tried. I tried so very hard. But you wouldn't listen, and now here you are.

Here we are, in the dark, together.

If my life was a movie, this is the exact moment—

(this space between frames, flickering past too fast to see, conveying only the illusion of forward motion in the service of a closed loop, a forever-predestined end)

—where I'd scream out loud.

Smash cut to black again; rewind, re-set. Another title card.
TWENTY-FOUR HOURS EARLIER.

Moments after Safie suggested I get myself to a TV set, Simon and I stood in the SickKids waiting room once more watching CITY TV's all-day local news coverage on the screen nearest the door, having managed to persuade the staff member managing the information desk to switch the channel. Or rather, *I* watched— iPhone still clutched in one hand with Safie on speaker, providing occasional commentary—while Simon surfed, cross-checking as many sites as he could on the iPad. Mom hovered beside us both, obviously still not happy with my previous behaviour, but having perked up considerably when we came back in.

"What's wrong?" she'd asked, seeing my expression; "I don't know," I'd replied. Then added, hastily: "Not yet."

Well, now we did, all of us—the story was pretty much the same on every media forum, and it was bad. It was, in fact, the very worst.

"Story's the same pretty much everywhere," Simon told me, which wasn't much of a surprise. I nodded, eyes never leaving the news anchor's face as the fifteen-minute mark passed, and the tale regurgitated itself once more:

Though their investigation has yet to be completed, Metro Toronto Fire Department spokespeople believe the fire broke out around 3:00 A.M. By 3:15, reports of the NFA offices being "engulfed in flame" were pouring in, and firefighters arrived on-site within minutes. It took until six this morning to extinguish the blaze, which appears to have started while a silver nitrate

selection from the BFA's Ontario Film Recovery Project was being
screened. Silver nitrate film is highly flammable, especially once
it's reached what experts call "the vinegar stage," a stage of decay
at which the film can literally combust if you attempt to screen
or copy it. . . .

Three A.M., I thought. That would've been right about when I
woke up, first noticed Clark looking ill, or makes no never-mind.
A moment before he vomited up what looked like half of Mrs.
Whitcomb's garden and kicked this whole trip off.

"You know what this means, right, Miss?" said Safie, over the
phone.

It meant that everything was gone, all Mrs. Whitcomb's films
in one fell swoop—the Hell Hole cache, the Japeries. Up in a puff
of noxious, toxic smoke, as though they—or *she,* for that matter—had never even existed. And why? Because some fucking
idiot just *had* to open the box. To run Schrodinger's Cat through
a projector and see with their own eyes whether or not it was
alive, dead, or (somehow) both at fucking once.

"Why the hell would they have been screening one of those
films in the first place?" I asked. "Jan told me they'd all been digitized already, half of them by Wrob Barney, remember? Totally
unnecessary to look at them again."

"Maybe it was from a new cache, nothing to do with our project at all."

"Maybe, yeah. Christ." I paused, poised to relax—but at that
very moment, something else occurred to me. "Wait, though . . .
where *are* those digital copies, anyhow? They're okay, right?"

Safie took an uncomfortably long beat before answering.
"Well . . ."

"Oh, you have *got* to kidding me."

Though I couldn't actually see her pained shrug, I knew it was
there, nonetheless. "Jan kept it all on the mainframe, which was
in the NFA offices. He told me that the last time we talked, right
after your—whatever-it-was. When I asked about backup. Said it
was the safest available option."

"What? I . . . didn't an *off-site* backup make more sense? I
mean, I'm not exactly an expert, but—the *fuck*?"

"Budget cuts." Adding, as I made an almost-indescribable noise: "Man, I don't *know*. But I'm guessing they probably weren't expecting *that* to happen!"

I nodded slightly, only then noticing I must have been unconsciously rubbing the middle, ring, and pinkie fingers of my free hand across the area between my eyebrows for some time—half grooming and half scratching, trying my best not to get obsessive with it. "Well, we're gonna have to get in touch with Jan, obviously," I made myself say, after a moment. "Set it all up again, the presentation; we could do it at Malin's maybe, right? Yeah, that'd work. Gotta think, gotta plan, gotta . . . gotta figure out . . ."

"Miss Cairns—" Safie broke in, gently, as I babbled on. "Miss, *Lois,* just listen, okay? Please."

Took a bit more effort, but eventually, I stopped and did. "Yes," I said, finally, while Simon and Mom watched me do so—equally still, equally careful. Equally worried by what they saw. Safie seemed to know it as well, which might be why she took a few beats more to let me calm down even further. Before she finally sighed, and explained—

"Jan was *in* there, Lois. When the fire started."

". . . Yes?"

"That's right, yeah."

"Uh huh, okay. And?"

"He's dead."

"I'm so sorry, Lois," Mom said, and I nodded, slightly; it was good of her, especially considering what a bitch I'd been not a quarter hour previously, but I could barely feel anything. Too many climactic revelations, I guess, with God only knew how many more yet to come—a kind of Hollywood shell shock, all plot twists and car crashes. Like the third act of a Michael Bay movie.

"Thank you," I replied, numb from the heart on down.

Remember, I didn't know about Wrob Barney's previous boyfriend at this point—the guy before Leonard Warsame, who told Leonard he suspected Wrob of having essentially burned down a section of Queen Street West just to force him out of Toronto. The guy who heavily implied that when pressed against the wall—or even sometimes when not—Wrob had little compunction about using any method that came to mind to get whatever he wanted done, with arson probably not plumbing the full depth of that particular bag of tricks.

As I stood there studying CITY TV's looped footage of the scene at the NFA, however—first engulfed in flames, then sodden, black and smoking, and eventually hollowed like a scooped-out gourd made from melted glass and heat-bent steel—all I could see was what they weren't showing: Jan Mattheuis's blistered corpse under a sheet, or shoved in a body-bag; Mrs. Whitcomb's life's work as a filmmaker wiped away like ash. Twelve thousand dollars' worth of grant money I'd already spent at least five of developing a documentary whose subject matter would now be even more difficult to "prove" than before—and how the hell I was going to pay that back, if the government decided to demand it after whatever enquiry was to follow, I simply did not know. Et cetera, et cetera.

Two weeks ago, I'd been high on potential, possibility. I'd gotten into a territorial pissing contest with Wrob over the phone, and then slapped his face with my metaphorical dick long-distance and run away laughing. And sure, within a few more days I'd been convulsing on the glass-house floor listening to my brain sizzle beneath the unbearable weight of Lady Midday's hot, invisible regard, but much like poor Art Whitcomb, I really hadn't known any better, not even then. And none of the weirdness I'd encountered along the way since had really ever challenged that initial sense of elation, of god-touched transfigurative *ekstasis*, of seeing and being seen . . . right up until the moment I realized I might not end up being the *only* person who suffered for being reckless and arrogant enough to drag the former Giscelia Wròbl's long-buried, literally damned art up into the pitiless noontime light, that is.

I could have borne it with equanimity if the only person paying the price was me—because on some level, I'd been expecting to pay a price for something, sooner or later. Knowing on some level that I didn't deserve any better, and never had; believing, on much the same level, that I probably deserved worse.

When did you figure out you hated yourself, Lois? I wondered yet again. *Or better still, and far more relevantly, in context . . . when was it you started thinking you were essentially unlovable, even by yourself?*

I mean, what the hell kind of person can't even manage to be their own friend, for Christ's sake?

Wrob did this, I told myself, looking at the damage the fire had left behind. But I was the one who gave him a "reason," fucked though it might be—the one who kicked him when he was down then laughed at him. The one who let him think this might be the only way left to win.

Which meant, in the end . . . this was basically my fault. Most, if not all of it; in thought, if not in deed.

"Wrob Barney do this?" Simon asked me sidelong, mimicking my own thoughts uncannily, as his parents arrived. I shook my head.

"No," I replied, just to hear it out loud. "*I* did, if anybody."

I knew he wanted me to elaborate, but there wasn't time—we immediately switched into meet-and-greet mode instead, his mom hugging me while his dad patted her back, eyes meeting mine, so forgiving I abruptly wanted to weep. Simon explained Clark's situation, or what little we knew about it, till he got to a point where Mom could comfortably take over, allowing us to move backwards, bending our heads together once more.

"Listen, hon," Simon began, quiet enough that hopefully none of them would overhear, "I really do get this has been a pretty bad day for you, in more ways than one—but considering it hasn't exactly been all wine and roses for me either, before you go ahead and take nebulous responsibility for all the drama in our lives, you maybe need to explain exactly what you just said."

I looked at him for a long moment, feeling a sort of existential despair at the very prospect. After which I pulled myself together, nodded, and replied, "You're right. It's . . . past time, really."

He blinked, possibly surprised by the ease with which I'd agreed with him. He nodded, jerking his head back toward the family group. "You take a john break, splash some water on your face or something—I'll beg some alone time, meet you wherever you want after that. What's your preference, Starbucks in here or that Tim's outside, on the corner?"

"Let's say Tim's. We need a bit of distance, probably, if I'm going to tell you everything."

"All right." Shrewdly: "And *are* you?"

". . . I'll try."

"Good enough," he said.

I had my stuff with me, of course, in preparation for that presentation I was now never going to give: the Mr. and Mrs. Whitcomb material, all ready for Jan's perusal, while Safie supplied the visual component. So I spread it out on the table in front of Simon instead, and walked him through what we'd discovered thus far. The basics took about twenty minutes, by which time Safie—who I'd texted from the SickKids' bathroom—had arrived, and my husband (*poor Simon*, as dead Iris Dunlopp W. would no doubt have called him) was starting to look more than a trifle existentially bitch-slapped.

"None of this can possibly be *true*, though," he protested. I just smiled a little grimly.

"That's exactly what I said, and more than just the once," I replied.

Simon opened his mouth again, but was distracted when his phone beeped. While he checked his text messages, Safie and I exchanged glances, one of her eyebrows hiking in a weird mixture of sympathy and humour—we were both used to this shit by now, at least halfway, which was kind of a scary idea in itself.

"Who is it?" I asked as Simon looked back up. His face had gone blank, white, apparently even more gobsmacked than before.

"Mom—Lee, I mean. *Your* mom. Says the doctor had an update on those tests."

"Great. And?"

"Um, well, the stuff he threw up? They say it was dirt, and, like, some sort of bulb—a flower, probably. Those can be poisonous, right?"

"Dirt, like, soil? Earth?" He nodded. "Simon, that's crazy; Clark doesn't eat that sort of shit, ever, not even when other kids do. I mean, we can barely get him to eat real food."

"I know."

"And flower bulbs? Where the hell would he have found *those,* in our neighbourhood, our building? In the middle of the night?"

"I don't *know,* Lois. Not from the ghost of Mrs. Whitcomb, though, I'm pretty damn willing to bet, or some kind of fucking not-so-dead pagan *god*—"

"Lady Midday," Safie put in, helpfully.

I hissed at her to keep quiet, almost automatically, but it was too late; Simon exploded. "Holy Christ, what's she supposed to be, Lord Voldemort?" he snapped, then caught himself, brought his voice down as people at neighbouring tables glanced curiously our way. "Lois, c'mon, here! You think all the blood vessels in your eyes broke because the *Poludnice* put her hand on you in your sleep? Think you had a seizure because you saw something you shouldn't have, something that doesn't even show up on regular film?"

"Not *that* time," I agreed. "But what we saw on Clark's iPad . . . that looked fairly visible to me. You and Mom sure thought so, anyways."

"That was a *glitch,* Lois—bent light, or something. Clark fucking around. It reminded you of this other thing, you freaked out, end of story."

"Don't you think I'd love to think that? But what about what happened to Clark, then—his seizure or whatever. A stomach full of mud and tubers, all over our bed sheets and floor—that's not an optical illusion, exactly."

"Not exactly, no, but it's not what you're saying it is, either. 'Cause it damn well *can't* be."

"Can't it?"

Simon sighed, frustrated. "No, Lois. It just can't. Because the alternative . . ." He trailed off then wiped his face and began again. "Look, God knows I don't write off the supernatural by default; I can't and believe what I believe. But even the supernatural has rules. Take demonic possession, right? There are patterns, stages—infestation, obsession, spiritual corruption, personality shifts, and then full-on pea soup crap. Look at it afterwards; it makes a certain sort of ill sense. All *this* stuff, though . . . it's contradictory, paradoxical. There's no logic to it."

"Yeah, well, maybe magic's like that. Metaphor made real."

"Fucking *magic?* Listen to yourself!"

"Well, what would *you* call it?"

"I'd call it you being already in recovery, overextended as all hell, upset over Clark getting sick, your project being derailed, your friend—this guy you pinned all your hopes on—being *dead*; traumatized, and understandably so! And trying to take control of everything, the way you usually do: by making up a reason, some problem to solve, something to fight. Making yourself—"

"Crazy?" I asked, toneless.

Simon looked at me then looked away, obviously struggling to choose his next words carefully; Safie simply sat there, silent, studying us both. ". . . I didn't say that," he eventually replied.

"You just think I'm making it all up, that's all."

"Miss Cairns," Safie hastened to point out, "he didn't say *that*, either."

A lag followed, during which I stared at my own hands clasped loosely in my lap. Thought vaguely about the odd fact I'd never previously noticed how my fingers and Clark's fit together in almost the exact same way, from crossed thumbs to slightly crooked little fingers; wondered if he, too, would have twinges of arthritis in his knuckles by the time he was my age, if he ever got there. Then wondered how it was he could have ended up with both Simon's long second toe and my own s-curved, squashed fourth one, so bent it almost fit underneath my middle, which I'd inherited in turn from Mom and she from her father. Genetics really are an amazing thing.

"All right," Simon began again. "Say what you're saying some validity—"

"Say it does."

"—even then, what're the odds? Mrs. Whitcomb had a direct encounter with Lady Midday back when she was a kid, right? She was touched, chosen—gifted. All you did was watch her films, find out her story, and Safie, here—she did those things, too." Switching focus: "Back me up, Ms. Hewsen; been seeing evil angels, hearing ghosts? Puke up any tubers recently?"

"No," Safie admitted.

"Okay, so there we go. Maybe the films aren't cursed, after all."

"Why'd she try and throw them down a Hell Hole then?" I asked.

He shrugged. "You said she probably wasn't happy with them—that they didn't do what she wanted them to. That's enough reason, I guess."

"Uh huh, sure. And then a fucking *tree* just happened to grow out of the hole around them, to make sure somebody like Jan Mattheuis could stumble across them. . . ."

"It's not impossible. Unlike some other things I could mention."

I blew out a breath, impatiently. "Holy *shit,* you can be a stubborn ass, Simon Burlingame," I snapped, which actually made him smile, at least slightly.

"Takes one to know one," he replied.

I'm not sure where the conversation would've gone from there, if anywhere. But luckily enough (for—as ever—certain values of luck), that's when my phone rang.

I picked it up, cleared my throat, pressed Accept.

"Yes?"

"Hi, Lois," Wrob Barney's voice greeted me, all too familiar. Gleeful.

"Thought I blocked you," I said.

"My old number, sure. This is a burner. I've got a drawer full of 'em."

"Very gangsta. What do you want, Wrob?" At the name, I saw Simon's eyebrows shoot up while Safie's face fell, appalled. I switched to speaker, so they could both hear what I was hearing. Wrob must've known, but he didn't seem to care; that didn't bode well.

"I'd like to meet. Face to face. Talk things out." Wrob's voice was smug, so relaxed he sounded almost benevolent. "Now that I know where you stand, and you know where *I* stand—or you will in a minute—there really isn't any reason we can't be more cooperative on this, right? I mean, given the amount of work you've already done, I'd be an idiot to cut you out completely."

"Out of what?"

With a theatrically heavy sigh: "The *project*, of course. All I ever wanted was proper credit, and now that that's all fixed, there's no point in being vindictive. If this is the only way forward for both of us, I'm willing to let bygones be bygones if you are."

I couldn't stop myself from reflexively rolling my eyes at his arrogance, no matter how oblique it might be. "Seriously, Wrob, what the actual fuck are you talking about? Yeah, this thing with the NFA—with *Jan*—it's a setback, but the material we've put together is still way ahead of anything you could've possibly . . ."

But here I trailed off as some sort of *oh-shit* realization signal suddenly popped up behind Safie's eyes; she began shaking her head frantically, pulled her laptop from her bag, flipped it open. "Hold on a minute," I told Wrob, curtly, while she dug out the DVD I'd seen her and Malin working with yesterday, popped it into the laptop's disc drive, and waited till the media-player program activated. With a glance back at me, she clicked PLAY, and I leaned in to watch, with Simon—intrigued despite himself—angling to look over my shoulder.

For a moment, the screen showed nothing but blue. Then it flashed to a stuttering, staticky ghost image of washed-out negative colour that broke apart in great swathes of smeared pixel clouds, then flashed back to blue, over and over again. Intermittently, I'd catch sight of a distorted image that looked familiar—Safie's face, the Vinegar House's outlines, a page of Mrs. Whitcomb's handwriting stretched out into spaghetti, a blur that might have been a painting of Lady Midday. Abruptly, however, everything cut to black, after which three words appeared onscreen in a large, white sans serif font, like a PowerPoint caption on an empty slide:

TEXT ME

WROB

"Shit," Safie blurted, slumping; Simon covered his eyes with one hand and turned away, muttering under his breath. I just stared, numb, face rigid. I picked up the phone again.

"How . . .?" I began.

"Same way as always, Lois—money."

He *was* gloating now, unattractively so, though I suppose that in a weird way, he had every right to. After all, he'd won.

It would be more than a year—summer after next, in fact—before Safie, who'd been fruitlessly trying to phone, text, and email her ever since she'd first reviewed the DVD, ran into Malin by sheer fluke on Yonge Street one afternoon, outside the Eaton Centre. Confronted, Malin would admit that when she'd left the studio that night she'd found Wrob outside, literally waving his wallet around. Ruining our DVD and turning over our files had netted her enough to finally pull off a long-planned move to Los Angeles, and she saw no point in lying about it, let alone apologizing. Frankly, she'd never expected to see any of us again.

"I didn't have anything to do with what happened to Jan, by the way," Wrob added after a moment. "Hell, I'm insulted you'd even *think* that, Lois; Jan and me . . . we had something. I'm gonna miss him every day. But I understand. You're not very a trusting person, I've found."

"Don't trust *you*, that's for sure. Which seems to have been a pretty good call, considering."

"Yes, well; that's all behind us now, or can be. And one advantage of working with me, by the way, amongst many—I've got a far bigger budget than the NFA, but not even a quarter as many rules about how best to spend it."

"Working with you," I repeated.

"Yup." He paused, probably for effect, before adding: "Well, okay . . . *for* me."

At that, Simon threw up his hands. "This is Simon Burlingame, *Mr.* Barney," he spat. "Lois's husband. I—" Here he stopped, and I could hear Wrob's voice cut in, tinny, snarky; I couldn't quite make out the words, but the mocking tone was clear. Simon's face reddened. "Yes, well, seeing you just boasted about ruining someone else's work, I'm not surprised that's your opinion—but it's also not much of an incentive to enter into *any* sort of business arrangement, either. So here's *my* offer: stay the hell away from my wife, or I'm getting a restraining order. And don't call this number again."

He slapped the phone back on the table and sat there fuming. Safie's eyes were wide; she shot me a look that could've been labelled "the fuck?" But I simply leaned forward, and asked, "What'd he say? The thing that got you so pissed off, I mean."

Simon huffed. "I don't see the point—"

"Humour me."

"All right. He said, 'Oh hey, Simon, nice to finally meet you. Too bad you married a full-on bitch.'" I laughed, which made his eyebrows lift. "This is funny to you?"

I felt like saying *Funnier than everything else, for sure*, but ended up simply shaking my head instead.

"Simon," I said, "I could give a flying fuck about Wrob and his drama—or the project, at this point, believe it or not. Right now, it's about one thing: doing what I can to get Clark out of harm's way. *Whatever* I can. You're with me on that, right?"

"Of course," he snapped back. "Look, whether I accept all this haunted film crap or what, we could still stand to spend a week or two away from here, in Florida, maybe; I could use my extra vacation days, the ones I was saving for Christmas." I shook my head again, making him trail off, groaning. "Oh, *come on*, man . . ."

"*No*, Simon. Look at the evidence—Mrs. Whitcomb changed continents, twice, and that didn't turn out to be a goddamn bit of help in the end. Besides which, the absolute last thing we need is Clark getting sick south of the border, down where health care's a pay-as-you-go game your insurance won't even cover!"

My voice rang in my own ears with this last part, and I suddenly realized just how loud I must have gotten, yet again—enough so that other Tim's customers were either turning around to look at me or trying to ignore me by "studying Mars," as my dad would've said. I rubbed my face and found it wet, felt a surge of guilty, painful rage that lit up my cheeks.

Christ, I thought, *I would cut this useless, stupid excuse for love right out of me this very minute, slash this choke-hold knot around my neck with a rusty fucking knife if I had to, if I believed doing it'd help, even a little bit.*

"Lo," Simon began, softer, but I raised a hand to stop him. "No," I replied. "Don't you get it? This is my fault, right from the start: me. Clark, fucking *Jan*—the Vinegar House, the NFA. My mistake, my . . . error. I kicked it off, I kept it going, I didn't listen, and here we are. So I have to do whatever I can to solve it, because it has to stop, all of it—it just has to. *Because it is my fault.*"

"No, Lois."

"Yes."

"*No,* Lois. It's not." Beside him, Safie seemed to be nodding as well, but it was hard to tell; my eyes were too blurry, the light too strong. "Lo, honey, look at me. This didn't happen because of you. Nothing that happens to Clark . . . nothing Clark does, or is . . . is specifically because of you. It doesn't work that way."

How do you know, though? I wanted to throw back at him. *How* can *you? 'Cause I know I don't, and can't.* Nobody *can.*

Then again, who fucking knew, right? Maybe it was that whole "faith" thing he was thinking about. Maybe *that's* what made him sound so sure of himself, the bastard.

"This does," is all I could manage by way of a reply—soft and choked, head bent, tears spilling over once more. "This does."

(*This is.*)

He rose then, pulled me up, folded me in; Safie stood too, putting one comforting hand on my shoulder. And we stood like that for a while, all three of us, me shuddering in the centre.

"Jesus, if only we could figure out what Mrs. Whitcomb was actually trying to *do* with those films," I said once I'd calmed down enough to resume my seat, "why she thought it wasn't working—maybe we could . . . finish it, somehow. *Make* it work."

"Complete the circuit," Safie said. Simon snorted.

I nodded. "Something like that, sure. I just wish we could *ask* her, directly."

Safie cleared her throat. "Well," she began, "we still can't do that, but I might've found something almost as good. I meant to tell you at the meeting, you and Jan, back before I saw the news: I found him, that guy, the kid Mrs. Whitcomb thought was gonna help her make the ultimate *Lady Midday* movie. Vasek Sidlo."

My mouth dropped open. Simon frowned. "Wouldn't he be like a hundred years old?"

"Over a hundred, yeah—checked it out, though, and it's definitely him. Started with whitepages.ca, then cross-referenced; there's only three V. Sidlos in the entire GTA, and of those, only one's listed as an interview subject and 'asset' over at the Freihoeven Institute's ParaPsych Department."

"The what with the what, now?" I said.

"Toronto's very own home-grown think tank for the Study of Weird-Ass Shit, basically. I got their name from Soraya, in case you're wondering." Which made sense, given Ms. Mousch's personal involvement in the general area of Weird Shit. I kept nodding as Safie explained further. "He's in assisted living at this point, paid for out of that trust Mr. Whitcomb set up for him; was asleep when I called, but the receptionist connected me with his personal nurse-practitioner. She says he's frail, but still pretty sharp, able to get around on his own . . . It'd only take us about forty minutes to get there in my van."

"And he remembers Mrs. Whitcomb?"

"That's all he talks about, most days, apparently. She definitely left a mark."

Of course she did.

"So," Simon said—and it was weirdly fascinating, listening to him audibly wrestle to keep his voice from sliding into disbelief— "you're thinking if you go interview the oldest man in Toronto, he'll tell you the magic formula for stuffing Lady Midday back in her box? Or . . . field, I guess?"

"Maybe."

Simon leaned forward, intent. "But what if he doesn't know? Or he's wrong? Or *you're* wrong about what's really happening here? Have you thought about what you're going to do then?" When I didn't answer, he laid one hand on mine, eyes soft, almost begging. "Why don't we just go back to the hospital, okay? You and me, so we can be there when Clark wakes up, with my parents and your Mom. They'd appreciate it—him too. Safie could check this out then get back to you . . . right, Safie?"

For a moment, Safie looked as though she wanted to agree, but I shook my head. "I get that you don't believe in any of this," I told Simon. "And that's okay, you don't have to; probably better for you if you don't. But I do, and I'm going—so unless you want to try and physically restrain me—" I pulled my hand out from under his "—nothing you say or do is gonna make me stop."

He drew back, sat there a second, dead silent; I caught the hurt flicker in his eyes before his gaze hardened. Then—

"You know," he began, carefully, "the one thing I've tried absolutely never to do in all our time together, ever, is give you an ultimatum. Which is why I'm . . ." a long pause ". . . very . . . *disappointed* . . . that you just gave *me* one."

"I understand. But if this works, I won't care . . . and you won't either, frankly."

Simon blinked. Clearly he'd been expecting me to backpedal, say something like *No, no, of course not, that's not what I meant.* "You're sure of that, huh?" he said.

I drew a breath then took his hand back. "I'm sure enough that I'm willing to count on you forgiving me." I could hear the hoarseness in my own voice. "Because you've been the one thing in my adult life that I've been absolutely sure I *can* count on. I don't see that changing. Do you?"

After a beat, Simon put his face in his hands and let out a long, tired sigh. "Okay then," he said, eventually. "Here's *my* ultimatum: I'm coming with you. I'm still pissed as hell," he added, as if either of us thought for a second I didn't know that. "But I'd never let you do this alone."

"Better call Mom and tell her then," I replied. "Or maybe your folks, because she's probably not gonna want to hear it from me."

"Probably not."

He didn't quite smile, and I didn't quite smile back, but the mood lifted, just a bit. Enough for me to turn to Safie and ask, "So. You okay with all this?"

Safie gave a small, tight grin. "I'm the one who found him, Miss, remember? You bet your ass I'm in." She held out her hand.

"Good," I said, shaking it.

SIXTEEN

I think back, remembering that old narrative-logic exercise of mine, the one I used to walk people through in class: the man, the tree, the apple, the bruise—gravity. There's only so many ways to tell a story, linearly or not, and that was something Iris Dunlopp Whitcomb always seemed to know, long before anyone else in her field.

So: knowing what I know now, or at least what I think—

(what I *believe*)

—I know, then perhaps this explains why Mrs. Whitcomb shot her films in ever more oblique, concave, complicated ways; through scrims and veils, cut-outs and paintings on glass with the empty spaces acting like a second lens, or even (in one case) a tank full of water with things floating around in it, paint and ink dropping down, unravelling, diffuse and sublimate. Reflections of reflections in mirrors or sheets of polished tin, cunningly bent to replace one image with another, or show two things at once, shimmering and slick and odd.

She did stuff other people wouldn't think up for decades, and none of it in service of making things explicit, making things easy. More like . . . the exact opposite.

I think I've said before how it was as if she didn't want you to see what she was looking at, or maybe as if *she* didn't want to see what she was looking at, let alone want it to see *her.* Yet to my mind, it's an observation that bears repeating.

In the end, I suppose, this will always be a story about the limits of what's known, or maybe of what can *be* known; one open to interpretation, not so much because it has missing pieces, but because missing pieces are all it was ever made from.

And if that's true, then I was a lost cause from the beginning, because I have a pattern-maker's mind—like Mrs. Whitcomb, like Hyatt, like Simon, like Clark. It's just how we're wired. Thus making me perhaps the single worst person who could've tripped across this stuff, with Safie running a close second. Because she could see what was *around* Mrs. Whitcomb's film, in total detail, and I could see what was *behind* it, eventually. But the thing itself, the trick being played? The shell-game signifier?

Which of us could ever have seen *that* coming, at least in time to warn anybody?

Then again, maybe there was no "thing itself," not really. Maybe there never is. Maybe there's just a shadow, a stain, a projection—a crude visual mimicry of something literally unimaginable moving behind the walls of the world, scaled down till it fits inside the limits of human perception. And when all's said and done, in the final analysis, all that good shit . . . the very hoariest of any and all possible hoary clichés . . .

Well then, maybe it isn't so much *that* you see what something is, but that *it*—

(or in this case, She)

—is what you *see.*

The place in which Vasek Sidlo had spent his last twenty years was a classic old-age home, indistinguishable from any other assisted-living facility you've ever run across: bright and airy, open spaces, light salmon walls, the vague smell of bedpans covered up with Glade. It reminded me of this really awful micro-job I'd had the summer I was nineteen, working for two hours every Saturday afternoon serving pre-wrapped kosher meals at a small Jewish hospice in Toronto's Bagel Belt. It involved wearing a hairnet, scrubs, and a lot of standing, while trying to simultaneously tune out the residents enough to stay sane yet keep alert enough to know when they wanted something from you: a napkin, more coffee, their tray taken away. By the end of my shift everything hurt, which I guess was sort of like being them for one day a week—except obviously far better, because I at least got to go home. Come late August, I was beginning to think they could not only tell that I thought this, but kind of liked it that way, too.

The woman to whom Safie had spoken ushered us down a long hallway, pausing by Sidlo's door. "He was awake the last time I looked in, but that was ten minutes ago, so I'm not making any promises," she told us. "You may need to be prepared to wait."

"We understand," I said.

"He's over a hundred years old, you know. It's amazing he's even . . ." She trailed off. "At any rate. I'm just down the hall, if you need me."

"Thank you very much, ma'am," Simon said. "We'll keep that in mind."

The door opened slowly on some sort of a restriction lever, probably to keep it from slamming. Vasek Sidlo sat in a wheelchair by the window, angled toward a shaft of light, dozing like an incredibly old, incredibly fragile cat. He was crepey everywhere you looked: skin worn so fine we could see through to his bones, where it wasn't covered by the green striped cotton pyjamas which were clearly all he ever wore; the shadows of sockets 'round his upturned eyes, cataract-blue and ticking slightly from side to side in his sleep. A few scant locks of hair still folded over his scalp, not so much white as colourless; blue veins bulged at either temple, and his Adam's apple pressed painfully against the front of his throat.

It was hard to watch, hard to be in the same room with him— mortality's naked presence pressing down on us like a weight, a full-body, lead-lined X-ray cloak. The kind of spectacle that made me want to fill out and sign my own DNR form, right then and there.

"Oh . . . wow," Safie apparently couldn't quite stop herself from remarking.

Simon nodded, wincing.

"Lois, this is cruel," he said, careful to pitch his voice low. "I mean, *look* at him. What can you expect to gain, aside from just . . . disturbing the poor guy unnecessarily?"

I shook my head. "I don't know."

"Well, then we should go, right? Let's go, hon."

"I can't do that, Simon."

"Yes, you can. It's easy: turn around, leave, don't come back."

"Miss, he might be right," Safie chimed in.

"I *can't*," I repeated.

"Oh," Sidlo said softly, at almost the same time; together, we turned to find him staring at us—me—with his supposedly useless eyes wide, an odd sort of yearning in every line of him. Smiling and trembling at the same time, as something wet spilled down his cheeks: rheum, maybe. Or tears.

"Oh," he said, again, re-angling his head to stare up over my shoulder, where nothing should have been except empty air. "It *is* you, after all. After all this time."

Yes, something replied from deep inside me, seemingly as glad to be recognized as he was to recognize it. *That's right, Vasek; you always did know me. Oh, my poor, dear boy.*

(*Yes, it is.*)

"Mister Sidlo," Simon began. "We're, uh . . ."

Sidlo nodded, eyes still on "me," or whatever stood behind me.

"I know what you're here for," he replied.

There's a VHS tape in the Freihoeven Institute's library that none of us would get to see until long after all this was over, and watching it can be an oddly wrenching experience, especially for those who happen to have met its subject in person first. Dated March 16, 1975, it's of an interview conducted by Dr. Guilden Abbott, now the Institute's acting director, who was then an intern working for its founders, the married parapsychologists Doctor and Mrs. Doctor Jay: Vasek Sidlo being put through his paces, asked to demonstrate whether or not his classic party trick would translate to a whole new type of technology—and what do you know, it actually does, with genuinely unsettling results.

The forty-years-younger Sidlo is still a gaunt old man, softspoken, with the same childlike intensity in his large blind eyes, though much thicker iron-grey hair, an upright posture, and wire-muscled forearms. The camera is focused on him, with Dr. Abbott nothing more than the half-seen back of a head and a pleasant voice whose clinical professionalism only barely hides his earnest enthusiasm. By contrast, Sidlo seems ill at ease—part annoyed, part bored. When I watched it, later, it took me a while to realize why his affect comes off so strangely: on the tape, Sidlo doesn't maintain the steady open-air stare you see in most blind people—instead, he casts his head around in small, constant jerks, like he's desperately trying to identify a noise he can't quite make out. Yet despite all this movement his eyes never once fall upon the camera lens itself; he seems, in fact, to avoid it reflexively, like he knows exactly where it is. Like he's afraid of . . . well, not of seeing it (being, you know, blind), but afraid of what might see him *through* it.

The transcript, which comes attached, runs like this:

DR. ABBOTT: Mister Sidlo, I'd like to begin by saying it's truly wonderful to meet you, on a personal level. I've been a great admirer of yours for years now, ever since the Institute began researching Kate-Mary des Esseintes' Ontario Spiritualist enclave.

SIDLO: Oh yes, the Mysteraeia.

DR. ABBOTT: I'm sorry?

SIDLO: That's what she called it, what she preferred to. In reference to the Delphic Mysteries, but also the Orphean Mystery cults. The descent into the Underworld.

DR. ABBOTT: . . . I see.

SIDLO: It sounds silly, I realize. But Kate-Mary was a firm believer in what she called Old Truths, which is why she used to give everything around her these . . . ridiculous sort of pseudo-Greek names. That cabinet of hers, for example, where she met with her spirit guide . . .

DR. ABBOTT: The Thanatoscopeon, yes. We've been trying to track that down, actually.

SIDLO: Her husband sold most of her things away, after. "Fripperies," he called them. And worse.

DR. ABBOTT: Very sad, of course, Miss des Esseintes' death;

so young. The child died as well, if I remember correctly. [Sidlo nods] But you'd left her group—the Mysteraeia—by then, I believe, hadn't you? You were—

SIDLO: Staying with Iris—Mrs. Whitcomb, I mean—in Quarry Argent; she'd seen me at the meetings, asked me to consult on a project she was contemplating. When I agreed, she made all the provisions for my travel and upkeep. She brought me from home, put me on staff, and gave me a room on the ground floor of her house. Mrs. Whitcomb was . . . very kind.

DR. ABBOTT: Consultation. On a psychic matter?

SIDLO: She had something she wanted removed, but preserved. From her mind.

DR. ABBOTT: An image?

SIDLO: A memory.

DR. ABBOTT: Of her son, no doubt.

SIDLO: [After a long pause] No.

Simon broke the silence first. "Mr. Sidlo, I'm Simon Burlingame," he said, half reaching out a hand as if to shake before realizing Sidlo couldn't possibly know what he was doing. He let it drop. "This is my wife, Lois Cairns, and her colleague, Safie Hewsen. They wanted to ask you some questions about your work with, uh . . ."

"Iris," Sidlo half-whispered. "Giscelia. I could never call her either to her face, Mrs. Whitcomb, not so long as she was another man's wife. We collect names as we get older, don't we? Too many, sometimes . . ." His voice wavered, then firmed. "Come in, please, all of you. Sit where you like." A trembling hand lifted, swept around the room; I took the only other chair, next to a small end table, while Safie parked herself on the end of the bed. Simon, visibly uncomfortable, stayed by the door, arms folded.

"Mr. Sidlo, I . . ." I began. "I'm—that is, my family and I— we're in a pretty bad place right now, which means I might as well cut to the chase: we need help, and I'm really hoping you can give it, 'cause . . . you're our only option, essentially. So if you can't—"

I stopped there, however; cut myself off as Sidlo reached across to grasp my hand, deft and sure, as though he already knew where it was. The feather-light fingertips, trembling slightly, felt papery on mine—cool, dry. Strangely soothing.

"You've been touched you, haven't you?" he asked. "By Iris, yes—but not her alone. By her, that other. *She, Herself.*"

Capital "S," capital "H." I heard Safie swallow; saw Simon's jaw work, as if he was biting back words. I opened my mouth to answer and suddenly found I couldn't; the thickness in my throat was as much relief as anything else. Somebody else *knew*, somebody *understood*. I *wasn't* insane. Not completely.

"Mr. Sidlo—" Head down, I couldn't see Simon anymore, but I could hear the sudden wariness in his voice, maybe spurred by my reaction. "When you say 'Her,' who are you talking about?"

"I think you know very well, Mr. Burlingame." Sidlo angled his head in Simon's direction, again with uncanny accuracy, and Simon recoiled. "You mock, since you have not been touched yourself; if you had, you would not ask at all. So tell me, will you play Arthur to your own Iris? Will you leave when the worst of it comes, your loyalty not worth admitting how little you understand?"

Simon flushed; his jaw set. "Never," he said, without hesitation. "I'd never do that."

I cleared my throat and looked up, meeting his eyes. "I know," I managed, and Simon gave me a painful sketch of a smile. From the corner of my eye, I saw Safie turn her head, deliberately staring elsewhere, while Sidlo nodded, slightly.

"Good," he replied. "After all, there's the child to think of."

"How—?"

"Because you came here, to me. You would have to be truly desperate to do that, far more so than on your own account. Someone else would have to be involved, someone you both care about more than you do yourselves."

"It's my son," I told him. "He's . . . special, like Hyatt Whitcomb."

"And has he seen Her, as well?"

My voice thickened once more, the words almost choking me. "I think so, yes."

"But he wouldn't know what he's seen," Safie quickly added. "Not really. He'd never know how to respond, or what she wants from him. If she does want anything."

"Oh, always—but what? That was Mrs. Whitcomb's question when I first met her. Some things simply want to *be* seen; Kate-Mary told me as much, in my very first days with her. But She, Mrs. Whitcomb's Lady . . . she wants more, far more, in return for her attention. A tithe, a payment for gifts received, whether those gifts were *wanted* or not." Sidlo laughed, a hollow, half-cracked sound, eggshell crunching. "All muses are cruel, some say, but She—She may be the cruellest. At least, so Mrs. Whitcomb contended, having studied the matter."

"Was Hyatt Mrs. Whitcomb's tithe?" I asked.

"She thought so, yes. It was . . . one reason. An understandable one."

"Because Lady Midday touched him in the womb, in the field. Chose him."

He nodded. "She fought the idea a long time, she told me. But then he was gone, and—there seemed no point in fighting it anymore. Better to proceed according to what one feared might be true, to assume it *was* true, than hope in vain for better."

I get it, I thought. Knowing, even as I formed the idea, that Simon didn't, couldn't—wouldn't.

"So what *does* this damn thing want then?" he demanded, arms crossed. Sidlo simply shrugged.

"Worship," he replied. "That was all she could figure, by the end."

"I friggin' knew it," Safie muttered under her breath.

In the Freihoeven Institute interview, Dr. Abbott reaches across to take Sidlo's hand and agrees to concentrate on an image inside his own head, one Sidlo can't possibly know about, while Sidlo (in turn) concentrates on the magnetic tape unspooling inside the camera trained on him throughout. What follows—as the image literally takes shape before the viewer's eyes, supplanting Sidlo and Abbott entirely—is a lot like watching a visual experience being reconstructed from MRI brain scan input; the details are definitely off, almost shorthanded, but the overall *shape* is astoundingly recognizable, far more so than in remote viewing experiments of yore. Full colour, for one thing, not sketched in black and white with the various components unstrung and drifting, like an encephalitis patient drawing whatever portion of a clock face their infection-swollen brain can process.

What's far more impressive, however, is the sheer clarity with which Sidlo seems to channel the sensory details of the experience, providing a tiny window into the moment in question: image as still frame in a mess of linked footage, one single moment culled from an inextricably linked, forward-moving mass. Instead of a cursory, surface-only browsing, it's as though Sidlo sinks deep beneath the crust of Abbott's chosen memory, culling out all the parts that tweak him emotionally: not so much the beach as the feel of hot sand slipping under rubber sandals; not so much his companion's face as the smell of her perfumed sweat, tiny soft hairs on the back of her arm brushing his; not so much the sea as the sound of in-rushing waves, the taste of salt. Not so much the day itself as the painful joy of it, their mutual intimacy already undercut with anticipation—accurate, as it later turned out—of future loss.

Then there's a cut, a lag, during which Abbott must have viewed the playback. When we return he seems shaken, slightly manic, while Sidlo appears . . . basically the same. Almost bored by his own powers, calloused over through constant interaction with the miraculous.

DR. ABBOTT: My God. My . . . God, yes. How incredible! How—that is *truly* remarkable. Isn't it? [As Sidlo gives him a look] Though yes, I suppose you have . . . no way of knowing, really.

SIDLO: Not as such.

DR. ABBOTT: And this was what you did for Mrs. Whitcomb?

SIDLO: More or less. She wanted the impression made on film, of course—silver nitrate, very particularly. Her medium of choice, though there *were* alternative stocks available by that time.

DR. ABBOTT: Interesting, considering its volatile nature.

SIDLO: Industrial alchemy, she called it. I knew nothing about such matters until she explained them to me, in detail.

Silver nitrate was once one of the most important ingredients in such processes, *lunar caustic* or *lapis infernalis*, the hellish stone; silver could be sublimated by dissolving it in nitric acid, *aqua fortis*—strong water. Evaporating the solution then produces silver nitrate crystals that when applied to an organic substrate—paper, for example—become photo-sensitive, depositing tiny silver-black particles on any area exposed to light. With the addition of common salt, it also turns into silver chloride, two of the most important ingredients in the history of photography: a moon solution, to reflect—and summon—its opposite.

DR. ABBOTT: Summon? Summon what?

SIDLO: You wanted to know what the memory was, the one Mrs. Whitcomb wanted captured.

DR. ABBOTT: . . . Yes.

SIDLO: She wouldn't tell me. But it didn't matter, no more than with you just then; I picked it from her head, let it run through me, bloom like frost onto the reel of film we both held. It etched itself into the silver. [Pause] I couldn't tell what she saw, not really. Being what I am isn't the same thing as *not* being blind; even if I could actually *see* through other people's eyes, I wouldn't know what I was looking at. But I remember what I felt, intensely. I can still feel it.

DR. ABBOTT: Describe it.

SIDLO: Lying down, in long grass. Scratchy everywhere. Bugs . . . cicadas in the trees, very loud. Hot. There are other people all around me, just lying there, not moving. A bad smell. *Very* bad. And someone praying. And then—someone else is there, all of a sudden. Asking questions. A voice like . . . I don't know. Terrible, brazen. Like a steel bell. Like nothing on earth.

DR. ABBOTT: And what happens then?

SIDLO: I start to cry.

DR. ABBOTT: Where did this person come from?

SIDLO: I don't know.

DR. ABBOTT: Who are the other people?

SIDLO: I don't know. I never knew.

DR. ABBOTT: Did Mrs. Whitcomb know?

SIDLO: . . . Yes.

DR. ABBOTT: She told you?

SIDLO: Not until later, but yes, she told me. Who she thought it was.

DR. ABBOTT: And who did she—?

SIDLO: *You know.* Her family, her father, Her. The Lady. The one who took her son, her Hyatt. The one from the field.

DR. ABBOTT: The field where Giscelia Wròbl's father died.

SIDLO: That field, and every other. She lives everywhere, you see, at least once a day—that's what Mrs. Whitcomb would say. Between the minute and the hour, at the very crack of noon. [Pause] She told me she was tired of thinking about that moment, so I took it out for her, as I said I would. And she was happy, and so was I—*very* happy, to have helped her, the best and most lovely woman I have ever known. I thought that would be the end of it, until . . .

DR. ABBOTT: Until?

SIDLO: She vanished. You've heard the story, surely.

DR. ABBOTT: Yes, we've done a fair amount of research into that, without much result. But you were there when it happened—what did you think? Did you expect her to be found?

SIDLO: [Quiet] No. I never did.

DR. ABBOTT: Why not?

SIDLO: Because I understood how it happened. Oh, not the exact mechanics, but . . . it would have been all right, I believe, except for one thing: the impulse to poke your tongue into an empty socket, to worry at a wound. Her memory was on the film, you see; she could have buried it, burnt it, never had to deal with it again. But she couldn't take it on faith. She had to see.

DR. ABBOTT: See . . . what?

SIDLO: To see if it was *there,* at all. To watch it. To know I'd gotten it right.

"I've had a long time to think about this," Sidlo told us. "And what I've come to see is that . . . she lied to me, Mrs. Whitcomb. Probably for good reasons, and yet: a lie, at the very heart of our dealings. If only she would have told me the truth, it might have changed everything."

Or not, I thought. But since I needed him to keep talking, all I said was, "What did she lie about, sir? Why?"

"Oh, as to *why,* I think she wanted not to scare me. And as for what . . ." He trailed away for a moment. "I now believe she was tired of waiting for Her to re-appear, of praying in vain for some answer to the question of what had happened to Hyatt. That, I think, was how the paintings and the films were meant—as offerings; Hyatt's own drawings, the paintings, the films, all meant to placate Her. But when that failed . . ." Sidlo turned up his hand ". . . she turned from propitiation to conjury. She wanted to open a doorway and find Her there, in that moment. The moment where She lives, always."

"In the field," said Safie.

"In *every* field, every appearance, every tale told, every dream. The Lady is not like you or I, miss, to say the least. Kate-Mary des Esseintes believed there were things that lived outside the boundaries of time, as we perceive them: ghosts, angels, demons. Gods."

I nodded slowly. "So when you made that film for her," I said, "you gave her a key to open a door from . . . wherever she was, to . . ."

"To there. To Her."

A moment passed, while we all digested that idea.

"Well," Simon said, at last, "that didn't seem to work out all too well for Mrs. Whitcomb."

Sidlo shook his head.

"Might be a lot of reasons for that," Safie pointed out. "Maybe she asked the wrong questions. Maybe she didn't take precautions."

"What *sort* of precautions?" Simon demanded. "I mean, does any of us know? If it was just a matter of getting a priest involved, or throwing holy water at her, or—" He ground to a halt, seemingly equal parts angry and afraid. "This is useless," he said, finally. "I don't know what you expected to find here, Lo, but I don't think we're going to leave happy."

I raised both hands, mind racing, and outright shushed him like he was Clark. "Let me think, Simon," I begged. "Just, just . . . *fuck.* Let me fucking *think.*"

Safie: "Miss—"

"*Quiet*, for shit's sake! I need—"

And that was when it came to me, right that moment: an idea so stupid, so hubristic and reckless, it could really only have been conceived by a person who'd been awake all night and stretched to their very limits, somebody hovering on the ragged edge of losing not only everything they'd ever had, but everything they ever *would* have. Like a spotlight on the brain, full blast—creativity erupting like madness, through the top of the head.

Like Hephaestus opening up Zeus's skull only to see Athena pop out, born full-grown and armoured, shining like a second sun.

The impossible made possible. The only option left.

Even then, though, I knew I couldn't just blurt it out, 'specially not in front of Simon. I had to wrap it up inside of something else, put things in place, then spring it on the others while he was out of the room.

Funny how time seems to slow in a crisis, isn't it? Or maybe it's that you speed up, all your neurons firing at once.

"Safie," I said, "do you have any film stock? In your van?"

She huffed, eyes widening as if dazed by the sudden swerve. "Um . . . yeah, yeah, I do. Got a whole reel of Super 16 Soraya gave me, along with a whole bunch of other shit I keep saying I'm going to put away." With a shrug: "I've even got some unexposed silver nitrate, as it happens."

Simon said, "Seriously?"

Safie flushed a bit. "Yes, seriously—I like dead tech, sue me. Why?"

"Would you mind going and getting it? Maybe a camera, too? Digital, I mean." While Safie frowned, I added as casually as I could, "Simon, if you could give her a hand, that'd be great."

Simon opened and closed his mouth, stuck in the classic Nice Guy's dilemma of clearly realizing something was up, but being unable to call me on it without knowing what it was. I only nodded at Safie. After a moment she sighed, got to her feet, and went to the door, tapping Simon on the arm en route. "Come on." He gave me one last tight-lipped look, and went with her. I waited

until the door had closed completely then switched my attention
back to Sidlo.

"You thought she shouldn't have opened the door, right?"
I said, my voice low. "The film you made—that that was Mrs.
Whitcomb's mistake, trying to go to Her?" He nodded, placidly.
"Well—what if you made another copy, right here, right now,
based on your memory of *her* memory? Could you do that? Am
I right in thinking it'd be just as good as the last one you made,
for Mrs. . . . for Iris?"

There was a long pause before he answered; not quite surprise—it was as if he'd known all along what I had wanted to ask
but hadn't actually thought about the answer till now. He said at
last, slowly, "I think so. Yes."

"On Super 16, or silver nitrate?"

"Silver nitrate would be more appropriate." He cocked his
head at me again with that weird accuracy. "But what do you wish
to accomplish, Ms. Cairns? Why would this time be different?"

"Because—" I caught my breath on a razor-edged gasp. "I
want to make a door that goes the *other* way. One where, instead
of me going to her, we make Lady Midday come to *us*."

Sidlo stared into space, blinking slowly; said nothing for so
long that I began to fear Safie and Simon would return before we
could finish. But then, finally, he drew a quivering breath.

"You have . . . no idea," he husked. "The repercussions . . ."

I kind of thought I did, but I wanted to hear it from him.
"Then tell me."

He shuddered. "Do you think She has ever really left me? I
am under Her eye, even now; I live there." He looked out the
window, sunlight turning his skin and hair semi-transparent;
weariness came off him so strong there was no room left for fear.
"At midnight, I feel the noonday sun shine on me. I have slept
only two or three hours a night for decades. Every sunrise is Her
attention fixed upon me once more, a hand on my shoulder so
hot and heavy I can barely rise, move, or breathe. Every day is
the same, waiting helpless for a death She will not *allow* me—I
am Tennyson's Tithonus, suffering forever, aging without end.
The woods decay, the woods decay and fall/The vapours weep their

burthen to the ground/ . . . And after many a summer dies the swan—" He let out a long sigh. *"Me only cruel immortality/Consumes,"* he finished, a near-silent whisper.

Okay, then great, the most hateable part of me crowed inside. *Even* more *perfect.*

I swallowed, refusing to stop. "Then maybe this is the way to break that streak, get rid of what's been haunting you all this time—this thing that isn't even yours, somebody *else's* ghost. And maybe . . . maybe this way, it can finally be finished. For Iris's sake, and Hyatt's. Their legacy." The words tumbled out of me, not particularly planned. "Lady Midday wants worship, right? She doesn't want to *give,* she wants to be *given*— that might've been Mrs. Whitcomb's other mistake—that she *demanded,* instead of placating. Well, I'm fine with doing whatever it takes to keep Her away from *my* kid, and She can have whatever She wants, in exchange. I mean I'm not going to *kill* myself, or anything—even going by the mythology, there's no earthly point to that. But if it turns out I have to spend the rest of my life making films about Her, or writing about Her, or telling people She bloody well exists in order to make her leave Clark alone—well then . . . that's okay, from my end. Not like I have another job, anyways."

(*This* is *your job, Lois,* Mom's voice disagreed, inside my head. But as ever, I ignored it.)

Sidlo blinked. "You have no idea that's what She wants," he countered. "No idea if this will work."

"Nope. But you know what else I don't have? Any other options." This time it was me who took *his* hand, gripped it hard, trying not to hurt him. "You saw how Hyatt vanishing destroyed Iris Whitcomb, and if I lost Clark—" The idea blindsided me, somewhat—an instant recipe for clogged sinuses and blurred eyes—but I choked my way through, nonetheless. "I'm not the world's best mother, Mr. Sidlo. Clark drives me crazy a lot of the time, and I let it show. I let him . . . He's mine, though. A piece of me—the best piece. I can't let him go."

A few moments passed, and I breathed in hard, letting the feeling ebb away. Then Sidlo moved his other hand across to cover mine. "My dear," he said, his own voice raw, "if I have anything to say about it, you won't."

Fast fade, wipe, dissolve. Cut to—

Us in the van—Sidlo, Simon, Safie, and me; Sidlo's wheelchair wedged into the back atop reefs of cable and equipment cases positioned to hold it still. And here is where, once again, a certain contextual ripple starts, filtering back from the inevitable point of contact between the "real world" and whatever lies sidelong, that hot silver reflection. A backwash, a storm forming, organizing itself around the seizure I can already assume is coming, once Lady Midday digs her fingers into my cortex yet again.

I think I remember being amazed my ploy had worked, at least thus far. That anyone—Sidlo, let alone Simon—had believed me. *Just let me get them home,* I think I remember thinking. *Let me put it all in place then see what happens. Let me* try.

Because I know now, like I knew then: it was never about surrender, placation. It was about attack, entrapment. Stuffing the ghost—the *god*—back in her box, then setting the whole damn thing on fire.

(Opposites attract; *lunar caustic,* that term I didn't even know yet. The moon tethering the sun. Industrial alchemy.)

Sidlo in the back, "watching" me from the corner of his filmy, flickering eyes. Safie driving, gaze on the road. Simon in the back, making sure Sidlo was okay. Me riding shotgun, a reel of precious, poisonous silver nitrate film in my lap, its case pressing cool against my legs—and my monkey-mind just racing, forwards and back at the same time, planning and scheming, unaware of its own impending danger. Always somewhere else.

(*Come back, Lois, goddamnit,* my father's voice demanded, from the past. *Don't take yourself away. There's more to life than dreaming, and it's here, right here—*)

I'm going to settle this, I thought, knowing on some level how stupid it sounded, even inside my head. *Settle it, here and now. Or . . .*

(What?)

Die trying, I suppose. Because that always seems so brave, when you're not thinking clearly. When you haven't even begun to consider what doing so—or, worse yet, *failing* to do so—might actually involve.

Let it work, let it work, I think I remember thinking. *God, Lady Midday, whoever; just let this work, and I'll never ask for anything again.* And—

Looking back, amusingly enough, I don't actually think I ever have.

But mainly because I finally know better.

SEVENTEEN

Hindsight being predictably twenty-twenty, the point of getting Safie to bring her camera soon becomes clear, once I take a moment to contemplate it—on some level, I must've known something like this would happen. That I'd more than likely be felled under the *Regenmöhme*'s heat-stroke once more, and need some sort of record made, to give me a clear idea of what'd happened while I was out. Smart thinking, me. I've always been kind of cunning that way, at least when it comes to covering my own ass.

Of course, it would've also helped if I'd actually been left in any sort of position to be able to *watch* said record, later on.

I remember dreaming that time, which was different. Not the smash cut to black and sudden splice that connected the trip up to Quarry Argent with waking in St. Mike's, heart all stuttery, eyes glued together and throat like a desert. Instead, there's a sort of . . . soft dissolve, fading from me in the van to me back at the Fac, either late at night or early in the morning, following those directional traffic arrows painted on the walls through its creepily carpeted corridors. That building was a serious petri dish, sick to its core; every fall we'd all get the same cold, like grade school kids, and pass it around till the new year. Not to mention how the whole place was laid out like a prison, with umbilicus-linked checkpoint doors only accessible with card keys, like contact gates. The studios were all nude concrete, which made it a lot easier to build and strike sets, and there was one particular classroom I always seemed to end up in, right in the centre of the place—triangular, glass on all three sides through which you could glimpse either eddying crowds or a lonely expanse of empty hall, classic J-Horror style; a haunting waiting to happen.

So: in the dream, I'm back in that classroom, standing at the board, giving a lecture. And as often happened in such cases, I've forgotten what the point of the exercise was—have to look up at my own handwriting to remind me, these scribbled notes done in dry erase marker. But suddenly even *I* can't read them. Is that my handwriting, or someone else's? The whiteboard's cool, slick gleam, familiar as my laptop monitor, or a stretched expanse of paper browned with age, liver-spotted like the back of a hundred-plus-year-old man's hand?

Oh, ah: Mr. Sidlo, I presume. How unexpectedly nice to find *you* here.

He's sitting in the front row, space cleared for his wheelchair, those filmy eyes "looking" up over my shoulder once again—at my words on the board, unintelligible though they might be. I turn, and of course now they're perfectly clear, or clear as anybody who spent ten years taking notes in the dark can really be expected to write. My own loopy shorthand: "th" reduced to a symbol like a crossed upper-case "L"; "and" consistently translated as a plus sign; "e's" and "o's" almost indistinguishable aside from context. A tree of observations, half blank verse, half equation, like so:

> technology = blessing + curse
> only way t/ make dreams palpable, but overwhelms/flattens in process
> inherently reductionist
> universal = myth
> dream to image = disappointment

Is it now? I wonder. *Is She coming?* I look at Sidlo, who shrugs.

How can we ever know? he seems to say.

Then there's a thump on the glass, from just outside: *Don't bang, there's no reason to* bang! And I glimpse Clark in the hall beyond, dancing and jumping, spinning in an endless circle. Singing, as he does: *Backwards, forwards, more and more/Every image is a door—*

A door, yes. My plan, or all that's left of it. Memory to film, dream to image, image to key, key to lock. Turning. Opening.

But doors open both ways, by nature.

This is how it happened, Safie would tell me, after everything. *Had* to tell me, just like she did about everything else—reminded me, I suppose, since I'd obviously been there, at the time. Summing up what I would've seen on the digital footage, if I'd only been able to.

Safie was already rolling when we set Sidlo up in front of the windows in our "living room," Simon hefting the ottoman aside, re-angling the couch to clear a path for his wheelchair then parking him with his back to the windows. Soon enough, Sidlo sat there sun-haloed, calm as a king enthroned. Since he claimed he'd need me close enough to touch, for an "anchor," I hauled one of the dinner table chairs over and set it down in front of him, while Simon pulled the blinds—flat, cream-coloured roll-ups, amusingly reminiscent of old-style movie screens.

"Not sure how much help I can be," I told Sidlo, voice kept low, as I deposited the silver nitrate reel's case on his lap. He simply smiled. "I mean, this is Mrs. Whitcomb's memory we're supposed to be imprinting, right? And between the two of us, *you're* the one who knew her."

"Certainly. But you share her experience, as I never did. You saw Her."

I shook my head, almost a shiver. "*Something*, maybe—I don't even know what."

"It doesn't matter. I feel the mark She left on you, as I did the one left upon Iris. More than sufficient impetus for a reading, allowing me to follow your own experience back into hers."

I bit my lip. Asked him, softer yet, "And . . . to open the door? Putting Her and me together, can you still do that?"

"Better to have more fuel than we need than not enough to build *that* fire. Wouldn't you agree?"

I nodded, slightly: *sure would,* I might have been thinking. Not that I'll ever know.

"Not much film on that reel, by the way," Safie leaned back in to caution me, pointing to the reel, unaware she'd even caught all of the above till she looked at it after. "Maybe ten minutes' worth at most, so if this doesn't work, I guess we'll have to go back to my studio for more."

Simon looked up from what he was doing, his mind boggling once again, at least a little. "Just how much of that crap do you *have*?"

"Not *that* much," Safie began, but stopped when Sidlo raised his hand.

"Ten minutes will be more than sufficient, Miss Hewsen," he assured her.

"Good," she said. "Anything else, before we go ahead?"

Sidlo nodded. "The lights should be turned off. All of them."

"Really?" This from Simon, who now stood hovering at Sidlo's shoulder. "I was under the impression filming without light made things kinda, y'know, hard to see."

"I wouldn't worry, Mr. Burlingame, given nothing literally visible will be recorded," Sidlo replied. "In this case, I *am* the camera—the images pass through me, into the film I hold. And since I already know you think me completely deluded on the subject, what can it matter whether the lights stay on, or off?"

"Good question," Simon muttered, but I shot him a look—of the fairly classic *just go along with this, okay, honey? please* variety—and he subsided. I sat, reaching to let Sidlo take hold of my hand again, as Safie began turning lights down around us. Meanwhile, Simon covered the areas beyond her immediate reach: bedroom, closets, kitchen, Clark's room. The apartment was submerged into dimness by increments, cold late-morning sunlight narrowing to leak 'round the edges of the blinds like fire.

"Okay, we're dark," I reported to Sidlo.

"Very well." He closed his eyes and lowered his head, breath slowing, finding a long, slow rhythm. "Miss Cairns, do not let go;

Miss Hewsen, please continue your recording. If you see anything unusual, be sure to tell me."

"Okay. Unusual like . . .?"

"I believe the sort of thing I mean will very quickly become apparent." To Simon: "Mr. Burlingame, I must ask *you* to make sure we are not interrupted before the process is concluded."

"How'm I supposed to—"

"Stand by the door, that's all; stay alert. Do not let *anyone* enter once we begin. The results might be catastrophic."

Simon's eyes flickered back to mine, as though checking for any sign I thought Sidlo might be joking. When he didn't find one, however, he simply nodded. "Understood," he said, turning his back on all three of us.

He passed me on his way to the door, Safie would tell me, *and you weren't looking, so you couldn't have seen . . . all caught up with Sidlo like you were, studying him like you thought if you watched him close enough you'd be able to see what was happening inside, reflected on his eyes or something. And your husband, he was putting up a pretty brave front, but if you got in closer, you could see he was starting to get scared. Same as a little kid who's just realized they're lost and can't see their Mom or Daddy anywhere—he didn't look like* him *anymore. Know what I mean?*

I do, yes. Did then, too. But I didn't see it. I don't know *what* I saw, really; can't remember, not even in my dreams. Unlike—

(*other things, so many other things*)

"I'm going to start now," Sidlo said.

You think that being blind is darkness, and sometimes that's true, yes. Mostly. Not always, though.

When I woke up back in St. Mike's, Mrs. Whitcomb's ghost voice in my ear and her bony hand in mine, the world around me had all gone hot and stark, consumed by the idea of brightness without any of its effects. Reduced to a vague tint of red, polluting an otherwise unbroken absence. And what I found was that this would wax and wane as time went on, with no apparent consideration for what time of day it was *supposed* to be, outside my own head—that 'round midnight I often seemed to orbit a weird, unblinking light, pitiless as some supermax prison cell's single bulb, while at noon things became still and quiet, colourless, nothing but gloom on gloom.

"Hysterical blindness," said Dr. Harrison's disembodied voice, intruding to anchor me where I floated, abandoned by everything. "Acute onset, since you don't seem to have any other type; probably an accompanying seizure, taking your additional memory loss into account. Conversion disorder, that's what Freud called it—apparent neurological symptoms with no identifiable systemic cause, produced by converting intrapsychic distress into physical symptoms."

"So it's all in my head, huh?"

"To some extent. The brain subconsciously disables or impairs a bodily function as a side effect of the original repression, thus relieving the patient's anxiety."

"I don't really feel all that *relieved,* per se."

"Well, no. You wouldn't."

Dry Dr. Harrison; thank Christ for him and his refusal to let me feel sorry for myself. If I hadn't had his snark to bounce off of, I don't know what I would've done.

He told me they'd given me another MRI, run all the same tests as before, plus more—stuff they hadn't thought of the first time 'round. Told me I was otherwise fine, no ill effects, aside from a certain basic inability to *see* any-fucking-thing. While I just sat there thinking about poor Derek Jarman, about that last film of his, *Blue.* What I'd have given to see a colour of my own, any colour, beyond red and black.

A blind filmmaker—that's a joke, right? That's irony. And a blind writer, one specializing in writing about *film* . . .

"What's the prognosis? Treatment?" I asked Harrison, who paused before answering, possibly to think. "Or . . . should I even . . .?"

"Oh, always better to know, Ms. Cairns," he responded crisply, over the slight break in my voice. "*Nothin' get ya nothin',* after all, as my old granny would say. So, for treatment—physiotherapy where appropriate; occupational therapy to maintain autonomy, as regards activities of daily living; treatment of

comorbid depression or anxiety if present, which I'd say they are.
Yes?" I nodded, throat tight, useless eyes burning. "As to prognosis, meanwhile . . ."

"Don't hold back, doc."

". . . conventional wisdom states most conversion symptoms
disappear within two weeks in hospitalized patients, which I
suppose bodes well. Twenty to twenty-five percent of patients
have a recurrence within a year, sometimes with further recur-
rences thereafter, but the statistics aren't really there yet, in terms
of prediction. Still, you've got all the hallmarks of a favourable
recovery—acute onset, clearly identifiable stress beforehand,
plus a very short time between onset and treatment. We could
start this afternoon, if you wanted."

"Sure. Hell, why not start now?"

"Well . . . there *are* some people outside who'd like to speak to
you first, unfortunately. From the police."

"What?"

"Yes, I'm afraid so. That's why you're still here, actually—they
don't want you going home, not till they clear what they're still
calling the crime scene."

"Crime scene?" Again, he fell silent; unavoidably, probably,
though he must've known how off-putting it was for someone in
my position. "But why . . . just what *happened* this time while I
was out?"

Another pause, though shorter, this time. "I think they'll
probably want to fill you in on that themselves," he said at last.

"What exactly is it you were trying to *do* with Mr. Sidlo, Ms. Cairns?"

The lead detective, who'd introduced herself as Susan Correa,
had a businesslike alto voice: Ontario native, stringently polite,
though the question held an inherent challenge. Her hand had
felt firm enough in mine to put her anywhere from thirties to
forties, but that was as far as I'd be willing to go, if asked.

"Interviewing him," I replied, quickly; wasn't a lie if it was the
truth, at least halfway. "For a project Safie—Miss Hewsen—and I
pitched to the NFA, the National Film Archive."

"Before the fire, I take it."

"Yeah, that's right. Our liaison there was one of the casualties, which means it's back-burnered, for now. But Safie had already tracked down Sidlo, and I wanted to keep going—guy was really old, so time was a factor."

"Understandable. I must admit, we're somewhat surprised you'd want to go ahead and do it while your son was still in hospital, though."

I could feel my face redden. "His grandparents were with him, both sides, and we all had our phones. They knew to call us if anything changed."

"And has it?"

"I don't know. You're the first people I've talked to, besides Dr. Harrison." A beat. "Actually, I'm kind of surprised my husband wasn't here when I first woke up."

"Mmm, well, we're sorry for that. That's because—"

"He's in custody," her partner's voice intruded, from further back—Valens, he'd called himself. "Her too, Safic Hewsen. Your *colleague*."

"*What?*" I blurted, stomach lurching, suddenly all cold acid. "Custody—like *jail*? Why?"

"Not jail," Correa hastened to assure me, playing classic *bon cop* to Valens's full-on asshole. "They're neither under arrest, just being questioned down at 54 Division—making statements, so we can figure out what happened. They're free to go at any time, as I'm certain they've been informed."

Valens: "We'd have you there, too, believe me, it wasn't for your . . . condition."

"You think I'm making this shit up?"

"Oh no, no, no—not the first two seizures, anyway; that's documented. Kinda convenient, you having another one, though, isn't it? Under the circumstances."

"Convenient," I repeated, trying my best to stay calm. I took a breath, made myself wait. "I wouldn't call it *that*."

"We really don't mean to be insensitive, Ms. Cairns," Correa said. To which I just snorted.

"Really?" I replied. "'Cause it kinda sounds to me like you do."

"I'm sorry you feel that way, ma'am."

"Okay, that's nice. Thanks."

She was probably making some sort of placatory headshake gesture right then, not that I'd know. Valens kept on moving around the room like he was pacing, trying either to trip me up or intimidate me, or both; the way my head snapped to follow him every time his shoes clopped across the floor must've looked pretty fucking funny, I guessed, though the casual disorientation factor was already getting old. Still, they call them micro aggressions for a reason, right?

"This Sidlo," Valens began after a moment. "Like you said, he was old—in a nursing home, right? You get permission to take him to your place?"

"He gave us permission before we left," I claimed, straight-faced, not actually knowing even vaguely if it was true. "He was glad we came, that we'd managed to find him in time to get him on tape. Been waiting years to tell his side of the story, so he wanted to do it as quickly as possible, someplace other than there."

"Yeah, all right—but permission from the *home,* that's what I meant. Quite a risk to the health getting yourself all twisted up like that, 'specially at a hundred-plus."

"Mr. Sidlo's an adult, detective. He knew what he was doing."

"Not most of the time, according to his caregivers—including Nurse Amy Bedard, the girl who showed you to his room. She says he was barely lucid, tired easily. Says she didn't know you were going to take him off-site, either, or she'd never have let you see him in the first place."

"That was Sidlo's idea, like I said," I claimed, digging myself deeper. "Why don't you ask *him* why he suggested it?"

"We'd like to, certainly," Correa said. "But we can't. Because he's dead."

"Why else would we be here?" Valens threw out, from yet another direction, making my neck twist so fast it actually hurt.

Dead. Jesus, no wonder they were pressing so hard.

"How?" I asked, finally.

"Natural causes, according to the paramedics," Correa replied. "But then again, at that age, any sort of death is bound to *look* natural. . . ."

"Are you implying it wasn't?"

"Was it?"

"I don't *know*," I bit off, teeth grinding slightly. "Not *anything* that happened, not after a certain point, just like the last time. Dr. Harrison would've told you how long it's been for me, right— a week ago, basically? When I fell down in a Quarry Argent glass house, almost cut my own throat?" No reply. "Paramedics, though . . . who called them? Was it Simon, Safie?"

"The paramedics came with the fire department, Ms. Cairns, responding to an alarm from inside your unit."

I half-rose, wobbling, only to find somebody—Harrison, it turned out—there to take my arm, pressing me back down while I struggled, panicked. "A fire alarm . . . something caught on *fire*? Is everything okay? Our place, all our stuff . . ."

"All that's fine, no casualties," Valens told me. "Except Sidlo."

"You need to tell me what happened, RIGHT the fuck now. Or we are *done* here."

"Calm down, ma'am—"

"Don't you tell me to calm down! Holy shit, what is *wrong* with you people? I wake up and I can't *see*, you tell me the guy I was talking to what seems like ten minutes ago is dead, my home might've burnt down, my son's still in a fucking *coma*—"

"I have to agree," Harrison said, from beside me. "I'm not sure just what you're trying to get my patient to confess to, but you're going about it very childishly, and I won't stand for it. Cease and desist, or I'll have you removed."

"Listen, doc—"

"Eric," Correa said, "he's right; that's enough. Drop it."

Ms. Cairns, you have our sincerest apologies. It's been a very long day.

The facts, as they told them to me, were these:

The Toronto Fire Department station that took the alarm at our building was #333, located on Front Street, less than a block from Sherbourne. The truck dispatched was probably the same one that seemed to turn up at our building every other week during the summer, when the change of weather plus the always-late switch to air conditioning meant stoves and grills started randomly overloading some apartments' capacity to process trapped heat. After checking in with security at the front desk, the firefighters ran upstairs, where they surprised Simon at his station, "on guard"—sure, the loss of light and the fans turning on had been a bit of a shock, but there was no way he thought *we* had anything to do with it. In a way, though, it's lucky he was there: they were all set to kick the door open till he reached in and demonstrated it was already unlocked.

Inside they found three things. Those were, in quick succession:

—Safie down on her knees, hands cupped under my head, desperately trying to keep me from knocking it on the floor as I trembled through another seizure; her camera, knocked over in the corner, was still recording.

—Sidlo slumped in his wheelchair in front of the drawn blinds, dead but not relaxed—taut all over, limbs slightly contracted as though electrocuted. The silver nitrate reel, clutched in both frail hands, seal intact and unbroken.

—Behind him, a scorch-mark spreading upwards across both blinds, like some giant, yellow-ashy pair of wings.

(Simon tells me the inmost part of it is still etched on the glass, black and slightly puffed, impossible to clean away. As though the very composition of its molecules has changed forever.)

Simon was the one who called the paramedics, once he saw what was happening with me. *Your eyes were all rolled back,* he'd later tell me. *Tonic-clonic, looked like; the full deal. You . . . pissed yourself, maybe more, I don't know. It smelled weird, like you'd been eating asparagus. Flailing everywhere, and this time you were chewing; I think you got your tongue a couple of times—*

Feels like it, yeah. Raw.

Well, there was blood, that's all I know. I almost . . . Here he stopped, had to, till he'd gathered himself enough to go on. *The paramedics waited till it stopped, then they rolled you on your side, got you onto a stretcher. Elevators were all unlocked again by then, so we took you down that way. And that's when we realized Lee and my mom and dad were already there, with Clark—had been since the alarm went off. They couldn't go up, obviously, so they just stuck around in the lobby, waiting.*

Turned out it was Lee, Simon Senior, and Bella who came with me to St. Mike's, though I couldn't remember them doing so. Simon and Safie would have come along, but they were prevented—one of the firefighters had tipped off building security, told them about Sidlo's body, and they were held till the cops got there. After which they got carted off to 54 Division while our place was cordoned off, Sidlo removed, with everything judged potentially relevant taken into evidence.

Correa insisted on playing what Safie had recorded for me on her iPad, once it'd been emailed over by the on-site techs. "There we go. Ms. Cairns, if you could—well, I suppose you can't *look*, but please listen. Tell me if any of this rings a bell."

I listened, hard. Straining for anything that would make sense.

On the file, in what passes for the dark of our apartment, Vasek Sidlo grips my hand tighter as his other set of fingers slips to touch the silver nitrate reel. He closes his eyes, or tries to; can't do it all the way, not anymore, thin lids straining together over bulging, occluded corneas. I simply sit there, Safie would later tell me, when we were going over it ourselves—my own eyes raising by very long degrees, seeming to focus on something over *his* shoulder this time. Something she can't see, and her camera doesn't register.

"The field . . ." Sidlo whispers, eventually, so low Safie's mic almost fails to catch it. "Light, heat . . . the insects, singing. That *smell*."

"Yes," I reply, my voice all of a sudden gone equally slow, equally sleepy. "I see it too."

"Oh, and that *voice*."

"*Her* voice, yes."

"Yes."

"And . . . the sun, high above. The noontime sun. You see it?"

"*Feel* it, yes. The dust cloud forming. Far out, where the stalks bend. Above the harvest."

"Yessss . . ."

A silence then. Probably not as long as it sounded.

Is it still playing? I asked Safie after a moment. *What happens next?*

Unable to see her shrug, I nevertheless still heard it shadowing her words when she finally spoke: *I'd say 'you tell me,' except you can't, apparently. But . . .*

This is where everything starts to go wrong, my brain supplied, as she hesitated once more. Knowing from the ever-so-slightly increased length of this next pause, that I *must* be right.

"Okay," Correa said, surface-patient as Valens tapped his foot somewhere behind her, arms probably crossed. "Explain again what's supposed to be happening with you and Mr. Sidlo, because that doesn't look like an *interview* to me."

I sighed. "He was psychic, or claimed to be—used to pal around with a Spiritualist group in the early 1900s, so that's how he met Mrs. Whitcomb. Supposedly, he could imprint images on film with the power of his mind."

Valens scoffed. "And you *believed* that?"

"I believed *he* believed it, and it's hardly the weirdest method I've used to get interview subjects to open up, either. We thought it'd be like . . . self-hypnosis, maybe; take him back in the moment, make it easier for him to talk. So we didn't have to do it again."

"Yeah, well, second kick at the can's not exactly gonna be an option now."

"You think I don't feel bad about that? He was a nice guy, from what I could tell. Not to mention I'm also not real happy about the idea of anybody dying in our apartment, no matter *who* he was. . . ." I trailed away. "But you can't think we *made* this happen, for Christ's sake."

"Can't we?"

Could they? I seriously didn't know; not only was I not a lawyer, it suddenly occurred to me I didn't even have one. Nor did I know what my rights were under the Canadian Charter, how they might or might not differ from your average *Law & Order* episode.

"Are you charging me with something?" I finally asked. "Or my husband, or my friend?"

Correa answered, "Not at this moment, no."

"All right, good. So why am I talking to you, again?"

"To find out what we know?" she suggested. "If you really can't remember, that is."

"I *can't* remember, anymore than I can physically see this shit you're supposedly showing me. Where's Dr. Harrison?"

"I'm right here, Ms. Cairns," the man in question answered, tone level as ever. "Since you detectives sound as though you don't believe she's really suffering, let me set your minds at ease to the extent that I can: yes, my diagnosis of conversion disorder spins on the assumption such a thing exists, and yes, it's extremely difficult to prove. It's also very hard to fake, however, and from what I've observed, Ms. Cairns *is* to all intents and purposes blind, though hopefully only temporarily."

"That sounds . . . very traumatic," Correa agreed, though in her mouth "traumatic" sounded almost exactly like "dramatic."

"It can be. Imagine yourselves in the same situation."

"Yeah, I can't see—" Valens shot back, or started to. To which Harrison retorted, coolly: "—that happening? Exactly. And neither can she for the moment, let alone anything else."

Now it was Correa's turn to sigh. "Very well. We'll check in with you later, Ms. Cairns."

I resisted the urge to shoot them a double finger, simply nodding instead. "I'll be here, probably," was all I could think to say.

Then I heard them all step out, Harrison softly shutting the door behind him, leaving me behind. I lay there in the not-exactly-dark, probably looking like I was staring at the ceiling, trying to think, to figure some way out of all this—my skull's domed confines, the sheer froth of monkey-mind frenzy making my brain chase its own mushy grey tail so fast I could practically feel sparks getting thrown off, only to fizzle wetly against the blood-slick sides.

And maybe I fell asleep then, drifting from one increasingly drown-heavy wave of panic to the next, because the next thing I knew I wasn't alone anymore. Somebody was there, breathing, slightly damp and cut with the occasional hitch—no corpse perfume, or weird floral stink of Soraya Mousch's installation, so not

Mrs. Whitcomb, thank Christ. Not Lady Midday, either—by all appearances, she'd be anything but quiet.

"Hello?" I rasped, reaching out. Waited a single held breath of my own, till somebody took my hand: warm, soft, familiar. Like coming home after a long absence, so long your adulthood peeling away.

"Lois."

I gasped.

Voice almost cracking: "Mom?"

She drew me in, and I came, willingly. We rocked and hugged a while.

"I'm sorry," I told her at last, when my tear-closed throat had widened enough to let me. Felt her hair stroke me lightly, back and forth, as she shook her head.

"It's all right," she said. "It's okay, Lois. Everything's okay now."

Aside from the whole hysterical blindness thing, I thought but didn't say. Because yeah, in that one moment, it really did seem like it almost was.

"Simon Senior, Bella?"

"They went back up to Mississauga—he has something tomorrow, some deacon thing . . . and Simon's not back yet either, though he texted me a few minutes ago, said they were letting him go. Still, there's somebody out in the hall I kind of think you'd like to s—uh." She broke off, momentarily flummoxed. "I mean . . ."

I opened my mouth, probably to say *I know what you mean, Mom,* or something similarly on-the-nose. But a second later, I forgot whatever it'd been when Mom raised her voice, calling, "Okay, bud, c'mon in."

Footsteps thumped over the floor to the accompanying beat of high-pitched hoots, and someone—small but heavy, and hot enough even now that I felt his warmth long before he actually reached me—clambered onto the bed. "Well, everyone, we hope you had a great time singing and dancing," Clark announced, his cod-Aussie accent echoing the end of one of his favourite Wiggles DVDs. "But there's one little problem: Mom's asleep!" Then, in a slightly different voice: "Oh, no—she must be tired from all that

dancing! Let's wake her up to say goodbye. One, two, three . . .
WAKE UP, MOMMY!"

I mock-jerked awake, blinking ostentatiously, trying to focus
my gaze his way. "Oh!" I exclaimed, feeling the words wobble in
my mouth. "Why did you wake me up? I was having such a nice
dream—"

(*I dreamed I had no boy*—those were the words I usually finished with, bending my simmering resentment into an in-joke,
and Clark had picked it up as quickly as any other. *No boy!* he
usually replied, triumphantly. But not today; today, the words
locked in my throat.)

Instead, I shifted to Dr. Seuss, oldest standby besides Mother
Goose. "Here, in the dark," I said. "Say, would you, could you, in
the dark?" And felt him nod, my hand still touching his cheek,
blessedly cool and fever free. "Look what we found, in the park,
in the dark," he responded. "We will take him home. We will
name him—"

"Clark," I agreed, voice gone suddenly ragged. "It's me, bunny.
Do you see Mommy?"

"I see her," Clark replied. "And now, it's time to kiss him."

"Sounds good. High-five?" I held up my hand.

"Whoo-hoo!" said Clark, utterly deadpan, whacking my palm
with his. "He will live in our house, he will grow and grow. . . ."

(*Will our mother like this? We don't know.*)

Once more, he smashed his lips onto mine without any warning but an exaggeratedly theatrical "MWAH!" Brief as a branding
iron, hard enough to almost hurt—but only in the best way. I
gathered him up and hugged him fiercely, trying to calm myself
by matching his febrile heartbeat to mine, till he finally started to
squirm. "You've to let me go!" he ordered, sounding like a Hong
Kong movie subtitle.

"I might," I said. "But there is a price, pretty boy, there is a
price. Do you know what?"

Reluctantly: "The price is hugging . . . and kissing."

"Exactly."

Clark had learned to accept these bursts of affection phleg-
matically, but this time he resisted even less than normal, just

letting his heavy, hard head rest on my breastbone. I could feel his grin, though; he knew this game, and liked it, as long as it didn't go on too long. So he kissed me again, lips smacking, and I managed to extort a third one before the door banged open again, causing him to break free.

"Who *is* it, Clark?" Mom called out, well aware he could tell even from here.

"Daddy!" he yelled back, scampering over. I heard Simon's grunt of effort; probably swinging him into the air.

"That's right, it's your friend Daddy. And topsy-turvy means . . ."

"*Upside dowwwwn!*" Clark yelled, and it was almost as if I could see it, imagining Clark arching back as Simon steadied him, making sure his hair only brushed the floor, instead of his skull colliding with it.

"Family happens at Swiss Chalet," Mom commented side-long, echoing another longstanding piece of echolalic emotional shorthand. To which I simply nodded, reduced to silence once more, throat tight, eyes burning.

"Yup," I agreed, eventually.

It was a good day after that, (lack of) eyesight issues aside. One of the best.

But all good things come to pretty much the same end, if you only wait long enough.

EIGHTEEN

A week later, I woke cold and shaking in the middle of the night. I pried myself out of Simon's grip and rolled to the bedroom floor, landing on hands and knees; the apartment seemed to reel around me, contracting and expanding, a seasick Hitchcock focus pull. What vestige of sight I'd regained over the last few days made everything around me just a series of vague lines and angles, but it was better than nothing. Good enough to navigate by, at any rate, as I felt my way up and into the living room, pulled my iPhone off its charge cord.

I thumbed it on, password disabled since Simon had been kind enough to download some voice-activation software, and coughed, clearing my throat. "Call Safie Hewsen," I told it.

She picked up on the fourth ring; saw my caller I.D., obviously, since the first thing she said was: "Miss Cairns?"

"That's right, yeah." I coughed again then swallowed. "We, uh . . . I mean . . . well, we might've made a really bad mistake."

There was a pause.

"Oh, you *think?*" she said.

Later, I'd realize I didn't remember falling asleep that night, not *per se*. Just what came after, and after that.

I knew it was a dream the second I raised my head and could see again, unoccluded. But I knew even more quickly that what I was dreaming must be a memory—a lost memory, *the* lost memory. My most recently lost.

First, a sort of light seed in the darkness, just beginning to bloom—the very start of an old-fashioned iris shot, unfurling outwards. And then I was back in the living room, my hand in Sidlo's, at the moment of breakage—the same micro-instant, before my second trip down into buzzing, burning absence took hold. We were still murmuring together, he and I, but somewhere to the left of me I could hear Safie, stuck behind her camera; maybe I was making a noise she didn't like, my words starting to slur, wincing as though in pain: *oh, ah, fuck meeee.* I couldn't hear what she heard, what might or might not be coming out of me. Couldn't do, or think, much of anything.

It was slowing down, all of it—everything slipping sideways into a kind of a pocket, a funnel twisting slickly. Like the gap where your tooth used to be, where your tongue longs to go: stick it in, twist it, taste the blood. *Because* you know you shouldn't.

Free will, that bitch of a thing. Given the freedom to choose, we human beings will always make the wrong choice, every damn time.

And then there I was, right there. With—

(*Her?*)

In front of me, over Sidlo's slumped shoulder, a figure was taking form, shouldering aside the blinds like two bloodless flaps of skin—an autopsy's Y-section, cauterized from within. Extruding out into the world head first, dragging its train through behind, its floor-skimming veil sewn with dangling mirrors, tinsel, and glass reflective from every angle.

On its head was a crown. In its hand, tip drooping, scoring the floor, a sword.

Lady Midday.

And here is where things start to shiver; here things blend and bend. Here is where things stick, like a frame of film through a projector's gate. Here is where things start to catch, and melt, and burn.

* * *

Inside the pocket, the whole rest of my memory's contents peel and whisk away, leaving nothing behind but a pitiless circle of light. Just me and Vasek Sidlo, frozen inside its circumference, with this phantom leaning in overtop, sliding one hand down under his shirt collar and cupping his frail breastbone, that lid beneath which his ancient heart beats.

I am abruptly hyper aware of the danger—my body, a mere meat-bone-blood-shit shell for my frenzied brain; a cage without keys. Sweat pricks my palms, my temples, muddies the small of my back. Pins and needles in my damaged shoulder, both arms clenching so hard the nerve cuts off, twangs like a pained string. My back hunches, furls, longs to grow wings.

Sidlo's looking up now, eyes narrowed, studying. Then they widen slightly, and—he smiles, the same way he did when I first walked into his room, at the home. As though he recognized me.

So long, so long I've waited . . .

. . . to see you, and not again, not really. No.

For the first time, ever.

Giscelia, that was my name, the painful burning figure hovering above tells me, as Sidlo relaxes against her like a tired child, head pressed to her bony, shrouded bosom. *Then Iris, then Mrs. Whitcomb . . . so many names, as poor Vasek says. So many attempts to reach you, after such long silence.*

I blink at her, so dry I can almost hear my lids click; wish I could cry, if only for purposes of hydration. Try to summon a suitable response—*any* response, really—but nothing comes. We are so far beyond all known maps, and I have no stars to guide me—no instinct, no tools. Not even a compass.

I shut my eyes tight against the light as death's breath meets mine, smelling of rotten flowers.

So very long, the figure repeats. *But time grows short, for all of us, and I have to show you something, sister, directly. Since you still refuse to listen.*

"I don't—"

Sssh, hush. Be quiet, that's all I ask. For once.

Now open your eyes once more, and watch.

*   *   *

I met Her in the field, when I was a child, trembling under my father's wrath—his God-madness. And that was the beginning of it, as you already know.

"Yes."

I grew up, possessed by Her image. I met Arthur and married him. Because he loved me, he took me there, to find out what it was I'd been seeing all those years—Dzèngast. "Home."

"I know, yeah. I found your—"

I let you *find it, sister, led you to it. Like She led your friend in the woods. As She would lead you elsewhere, if I did not stand between.*

I frowned. "Stand between . . . So everything up till now, everything that's happened—that *wasn't* Lady Midday after all? That was—?"

Yes, sister, me. Hurting you to spare you further hurt. Visiting harm on you and yours, in the service of saving you from harm.

"*You* killed Jan, that's what you're saying."

Something I'd mourn, if I still could. And yet.

(And yet.)

Now: are you ready to see?

"See . . . what?"

What you did not want to then. What you blinded yourself in order not *to see.*

Something you'd rather sit in the dark with forever than look at directly. That'd be bad, man. Really bad. I didn't know if I was capable of looking at something like that, or anything else. If I was—capable, at all. If I ever had been.

I kept my eyes closed in the field when She came; you keep your eyes closed now. But you can only be selfish so long, sister.

Mrs. Whitcomb's skeleton hand slipped further down to rest lightly over Sidlo's hidden, fluttering heart.

This world is full of terrifying things, yes—far more than we ever thought; things that make us want to run, to hide, to dig ourselves deep and pull the earth up over, a child under blankets. But being a mother must put paid to all that, don't you find? It's like being born again, your heart on the outside of your body.

It all sounds so simple, because that's how I'm making it seem—so glacially paced, when it actually went by in a drunken rush, a neural pop. Because when one mind touches another, even through the medium of a third mind, things happen at absolute top speed; essentially indescribable, even when you struggle to. Particularly then.

Be bold now, Lois—for Clark's sake, if not your own. Please.

(A classic fairy tale instruction, with its provenance daylight-clear: the sign over Mister Fox's murder warren, that grim den of bones, warning unwary potential brides away. *Be bold, be bold, but not too bold, Lest that your heart's blood should run thick with cold.*)

"What do I have to do?" I made myself ask.

What are you willing *to do?*

"What's necessary?"

I meant it as question, but she took it as a statement. And there she was, all of a sudden—closer yet, engulfing Sidlo, who gasped in pleasant pain: *Oh yes, oh thank you. At last.* Her shrouded face pressed up to mine, teeth to lip, so near my nose almost fit the hole where hers should have been.

Listen to me, she repeated—a whisperless whisper, so strong I felt my whole head resound. *She is not here, not yet, but soon; call me Her harbinger. She shone her light on me and I became her reflection, her crooked shadow. But I am not even one-tenth of what she is—a ghost, not a god. You would always rather deal with a ghost than with a god.*

"I—yes, yeah. I agree."

And the reason She is coming is you. Accept that. Because you wouldn't turn away. Because you kept going when everything—when I—told you to stop.

"I understand," I admitted, not wanting to.

You made a door for Her, and it will open, unless you close it. Or the only control you have left will be over where She arrives, and who She shows Herself to.

Time to do the unselfish thing, in other words. Unlikely as that was.

Mrs. Whitcomb's ghost looked down then, or seemed to—hard to tell without eyes. *In Dzèngast, when I asked the Kantorka*

*how I might yet escape, she laughed at me. As she was right to.
What she told me was this, and I have remembered it ever since,
though I never wanted to believe it: "Only do your duty and you
will not be chosen—that is Her promise. Unless She decides your
duty is to be chosen."*

I cleared my throat. "Will you leave them all out of it if I do?"

Yes, sister. To the best of my ability.

"Will She?"

I cannot know. No one can.

No surprise there.

So I bent my head in the dark, not daring even to pray. "Show
me," I told her.

I opened my eyes. I saw.

I was seen.

And like my self-proclaimed "sister" before, I knew I would
never again be *un*-seen.

The blinds behind her were sealed back together now, narrowly
bisected, daylight threaded. I saw images spill across them, flaring like a plume of steam—memory as movies, pulled straight
from her head through Sidlo's, black and white and silver burnt
all over. Reflections in the mind's eye of a long-dead woman.

The images were constantly oscillating, rendering them impossible to understand for a few seconds, till I recognized a particular pattern of rhythmic blur: the way sunlight flickered through
the GO Train windows when we took it down to Mississauga on
a summer afternoon so Clark could spend time with Gran and
Granddad, Simon's folks. Which, in turn, snapped everything into
focus, an optical illusion flipping from nonsense to meaning.

A dark-panelled train compartment with cushioned benches,
smaller than any I'd ever travelled in—Victorian, Edwardian
maybe. One door, one window; a cream-gloved hand (mine?)
pushed in the last of a series of pins fastening a sheet across
the already-drawn blinds, shutting out the last of the popping,
scratching, flickering outdoor light. But the haze around me
wasn't *all* darkness—there was something else in my way, a sort

of swaying scrim, lightly floral patterned. Cream too, or even white, dimmed down to dirty grey.

(A veil.)

Squeezing back past the projector, set up on the compartment's tiny side table, I watched "my" hands travel up past my face, then peel the occlusion free from my head on down, like shedding skin. The image immediately sharpened overall, lightened, though only slightly. The bulk of it fell sidelong, topped with the flat, broad-brimmed beekeeper's hat it'd swung from, trailing over the closest disused row of seats.

There was one further, small pause, time enough to wonder if "I"—this memory-movie's unseen protagonist—might be nerving herself up for something. Then, all at once, the gloves reached out once more, snapping a series of switches; the clacking, whirring sound of a film reel kicking into motion, rattling gears mimicking the train wheels below as light splashed against the haphazard sheet-screen in a blaze. And underneath: harsh breathing on the ragged edge of sobs. It rose over the camera's whir, keeping a gross sort of time.

Don't look, I thought, as though I had a choice. *I'm not going to look, I won't—*

But the real laugh of it was there was nothing there *to* see. Not immediately.

(*In the field, when she came, I kept my eyes closed. My first sin, in a long line of them.*)

Just darkness at first, close and hot as the train itself, muffled somehow—only the barest lines of light available to become gradually arching upwards, outwards, the veins of two crossed leaves. A tiny, uneven triangle near the top, centre-hung—a sort of upside-down diamond. But watch long enough (you couldn't not, I soon found), and things got ever more recognizable, in tiny increments. The lines thickened, greying, back lit flesh over bone. Ten fingers separating with slow discomfort, reluctant, as though under orders; that flesh diamond stretching, breaking open, wider, wider, wider: Hell's own peep-hole, framing an uprooted, alien world. To show, at last—

A denuded field, bare to the tree line. Dust on the horizon. Ash from a burned-out barn.

Humps of clothing, some hugged together, burnt and swollen faces turned away. Flies rising, probably buzzing, though the lack of sound made it hard to tell.

And bright, *so* bright, but . . . slanted, somehow. Not lit so much by the still-noontime sun above, burning stationary at its centre-most point—the time between the minute and the hour, according to Dzèngast's long-dead Kantorka—as by something located just off-screen and widdershins, on the sinister left-hand side.

Cameras stayed stationary in the earliest films, but this was memory, no matter the trappings. And Mrs. Whitcomb . . . Iris Dunlopp . . . Giscelia Wròbl . . .

Her head was already moving, even as her hands dropped. Swinging 'round, eyes slightly squinted, to finally see, to face—

The sword, and its bearer. That burning crown. That molten hair, falling to brush those bare, brass-nailed feet. That face—too beautiful to not stare at, yet almost too bright to perceive clearly, without threat of damage. That looming body, silver-white shrouded and figured all over with white-hot gold, a slice of sun itself.

This, *this* was the real thing, obviously. Real enough to wound. Real enough to tear the wall between worlds like flesh.

Light roared through the gap, a blinding torrent. "I" threw up my hands—sheer instinct—before forcing them and "myself" back down, to one knee. From somewhere, a word came:

Lady.

Nothing remotely feminine—or even human—in the massive force glaring at "me" through that awful gap, so the term rang both hollow and foolish, like calling a volcano "Sweetheart." Yet it was all "I" had, and apparently, it was enough to merit a reply.

(daughter)

At the sound of it, so killing-soft, so—*deplorable*, equally bruising to the ears as its speaker was to her own eyes, brain, *soul*—I felt Mrs. Whitcomb reel, momentarily deafened, almost passing out. Then she pulled herself straight again, still kneeling, and repeated:

Lady, please. I beg you.

So terrible, to be under a god's eye, her attention. To be pierced through, pinned, like an insect.

(*daughter of liska, daughter of handrij, I see you, yes*)

(*I know your name*)

(*what would you ask of me? what would you*)

(*offer*)

Not *quite* so overwhelming, this time, but still a skull-rattling cacophony, still utterly soulless. *You know,* "I" cried back at her. *My son, Hyatt. That he be here, or I be there, with him. I no longer care which.*

(*ah, but that cannot be*)

(*he does his duty*)

(*poor broken thing, gone to feed the earth, and happily*)

(*knowing, at last, he has a purpose*)

The train rattled on, as did the projector; the sheet-screen burned still, heatless, unconsumed. And I felt Mrs. Whitcomb rock back on the heels of her high-buttoned boots as though slapped, kick-skirt flaring; felt her lips tighten, her heart skip, her ears burn. Felt her give a long, ragged breath, before gathering enough courage to ask the terrible thing before her—

What?

(*you heard me, daughter*)

I'd never seen a photo of Hyatt; there weren't any that I knew of. So instead I saw Clark, of course—grinning sly over his shoulder, trying to catch my gaze so he could spout a string of well-memorized advertising jargon and have me sing it back to him in the same slurred, jazzy way, all inflection, no real content. A bare sketch of conversation, pared down to the simplest of all emotions: contact, acknowledgement, affection. I see you, Mommy; do you see me? I—

(*love*)

The idea, sweet Jesus. The very fucking *idea* of something, *anything*, telling me that, about Clark . . . it lit me up, inside. Or was that *her*, Mrs. Whitcomb? All that fear, all that awe—

—and now, anger, sweeping it all away. Plain human rage, like a landslide. Like a flood.

You took my son, she said, toneless. *And you killed him.* Continuing then, for all she must have known it meant nothing: *How long ago? Was it the same night, or later? Did he live with you, here? Was he happy, even for a little while? He* loved *you, you vile thing; I saw the evidence—his drawings, his trances, his tiny ecstasies. God damn me, I loved you too, in my way.*

I was never given a choice not to.

And here I remembered an interview I'd read once with Larry Cohen, non-practising Jew and director of many fine no-budget horror films (*The Stuff, Q: The Winged Serpent, It's Alive!*), in which he said that if any of us really believed in God then every time we prayed, the only thing we'd ask for would be for Him to leave us the hell alone.

To all of which Lady Midday didn't quite nod, but neither did She—did It—completely disagree. Only replied, in that same dreadful voice—

(*he does his work, yes, for which he was chosen*)

(*as you do that for which* you *were chosen*)

(*as you complete it, now*)

And again: *What?*

The film, of course: Mrs. Whitcomb's ultimate vision of Lady Midday, plucked straight from her head and packaged for mass consumption, with Vasek Sidlo's unwitting help. The image that forms a door, opening from both sides, to let Lady Midday— her inspirational muse's gaze, her inquisitor-executioner's judgements, her ceaseless thirst for sacrificial blood—back into an unwarned, unprotected, supposedly safely disbelieving world at last.

To take possession of someone capable of mastering this language of images and illusion, almost from birth, and use it to create something that could seize an entire audience's hearts and minds at once, restarting the cycle of worship in an altogether new way.

Dzèngast had been destroyed during World War I, I vaguely recalled from my research, long after Mrs. Whitcomb's ill-fated honeymoon. Which meant that our all-powerful She had already been effectively busted back down to a fairy tale by the 1920s, one unlikely to be told outside Wendish circles, with fewer and fewer people identifying as such. So how else could She expect to gather together another patch of "old heathens" to feed Her the elderly and compromised, to chuck their exceptional offspring into the earth's open maw, if not through the wildly flourishing new international church of cinema? Where else could She hope to find and train a fresh Kantorka, one whose Cult of Lady Midday-proselytizing songs and stories might reach millions without Her even having to open Her mouth?

And Mrs. Whitcomb had played right into it, trying to save Hyatt, trying to save herself. Trying to placate this creature that chased her from cradle to grave, from the murder field in Lake of the North District, where she'd first felt Her touch, to this fast-moving Toronto-bound passenger train she stood in now, watching reality's skin peel away under the toxic weight of her life's "work."

Thinking: *I saw You. I saw Your reflection. You were behind me, like a light, on fire; You cast me like a shadow, and then I disappeared. And since then there has been nothing but light, and the light is still here, and I just want it to stop, all of it. I want to sleep, to lie down in the dark. I want it to stop.*

Poludnice, a little sunstroke, under whose scrutiny this shell of delusion in which we cocoon ourselves becomes nothing but dust and ashes. That moment of knowing things are literally irreparable, a last jolt before nothingness, as you shrink down to an easily extinguishable spark.

Was this what you saved me for, from my father? Mrs. Whitcomb asked. *Was this the game, all along? Was I never anything but a key to you, and my boy the key to me?*

Those pitiless eyes. That unforgiving glare. These words, soft as death, and just as inescapable.

(*what else?*) was all Lady Midday could apparently think to ask in return.

The film blazed on, impossibly bright. No darkness anymore, no contrast. Around it, the train compartment had begun to bleach, to lose consistency. Because Lady Midday was so close now, close enough to touch the screen from its other side. In a moment, she would climb through, and Mrs. Whitcomb could do nothing to stop it—tear down the sheet, perhaps, and stuff her back inside? No. The wall beneath would split; the train would crack in half. The sky would crack, and take the earth with it.

I did this, I watched Mrs. Whitcomb whisper to herself. *I am doing this. I let this happen.* Hearing, as she did—

(*yes, you did; you do*)

(*you do my work, for you are mine*)

(*you always were*)

(*you always will be*)

No malice in that statement, or even passion, save the faintest possible hint of satisfaction; no cruelty except for that found in nature, occasionally rebalancing itself to the tune of a couple of hundred thousand extinctions. And while I'd never actually tell Simon this out loud—though since he's eventually going to read this I guess the point is rendered somewhat moot—the closest I've ever come to believing like he and his family do is when I think about what happened next. How it was a random fluke, a complete coincidence, which somehow kept the world going on as it always has, instead of ripping apart like a bad episiotomy as Lady Midday birthed herself back into what we view as reality.

The fact is if Mrs. Whitcomb's compartment had been fitted with those newfangled electric light bulbs instead of the old-style Pintsch gas lamps, which most trains were already in the process of switching out, there wouldn't have been any matches in that little tray beside the sconces on her wall. Which means she, in turn, wouldn't have been able to grab one, scrape it 'cross the nearest hard surface—the top of that same side table—and then throw the lit match into the heart of her projector's exposed gear work, thus causing Vasek Sidlo's mentally-imprinted silver nitrate film, already overheated, to literally explode on contact.

The sheet-screen caught fire, and in almost the same instant, a great howl of cheated rage seized her, gathered her up, bore her up and away and forwards. The world folded in on itself, wiping away sight, sound, smell—everything. No pain followed, only darkness, pressure, cold and damp; ground sealing fast overtop, grit of soil everywhere, a smothering weight of earth on her back. The field again, though from a very different angle.

("he here or I with him," *daughter: do you remember?*)

(*you no longer care which, or so you say*)

Reaching out, blindly, barely able to move, till she felt the pressure of something against her outstretched fingers, just out of reach: tiny, sharp, hard. Like bones.

(*all I want is your toil, your duty, as promised*)

(*so many others ask for much more*)

(yet *if you make yourself useless to me, I will give you for gift something very different indeed*)

The twenty-seven secret bones of a dead child's hand, almost seeming to fold themselves into hers, in that last mocking second before she breathed a double lungful of dirt.

"Holy shit, Miss—Lois—that's an *awful* fucking story, right there." Safie's face wasn't much but an olive-toned blur, but I could imagine her expression from the sound of her voice: half appalled, half dazed, close to numbness.

"I know, Safie."

"And you, what, *dreamed* all this? *That's* why you called me last night?"

"I'm pretty sure it's what actually did happen, during the seizure, but I definitely get how you might not want to believe me on that one. Same way I'm sure you get why *I* didn't want to tell you the whole thing over the phone, at least not before you agreed to see—to meet with me."

Safie shook her head slightly, whistling through her front teeth. "Jesus," she said, after a moment. Then: "Okay, fine. So our really bad mistake was getting Sidlo to make another memory-film."

"Because it can be used as a door for Lady Midday, right."

"Which was—why we made it, I kind of thought."

I sighed. "Sort of. You know, what I said I was trying to do . . ."

"Talk to Lady Midday. Get her to leave your kid alone."

"Yeah, well—that was basically bullshit, on my end. I was

actually going to try and trap her, maybe even kill her. Get Sidlo to put her on film again, then burn it without looking at it like he said Mrs. Whitcomb should've, back when."

Safie rocked back as if I'd shoved her. "And Sidlo was down with this?"

"Sure. I mean, he would've been. He hated Lady Midday, right? For ruining Mrs. Whitcomb's life." I paused. "That said, I didn't really . . . tell him that part, as such."

"You thought you could trap a *god* in a freakin' *roll of film*," Safie repeated, understandably stuck on that particular part of the equation.

"A little god, by your Dédé's standards," I pointed out.

"Uh huh. Still . . ." Safie shook her head again then, as best I could make out, looked straight at me. "That was possibly the dumbest damn idea I've ever heard, Miss."

I hissed, rubbing the bridge of my nose where my glasses would usually rest if I were wearing them. "Christ, I know that *now*. Didn't, then. Not to mention I was also kind of out of my fucking mind at the time."

"True enough," Safie agreed, sipping her coffee.

We were downstairs again, at Tim's; it'd seemed the easiest option, especially since I still needed Simon's help to get down there. He was off at the nearest local park with Clark, waiting for me to text him whenever I wanted to be taken back up. Today was comparatively good on the sight front thus far, in that I could not only make out most things held a few inches from my nose, so long as I studied them a while, but could also tell the difference between static and moving objects—more like blundering my way through a fog rather than being blindfolded, or having everything I encountered look like it was encased in white plaster.

"So what happened to Sidlo in your dream?" Safie asked.

I thought back. "He . . . said he was sorry," I began, slowly. "And she said it wasn't his fault, or mine, or hers. *My sin brought you to Her attention, so She would not let you go till you had served Her ends once more. But I can make sure She never touches you again. . . .*"

And then I was back there, for a split second, watching Mrs.

Whitcomb's ghost slide her hand inside Sidlo's chest, arm stiffen-
ing to the elbow, squeezing something. Saw Sidlo gasp, lift his
head and smile, then slump sideways, blind eyes fixed; *thank you,*
his lips shaped, silently. Mrs. Whitcomb remained motionless,
fist still sunk wrist-deep between his ribs, as though reluctant to
release whatever she was touching.

You have to do it, Lois, she told me. *Find the film. Destroy it.*

"I understand."

She will not make it easy.

I remember opening my mouth to respond, maybe snap
something stupid, like *and why am I not surprised?* But something suddenly stopped me, struck me hard, a punch to the
stomach so deep it made me physically unable to breathe: light
and shadow folding together, deep beyond the blinds' narrow-
thread window, like the flicker at the end of a tunnel. Vibrations
in my feet, heralding an approaching train.

"Is there . . . something . . . behind you?"

Sister, this much is certain: something *lies behind everything.*

Under the veil, once more fallen shut, Mrs. Whitcomb's skull
seemed to smile, sadly. Light mounted, wiping her features away.

"Yes," I managed, tongue dry to cracking. "But, what I mean
is—is that—?"

(—Her?)

Yes. Which is why you should wake up.

Now.

I emerged from my fugue to find Safie snapping her fingers
near my right ear, quick but discreet—eyes intent on mine, trying to catch my gaze without making a scene. "Miss," she was
saying, low and worried. "Miss, Miss Cairns, hey. Lois?"

"Here," I replied, at last.

"Um, good. What just happened?"

I shook my head, to clear it. "Not all too sure. Harrison said
I might have episodes, like little drop-outs—sort of *petit mal,*
but not a big deal, comparatively. Sorry to worry you, if I did."
She restrained herself from questioning what had happened.
"Okay, so. The film's in custody, right? And we can get it back
now that they're not gonna charge us with anything . . . They

do have to release it, right? The reel belongs to us, after all—to you."

"Yeah, 'course. We can go down right now, easily."

I nodded. "And then we destroy it. We don't watch it, don't file it, none of that. Just burn the bastard up till it's gone, pure and fucking simple."

"Co-fucking-signed," Safie agreed, without blinking. We shared a sort of mutual half-grin, well aware how our lives had morphed into some unlikely genre mash-up—Quentin Tarantino does supernatural *giallo*, maybe, or a Guillermo del Toro sitcom, both with a CanCon twist.

And then we were in a cab, me voice-texting Simon as to where we'd gone, him responding almost immediately: *Wish you'd told me first but okay, love.* And then we were getting out in front of 54 Division, Safie leading me by the sleeve, like the world's largest five-year-old. And then we were talking to a constable on the front desk till, eventually, Detective Correa appeared.

"Miss Hewsen, Ms. Cairns," she greeted us, polite as ever. "You look—better, overall. What can I do for you?"

"I'd kind of like my stuff back," Safie said, which was an almost exact précis of what we'd already told that relatively nice-sounding uniform now busy answering the phone a few feet to our left. "Didn't know who else to talk to about it, really. So."

"Hmmm," Correa replied, not seeming particularly put out. "Well, as it happens, things are slow right now. Wait here."

Safie ushered me over then went to get us both more coffee, not that we needed it. I sat there for what seemed like longer than necessary, listening to the station's din like it was a really extended John Cage piece; the coffee, when it arrived, was hot, grainy, Java-flavoured water. Eventually, I heard Correa's sensible shoes tapping back down the hall, and sat up straighter.

"I have some rather disappointing news," she told us.

NINETEEN

Tired, holy Christ, *so* tired. It's a long time since I've had to think about all this deliberately, or with any sort of genuine detail; at least the bulk of two years since I've even *allowed* myself to, and part of that is mere self-protection—for the child of two actors, amusing enough, I'm a remarkably shitty liar. Which means I basically have to all but convince *myself* whatever agreed-upon fable I'm currently parroting is true, in order to even attempt to put it over on anyone else.

I don't know who I expect to see this, or when. After I'm dead, maybe. But then again, how plausible is it, really, except as a litany of hallucinations and existential crises—the testimony of a woman who lost both her sight and her mind, at least temporarily, while getting caught up in forces far beyond her own control? It doesn't even have to contain anything truly supernatural if you just consider it from the correct angle: already under intense psychological pressure, I experienced a series of sad but explainable traumatic events while researching a similarly eccentric and unstable woman who held odd, creepy beliefs which caused her to attribute every bad thing that happened in her life to a long-dormant monster goddess's malign influence. A type of transference occurred, thus causing me to develop a version of those same odd, creepy beliefs myself. QED. And all that's without even going into Wrob Barney's contribution to the whole affair. . . .

Oh yeah, right. I should probably start doing exactly that.

What had happened, Correa was eventually forced to admit, was that Safie's effects—Sidlo's reel very definitely included—had somehow disappeared from their designated space in 54 Division's otherwise hyper-efficient evidence processing and storage department. At first, they thought perhaps it was a matter of misfiling, of someone screwing up protocol, even filling out the paperwork incorrectly; Hewsen's not *such* a weird name, in context, but Safie sort of is. And I've certainly heard myself called "Miss Korns" over enough P.A. systems to know how difficult it is to believe what's right in front of you sometimes, especially if you're afraid of embarrassing yourself by pronouncing it incorrectly.

"So what now?" I asked Correa, who shrugged, though somewhat uncomfortably. "Wait and see," she proposed. "We have a pretty good system here, you know—even when things do go astray, they tend to turn up fairly fast later on, once we start looking."

"There's . . . a bit of a time element involved, Detective," I said.

"How so?"

Which probably wasn't the world's smartest tack to take, considering it was the reason we spent a good deal of the next few hours explaining why we hadn't warned the officers on scene they were handling a potential fire hazard. After a while, Correa's perennially bolshy partner got involved and started tossing around phrases like anti-police terrorism, but she thankfully shut him down before it could go much further—maybe she figured out that grilling a legally blind woman who's just gotten out of hospital over something you already know is bullshit wouldn't end well, especially when they're a former journalist who implies they have enough press contacts to get it looked into afterwards.

Simon was waiting for us when we at last exited the station, alone, arms crossed. "I dropped Clark off with Lee," he told me. "So, how'd you like the nickel tour of their interrogation suites?"

I reached out for his hand, hoping my facial expression looked mainly apologetic rather than annoyed. "Don't suppose you'd believe I got so jealous Safie and you had already been through once that I just had to experience it for myself."

He snorted.

"Not really, no."

I sighed. "Should probably tell you the truth then, I guess."

"My dad tells me it's a good policy in general, Biblically speaking."

We ended up in the Queen Mother Café, up near Queen Street West and Beverly. Three orders of Pad Thai later, Simon was up to speed and looking better fed, if not entirely convinced. "Importance of the film as an artefact left aside for a minute," he began, "what do you think happened? Wrob Barney and his magic chequebook again?"

"We don't have any proof of that," Safie pointed out.

"No," I agreed. "But I wouldn't put it past him."

Now it was her turn to sigh. "Yeah, me either."

"Well then, that's at least an investigative starting point," Simon argued. "You've already got a documented pattern of him interfering in your project. We can call Correa, tell her about Malin Riegert, the NFA, the stalking—point the machine at Wrob and let it take over. Do what it's supposed to do for *us*, for a change." He pulled out his wallet and extracted a card, holding it up before me like a magician doing a trick. "She left contact information, last time we talked. I say we use it."

I looked at Safie, her expression unreadable in the dim light; seemed like as good an idea as any, and I said so. But just as Simon went digging for his phone, Safie's started to ring out from our side of the table; Safie jumped to answer it. "Yes? Soraya, hi, yeah. What? No, haven't had a chance. We were—" A longer pause followed, and when she spoke again, her voice had gone grim. "I'm actually with Ms. Cairns right now, and her husband. Can I put you on speaker? . . . Okay, go ahead."

"Hi, Lois," Soraya Mousch said, her lovely, low tone unmistakeable. "And Mr. Lois."

"Simon, thanks."

"Simon. Sorry to interrupt you all, but I forwarded Safie an email yesterday, which I gather she's just getting around to now. It came through an old distribution list, one of those things Max and I—well, at any rate, I keep forgetting to unsubscribe. I thought I'd better follow up; you and she will both want to know about this, given what you've been working on."

Simon rolled his eyes. "Or, you know, you could *tell* us what it says, just for the hell of it—" He cut himself off as Safie stiffened in mid-scan, sat up and spat something vicious-sounding, probably in Kurdish. She almost handed the phone to me automatically, then thought better and passed it to him instead. "Read this out loud," she told him.

Simon took it from her, squinted down at the screen. "*Ursulines Studio, 8:00 P.M., November 15, World Premiere,*" he read. "*Be one of the first to see a lost piece of Canadian history. . . .*" His voice slowed, incredulous. "Untitled 14, *by Wrob Barney, uses original antique technology to recreate the never-before-seen work of Canada's first female filmmaker, Iris Dunlopp Whitcomb*—oh, I don't *believe* this." He shoved the phone back at Safie, raking both hands through his hair. "That *asshole!*"

"Ah," Soraya's voice observed. "So it *is* a surprise."

"To put it mildly." I tapped forefinger to teeth, literally staring at nothing. "Classic Wrob. He's going to pass her stuff off as his own—and ten to one he'll use Sidlo's whole reel, too, not just what he digitized from the cache Jan found." I tried to laugh, but couldn't manage much more than a grunt. "Talk about disrespect for somebody else's work; can't think Lady Midday's gonna approve of *that.*"

"Lady who?"

Safie grabbed the phone again, breath quickening. "Soraya, I'm sorry, we have to go," she said. "But thank you, so much—bye." She disconnected, cutting Soraya off mid-farewell. "Lois, that's less than half an hour from now, right in the middle of the Market; be a lot of people there, and none of them know better. We have to stop it."

"We," I repeated. "Like, you and *me*, you mean. The almost-blind person."

"That might be an advantage."

"*No.*" Simon slammed his palm down between us, startling our nearest neighbours. "Look, if the both of you are convinced then we'll *all* go. But no matter what, Lois—" He leaned forward, tone calm but hard, my hand abruptly in his. "No matter *what,* I want you to promise me you'll stay back and let me handle it. I don't want you risking yourself. Am I clear?"

For once, someone else's display of temper didn't spark my own; I was too far into terror for that, so far beyond anything I'd felt before that it lent its own weird clarity. So I squeezed back, replying, "Simon, baby, yes—you *are* clear, absolutely, but you're *wrong.* You still don't really get what you'd be in for."

"And you do?"

"Well, yeah. Like you say, stuff's happened. You *saw* it happen, some of it."

"I saw stuff happen to *you*, which is exactly why I don't want you near it again; no more, Lo. No more." He released my hands, rising, bag heaved over one shoulder. "I'm going to go settle up. When we get back, we'll take a cab up to this place and Safie and I will shut this down while you wait outside." To Safie: "Might be a good idea if you called Detective Correa, keep her in the loop. . . ."

She nodded and he turned away, rummaging for his wallet as he rounded the next corner, heading for the bar. Left alone together, we only had to glance at each other—a blurry twist of what I assumed was her head—before I stood, too, coat already half on.

"You in?" I asked her. "Tell me quick if you are."

"Lois, c'mon. All you have to do is wait."

"Yeah, sure—and then he runs in half-cocked, so Lady Midday can pick her teeth with him. Screw that noise. Plain truth is, if Clark has to lose one of his parents, it's better if it's me." Saying it out loud sunk a phantom needle through my chest; she tried to protest, and I cut her off mid-word. "No, just shut up, okay? I may not be as shitty a wife and mother as I think I am, but if I'd only agreed to leave well enough alone, we'd be laughing; Simon'll gladly kill himself getting me out of all this, and that's not something I'm willing to live with. So help me, please." I held out my hand shakily, barely able to see where it went. "*Please,* Safie."

Safie let out a long, stuttering breath. "Going by every horror movie ever, there's no possible way this can end well, for either of us," she said at last. "But . . . my Dédé always told me it was important to stand up, fight evil wherever and however, whether human or something else. Not to mention I guess some of this is on me, too."

"Hey, no fair," I retorted. "I got funding, remember? Which makes your part of the proceedings a job, not an obsession."

"Least I'm getting paid," she agreed. "Hell with it, though—let's just do it, and call it even."

Up and out, through the back door and onto the patio, Safie steering me into the alley. We emerged northbound onto McCaul at a sort of loping run, pausing to hail a cab. We'd only been in it for a few minutes when my iPhone began to ring: Simon, who else? We headed up through tree-lined side streets toward the Kensington area. I hit the "ignore" button once, then again, and one more time. After that, he switched to a series of texts heralded by impatient chimes, text-to-talk's vocal software growling at me in all-caps like a pissed-off Wookiee: LOIS DONT, LOIS STOP LOVE YOU, JUST FUCKNG WAIT GOD DAMN IT. I finally raised it to my lips and dictated three messages in quick succession: *Sorry, I have to, Love.* "Now send to Simon," I told it, before I turned the whole thing off.

The Saturday-night traffic was heavier than expected. I swore under my breath. "What time now?" I asked Safie, barely visible against the window, what with Chinatown's lit-up heart whipping by outside.

"Seven fifty-three."

"We're not going to make it."

"We might. Hey, you know Wrob; he likes to waffle. If his introduction runs long enough, then maybe . . ." Safie sighed. "Then again, maybe it won't even work for him. *He* wasn't 'touched,' not like Mrs. Whitcomb, or Sidlo, or you; probably doesn't know Lady Midday from her picture on the Vinegar House wall. If so, then for him, it'll just be a film."

For a moment, I wondered what the cab driver thought of all this, if he was even listening.

"Maybe," I said. "But I don't want to bet on it. Shit, he stole the thing She wanted to use as Her bible, Her doorway, then claimed it for his own—that's gotta piss her off. Hell, this *world's* going to piss Her off, the level of disrespect She's going to face on a daily basis."

(Big "s," big "h," without thinking twice about it. Christ, I was starting to sound like I came from Dzèngast.)

"I don't think it's about disrespect," Safie replied. "Not really. I mean, yeah, She doesn't *like* it, but it's more people who aren't . . . doing what they're supposed to, neglecting their responsibilities. People with no vocation." She paused. "Then again, how many people in that room—any room—know exactly what they're *meant* to be doing?" I heard her swallow. "I mean, *I* sure don't, and Lady Midday, She's not exactly Jesus; no Hail Mary rain cheques in *Her* church. She doesn't forget, or forgive."

I took a breath, felt it tremble in my chest, resonating: all fuzz, like some cordless speaker. Then whispered, the sound barely audible outside my own skull,

"Well, fine—can't really blame Her, not all that much. I was never very good at any of that crap, either."

By the time the cab let us out at the bottom of Augusta Avenue, into the unseasonably bitter November cold, it was already two minutes past eight. The streets were empty, and all I could see around me was a shifting black background pierced by blurred squares of yellow light. Safie paid, and the cab peeled away with unnerving speed; maybe the driver had decided he didn't want anything further to do with the crazy-talking ladies . . . or maybe he could sense the same thing I could. Something in the freezing starless air felt *strained*, like a weak spot in a balloon where the rubber looked uneven, splotchy and thin.

"Come on," said Safie, and I felt her grab me by my wrist, the same way I'd grabbed Clark a thousand times or more: *Enough fucking around, let's move.* I ran as best I could, blindly, trusting Safie's path and stumbling from time to time. Once I tripped and went down completely, banging the hell out of my knee, but the adrenaline stifled the pain and I was back on my feet before

Safie could fully stop. "No, I'm fine, I'm okay," I gasped, and we resumed our run. The noise of College Street came over the rooftops, nearing as we closed in on the Ursulines, but strangely distant. If we passed anyone else, I never saw them, or heard them; all I could hear was Safie's ragged breathing, and my own. We might have been alone, the city as empty as every post-apocalyptic vista ever: *The Walking Dead*'s Atlanta, *28 Days Later*'s London . . .

(Neither of which were really empty, of course. Which was the point.)

I recognized the Ursulines not by the shape or colour of its light but by the quality: the rattling flicker of a film in motion, leaking around black squares of drawn shades on the upper floor of the big square building. We staggered to a stop below those windows, staring up in dismay. "Shit," I choked, trying to get my breath back, "they've already started. Come on!"

Safie let go of my hand, ran to the front of the building; I heard rattling, banging. "Doors are locked!"

"That's the bike shop! You go up the fire escape, 'round the back—I think it's to the left . . . no, *right*." I raised my voice as footsteps scampered past, startling myself: "Safie, don't *leave* me!"

"Shit—sorry!"

Her hand seized mine again and I clutched it hard, too scared for shame.

We clattered up cast-iron steps to the landing, turned. A tall rectangle of lead-coloured light hung before us: the doorway to the studio was propped open. The short hallway beyond led to a set of double doors between whose seams the flickering light danced.

This is taking too long to tell. Longer than it took to happen, by far.

What I heard next I recognized from my "dream": the brazen bell, a slow, awful tolling; the fast, terrified breathing, thick and raspy with the air it gulped. A racketing thunder, more like a train hurtling along tracks than a film chittering through a projector's reels. And all with the faraway tinny sound of a gramophone recording, despite the fact that I knew, *knew*, the film should have been *silent*—the silver nitrate stock we'd given Sidlo had no track for recording sound. And somehow beneath, around and surrounding all this noise, the utter, hypnotized stillness of an audience caught completely in a film's spell—the stillness of a mouse before a snake, a rabbit before a stoat.

Oh God, I thought, while beside me, Safie was whispering something in a sibilant, guttural tongue. None of it made sense till I caught one name—*Malak-e-Tâwus*—and realized she, too, was praying. I shook her by the elbow.

Our first step forward felt like we were lifting our feet against gravity ten times that of Earth, the barely visible doors stretching away in a classic *Vertigo* push-pull zoom. Then we were past the threshold.

A thunderous *WHAM* of light and heat smashed against us, almost knocking me on my ass, but the noise that followed pulled me right back up, like a cord.

Screaming.

The first person we found as we fought our way into that sudden inferno was Leonard Warsame, who'd been doing doorman duty—unobtrusively helpful to the last, like a good boyfriend should be. He was collapsed on the floor near the doors, hands over his ears; we helped him up, turning our faces away from the horrible radiance pouring out of what had once been the screen. I remember shouting, but I don't remember what; later, in a *Toronto Star* article about the "disaster," he was quoted as saying: *Lois Cairns told me, "Don't look," and I said, "Believe me, I won't!"* At the time, all I saw was him nodding then following us back in, hunched over to stay below the smoke rapidly collecting against the ceiling. The air tore at our lungs as we bent, again and again, stumbling over knocked-down folding chairs, hauling up people lying limp or shaking in spasm, bleeding from noses, ears, eye sockets. I wound up with bloodstains on my palms, warm and coppery, as I had to feel my way over people for a handhold. Some bore bright, shiny burns on their faces and hands, eyebrows and eyelashes gone as if they'd been cooked. One man was having what looked like a full-bore fit, flinging himself up and down; it took me, Safie, and Leonard

together to drag him toward the doors, and when we got there
I collapsed, coughing.

"Got to stop it . . . at the source," I wheezed to Safie, who nodded, hacking up black phlegm. "The projector. Can you see it?
Don't look at the screen!"

Safie nodded, covering her eyes with one hand and tilting the
bottom edge up slowly, head ticking slow from side to side. At
last she pointed, shouting: "There! Straight ahead. Lots of chairs
in the way, and people. I'll yell when you get near! Go!"

I plunged back in, the smoke so thick it almost masked even
the burning screen's light. Faceless shapes stumbled past me, vanished. I tripped over a chair and just stayed down, crawling over
the hot hardwood floor on hands and knees. For half a second,
the slightly cooler, cleaner air was a blessed relief, till somebody
crunched what felt like a size-sixteen boot down onto my left
hand. I screamed, curling 'round the injury, then forced myself
to straighten and kept crawling, sobbing, this time on only one
hand, the broken one sweeping side to side. When it smacked
into the projector stand I gave another yowl but didn't stop—
grabbed on with other hand, got my knees under me, then my
feet. Forced myself up, tear-blind, the projector's rattle a deafen-
ing roar. And then—

The noise stopped.

Everything stopped.

My eyes snapped back into focus, clearer than they'd been
since I was five. Like I was wearing glasses with an absolutely
perfect prescription. My hand—red and swollen, one finger bent
sideways at an angle—stopped hurting. I took a breath but tasted
no smoke even though I could still see it everywhere around me,
frozen in mid-air like blackish-grey wool muffling moviegoers
caught in impossible poses, still trying to escape. Plus, cringing
against the wall with one eye peeking through his splayed hands,
Wrob Barney himself, paralyzed, appalled. Like Todt before the
lost Ark of the Covenant.

The moment between the minute and the hour, Vasek Sidlo
seemed to say, in my mind. And the screen's light shifted, brightening till it glared down from overhead, furious: the stark and

pitiless noonday blaze of the fallow field, the wasteland, turning everything around it to a cut-out silhouette—reflecting something entirely outside the world I knew.

I did then what I'd ordered Leonard not to—what I suppose I'd always known I *would* do, anyway: I looked.

It was only a film, after all. Right? A permanent record of a single string of linear time, "cut" in camera to pull seconds together, to create a reality of its own, encapsulating a larger one. Its emulsion scored by nothing so crude as waves of lens-bent light, but by thought itself, because nothing else could part reality's layers deeply enough to reveal what *truly* lay beneath: what was even now stepping down from that screen, towering up impossibly far beyond what the smoke-shrouded ceiling should have permitted.

For two or three heartbeats, I tried to pretend it was nothing but Iris Whitcomb's ghost again, in full Lady Midday drag—but all that stopped when the figure lifted its hand, simply wiping away that illusion, that glamour-shroud cocoon. What emerged was a thousand times more vast—the face, not the mask, or even the mirror: the Eye of the World, the still point, the muse. The thing that opens your own eyes from the inside, killing you with its glory.

The truth, plain and simple: that every idea—good *or* bad—comes from someplace entirely other, knocking on the inside of your skull, trying to get out. And not everyone survives its scrutiny.

(*what sad damage she's done you, that daughter of mine, in her raging. and all to keep you from me*)

(*a thankless task*)

(*your curiosity draws you to me, like moths to light. you see. you are seen*)

Not words, so much, but their meaning, placed directly into my brain by something for which speech was an impediment, not a tool. And on the same level I thought back, desperately:

The hell do you want, *anyhow?*

(*what is due, only*)

(*feed me. love me, and die of it. feed the earth, make it grow*)

(*do your duty*)

Yeah, no, I thought back, before I could think better. *Fuck that mediaeval bullshit, right in the fuckin' ass.*

Then cringed, expecting annihilation. But it didn't come; only stillness—a long, long no-moment. Followed by something I hadn't expected, at all.

(*then choose another duty and know my favour, for those who serve will be blessed beyond dreaming*)

(*ask, and you shall receive*)

Like . . . what?

(*let me show you*)

My brain peeled open.

There's this dream Mom has sometimes, and in it, Clark is an adult: tall, handsome, able to talk in complete sentences. They have a long, satisfying conversation in which he answers all her questions—he tells her he's happy, tells her he's always understood what we were saying to him, that he knows why we did the things we did and that he doesn't blame us for anything. He tells her he loves her, always has, always will.

It's a beautiful dream, and it obviously means a lot to her, but I've never had anything like it, and I never expect to. Which makes me sort of sad, considering I'm Clark's mother—what the hell does that say about me, in the end? After all, it's a hope, not a lie; it might even turn out to be true, eventually. One day.

And . . . here it was, at long last. Close enough to touch, or be touched by.

Like a memory of the future, a history-to-be: I saw days blur into years, like frames in film—the sudden breakthrough, Clark's speech and social skills exploding, years of delay caught up on overnight. I saw Simon promoted at his job, rich yet unchanged, still the same man who'd persuaded me to marry him by making it impossible to believe he'd ever leave. Rows of books, all with my name on them. Myself on stage, reading aloud to massive audiences, utterly pain-free. My mom, bragging proudly about me; people telling me what a difference my writing had made to their lives, how much I *mattered* to them. And then Clark onstage, too, performing, singing, *his* music spilling out of him, touching the world. Saying *I love you, Mommy*, with perfect clarity, perfect eye contact. *I've always loved you—this is for you, because of you, all of it. Thank you, for my life.*

But—*no.*

I put my hands to my eyes, felt the tears pouring down. Felt myself tense, suddenly head-to-toe rigid.

That's not my *son.*

Because sure, She could show me something like him, maybe even *give* me something like him, like what he might have been— but it would be forever a fake, nothing but a doll, made from dreams and dead flowers. *And I won't let you back in, not for that,* I thought. *Not if it means I'm responsible for everything you'll do after, sitting on a throne made from the bones of other people's kids— whoever* you *think is useless—to save yourself from being forgotten.*

All gods who receive homage are cruel, Zora Neale Hurston once said, and, Christ, wasn't *that* still true, like it always had been. *All gods dispense suffering without reason, otherwise they would not be worshipped. . . .*

But what is equally true, today as it was then, in that one second, is this: that I will always want to *earn* what I get, however much it hurts; that I want it *because* it hurts, because pain gives life a point, and without it life isn't even death, just . . . nothingness. And I will always want my son to be who he *is*, not how I'd like him, because it works both ways or not at all. Because if I'm not me, then who the hell am I?

I may not love myself, I thought, *but I do know myself. And you—don't.*

All of this I flung back at Her, Lady Midday, in far less time than it took to write it down. Which may be why the pause She took before replying lasted longer than almost anything that had gone before.

(*but i can make you . . . better*)

(*if*)

Yes, of course. *If.*

Small gods tempt, like Safie's Dédé said; they take what's already ours then offer it back to us at twice the price, bountiful and cruel at the same time, for no good reason. The sort of gods whose attention brings inspiration inseparable from torment. And if we see too much, if we feel too deeply, are exalted, are set apart—we will never be comfortable, only blessed.

Which means the best they can do for us . . . the closest they can ever come to doing "good," as the Peacock Angel supposedly does . . . is to force us to make our own distinctions between right and wrong. To discover what we truly value, by asking for it as payment.

It was over, then. I knew it; She knew it. But She didn't like it.

Reality slipped, stuttered and jerked like film caught half-on and half-off its sprockets; pain smashed into me and I went down, clinging to the projector stand, struggling to hold myself upright, with smoke in my once more useless eyes. Unable to see anything except for *Her*, still searing bright and impossibly tall, her molten sword hefted in one taloned hand. Rising, slowly, up over me.

(*do—your—WORK*), She told me, Lady Midday. And I coughed out something I knew She'd know was a laugh, even if nobody else could have recognized it.

"Oh, I'm gonna," I told Her, this time out loud, voice raw. "But it's gonna be *my* work, not yours. And whether or not it's worth it? *You* don't get to say."

The rising sword paused, as if surprised at last. Maybe nobody really had said no to Her before, or never as firmly as this.

(*you wish to matter*), She reminded me. (*my chosen stand apart. for others, nothing—but for my chosen, special favour*)

"Special like how, exactly? Like Special Ed-type special?" I laughed again, choking. "Lady, I've been like *that* my entire life— just like Clark." I hauled myself up far as I could, determined to go out standing. "So I don't *want* anything, not from you. Take it all back, and everything else, too, while you're at it. From now on, my *work* will be to make sure no one ever remembers you again."

A long silence, broken only by the crackling of flames, and a whirring sound in my ear: the film had run out, whipping 'round and 'round the projector's take-up reel. Nothing else mattered, not except Lady Midday, and that blazing sword high above.

(*be blind then. forever.*)
The sword swept up—

At the last minute, though, came the weirdest thing I've ever seen, or ever expect to see: Wrob Barney, of all people, charging in to knock me aside. Wrob Barney screaming into a goddess's face with only a folding chair raised between, for the world's most ridiculous weapon—*no, you do NOT, it was ME all along, not her, not* her! *It was supposed to be ME!*

Choose me, choose me, choose me, like a kid on a playground. Like the teams were all matched up for kickball, but nobody had picked him.

I mean, I didn't *like* Wrob, and I still don't, not even now. Not even after he obviously saved my life, if not—for all I know—my soul.

Christ Almighty, though. What a pitiful goddamn way to die.

I remember lying on the floor, contorted in pain, as the projector fell away from me, Sidlo's film sparking, going up like a Catherine Wheel. I remember Wrob falling the other way, in two pieces. Lady Midday, first there, then gone. Her sudden absence left a scar on the world, white hovering over black, reversed.

Somebody who later turned out to be Safie turned me over, drawing a scream. She slid her arms up under mine and hugged me around the chest, dragging me back toward the doors, where she was met by Leonard Warsame and somebody else—Simon, staring down at me white-faced, grabbing my ankles. They heaved me up, then headlong down the stairs and out, under the stars.

(No, I couldn't see them, obviously. But I knew they were there.)

The night air was cold, but clean. I breathed in, coughed, breathed in again. Felt everything around me narrow like a D.W. Griffith signature move, so damn old it was new all over again: up, back, down. My mental camera's perspective, dollying straight in on my own shrinking pupils, employing first a slow pull into focus, then an equally slow pull back out of it. An iris, shrinking inward, taking everything with it.

Simon's lap was warm, comforting. He and Safie were talking to each other someplace far above my head. He stroked my
hair, possibly not even knowing what he was doing. Soon enough
there were sirens, coming closer.

I lay there a few minutes more, contented, until I finally fell
asleep.

CREDITS

In their forensic analysis of the Ursulines Studio fire, the Metro Toronto arson team's report implies that something almost as flammable as silver nitrate itself—a casually thrown joint, perhaps, though the screening room was supposedly a non-smoking space—must have hit the projector in mid-rotation, thus causing *Untitled 14* to ignite. And certainly, a few witnesses do claim they saw it burning merrily in the moments before that last explosion, the one which supposedly ripped Wrob's head from his shoulders with one single, weirdly level blast, cauterizing his neck from throat to spine. Of course, none of that really explains where his head actually went after that, or how it eventually came to be found buried two feet down in the concrete floor of the bike shop, a whole storey beneath where the rest of his body fell.

Construction workers finally drilled down into it during the rebuild, five years later, when that whole block was being turned into a condo everyone else in Kensington Market almost killed themselves protesting. The end of an era, some said. The end of something, anyhow.

By then, the book Safie and I did indeed end up co-authoring was into its third printing, and still going strong: *Highly Combustible*, a weird—and in the event, award-winning—mixture of true crime and lost Canadian cinematic history; the story of how one filmmaker's obsession with curating another's legacy ended

in literal disaster, accidental mass murder, and equally accidental suicide. I think the real cornerstone of our pitch, once we'd
recuperated from the fire's aftermath, was having returned to
Quarry Argent and confirmed—via Val Moraine, natch—that
the unlucky "kid from Overdeere" who fell through the floor in
the Vinegar House and got stuck there overnight while researching his thesis had been, in fact, Wrob Barney himself. He'd been
enrolled in Brock University's film studies program under a different name, doing his courses on a correspondence level, while
simultaneously amassing a move-to-Toronto fund by working in
one of his family's stores.

In hindsight, it all looks remarkably straightforward: this
traumatic experience obviously formed the cornerstone for
Wrob's lifelong jealous obsession with Mrs. Whitcomb and her
art, which led in turn to him trying to seize it and make it his
own, both literally and figuratively. With Leonard Warsame's testimony backing us up, we can retrospectively assume that Wrob
had already found and planted the cache of Mrs. Whitcomb's
films, to which he led Jan Mattheuis, having done all the necessary legwork while tracking down Japery's old pit stops and
discovering the Quarry Argent collection. Building on the same
theory, we can likewise assume that Wrob somehow arranged for
me to be there to review *Untitled 13*, expecting me to imprint
on his use of Mrs. Whitcomb's clips and become his champion,
making sure he was credited for her discovery. Then, when I not
only didn't but tried to co-opt "his" project as my own, he got
progressively more unstable: bribed people to stalk me, arranged
burglaries, maybe even stage-managed the NFA fire and Jan's
death. That last part's not strictly provable, so we didn't end up
going too far with it, in the end—but then again, we didn't really
have to, once it became clear the Barneys had no interest in suing
us for defaming their familial black sheep's name post-mortem.

It sounds ridiculous, obviously, given what I've already told
you. I'm well aware of that.

Funny how eager people will be to believe almost anything,
though, especially in the face of tragedy, so long as it sounds even
mildly plausible.

The book sells well, even now, and I'm proud of it, which I suppose only makes sense—it's made me more money than anything else I've ever written, hands down. Too bad I can't ever tell anybody outside my own home that it also happens to be my very first stab at fiction.

When I woke up after the fire, back in hospital yet again, Detective Correa was standing over my bed. I saw her indistinctly, as through a mist, and smiled—mainly because I was surprised to be able to see her at all.

"Ms. Cairns," she said. "You're either the luckiest woman I know, or the exact opposite."

I coughed, throat rough, semi-cooked. "Six of . . . one, I guess," I whispered, unable to stop grinning.

She told me thirteen people had died in the fire, which seemed surprisingly low, considering what Safie and I'd stumbled across on our way in. But while the injury toll was far higher, and almost nobody involved had escaped without damage, the people we hadn't been able to save had either all died before we got there, or been unable to escape for other reasons. One guy, for example—his name was Hartwin Tolle—had somehow managed to get his arm stuck halfway *inside the wall*, as though it had suddenly become so hot the plaster itself had started to melt. I didn't even know if that was strictly possible, according to the normal laws of physics, but it didn't really seem like something worth bringing up at the time.

Only two of the dead remained unidentified, Correa said, a pair of skeletons found near where the screen had once hung. Both were totally denuded, fleshless, and old, though one appeared to be older than the other—a mature woman and an immature child, probably male, possibly around ten years old at the original time of death. Did I have any ideas about who they might be?

I allowed that I did, but that the idea might sound a little nuts, even in context. To which Correa just crossed her arms, eyebrow hiking only slightly.

"Go on," she said.

Eventually—a relatively long while later, at least by *CSI* standards—authorities were indeed able to match the DNA of the late Arthur Macalla Whitcomb's surviving relatives to the child's, thus proving he was probably Hyatt, while similar tests matched *his* DNA with that of the woman, revealing her to have once been Iris Dunlopp Whitcomb, née Giscelia Wròbl. What demented satisfaction Wrob Barney might have gained from digging up their bones after somehow finding out where they were both buried, meanwhile, remains a mystery, as does the exact cause of Mrs. Whitcomb's death—let alone how she ended up back near Quarry Argent after having disappeared, while still in transit, from a Toronto-bound train. But given how much other cracked-out shit Wrob'd been posthumously charged with, in the interim, I suppose everyone involved just sort of agreed to let it slide.

It's like I've always said: re-frame any story with its end in mind, as a *fait accompli*, and it all suddenly becomes very logical indeed. Besides which, what did anyone really have for evidence to the contrary? The testimony of a two-time seizure survivor who says a ghost told her in a dream a dead goddess did it? No, that was obviously my own subconscious playing games, solving a crime before it even happened; that's what I wrote, and that's what I'm more than happy to keep signing off on, so long as it keeps bringing in the bucks.

I have a son with special needs, after all, and 25 percent of everything I make goes into a fund for him, to keep him well looked after, once Simon and I are gone. Which I guess makes being legally blind for the rest of my life look like a pretty good trade-off, inconvenient though it may be in daily practice.

As things stand now, I've got my career back, and better than ever. I can kind of write my own ticket, in a way; I'm programming for festivals here, interviewing and being interviewed there, hosting special screenings. I'll never be able to learn to drive now, not even if I wanted to, but my eyesight does keep on improving steadily; the other day I woke up and realized I was *looking* at the ceiling, actually able to see all the cracks, the stippling, the stucco-shadows . . . Christ, that was amazing. I didn't stop crying for the next half hour.

"The great part," I told Simon, just the other week, when he, Safie, and I got together for dinner, like we do almost every other month, "is that most of the stuff we found out about Mrs. Whitcomb I can still talk about in public without looking insane, 'cause it's just true: her dad killed her family, she grew up obsessed with fairy tales, made art, lost her son, talked to ghosts. She made films."

He frowned. "All that information about Lady Midday, though—it's still *in* there. Somebody could go look it up, pursue it, if they wanted to."

"Yep," Safie agreed, pouring some more wine. "But why would they? Factor Wrob's actions in on top, it all just becomes a bunch of crazy shit Mrs. Whitcomb happened to believe in, stuff *she* thought was true, because of all the bad things that happened to her. Sad, for sure. Totally. But nobody's gonna be burying anybody in fields over it anytime soon."

I nodded. "'Just because you think something's real, doesn't make it so'—they say that about all sorts of religions, all the time. And a religion without miracles doesn't tend to leave much of a footprint, does it?"

"Hmmm." Simon lifted a finger, the old aha-gotcha twinkle back in his eyes. "What about Scientology?"

"Scientology doesn't count," I replied. "Not when it comes to old dead religions requiring human sacrifice. That's common knowledge, man." And I kissed him.

Later, Safie told me the producers she'd been working with had finally managed to net a bit of Telefilm funding, though not for her long-deferred Yezidi film. "They want to do the book, adapt it," she admitted, reluctantly. "Like, *semi*-fictionalized— sort of a braided narrative, back and forth through history. Mrs. Whitcomb juxtaposed with Wrob. Like *The Hours*, but with setting yourself on fire."

"Aaron Ashmore in a fake nose?" I suggested, laughing when she shuddered.

For myself, I know I see things differently, literally, since that night at the Ursulines, that day in the Vinegar House. That on the one hand, I no longer reckon my own worth—or lack thereof—by the same standards; while on the other, I know beyond a doubt that the world is full of holes behind which numinous presences lurk—secrets no one should ever have to see, or want to. And those who do will never be the same.

Maybe the iconoclasts were right—any image is an anchor, a trap, an open invitation. When you see the god, *a* god, you either forget or you go mad, trying to forget—*ekstasis*, the Greeks called it, "to stand outside oneself." A removal to elsewhere.

But there's a third choice, or at least I've found so: remember, no matter how it hurts to, and deal with the consequences of remembering. Submit, and bear your scars proudly.

I work on doing just that, every day, give or take. I work *hard*. And what will it get me, in the end? Will I be allowed to escape or be pulled back in, falling between the cracks? Into the places no one wants to think exist, to face what I *know* lives there?

I don't know yet. I can't.

I may never know.

What I didn't tell Simon, though, in our conversation—what I'll tell *you*, now—is how you'd be infinitely surprised what people will accept as a miracle, so long as it gives them something they really want: forgiveness of sin, unconditional love, the idea that your wounds make you special. That doing your art—your *work*—can help you save your own life.

Miracles, black, white, and grey all over. Like light on a wall, telling a story; like magic. Like cinema itself.

But, and still, and even so: it's the things you don't see, in this world or any other—the hidden things, unseen, lost between frames—

—that will always make all the difference.

STING

Soraya Mousch sent me this last part. It's something written at the Freihoeven Institute, during a "free imaging" session, a sort of channelling course for mediums. This chick Carraclough Devize teaches it, apparently—so maybe she wrote this on some-one else's behalf, or maybe it was one of her pupils, at the behest of similarly unseen powers.

One way or the other, I'm pretty sure I recognize the style.

It is so hard from where I am, it begins, & so difficult to reach you, so near & yet so far—

—but then again, I do not even know where I am. So I try to warn you & you do not hear, you never hear, not any of you.

Seeing is more important than hearing, though. & that is why I made it, made them, though I knew that I should not. Because. Because.

So hard, but I keep trying.

I did not look up, you see, not even when She touched me, & yet I know, now, what I would have seen. I have always known.

& so I tried to cut it from me, cast it far away. To show you all, though it is always better not to see, not to know, by far—

I can show you, now: what I saw, or almost. A black miracle, done brightly. A flame, once lit, burning everything it touches.

But no, don't: look down, not up—shut your eyes & keep them shut, no matter what you hear. No matter who comes, or what they ask you.

I was wrong to make them, I know that now, any of them. They are not for you, or me.

They are for no one.

My father was convinced that the world would end and we with it, unless we followed after this Call of his. But it did not, & now I think the tragedy is that the world never does end, ever. That it goes on & on, forcing us to go on along as well, until at last there is nothing else, nothing more. Until there is only what was, same as what is and what will be—

Only the truth, which never changes. Truth not made flesh but image, for anyone to see.

For a thought cannot be un-thought, anymore than the world can be un-made, & thus we can never escape the consequences of our mistakes, not without great price, & cost, & pain. Or perhaps not even then.

Oh so hard & all for nothing, all of it, for you will look, no matter what. You must, it being your nature—all our natures.

We always do.

ABOUT THE AUTHOR

Gemma Files, a former film critic, journalist, screenwriter, and teacher, has been an award-winning horror author since 1999. She has published two collections of short work; two chapbooks of speculative poetry; the "weird western" Hexslinger Series; a story-cycle; and the standalone novel *Experimental Film*, which won the 2016 Shirley Jackson Award for Best Novel and the 2016 Sunburst Award for Best Adult Novel. Files also has several story collections and a collection of poetry forthcoming.

GEMMA FILES

FROM OPEN ROAD MEDIA

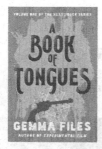

OPEN ROAD

INTEGRATED MEDIA

Find a full list of our authors and
titles at www.openroadmedia.com

FOLLOW US
@OpenRoadMedia